OTHER WORKS BY ELIZABETH CUNNINGHAM

NOVELS

The Return of the Goddess

The Wild Mother

How to Spin Gold

THE MAEVE CHRONICLES:

Magdalen Rising

The Passion of Mary Magdalen

Bright Dark Madonna

Red-Robed Priestess

POETRY

Small Bird

Wild Mercy

So Ecstasy Can Find You

MUSICAL WORK

MaevenSong: A Musical Odyssey Through The Maeve Chronicles

MURDER AT THE RUMMAGE SALE

Elizabeth Cunningham

IMAGINATION FURY ARTS
ALBANY, NY

Murder at the Rummage Sale © 2016 by Elizabeth Cunningham

ISBN 978-1-944190-00-2 (HC)

ISBN 978-1-944190-01-9 (PB)

ISBN 978-1-944190-02-6 (EB)

Printed in the United States of America

Book and cover design by Ray Curenton

Church art by Johanne Renbeck

Publisher's Cataloging-in-Publication data

Names: Cunningham, Elizabeth, 1953-, author.
Title: Murder at the rummage sale / Elizabeth Cunningham.
Description: Albany, NY: Imagination Fury Arts, 2016.
Identifiers: ISBN 978-1-944190-00-2 | LCCN 2016942972
Subjects: LCSH Churches—Fiction. | Rummage sales—Fiction. | Murder—Fiction. | Mystery and detective stories. | BISAC FICTION / Mystery & Detective / Amateur Sleuth.
Classification: LCC PS3553.U473 M97 2016 | DCC 813.54--dc23

First Edition

Imagination Fury Arts

P.O. Box 66265

Albany, NY 12206

imaginationfuryarts.com

Advance Praise for *Murder at the Rummage Sale*

Murder at the Rummage Sale delivers all the pleasures of a good village murder mystery and considerably more. The author knows her setting intimately, cares about her sharply drawn characters, keeps up the suspense patiently, and divides the innocent from the guilty artfully. As with all Ms. Cunningham's novels, *Murder at the Rummage Sale* is well told, thoughtfully written, cleverly and propulsively plotted, and features her signature concerns with religion, magic, childhood, humor, good will, humane openness, and moral seriousness. Readers are in for plenty of fun, vicarious guessing, and delight on the way to the book's satisfying resolution.

— Robert Wexelblatt, author of *Zublinka Among Women* & *Heiberg's Twitch*

With her characteristic wisdom, whimsy, and extraordinary attention to quirky detail, Elizabeth Cunningham transports readers to the 1960s. Think: "Mad Men" Meets Church. *Murder at the Rummage Sale* features the mainline church of rummage sales, privilege and ironic despair, as well as glimmers of light. *Murder at the Rummage Sale* is a whodunit in the grand tradition of rollicking mysteries with memorable characters who keep readers turning pages and wondering about the ending long after the mystery is solved. Love this book, more please!

— Meredith Gould, author of *Desperately Seeking Spirituality: A Field Guide to Practice*

PROLOGUE

No one understands this pleasure. She doesn't care. She feels no shame.

It's early Sunday morning. She's had a lovely walk. Who would want to drive such a short distance at a time of day that's always fresh, dew winking in the grass, spiders going about their business, morning glories blue as the September sky just beginning to open? Most people are still asleep; if awake, they are making coffee, picking up the Sunday papers. No one will disturb her. She has the key to the parish house and no intention of returning it when the rummage sale is over. Or if she has the intention, she will forget.

She unlocks the door and steps inside, not bothering to lock it behind her. Today is the great rummage sale sort. After church, the women will swarm the place, busy as ants or bees, and she, their queen, will preside as they make order. But it is the mad jumble she loves, the flotsam and jetsam of so many lives crammed in one place. The air inside is stuffy, holding yesterday's heat, smelling of must and dust and secrets.

She starts to hum as she makes her way upstairs, stopping to peek in half-opened boxes. Oh, she missed it yesterday, an old jewelry box full of trinkets, a brooch shaped like a fan, a three-strand rhinestone bracelet with a silver clasp. Oh, look, an antique handkerchief, stained at the center, but edged with what appears to be handmade *point de Gaze* lace! Best of all, a locket. Patiently she pries it open as if it were an oyster about to disgorge the pearl of great price. Empty? What a cheat! She tosses it back, but the lovely old handkerchief finds its way up the sleeve of her jacket.

Upstairs, where clothes have been piled, she happily paws through pockets and linings. The things people cast off, unknowing, a compact for rouge inlaid with mother-of-pearl, a shopping list, hotel receipts some wife failed to ferret out. Her own troubles can be forgotten just as easily. There is no need for a fuss. She will find a way to make it all right with the bank. She always does.

Too soon it's time to go. Duties await her. People rely upon her, look up to her. They always have. She heads back downstairs, forcing herself to walk past still-unopened boxes, though she can't resist a quick pass through the room where notions and other unidentifiable small objects will be displayed. She pauses to peer out the window. Good. No cars in the driveway yet. Perhaps she can steal a few more minutes. It occurs to her it might be fun to have a private peek in the parish house offices; the rector's study door opens onto this room. Of course it ought to be locked with so many people coming and going during the rummage sale.

How careless to leave the door open, reprehensible, really. She begins to hum again as she walks through the rector's study, pausing to knock the ashes out of one of his ubiquitous pipes, this one carved with a face. Handsome, but—she takes a sniff—too smelly to carry anywhere on her person. She sets it down and proceeds to the secretary's office. Gracious, the file cabinets are not locked either! She opens one and with a sigh of deep contentment, she delves into this unexpected trove of treasure—the funeral plans parishioners are encouraged to file, the records of annual giving, who gets handouts from the discretionary fund. What else might she find!

Almost purring with pleasure, she does not hear the front door click open or closed. She's left the doors to the offices ajar. (She may be a snoop, but she's no sneak!) She does not hear the careful, almost silent footsteps. Then suddenly a hand on her shoulder. She startles but recovers quickly. She's been caught before. She doesn't care. She has no shame. Smiling, she turns to see who it is, utterly confident in her charm.

What she does not know, what she cannot consider (since no one asked) is this: If she could choose the last face she would ever see, would this face be the one?

PART ONE:
LIFE

CHAPTER ONE

Lucy popped the bonnet of her old, blue Volkswagen Beetle, all the more bonnet-like for not shielding the engine, which was in the back where the boot was in most cars. She knew Americans said hood and trunk, not bonnet and boot, but she had spent so much of her early life in England it felt more natural to use English words—if there were anything natural about cars, German cars in particular, named by Hitler, no less. But here it was, fifteen years after the war and they were all over the road, usually driven by women of a certain age who had no need of those vast, lumbering station wagons crammed with children.

There was Elsa Ebersbach's car, a case in point, exactly like Lucy's but tan, parked in its usual place by the choir room door. Lucy paused to listen for the organ, a chorale prelude, "Come Thou now to Save Mankind," Lucy thought, probably for this Sunday. If Elsa was still there when Lucy had dropped off her donation for the rummage sale, she might stop to listen. Elsa wouldn't care as long as she was quiet, and she wouldn't stop playing, even if she sensed Lucy's presence. It was one of her rules. Practice ceased for no one. Lucy knew that some of her fellow parishioners found Elsa abrupt to the point of rudeness. She dressed mannishly, wearing slacks except on Sunday, had short greying hair, just long enough for her to push back distractedly with her fingers. She made no attempt to soften her German accent or manner. Lucy didn't mind. She was one of the few people at the Church of the Regeneration who knew Elsa's story, what she had gone through during the war, how she had become a refugee. And Elsa knew more about Lucy than most people did.

Not everything. No one knew everything. In fact, Lucy doubted it would occur to anyone that she had what used to be called "a past."

Propping open the hood, Lucy reached in to pick up her mother's old winter coats, still in their plastic bags straight from the drycleaners. It seemed almost an affront to these coats, some of them dating back to the First War, that they should be swathed in see-through plastic instead of an old-fashioned quilted garment bag. But Mother herself hadn't worn most of these monstrosities for years (some monstrous indeed with the heads and teeth of mink snarling from the collar). The smell of camphor had given way to must and even mildew, so Lucy had salvaged what she could and taken them to be cleaned in time for the famous annual Church of the Regeneration Rummage Sale.

Mother had been gone now for more than two years. Lucy had taken time sorting through her mother's things, perhaps because Lucy had been a nurse in the war where death was so often sudden, indiscriminate. Here today, tomorrow in a body bag or, as bad, a young boy trapped in a body that would never again be whole. It had been an odd kind of a balm to care for her mother through a ripe old age that ended in a quiet death. No air raid sirens, no bombs exploding. Not even an ambulance. When her mother died in the middle of the night, Lucy had called no one. She'd just closed her mother's eyes and then dozed beside her till the birds woke her to a grey spring dawn.

Now it was a late afternoon in August, warm and breathless, the birds too hot to stir from whatever cool branch they'd found. Only the cicadas sang their long hypnotic note, a sound that seemed synonymous with the end of summer. It was so hot that Lucy had allowed herself to wear a sleeveless blouse, something she did not normally do. Though Lucy was still trim, she knew that nothing betrayed a woman's age like her neck and her upper arms. Her mother would have considered such minimal covering unthinkable. As if proving her mother's posthumous disapproval right, a trickle of sweat began a meandering journey down her arm as she tried to lift the whole pile of coats at once. She set them back down and felt for the handkerchief she carried in her breast pocket. Before she could undo the damage, she heard footsteps behind her on the gravel. She turned and saw Frank Lomangino, the church sexton, approaching her.

"Hold on, Mrs. Way. Let me carry those for you."

It used to bother Lucy when people called her Mrs. instead of Miss. It had made her feel old, but now, well, she was old. And there was something courtly and old world about Frank Lomangino. "Mrs." from his lips sounded like respect instead of assumption, the way in France she would be addressed as Madame. No one wanted to be called Mademoiselle at the age of fifty-seven.

It was rather flattering that Frank knew her name at all. He hadn't been working at the church for long. Ancient Amos McCready had finally retired last spring when he fell off a ladder and broke his hip, poor thing, though amazingly he was now getting around with only a cane. Lucy knew that some people on the vestry had been opposed to Frank's appointment. No one objected to his being Roman Catholic—or they didn't say so; after all, an Irish Roman Catholic was running for president. But that he'd served time in prison for something to do with illegal gambling raised some eyebrows.

For Gerald Bradley, their outspoken liberal rector, Frank Lomangino's criminal record was his chief qualification. Mr. Bradley (he refused the Anglo-Catholic title "Father") had even worked the matter into a sermon on Matthew 25. "I was jailbird and ye gave me a job, inasmuch as ye have done it unto one of these least of my brethren..." And of course it helped that Joe Petrone, the town deputy constable, was Frank's brother-in-law. No doubt Joe had approached the rector on Frank's behalf over a beer at the firehouse where Mr. Bradley volunteered, something none of his predecessors had ever done. Gerald Bradley liked upsetting his parishioners a little too much, Lucy thought, but she respected him for acting on his convictions.

"Why, thank you, Mr. Lomangino."

Lucy believed in according everyone the respect of a title, even if he was wearing a white undershirt that made him look like Stanley

Kowalski in *A Streetcar named Desire*. It was a very hot day, and, to be perfectly honest, a young man's muscular arms were not an unpleasant sight.

"For the rummage sale, am I right?" Frank tossed the coats over one arm as if they weighed nothing. "My wife can't wait for the rummage sale. She's a real bargain hunter. She gets most of the kids' clothes there. Except the school uniforms, of course. She's found some swanky outfits for herself, too. She's a real looker, my Teresa, even with all the kids."

You had to like a man who admired his wife. She followed him up the roofed steps to the parish house.

"How many children have you, Mr. Lomangino?" she asked as he opened the door and made a gracious gesture, inviting her to precede him.

"Four and counting."

She caught a look of mixed pride and worry on his face. Poor Mrs. Lomangino. He must have gotten her pregnant again as soon as he got out of prison. She knew he also worked as a janitor as St Alphonse's. (Perhaps his brother-in-law thought working at churches would help keep him on the straight and narrow.) But even with two jobs it must be hard to keep food on the table. She hoped his job at St Alphonse covered parochial school tuition.

"Frankie, Junior is around here somewhere. My only boy so far."

"Yes, I believe I've met him. A handsome young man."

Lucy did not add, like his father, although it was true. She disliked older women who flirted so obviously.

They had both paused in the relative cool of the parish house hallway. The place was starting to fill up with, well, it could be called junk, though there was always treasure hidden in the boxes of bizarre castoffs of all descriptions. Donations started coming in as soon as the mid-August portion supper was cleared. Sorting began right after church the Sunday after Labor Day and preparations went on feverishly for two weeks, women working all day, every day, men being corralled to help with the larger donations, furniture and machinery, on the weekend. Everyone in the parish got involved in one way or another, and people from other churches helped as well. Volunteers got to go to a workers' sale and fight (sometimes, alas, tooth and nail) for items they'd staked out or even squirreled away.

The hallway was already piled with boxes, and more donations lined the stairs to the second floor. Lucy noted with amusement that someone had contributed a toilet plunger and brush. They stood neatly on the stairs between boxes of costume jewelry, old linen handkerchiefs and some faded folding hand fans. Yet despite the chaos and incongruence, there was a sense that order would return and prevail. Frank Lomangino must take his job seriously.

"Katherine!" came a child's voice from outside. "Come *on*! You can do it. Give me your hand, I'll pull you up!"

"Speaking of the little devil," said Frank. "Excuse me a moment, Mrs. Way."

He set the coats down on some boxes. Curious, Lucy followed him into the parish house library sitting room where people over-flowed during coffee hour. The room was connected to a porch that was almost two stories high, as the parish house was built on a rise with a windowed basement on one end. Through library windows, they could see Frankie, Junior, a sturdy black-haired boy, reaching over a wall as high as his chest, holding tight to another child's hand.

"He's going to pull her arm out of the socket! I told them not to climb up there. Frankie, hey, Frankie, Junior. I'm talkina*you*!"

"Don't," cautioned Lucy. "He might let go suddenly and she could fall."

Just then another arm threw itself over the railing and Katherine Bradley, the minister's daughter, hauled herself up and over as Frankie, Junior staggered back.

"Hey, you kids!" shouted Frank, Senior, advancing on the door.

He was trying to sound angry, but Lucy could tell he was strug-gling to keep from laughing as Frankie and Katherine ducked below window level, fruitlessly trying to hide. She couldn't help laughing herself, especially when Frank discovered the door to the porch was locked. She was fairly sure he was cursing under his breath, perhaps in Italian, as he searched his pocket for the keys.

"He's coming to get us. Come on, Katherine!"

Frankie, Junior vaulted over the edge and disappeared. Katherine, slightly younger and smaller, perched uncertainly on the railing. Her shorts and T-shirt were grass and dirt-stained and her straight brown hair had come loose from her barrettes and was plastered to her flushed face. Lucy was fond of the child, though she didn't know her well. Katherine was a bit aloof, not a child who performed for adults. The twins, Katherine's younger brother and sister, were more popular in the parish. Lucy did not know whose idea it was to eschew nicknames like Katie or Kitty or Kathy. It was unusual in this day and age, but the more formal name suited the rather solemn child.

"I better go outside. Make sure she don't hurt herself."

But just then, Katherine took the leap. By the time Frank and Lucy reached the steps and looked outside, Frankie, Junior and Katherine were nowhere in sight.

"Kids!" Frank, Senior shrugged. "Where do you want them coats, Mrs. Way?"

"Oh, don't trouble yourself any further, Mr. Lomangino. You'll want to check on the children."

"As long as they ain't hurt, I'm not going to wear myself out running around after them. It's no trouble, Mrs. Way. It's my pleasure."

Lucy supposed she ought not to approve of his laxness with his son, but she couldn't resist his gallantry.

"Thank you, Mr. Lomangino. Coats go upstairs, I believe."

Any lingering cool air had decidedly not come up to the second floor, a high raftered room lined with windows. With the afternoon sun beating in, it was worse than an oven; ovens were dry and this heat held moist heaviness that could only be relieved by the cataclysm of a thunderstorm that might not come for days yet. Boxes and piles of loose clothes were everywhere, and Lucy shuddered to think what more might be lurking behind the curtains of the stage.

"Just put them anywhere." Lucy felt weary and longed for the cool of the church. She'd rest there before getting back into her sweltering car.

"Looks like there's room to hang 'em on this rack over here."

"Frank?" a woman's voice called out from behind the curtain. "Frank Lomangino, is that you?"

"The one and only," he answered grandly, apparently forgetting the existence of Frankie, Junior.

And to Lucy's dismay, before she could turn and slip away unseen, Charlotte Crowley thrust aside the curtains and emerged from behind the stage, as if she were a leading lady, which no doubt in her own mind she was and always would be. A handsome woman in her late fifties, with a well-placed shock of grey in her auburn hair, Charlotte was the reigning queen of the Women of the Church of the Regeneration. In the pecking order, she outranked even Anne Bradley, the rector's wife, who could have fought her for first place but had surrendered without a struggle to Charlotte's prominence. Lucy felt her habitual twinge of guilt at her dislike of Charlotte. She had to admit there was nothing mean about Charlotte. She meant well, *awfully* well.

"Why, Frank, what on earth are you wearing?" Charlotte goggled.

But Charlotte had no tact, none, Lucy reminded herself with satisfaction.

"I hope you'll excuse my appearance, Mrs. Crowley," said Frank, who looked embarrassed and might even be blushing under his swarthy complexion. "It's just that it's so da—" he stopped himself from uttering a mild curse word. "So hot."

"It *is* hot." Lucy stepped in. "I am surprised that you are working up here today, Charlotte. Aren't you overheated in that smock?"

"Keeps the dust out." Charlotte waved away Lucy's concern.

And it had lots of pockets, Lucy observed. And some of them were bulging. Everyone in the parish knew that Charlotte was, well, light-fingered was one way to put it. Kleptomania was the fancy word. Lucy in her more charitable moments thought of Charlotte as a magpie—curious, a little mischievous, unable to resist anything shiny, whether an object or a secret. If anyone else had such a compulsion, she might have been a social pariah. But Charlotte was Charlotte, the soul of shabby gentility, the one who lent an air of gaiety and class to any gathering.

"I'm just taking a quick look at what we've got already," Charlotte went on. "You know I am in charge of the rummage sale this year. Or did you miss the last WOR meeting?"

WOR being short for Women of Regeneration.

"I was there," Lucy said dryly.

She had, as usual, sat quietly in the back with some needlework, hoping not to be noticed or volunteered for anything she would rather not do.

"Excuse me, ladies." Frank took his chance to exit. "If there's nothing either of you—"

"Now, don't run away, Frank." Charlotte descended from the stage. "Mr. Crowley and I were just talking about you this morning. Our yew hedge has been getting a bit out of hand and we were wondering if you might tackle it for us if you're free one day."

"Well, I'm no gardener, Mrs. Crowley."

"Oh, but you are so clever, Frank."

Lucy did not want to, but she could not help watching Charlotte put her hand, just beginning to show age spots, on Frank's bare arm. The gesture struck Lucy not so much as flirtatious as overly-familiar, even condescending.

"We see the wonders you've worked around here. We'd like to steal you for a bit."

Lucy felt like blushing for Charlotte, but really it was too hot and past time for her own getaway.

"I'll see you at altar guild, Charlotte," said Lucy. "And thank you for your help with the coats, Mr. Lomangino."

She wished Charlotte would feel reproved by Lucy's formality, but she knew the hope was in vain.

"It was nothing, Mrs. Way."

"Oh, did you finally go through Elizabeth's things, Lucy?"

Why must Charlotte say Elizabeth? Why couldn't she say your mother? After all, Charlotte was Lucy's contemporary, and yet she acted as if she and Lucy's mother were the peers. Because Lucy was a maiden daughter, and Charlotte was a married woman, that's why. Lucy knew she was overly sensitive on the subject, but silent indignation was swiftly obliterating all other feelings.

"You know I was sincere in my offer to help sort through Elizabeth's things, Lucy. Such a difficult task. Do let me know if you ever need anything. Gracious, you must be so lost all by yourself in that big house."

"Thank you, Charlotte." Only Lucy's good breeding and strict early training kept her tone civil. "There are some things I find it best to face alone."

The air downstairs no longer felt cool, but stagnant, trapped. At least the heat outside was alive, Lucy thought, as she opened the heavy doors to find herself face to face with the excessively handsome Mr. Foster. Perhaps blond men of a certain height and build did not sweat, Lucy considered. He looked as though he had just showered and shaved. His eyes lit up with recognition. He was one of those men who always made you feel important. A good asset for an aspiring, not to say ambitious, politician. Mr. Foster was running for Congress, as a Democrat, no less, and in a decidedly Republican district. She did not know how he found time to be an active church member, but he and Gerald Bradley were good friends, and perhaps more than that, allies. Rick Foster was on the board of the interracial children's camp Gerald Bradley proposed to build when he had raised sufficient funds to secure a location.

"Ah, Miss Way." She believed he would have tipped his hat had he been wearing one, his bare head his only concession to the heat. "How do you manage to keep so cool and collected in this weather?"

Could this be a reference to her sleeveless blouse? Surely not.

"I might ask the same of you, Mr. Foster."

"Appearances can be deceiving." He laughed. "Say, have you seen Mr. Lomangino? Mrs. Jones said she thought he might be in here."

Titles for Grace, the church secretary, and for Frank? Lucy wondered if Mr. Foster always used formal address or if he had merely observed that she did. Either way, she was impressed with him.

"Yes, he's upstairs with Mrs. Crowley."

"Better and better. I need to talk to them both. I've been volunteered to man the tent of furniture and appliances." He didn't exactly wink, but his tone was pleasantly conspiratorial. "I understand Mrs. Crowley is our superior officer."

"Indeed she is, Mr. Foster. A regular brigadier general." She hoped she did not sound too flippant, but after all she, too, had served in the armed forces and surely where Charlotte was concerned everyone was allowed to gently press their tongue to their cheek. "I wonder you can spare the time during campaign season, Mr. Foster. It's awfully kind of you."

"Oh, don't think too highly of me, Miss Way. Where else but at the Church of Regeneration Rummage Sale would I get to press so much flesh. I don't mean I'll be handing out leaflets, but half the district will be there."

"True enough," agreed Lucy. "Good luck to you, Mr. Foster."

And he didn't have to hand out literature, she thought to herself. His face and his charming manners would be more effective than any campaign literature.

"On another note, Miss Way, my wife and I are hosting an informal barbeque this Sunday afternoon. Nothing official, just for friends. We'd be delighted if you were free to join us."

Lucy rather doubted that Rick's wife even knew who she was. Sybil Foster was a socialite from the upper echelons of New York society and made rather heavy weather of small town life. The rumor among the WOR was that Sybil Foster would have preferred to attend the tonier St Luke's-in-the-Fields. Lucy hoped for Sybil's sake that her husband won the election and she could remove to Washington.

"Why thank you, Mr. Foster," said Lucy, without committing herself. "Shall I phone your wife to let her know if I'm able to attend?"

"No need," said Rick. "Just come if you're free."

He gave her a smile—his smile reminded her of someone but she couldn't think who—and a nod that was almost a bow and went inside. Well, all right, maybe she would go to the barbeque. It would make a change.

Elsa's car was still there, Lucy noted, but as she reached the bottom of the steps, Mildred Thomson's Citroën pulled in right where Lucy would have to encounter her if she walked up to the church. Lucy thought longingly for a moment, not just of the cool of the church, but of the peace she found whenever she rested there, the dust motes in the shafts of filtered light, how the eyes of Christ Triumphant (her gift to the church in memory of her mother) always seemed to seek hers, to share some tender secret. Then Mildred spied Lucy as she got out of her car and called out a "Halloo, Lu-cee." (Yes, she did.) Lucy abandoned her plan to listen to Elsa practice.

Lucy felt sorry for Mildred, everyone did, poor thing. Though Mildred was a widow, she seemed far more never-married than Lucy. No one could remember Mildred's husband, and she had an air of long-preserved virginity that Lucy hoped did not cling to herself. Mildred was no doubt here to discuss her spiritual life with the rector, but if she could not find him, Lucy would do. She could not bear a discussion about original sin or about salvation by faith or good works. Not today. She waved to Mildred apologetically and gestured that she was in a hurry. (Does a gesture count as a lie? Lucy feared it did.)

Dear Lord, she prayed, as walked quickly to her car, *forgive my hard heart. Make me more charitable, but not yet,* she ruefully echoed St Augustine. Out of the corner of her eye, she glimpsed Anne Bradley behind the honeysuckle hedge that was supposed to protect her family's privacy. She was taking down laundry from a clothesline. She waved to Lucy but did not call a greeting. If Lucy could have, she would have cried out a warning to Anne. For Mildred, seeing that the rector's car was not there, had begun to wander, with an odd mixture of diffidence and determination, in Anne's direction.

Lucy ducked into her car, left the windows rolled down, and drove away, her damp, white curls (snow white, and yes, she was vain of them and how well they became her green eyes) flying in the hot breeze.

CHAPTER TWO

Katherine and Frankie crouched, hiding in the long grass beyond the burn barrel just outside the back door of the parish house. The sun was on the other side of the huge building, so the long shadow further concealed them.

"He'll never find us here," whispered Katherine.

Deep down, they both knew that Frankie's father had stopped looking for them, except that of course, he wasn't Frankie's father at all. He was really a pod person from outer space. He wanted to suck their brains out, Frankie had explained, and turn them into robots.

"With a straw?" she had asked.

"What are you talking about?" Frankie wanted to know.

"Will he suck our brains out with a straw?" Katherine was trying to picture it. In her mind she saw one of those straws with the crinkly bend in it, the ones she drank ginger ale through when she was sick in bed. Would a brain squeeze through those?

Frankie made one of those noises that meant she was crazy and didn't know anything.

"No, dummy, they have special laser beams for that. It would just be presto bingo alakazam! And your brain would be gone."

"Oh yeah, laser beams," she'd said, like she'd known all along.

She didn't like it when Frankie called her dummy, but she did like Frankie. He was eight and she was seven (even though they were both going into second grade). She was lucky he wanted to play with her, and their games were the most exciting. They were always in danger. They were always running and hiding.

"We're not safe yet," Frankie whispered back. "He could come out here and trick us. He'd pretend to be burning the trash. But really he has x-ray vision. He'd see us. We need to go far, far away, where he could never follow us."

Katherine knew what Frankie meant, and now she felt scared for real. And excited. They both wanted to go there, almost more than they wanted anything else.

The woods. The woods where they were not allowed to go.

"Come on," Frankie hissed a command.

He dropped to his belly and began pulling his way through the grass like a snake. Katherine followed, fleetingly aware that her mother might scold about grass stains. But soon the world of mothers and fathers, clothes and stains fell away. She and Frankie crouched again, peering over the stone wall into the wood. Air that was not quite a breeze came toward them from that world, smelling of water and pine, of stone and moss. The world on this side of the wall was a white glare of heat. In that other world light and shadow shifted, playing tricks on your eyes. Katherine believed the flashes of light were fairies not quite letting themselves be seen. She knew fairies drank out of acorn cap cups and made homes in the hollows of trees. This wood must be where they lived.

"Let's go," urged Frankie.

Without looking back at her, he reached for her hand and began to pull her after him to the top of the stone wall. She almost lost her balance on a loose stone, and with her free hand, she grabbed hold of a tree on the other side. That's when she saw the sign nailed to the trunk a little higher than her head.

"Frankie," she said. "Look! There's words on the tree."

"So? Who cares?" Frankie dropped Katherine's hand, and she almost lost her balance again.

"I think we should read them," she said.

Frankie began kicking at loose pebbles on top of the wall.

"Who cares about stupid old, dumb old words."

Katherine did. She had cared about words ever since she knew they could make the pictures in her storybooks come to life. She wasn't going to say that to Frankie, but she was going to read the words on the tree, whether he wanted to or not.

"No," she began. That was easy, but the next word was long, longer than any of the words in her books. "No tres-pass-ing," she sounded it out. "No Trespassing."

Katherine suddenly had a sick feeling in the pit of her stomach. There were a lot more words in smaller letters, some of them even longer than Trespassing. But those were the big words. NO TRES-PASSING. Katherine knew what they meant.

"What's trespassing?" demanded Frankie angrily. "Why shouldn't we trespass? I want to trespass."

"God," whispered Katherine, even more softly. She moved closer to Frankie and took his hand again. Even though he sounded mad, he let her.

"What's God got to do with anything?" Frankie asked, but he was whispering again, too.

Frankie liked to act tough, but they both knew God was every-where, always watching, like Santa Claus, like her dead grandfathers in heaven. She wished God would leave her alone.

"God doesn't want us to go in the woods."

"How do you know?" He sounded more curious now than angry, and maybe just a teeny bit scared.

"Because it says: No Trespassing. You know like in Our Father who art in heaven. Forgive us our trespasses."

Katherine knew the prayer by heart, not only from church where everyone said it together like I Pledge Allegiance in school, but because her mother and father sang it with her and the twins every night before bed right after they sang Jesus Tender Shepherd. She had asked what trespasses meant. "The things we do that are wrong," her father had explained. It is another word for sin." Sin, a short word but a scary one that her father usually said only in church. It meant bad, very bad. Trespassing was the long word for it.

"Trespassing means sin." Katherine tried the idea out loud.

"Does not," Frankie shot back, the way he always did.

"Does so," Katherine said automatically.

"Well, is it Latin?" Frankie demanded.

Katherine felt uncertain. Latin was a touchy subject. Frankie insisted that God spoke only Latin, but Katherine knew that couldn't be right.

"Yes." She took a risk. "It must be a Latin word. Look how long it is."

Frankie made a noise that sounded like a fart. He'd taught her how to do it, but when her mother caught her showing the twins, she got sent to her room.

"It is not Latin," he decided. "It is not in the Mass."

Frankie talked about the Mass a lot. That's what they had in his church. She couldn't help thinking of Mass as mess. She saw Frankie's church as having a lot of dirty socks on the floor, toys not put away, plates with half-eaten peanut butter sandwiches. She wished she could go there and see what it was like. There were nuns in his church. She saw them downtown sometimes, wearing long black robes, like her father's. But their robes had headdresses all white and stiff and starchy, standing out around their faces. Frankie called the nuns penguins. Katherine thought they looked scarier than that.

"Anyway, I know what that sign means. No Trespassing." He broke it down. "No trees pissing. Get it, Katherine, get it? It's a dumb sign because trees don't piss anyway."

"Don't say piss, Frankie!" Katherine started to giggle.

"Piss," said Frankie more loudly. "Piss, piss, pissing. No trees pissing."

"Piss, pissing, pissing!" Katherine boldly echoed.

And they both laughed so hard, they lost their balance and tumbled back into the church yard. What if they had fallen onto the other side? Katherine sobered up as she caught her breath. Maybe it was a magic wood, and if they went in they wouldn't be able to come back. Lucy and Edmund went back and forth from Narnia a few times, but then they all stayed there, for a hundred years. Till they were grownups.

Katherine lost all awareness of everything as she thought for a moment of her and Frankie gone away to another world, fighting witches and werewolves until they grew up to be king and queen. But it was winter when Lucy went to Narnia, and it was still summer in the woods.

Katherine glanced over at Frankie. He had lain all the way down in the grass on his back. He was looking up at the sky, squinting, as if he could see something there. Flying saucers. Frankie was always seeing them, waiting for them to land. Frankie wanted more than anything to go to another planet.

I'll go if you go, Katherine thought in her mind, and she didn't know if she meant the woods, Narnia, or outer space. If she went with Frankie, she thought she wouldn't be too afraid.

"Katherine!"

Someone was calling her back, back from almost stepping over the wall into Narnia. Someone was always calling her back.

"I guess I had better be going, then," said Mildred Thomson, still hovering next to Anne, even though Anne had walked out into the driveway, in the general direction of Mrs. Thomson's car, to scan the lawns for Katherine.

Anne knew it was borderline rude to call for her child while Mrs. Thomson so clearly still wanted to talk. But then, Anne considered, it was rude of Mrs. Thomson to approach her in her private back-yard where she was taking down her laundry while the twins finally napped, exhausted by the heat. She hadn't actually planned to call Katherine in yet. It was so hot she felt she didn't have the energy to load the children into the car and take them to the pool. She had intended simply to turn on the sprinkler in the backyard and let the children run in and out of it, but Mildred Thomson had driven her to it.

"Hello there, Mrs. Bradley," Mildred had said, adding some obligatory remarks about the weather. "I was hoping to find Father, I mean *Mr.* Bradley in today. Do you know when he might be back?"

Anne did not. In fact, she realized she did not even know where he was. Hospital calls? A diocesan meeting? Surely she would have remembered if he'd gone all the way to New York. He had probably told her, and she had probably not listened. He was not there most of the time, or if he was, he was not available, not to her or the children. He stayed in his study in the parish house where no doubt Mrs. Thomson had hoped to ambush him.

"I'm afraid I don't, Mrs. Thomson," said Anne, feeling for her cigarettes in her apron pocket. Hell's bells. She must have left them in the back hall on the shelf above the washer.

Anne had turned back to the clothesline. Three children meant a lot of laundry, though in the summer the load was a little lighter, shorts and short sleeves, not so many filthy elbows and knees. There were always Gerald's shirts. Short or long-sleeved, they had to be ironed, something she could not even contemplate till the cool of the evening. Perhaps she could ask Bernice, her half-blind cleaning woman, to do the ironing tomorrow while Anne relieved her of other tasks she wasn't really fit to perform, either.

"Did you have an appointment with him?" Anne had asked, hoping the question did not sound too much like a reproof.

"No, no," Mrs. Thomson said vaguely. "I just happened by. I suppose I ought to make an appointment. I never did with Father Roberts. He never minded my popping in."

That was definitely a reproach. Anne felt almost sorry for her husband, almost. But it was part of his job to listen to parishioners maunder on, as much as holding services on Sunday and galvanizing his congregation to do good works in the community.

"Mrs. Bradley, may I ask you a personal question?"

Could she say no, Anne wondered? Or at least, excuse me while I get a cigarette? But Mrs. Thomson took her hesitation for consent.

"Do you ever struggle with your prayer life?"

Anne bit back a bitter laugh. She could hear it in her head, a sound a dog might make, something between a yelp and a snarl.

"I suppose you don't," Mrs. Thomson said wistfully.

No, I don't, Anne almost said. I don't have a prayer life. I am not on speaking terms with God. But she couldn't say that to anyone, certainly not to Mrs. Thomson.

"Why would you think so?" she asked instead, almost curious.

"Well, I don't mean to presume. I just thought that, well, being married to a Man of the Cloth, your faith must be very sure."

Anne had stopped for a moment, stunned, holding Gerald's plaid boxer shorts in midair. She fought an impulse to hand the undergarments to Mrs. Thomson. What the Man of the Cloth wore under his priestly robes. Temptation passed and she folded the rector's underwear neatly and discreetly into the basket.

"We all struggle." Anne hoped that platitude would suffice.

Anne reached for one of her own undergarments. Really, the woman was impossible. Couldn't she see that Anne didn't want to air even her clean linen?

"Oh, my dear, I am so sorry. I forgot for a moment—"

Anne felt that familiar pressure behind her eyes: the world going red, as if all the blood in her heart, in her always cold extremities had rushed to her head. She wished she would just explode, bits of brain and skull splattering Mrs. Thomson.

"Excuse me," she heard herself say through the roaring. "I just realized I've lost track of Katherine. The twins will be up from their nap any minute. I promised the children I'd take them to the pool this afternoon."

Which was a lie, she hadn't promised, but it didn't matter. Briskly and efficiently, she'd yanked down the last garments instead of turning and ripping Mrs. Thomson's throat out. Then she stepped into the driveway and called for Katherine.

"I can see that you are busy, Mrs. Bradley," sighed Mrs. Thomson. "I'll run along now. Perhaps I will go and see if Charlotte needs my help. I do believe that's her old Packard down by the parish house.

Poor dear Charlotte. She's had that car since before the war. How it still runs, I don't know."

Poor Charlotte indeed, thought Anne, though poor wasn't a word she usually thought of in connection with Charlotte. She found it odd—and mildly intriguing—that a woman everyone thought of as poor Mildred seemed determined to pity the reigning queen of not only the parish but the whole county, never mind that she drove a rusted out battle wagon.

"I'm sure she'd be glad of your help, Mrs. Thomson." Anne hoped she did not lie. "I'll tell Mr. Bradley you were looking for him."

Which is to say, warn him.

"Oh, don't trouble yourself. It's nothing important."

Mrs. Thomson's humility sounded (for a moment) so genuine, Anne felt an unexpected rush of penitence. How dare Gerald—or herself for that matter—make fun of this woman, think her suffering any less significant than anyone else's?

"Of course your prayer life is important." Anne turned toward her. "I am sorry I could not be of more help."

But then, Anne thought, I am not a Woman of the Cloth. My undergarments are plain and made of nylon.

"Why, thank you, Mrs. Bradley."

To Anne's discomfort, the woman's eyes welled with tears. (*She cries real tears*, a line from an advertisement for a baby doll went through Anne's mind.)

"You are a genuinely kind person," she quavered.

Then before Mrs. Thomson could embarrass either of them further, Katherine appeared, and Mrs. Thomson, who had always struck Anne as frightened of children, murmured something and turned away.

Katherine's shorts and tee-shirt were covered in grass-stains, her knees filthy, and to Anne's dismay, she had Frankie Lomangino in tow. The boy's clothes were as dirty as Katherine's. He stood beside Katherine now, kicking at stones in the driveway. She wished she liked him better, since Katherine seemed to. But she didn't; she couldn't. She hated seeing Katherine tagging along with this boy. Frankie wasn't as old as Hal would have been, but he was big for his age, so from a distance...

"What?" Katherine demanded.

"Don't say 'what?' like that, Katherine. I've told you before, it's rude."

Now Katherine looked down at the driveway and began kicking dirt. Frankie stopped and looked up at her as if she were speaking a foreign language. His expression was not as sullen as she expected but almost curious.

"It's time to come in now and get cleaned up," Anne said. "I'm sure Frankie's father is wondering where he is, too."

Katherine stopped kicking stones and met her mother's eyes with a gaze Anne found particularly disconcerting, her grey-blue eyes, so like Hal's. It was not a defiant or questioning look, more a distant one, as if there were some horizon beyond Anne that only Katherine could see.

"I told the twins I would take them to the pool after their nap."

Why this lie again, she wondered?

"Can Frankie come?"

The inevitable question, and her answer would be no. With their honorary membership at the country club (traditionally extended to the Episcopal rector and his family) they were, of course, allowed to bring guests for a nominal fee. But not Frankie, Anne decided, not Frankie Lomangino.

"Frankie doesn't have his bathing suit with him," Anne began.

"But we could stop at his house and get it!" Katherine reasoned.

"I said no, Katherine."

She hadn't actually said no, but that is what she'd meant, and Frankie knew it.

"I don't want to go to any stupid old pool," he offered with a strange mix of rudeness and gallantry. "My pops is going to take me to get ice cream."

With that, Frankie turned away and went to look for his father.

"I want to go with Frankie," Katherine said, wistful and defiant.

"Another time, sweetie," said Anne. "Come on. You can have a popsicle while I get the twins up."

She slipped her hand into Katherine's and they walked towards the back steps, Katherine dragging one foot as they went.

CHAPTER THREE

Gerald Bradley pulled into the driveway in his VW bug, the car he used when he traveled for work, leaving Anne and the children with the station wagon. He probably should have waited till he was inside, but it was so hot, he pulled off his dog collar as soon as he stepped out of the car. He'd already shed his light-weight seersucker jacket and left it crumpled on the passenger seat. He stuffed the collar in his pants pocket, and then forgot all about it. Automatically, he looked to see if Anne's station wagon was in its usual spot near the front porch of the rectory. It wasn't. He felt a wave of relief that was almost as good as a cool breeze; following that, a barely acknowledged wave of guilt that made him feel all hot and sticky again.

He'd just come from a lunch meeting with three other Episcopal priests from the area. They'd gotten together in the back room of a local restaurant where they didn't have to run into parishioners or involve any wives. Their official topic: forming a team ministry to better serve each of their parishes and the whole region. Andy Wheeler, in the eastern part of the county, wanted to start a ministry to migrant workers most people at the Church of the Regeneration didn't even know existed. Tom Manning had a prison and a men's rehabilitation center near his church and wanted to get his parish involved in volunteering. As for Gerald, his church already had a ministry with the state institution for the mentally retarded, but he had greater ambitions than working in institutions that already existed. Though it was still little more than a glimmer in his eye, he'd already found some powerful board members for his dream of an interracial, interdenominational summer camp for inner city kids.

His brother priests had all been impressed with his success at integrating the Church of the Regeneration without losing more than a couple of very conservative parishioners. That is, all but Alfred Channing, the rector of the tiny wealthy church to which said members had decamped. Though the church's official name was Saint Luke's in-the-Fields, some of the priests (out of Alfred's hearing, of course) called it the Church of the Horse and Hound. Almost all Alfred's parishioners were members of the White Hart Hunt Club. One of Alfred's arcane pastoral duties was the blessing of the Hunt on opening day. He had the privilege of handing the hunt master the stirrup cup as if it were the Chalice—which for the hunters it was. The fox's blood, too, was holy, and if the hounds ever killed one, which was rare, new members were "blooded."

"Best not to force things," Alfred had commented with deceptive mildness. "There's always trouble when Man insists on his own timing instead of God's."

When people invoked God that way, Gerald saw red (in more sense than one, Alfred might have joked; liberals were always in danger of being called commies).

"Who else does God have but us?" Gerald challenged, somewhat belligerently. They had dispensed with most of the business and finished their hamburgers and club sandwiches with their sides of fries, but they were all still drinking gin and tonic (it being a hot summer day). For lo, hadn't Jesus said: whenever three or four Episcopal priests are gathered together, there will be a fifth? "If we don't follow the teachings of Christ, who will? Look at the Negro clergy. Martin Luther King, Jr., and Ralph Abernathy. They're the church leaders who are living the Gospel."

"Bus strikes, lunch counter sit-ins." Alfred further infuriated Gerald by stifling a yawn.

"Turning the other cheek. Nonviolent resistance!" Gerald was tempted to pound the table with his fist. "It brought down British rule in India, and it will bring down Jim Crow in the South. Nashville,

Nashville, think of it, all lunch counters integrated. In Montgomery a tired domestic can take whatever seat she likes."

"Did you hear about what happened in Jacksonville on Saturday?" put in Tom. "Two hundred white men trying to bash in the demonstrators' skulls. Hard to turn the other cheek with a baseball bat coming down on your head."

"They're saying the Ku Klux Klan is behind it," added Andy.

"Of course," said Gerald. "The Klan is going to use every means they can to intimidate the Negroes and anyone who supports them. Starting with violence."

"That's my point," Alfred said. "It's going to be a battle, bloody, bitter and divisive."

"Not so different from leading your people out of Egypt," said Gerald. "Or being nailed to a cross."

Alfred had given Gerald one of his ironic looks. Then he drained the dregs of his drink, the melting ice sliding down the sides of the glass as he set it down.

"Game. Set. Match," Alfred smiled. "Till next time."

Gerald raised his glass and downed it. He couldn't help but like Alfred, even if he was stodgy. He was a man of his time and generation. The same generation as his own father, Gerald reminded himself. But his father would have been at the forefront of any liberal movement. During the Depression his father's church had opened one of the first soup kitchens in Boston. He helped hoboes find work and even organized temporary shelters. If he were alive today, he might have gone down South and joined a demonstration himself, brought his whole congregation with him.

Maybe one day soon Gerald would do the same, even if he was stuck in some sleepy small town away from all the real action in the world. Gerald looked around the church yard and felt suddenly overwhelmed with sleepiness himself. The lunchtime drinks were wearing off, leaving him thirsty and dispirited. He missed New York. The city could be exhausting but it was stimulating, too. He'd always felt at the heart of things there. He didn't have to search for relevance; he lived in its midst. But he had done what he had to do coming here, for Anne's sake. Really, after Hal, there had been no choice. The bishop had agreed.

Gerald did not follow the thought further. It led nowhere he wanted to go, nowhere he hadn't been a thousand futile times. So he veered away, wandering uncertainly towards the parish house, wondering what to do next. It was too late for a nap, too early for another drink. His secretary Grace had left for the day, keeping her same meet-the-school-bus schedule, even though it was still summer, and her kids were teenagers now. (He helped her find them summer jobs, and the youngest daughter was always willing to babysit for him and Anne.) But Grace might have left messages for him. He ought to check. Elsa's car was still here, but he knew better than to interrupt her, even if she wasn't practicing the organ. She might be going through files of music, or even writing her own arrangements for the hymns. She held a degree in musicology from Heidelberg, he believed. She took her job with ferocious seriousness.

Maybe he could just retreat to his study in the house, enjoy the rare quiet with the children gone. He'd mix up some lemonade. Anne kept concentrate in the freezer—something his mother would never countenance. He could sit in his easy chair, make notes for his sermon, and if he happened to doze off...well, when he woke up it would be time for a drink. Then he spied Amos McCready in the flower garden, leaning on his cane, but still bending down now and then to pull weeds. Retired or not, Amos couldn't keep away from the garden. At least it was shady there now. He'd better go talk to the old coot. Make sure he didn't have a stroke on church property.

"Dahlias are coming along, Rev," Amos greeted him, without looking up.

Gerald went to see. He had planted the dahlias himself. Amos knew, without having to say anything about it, the pleasure they gave Gerald. He stood next to Amos now, admiring the hardy leaves and the buds that in September would rival any foliage for splendor, yellow dahlias bigger than sunflowers, white ones, smaller, but as fresh as any spring flower. But the black dahlias were his favorite, a deep velvety red you could get lost in. Women should wear dresses made of that color and texture—though Anne wouldn't, unless there was a lot of navy or beige mixed in. Funny how he felt about flowers. Usually, it was the wife's domain. Certainly flowers had been the only sort of beauty his mother had ever cared about. Roses, especially. But Anne never spent any time in the garden or outside at all, unless she had to watch the children. When they'd first arrived, he'd suggested she join the garden club to get to know more people in the community. She hadn't said anything. For days. That was her answer.

"Frank Lomangino not keeping things up to your standard?" Gerald asked, as Amos bent to pull another weed.

"Oh, the lad's all right." Amos paused a beat. "For a Wop."

Gerald suppressed a smile. Amos liked to shock. A veteran of both wars, though in a Scots unit of the British army during the first one, he had a lexicon of common and obscure slurs that he applied to almost everyone. (One of Amos's favorites was Cheese-Eating-Surrender-Monkey for anyone he suspected of being French or, as Amos put it, Frenchified.) He referred to himself as a Jockie (slang for Scot). He was so universally offensive, it was hard to take offense. At least for Gerald. Some of his parishioners were not as tolerant of the old curmudgeon.

"Schooled the Dago on how to expunge aphids. Soap, water and whiskey. Brought him a batch, warned him not to tipple."

Gerald thought idly of a sermon he'd once given on the Good Shepherd. Everyone loved to think of Jesus as cradling a snow white lamb in his arms. They didn't think about the Good Shepherd plunging his pest-ridden, shitty-assed (not that he'd used that term) sheep into...

"Sheep dip," Gerald said out loud. Then he added, "Isn't that what you Jockie's call your moonshine?"

"Aye, that's about the size of it," agreed Amos. "Sheep dip is all very well, Rev. But what you need around here is hen-dip, old biddy-dip to be exact."

Amos was also notorious for his scorn of women. They returned the sentiment. The year Charlotte Crowley was head of the Sunday School, she had lobbied to get Amos removed from his self-appointed post as the only one who could teach the prophets to fifth graders.

"He tells them dirty jokes!" she had protested.

But no one else wanted to teach fifth graders anything, so Amos had remained a Regeneration tradition. Whenever Gerald thought of the prophets he pictured Amos on a rant or Amos smoking a pipe under his gourd vine, waiting for the Lord to deliver retribution to the wicked. He would have been just as peeved as Jonah when Nineveh was spared. And of course the prophet he'd been named for was famous for frothing at the mouth about Israel's whorish ways. Gerald prepared himself to listen to a tirade on the sins of woman-kind, Jezebels all. Instead Amos just gave a quick nod of his head in the direction of the choir room. Gerald turned just in time to see Elsa walk out the door, slamming it behind her. Her gait was a little unsteady.

"Quick, hide behind me, Rev. I'm taller than you."

The offer was tempting, but came too late.

"Gerald!" Elsa called out; she must have been drinking or she would have called him Mr. Bradley in public, or semi-public. "A word with you, please, if you don't mind. When you are finished talking to the Scotchman."

It wasn't an epithet, but she made it sound like one.

"Scotsman," he corrected, "you little schnauzer," he added under his breath. "Scotch is what you drink."

"No, it's what *you* drink," she corrected him.

Gerald looked around to see if anyone else was hearing this exchange. The neighbors on the other side of the church were not Episcopalians or even Catholics. In fact, they were teetotalers, he had discovered to his dismay when he and Anne had invited them to dinner.

"I prefer vodka," Elsa informed him.

"You don't say?" said Amos.

She planted herself in front of Amos and stared belligerently. Gerald had to admit she did look rather like a small, riled dog.

"Gerald, if you please," she said.

"Excuse me, Amos. And take it easy in this heat."

He could hear Amos lighting up his pipe, and Gerald began to feel in his pocket for his own pipe with his right hand as Elsa linked her arm through his left. (How a gesture that could have been intimate was so lacking in seduction and flirtation Gerald could not explain.) All he found in his pocket was his dog collar. Damn, he must have left his pipe and cigarettes in the car.

"That woman," Elsa dramatically lowered her voice as she led him across the driveway to the entrance to his office, "that woman should be executed. She should be taken out, placed in front of a firing squad and shot at dawn."

She released his arm and pulled her own cigarettes and lighter out of her pocket.

"Here, have one of mine."

She handed him a Camel unfiltered (not his brand but never mind) and she lit both their cigarettes.

"Which woman?" he asked, wondering if he should attempt to say anything about Christian forbearance but immediately dismissing the idea. It would only encourage her to be more outrageous—and he supposed he shouldn't, even though he was rather enjoying her rage.

"Charlotte Crowley," she stated. "Who else? I would like to cut off that long snout of hers, make it into Bratwurst and feed it to her for breakfast!"

After she'd been executed? Gerald did not say.

"What now?" sighed Gerald. "Did she complain about the hymns again?"

Elsa had impeccable taste. His wife Anne loved her for it, even though she found Elsa intimidating. Now that the twins were old enough to go to Sunday School, Anne had joined the choir. It was the first volunteering she had done voluntarily. But some of the other parishioners missed some of the old Victorian chestnuts that Elsa refused to include except when he threatened to fire her, which he did about once a month.

"The woman is a public menace. J. Edgar Hoovering should resign and give her his job."

Then to his dismay, Elsa burst into tears. She must be more upset—and drunker—than he'd thought.

"Somehow or another that old *rotzunge* has found out about Clara."

CHAPTER FOUR

Anne knew Gerald was having drinks with someone even before she went into the house. She had hoped the driveway would have been clear of cars by the time she got back from the pool, but someone was still here, someone who drove a medium-sized tan car. She could never identify the makes of cars, and remembering who drove what wasn't her strong suit. Gerald and his visitor were sitting on the screened porch, obscured by late afternoon shadow and wilted morning glory vines. She could hear laughter, masculine, she thought, and the sound of ice, perhaps just freshened, in glasses. They were drinking gin and tonics, most likely. And here she was with three hungry, querulous children, a carryall full of wet bathing suits to hang on the line—and two separate suppers to fix.

"Where's Daddy?" Janie asked.

"Where's Daddy?" Peter echoed, whether because he wanted to know or because he was still playing repeat-everything-Janie-says as he had been on the way home, Anne wasn't sure.

Funny how seldom Katherine asked about her father. Long ago (if there was such a thing in a seven-year-old's life) when she was a baby, really, she had been Gerald's favorite, and Katherine had certainly preferred her father.

"He's with a parishioner," Katherine informed the twins, as if she were the grownup.

"I don't like pishners," announced Peter.

"Parishioner," Katherine corrected.

"Panishuner," Janie said proudly.

"Parishioner," Katherine insisted severely.

They were all three massed on the landing now between the front hall, kitchen, and stairs. Anne wanted to get the bathing suits hung on the clothesline and change her clothes before she had to greet an unwanted and possibly tipsy guest.

"All of you, go upstairs and play until supper's ready."

"Can't we go outside?" Katherine asked, her tone just shy of a whine.

Anne had had enough of dirty knees and grass stains. They were all clean from the pool, and if they stayed that way, she could skip the often chaotic ordeal of baths. Besides, she wanted a moment outside alone. Gerald thought she didn't care for being outside—and she didn't during the day. It was too public. But all at once, she found herself wanting to look at the patterns of light and shadow. Hear the long, repetitive call of the mourning dove.

"Television, television, television!" Peter's voice rose steadily.

But the television was in the dining room, which had windows that opened onto the porch. If Gerald had been alone, she might have risked it, but not with company.

"Katherine, would you read the twins a story?"

"Yes, a story," agreed Janie, Anne's most reliable ally. "Read to us, Katherine, read to us!"

Katherine appeared to consider. Anne knew she had found Katherine's weak spot, or rather her strength. Katherine was very proud of her skill at reading.

"*Mike Mulligan and the Steam Shovel!*" shouted Peter.

"No," said Katherine, exercising her small power. "I will read you...*The Tale of Two Bad Mice*!"

"Bad Mice! Bad Mice!" Both twins jumped up and down.

Anne smiled, impressed with Katherine's choice, winning Peter over with the badness of the mice, while satisfying her own desire for more challenging vocabulary. Long before Katherine could read, Beatrix Potter had been a favorite of hers. Anne could remember Katherine at the age of two informing her older brother that she was "affronted" just like Mrs. Tabitha Twitchit.

"Off you go, then." Anne herded them towards the stairs. "I'll call you when supper's ready."

She felt a pang as the twins each took one of Katherine's hands, as if she were much older than she was, not really another child. Peter and Janie were such a self-sufficient unit, playing their own private (and to Katherine idiotic) games. Unless she assigned Katherine a role like this one, she was often left out. It touched her to see Katherine wear the mantle of older sister, so gravely and forbearingly. Katherine had come into this world as someone's baby sister.

Stop, Anne told herself. Stop. Remember what Dr. Aiken had told her. Grief is normal, but don't become morbid. Don't dwell. The tranquilizers he had given her didn't help much, just made her feel woozy, so she had thrown them away. But she did take the sleeping pills. It's just that she cared so little about waking up. Stop, Anne told herself again. And she picked up the bag of wet suits and went out into the yard where the mosquitoes had started biting and the doves had fallen silent.

Katherine was still reading to the twins as Anne changed into a fresh, somewhat more formal shirtwaist dress, dark blue with subdued paisley patterns in dark gold and red. She decided to go greet Gerald's guest before putting on the children's hamburgers. That way she could excuse herself after a brief exchange. As she passed through the kitchen, she noted the open gin bottle, the tonic water left out instead of put back in the refrigerator, an empty ice cube tray, little puddles on the counters, and a can of cocktail peanuts, almost empty, also left open with traces of red peanut skins everywhere. Typical Gerald, who could not put a lid back on or put something away to save his life—or hers.

She fought the almost overwhelming urge to stop and set everything to rights and kept going through the little pantry-breakfast room and the dining room where she could see through the windows the Kennedyesque hair of Rick Foster. That is how she thought of it.

It was actually quite a bit lighter than Kennedy's but just as abundant and combed the same way, giving that impression of youthfulness and vigor that Nixon fell so short of though he was the same generation. Rick Foster and Gerald were laughing now, a trifle too heartily, she thought. Then she reproved herself for begrudging Gerald this jovial camaraderie, the obvious relaxation he found in having a drink with someone who was more a friend than a parishioner. Too bad for Gerald she didn't feel the same way about Rick's wife, Sybil. And too bad she couldn't tolerate more than a sip or two of sherry. It made their obligatory social life more than a little fraught.

"Hello, Anne!" Rick stood to greet her and smiled at her with what seemed like genuine pleasure. "I'm afraid I could not resist inviting myself for a drink with your good husband here."

Gerald, too, half-rose from his seat, then sat down again, seeming a little flustered, as if unsure whether he was supposed to stand for his own wife in his own house, but wanting terribly to make the correct gesture.

"I'm sure it was all Gerald's idea."

"I hope we can persuade you to join us," Rick invited her.

How much more at ease Rick seemed than Gerald did. She looked from the tall blond man to her husband, who was by no means short and had most of his brown hair. But at forty he still had a round face and a snub nose that made him seem not youthful, but immature.

"Would you like some sherry, dear?" Gerald rose again.

His pleading tone set her teeth on edge. She did not know who she hated more for the way she felt—herself or him.

"Rick came by to tell me a marvelous idea he has about a location. For the camp. A real brainstorm."

The camp. His memorial for Hal, his amends to Hal. Amends that as far she was concerned could never be made.

"I look forward to hearing about it later," she said politely. "I'm afraid I'm in the middle of things in the kitchen. It's time for the children's supper."

Rick, a true gentleman, took the hint and looked at his watch.

"Same thing at my house," he said. "I promised Sybil I'd be home early to see the boys before I go out. I'm speaking to the Rotary Club tonight."

"Wall to wall Republicans," Gerald laughed. "But if anyone can convert 'em, you can."

"Good luck," said Anne, ready to retreat. "It is so kind of you to be thinking of Gerald's project in the midst of your campaign."

"Not at all," said Rick. "It's my project, too. Say, I'm going to be taking an afternoon off from campaigning on Sunday. We're having a barbeque, just a few good friends. If you're free, I'd like you to join us. I thought I might see if I could get Mildred Thomson to bring her nephew. Chance for a casual chat about the property. I'm going to ask the Crowleys, too."

How is that an afternoon off? Anne did not ask, already picturing the well-coiffed crowd around the Fosters' patio by the swimming pool, the casual but calculated introductions.

"Love to," said Gerald. "We're free aren't we, Anne?

Her eyes flickered over his. He had forgotten her request for a day without social obligations, a day with the children, so that they could take them on a picnic, somewhere by a stream or a lake.

"As far as I know," she said.

He had forgotten, but she would not, even if she never spoke of it to him. It would be recorded in the Book of Betrayals, a private book that existed only in her mind, but it was very long and detailed, with well-worn pages.

"That's settled then!" said Rick. "Oh, and feel free to bring the children. We've hired a sitter for the afternoon. The kids can swim."

Rick Foster smiled at her so warmly, as if he knew, perhaps even sympathized, and was ever so grateful for her sacrifice.

Katherine looked at her mother's back as she stood at the stove cooking dinner for the grownups. It was almost the same dinner as theirs, but the hamburgers were a different shape, because they

were really lamb patties. And instead of potato chips, they were having rice that was white as clouds and should have tasted like clouds
but didn't. And they were having green beans from a frozen package
with pictures of green beans that looked much prettier than the real
beans. Katherine had tried green beans once, and she had gagged.
Her mother never made them eat anything they didn't want to eat,
which made her father mad. He said she and Peter and Janie were
spoiled. Her Nana said so too. She was the one who had made her
eat the beans.

Katherine did not like to see her mother's back that way with
the shoulders raised and the bones where people used to have wings
(so Katherine believed) all hunched and hard-looking. She could tell
that the front of her mother was closed, and her face had the look
that scared Katherine. It wasn't mean exactly, but you knew someone
had done something wrong. It might have been her. She could never
be sure. She did not know how to ask. When her mother's back and
face looked this way, her mother didn't talk. Her not-talking filled the
whole house. That was one reason Katherine liked outdoors better. It
was too big for anyone to fill it.

The twins were blowing bubbles in their milk through their
straws. They weren't supposed to do that, but her mother hadn't
stopped them. Katherine thought about telling on them, but decided
she would blow bubbles, too.

"Stop that, all of you!" her mother said without looking around.

The pan sizzled as she turned over the lamb patties and then patted them into the pan. Was that why they were called patties, because
you patted them? Katherine would rather pat a real lamb.

"Goddamn it!" their father suddenly roared from the other room.
"Goddamn son-of-a-bitch!"

Their father was loud. Loud as thunder. Loud as God. Loud as
the gasses he made in the bathroom next to her bedroom. He had
probably stubbed his toe. It was terrible when he stubbed his toe.

"Finish your supper," their mother said.

Then she stabbed out her cigarette, turned off the stove and walked quickly into the other room. It was as fast as her mother ever went. Katherine had never seen her run.

"They should put their toys away before dinner," they heard their father saying. "No dear, don't you do it. Janie! Peter! Katherine!"

They all put down their cups and ran through the pantry and dining room to the living room door where they stopped for a moment, watching their mother pick up Lincoln Logs that had rolled across the floor and under the couch.

"Daddy knocked my fort down," whimpered Peter.

"Get down and help your mother!"

He took a step towards Peter. For a moment Katherine felt like she could not breathe, like she could not see. Everything was happening too fast and too slow. Then without thinking what she meant to do, Katherine stepped between her father and Peter.

"Mommy said he could leave his fort up," she told her father.

He could kill her if he wanted to. In that moment she did not care. Her father was being mean.

"Katherine," said her mother sharply, angrily. Why? What had she done wrong? And why hadn't her mother told her father that Peter was allowed to have his fort? "Go get some paper towels. Your father has spilled his drink. Peter, Janie, help me put away the logs."

They all hurried to obey, leaving her father standing there. Like a bear, Katherine thought, like a bear who has gotten lost and does not know how to find the honey.

It was one of those evenings, and Gerald knew it was all his fault. He just didn't know what to do about it. If he apologized for whatever he had done—and he was never quite sure—that would be wrong. If he defended himself, that would be even worse. If he knew how to placate her, he would. He had already denied himself a refill of the spilled drink—he knew she did not like him to drink too much—but if she noticed or appreciated, she did not show it. He had offered to take the children upstairs while she finished cooking dinner, but she insisted it was unnecessary. Dinner was almost ready. She had sent the children upstairs alone to play quietly. They seemed eager to go. He did not want to let himself know what he knew: they were frightened of him. He could not help resenting Anne for it sometimes. She spoiled them. His own mother said so. She had turned them against him. All without saying a word. Because she believed it was his fault. Everything.

And maybe it was.

Dinner was over before he could think of anything to say that would not be met with more silence. They both ate too quickly, barely chewing their food. That was the way you had to eat in the army. She blamed dormitory life, but she had attended a small women's college where surely you could linger over your meal. He suspected it was more that she took no interest in eating. Smoking was a more reliable pleasure. But she wouldn't even allow herself a cigarette until she had cleared away the dishes, scraped and stacked them.

"That was very good, dear," he spoke to her back as she retreated into the kitchen.

It wasn't even true. There was nothing special about the meal, but it was true that he needed to say it, needed to send good words and will after her. Maybe it helped. After they had finished dessert (lemon sherbet) she took out a cigarette, and he lit it for her.

"What did Rick Foster have to say?" she asked, after her first puff.

Salvation by grace suddenly seemed more than mere doctrine.

"He had a conversation with Mildred Thomson. Did you know that Rosewood belongs to her family, extended family, really? It was her great uncle who deeded land to the church."

Anne made no comment, but seemed to be listening.

"Mildred didn't inherit, wasn't in the direct line, although she's plenty well off from her own parents' estate. There are heirs to Rosewood from a couple of different branches from the family. That's why nothing's been settled. Rick gathered from Mildred that the heirs might be interested in selling or leasing the property. It's become a bit of a white elephant, apparently. Mildred Thomson said she would introduce them to Rick, or, well, to us both." Gerald took out his own cigarettes, trying to hide his excitement. He would really prefer a cigar after dinner, but that would be pushing his very tenuous luck. "Rick also thinks he's found some wealthy donors."

Anne took another puff of her cigarette, seemed to be debating putting it out half-smoked, and then changed her mind.

"That's nice, dear."

Her voice was as flat as a vacant city lot, where bits of trash blew nowhere and snagged on wire fence. He did not know why exactly, but the camp was not a safe subject. So he changed it quickly.

"Rick came along at just the right moment to save me from one of Elsa's tantrums."

Anne almost smiled.

"I bet someone criticized the Distler anthem," Anne guessed. "Some people don't have an ear for dissonance. Charlotte Crowley looked so indignant last Sunday, I thought she might walk out."

Oh, but this was wonderful, wonderful. So many words from Anne at once! Every muscle in his body relaxed. He felt almost as if he had had that third drink—and maybe he would, after they finished their coffee, just a small one, to celebrate.

"As a matter of fact, her conniption fit was about Charlotte Crowley. She said Charlotte had found out about her and Clara."

"Found out what?" said Anne. "That they're lesbians? I've always thought they were."

Gerald realized he may have stumbled. Anne probably didn't know about Clara's mental illness, how Elsa had fallen in love with Clara when she was a patient at the Gables where Elsa had worked for a time teaching music. Elsa had told him the whole story once when she was very drunk.

"Charlotte probably asked a lot of insinuating questions," said Gerald. "It doesn't take much to get Elsa into a tizzy. Before she could tell me what happened, Rick came along and Elsa stormed off. I am pretty sure she'd been drinking in the choir room. She said Charlotte should be shot—at dawn."

Gerald laughed. Surely Anne would laugh with him at Elsa's outrageous histrionics. But she didn't. She took a last drag and put her cigarette out, dumping it from the holder into the ashtray.

"Elsa's right about that." Anne spoke quietly. "Charlotte Crowley should be shot—or at least accidentally pushed down a long flight of stairs."

Gerald was taken aback by Anne's venom. Where had it come from? But before he could think of what to say, she had cleared the plates, with an efficiency that seemed almost ruthless, and made her way to the kitchen.

CHAPTER FIVE

Lucy sat on a wrought iron garden bench enjoying the moon-flowers that climbed a trellis just outside the French doors. The flowers had only begun their exotic night blooming now that the sun was setting earlier. The hot, humid day had not cleared exactly but softened with darkness. Undimmed by the waxing moon, the stars shone all the more lustrous through the hint of moisture in the air. A breeze made the lingering warmth seem caressing rather than oppressive. It also kept the mosquitoes at bay. Her old tabby cat Tabitha sat at Lucy's feet, content for now just to listen to the night rustlings instead of pursuing them as she once might have. Lucy had brought out with her a glass of claret. The dark wine gave back the night sky, and she sipped the reflected light of stars.

Behind her, the old house dreamed, waiting to fold her in its embrace when she went to bed. She knew people wondered why she stayed on here alone after her mother died. Some hundred years ago the house had held a large Quaker family. It had been a stop on the Underground Railroad with a secret room off the big country pantry. One day, Lucy would have to sell the house, perhaps to another family. But not yet. She and the house had become such good friends. They knew each other's ways, each other's sighings and creakings, each other's ghosts.

She had not grown up in this house, far from it. Her childhood had been migratory, beginning in France, where her American mother had met and married her father, and then on to England, when the First War broke out. There were sojourns back in the States after her father was killed in action, then more schooling for Lucy in England and Switzerland. At last her mother, weary of rambling, stuck a pin in a map. It landed here in this tiny hamlet a couple of miles from the village of White Hart. Lucy's uncle had joined her mother, and they had kept bees and grown vegetables together. They gave the house and land the rather fanciful name of Falling Star Farm because of a hill at the edge of the property where a large flat rock permitted an excellent view of the Perseid showers. Lucy had taken blankets and lain out on the rock last week, as she had every summer since she returned from overseas. Her uncle had died just after the Second War, and her brothers were married, so it had seemed only right for her to become her mother's companion.

Now the house was Lucy's alone, though she still slept in the back room intended at one time for a maid, a preference that had irritated her mother, who in every way had wanted Lucy to make more of herself. She had given up trying to explain to her mother why she loved the back room, which she had painted pale lavender, just a shade lighter than the lilacs that grew outside the window. Beyond the lilacs was the kitchen garden where she grew rosemary, basil, and thyme, along with a few tomato plants each summer. The room was big enough for a single bed and a wash stand with a porcelain basin where she kept a pitcher of water and witch hazel on hand. What clothes did not fit in her small dresser or closet could be stored in one of the downstairs closets or in the trunk at the foot of her bed. She had a bedside table with a lamp and a small bookshelf with her favorite novels and volumes of poetry as well as *The Book of Common Prayer* and the King James Version of The Bible.

"An old maid's room," her mother had lamented.

"*Chere petite maman*," Lucy had laughed, past minding. "Face it. I am an old maid."

At least as far as her mother knew, and Lucy had no intention of enlightening her. There were secrets she would take to her grave.

"But you needn't have been," her mother sighed. "You were so pretty with your green eyes and chestnut hair, and so accomplished."

"My eyes are still green," Lucy would say with just a hint of mischief in her voice. "I can still speak three languages, and I can cook as well as any French peasant."

Her mother would look at her and place her hand on her cheek.

"You are a treasure," she would say. "You are my treasure. I blame the war," she would inevitably conclude, vaguely yet emphatically.

The war she meant was the First War, the one that had widowed her mother and made old maids of many others in her generation. Not Lucy's generation. Lucy had come of age between the wars, the wild self-indulgent twenties (though Lucy had never been a flapper) followed by the Great Depression. But she knew what her mother meant. The world of her mother's youth, and of Lucy's earliest memories, had vanished, never to return. It had not been a perfect world, or a just world, Lucy knew that. But her few memories of her parents (they had been so young, Lucy realized now) were sealed in something like those toys children loved—a little scene in a globe. Shake it and snow would fall gently, making it come magically alive. In some ways, despite being widowed and raising three children alone, her mother had stayed in that idyllic world. Lucy still longed for it, despite or because of her embrace of all that was practical, her headstrong insistence as a young woman (secretly ruined) that she should be trained in useful work.

Lucy, made fatherless by the First War, had seen the Second War first hand, stationed at a hospital in London during the blitz. Though so much had changed in the way war was waged, in the scale of things, the Second War in many ways seemed the continuation of the first. She had witnessed horrors she would never forget and that she, like others who had been in the war, would not speak of lightly.

She did not regret her service. She would never forget being on night duty and suddenly sensing the presence of her father. She was caring for a young soldier who'd had half his body ripped away. She was making her rounds, checking vital signs, giving medications when she sensed that this soldier was losing ground, but he was conscious or at least his eyes were open and looking into hers. She made soothing sounds, hardly words, and pulled up a stool so that she could sit with him. It was when she took his hand that she felt her father there, next to her, both a young soldier himself and, more strangely, an older presence, as if he had lived and knew her in this moment as the woman she had grown up to be.

He stayed with her while the soldier died, and then they were both gone. For a moment, Lucy minded being left, and then she folded away the memory, where she could always touch it when she needed to, and went on with her work.

It seemed extraordinary sometimes that she could be here, alone in her garden, without fear, with the loudest sound the song of crickets, with her memories that held sorrow but no terror—unlike poor Elsa. Lucy felt concerned for her friend. She took a sip of her wine, feeling its gentle comfort deepen her breath, loosen the muscles around her heart, and she murmured an impromptu prayer. *Defend, O Lord, thy servant Elsa from all the perils of this night—and from the perils of her nightmares.*

She'd had supper that evening with Elsa and Clara in their little cottage on a remote back road. A few years ago, Lucy had advised them on what flowers might grow in their shady yard. They always made a point of inviting her over in late summer when the delicate fall cyclamen began to bloom and the showy pink sedum was in its glory. Elsa's favorite was the tall, white ghostly looking bugbane, which sounded more dignified by its German name *Bärenklau-Silberkerze*.

But the after-supper tour of the garden had not been peaceful. Elsa had been full of agitation, the cause of which she refused to confide in Clara, though clearly Clara sensed it. Elsa dismissed Lucy's offer of help with the dishes and made a point of taking her outside, leaving Clara to clear the plates and put away the leftovers of cold salads and smoked ham (an extravagance for their little household). Elsa had, alas, had quite a bit to drink by then (not just the chilled Riesling she had served with dinner, Lucy suspected) and she was not fully coherent. From an emotional account full of German and English expletives, Lucy gathered that Charlotte Crowley had made menacing and insinuating remarks about Clara, whether about Clara's sojourn in a mental hospital or the nature of her relationship with Elsa, Lucy wasn't quite sure.

"Elsa dear," Lucy at last got a word in edgewise, "Charlotte Crowley is a nuisance, I quite agree, but she means no harm. She just likes to know things. I confess that I have never been able to like Charlotte, but in fairness I can't say that she gossips, or at least not more than anyone else. She is just inquisitive—and acquisitive—in this peculiar way."

Lucy took Elsa's arm to keep her from tripping over rocks and roots and steered her towards a garden bench. Elsa lit a cigarette and drew on it as if it were the only way she could breathe.

"Oh, don't be naïve, Lucy!" Elsa exhaled with a vehemence that made Lucy think of a dragon. She could be breathing fire instead of merely smoke. "Don't you see? This is how it starts. It is all starting again."

Lucy took one of Elsa's hands and patted it. Night had come early to the secluded garden. Only the bugbane held the light, its tall tapering shape glowing eerily. Fairy candles. That was another name for them, she remembered.

"What's starting again, Elsa?" Lucy asked.

Elsa just shook her head and muttered something in German that Lucy didn't catch.

Lucy thought she could guess at Elsa's meaning. Neighbors betraying neighbors to the police. Whole families disappearing in the middle of the night. Elsa never talked about the war unless she was very drunk. Only once had she told Lucy about Annaliese, her Jewish, well, why not say it, lover. They had roomed together in Heidelberg, both music students. Though the university itself did not accept women, it was possible to study privately. Like Clara (surely not a coincidence), Annaliese had been a pianist. And not only a musician but a composer. "She could have been the most brilliant composer of our generation," Elsa had said over and over again the night she'd confided in Lucy.

When word came that Annaliese's family in Berlin had been rounded up and taken by the Gestapo, Elsa had drugged Annaliese to prevent her from going to look for them and getting herself captured or killed. Elsa had used her own considerable family connections to get Annaliese fake papers. They were on a train to Switzerland doing their best to look like two carefree students on holiday. At the border, the SS boarded the train; there was an altercation about Annaliese's papers. Possibly someone in Elsa's own family had betrayed them. The last thing Elsa remembered was a blow to her head. She woke up in a Swiss hospital and never saw Annaliese again. Only after the war did Elsa learn that Annaliese had died at Bergen-Belsen.

"I tried to tell Gerald today. He should do something about that woman. But before I could finish that damn Nazi came along and interrupted. Gerald always has time for *him*."

Lucy felt alarmed. Some people nowadays used the word Nazi far too frequently and casually to describe anyone whose politics they disliked. Just as others called people communists. Surely Elsa who had known Nazis first hand would never use the word lightly. Was Elsa starting to hallucinate? Lucy had worked at a VA hospital for a time. In all wars, there were people who experienced things so terrible they lived in a recurrent nightmare. Lucy knew Elsa drank too much. Drink was an obvious escape, but perhaps it was turning on her.

"Darling, surely there are no Nazis at the Church of the Regeneration," Lucy said. "And if there were, you can be quite sure Gerald Bradley would give them no quarter."

"Well, he's German anyway," said Elsa, less certain but still belligerent.

"Elsa, you know better than anyone that not all Germans are Nazis!" Lucy remonstrated. "I can't think who you mean."

"Now, Lucy, you know perfectly well who I mean," Elsa insisted unreasonably. "The politician. Running for Congress."

"Rick Foster?" Lucy was startled. "Good heavens, Elsa! Have you paid no attention to his campaign? He is running as a liberal

Democrat! And he is outspoken about integration. He is on the board of the interracial children's camp Gerald Bradley wants to found."

In fact, Gerald Bradley had asked Lucy to serve on its board. She wasn't sure why. Perhaps he thought she was wealthier than she was or perhaps it was because it was the sort of thing her mother would have done. Her mother had a strong sense of noblesse oblige. Though she had never been a supporter of women's suffrage or other modern notions, as she dismissed so many things, her mother liked to take a public role and had served on many committees and boards in her day. Lucy had made a half-hearted attempt to take up her mother's mantle, but she quickly retired it among mothballs—or rather dropped it off at the rummage sale. In any case, Lucy had politely declined and made a generous donation to Gerald's cause instead. Perhaps that was why Rick Foster had invited her to his Sunday barbeque. Spinsters did not usually receive such invitations. Now, as always, they were extras, causes of imbalance to numbers at tables. But perhaps at a barbeque, there would be no tables?

"Well, I suppose you are right." Elsa took a last deep drag from her cigarette. "I don't know why I dislike him so. I do know he doesn't like me, either. Gerald said this Fosterling person accused me of being drunk on the job."

Lucy stayed quiet for a moment, wondering if she should speak.

"*Cherie*, forgive me for saying so, but Mr. Foster would not be the only one who has noticed that you are a little too free with the bottle. You really ought to wait until you are at home to have a drink. You put your friend Gerald Bradley—and you know he is your friend—in an awkward position. I think you may have had a little too much today. Perhaps it showed. Gerald might have done you a favor steering Mr. Foster away from you, especially if you were upset. He might have been protecting you."

Lucy braced herself for an indignant outburst. Instead Elsa hung her head and even leaned against Lucy a little.

"Yah, yah," she sighed gustily, as if she were exhaling, though her cigarette had burned down to her fingers and gone out on its own. "You are right. After that Crowley woman accosts me, I have a drink, just to calm my nerves, but maybe more than I should. That woman makes me so angry, so angry. People don't understand Clara. They say she's queer in the head. They think, well, you know what they think, Lucy. And what gives them the right? What gives them the right to judge? They don't know what we've been through. I won't let anyone hurt her. I won't let anyone take her from me, not ever, not ever again. I'll kill them first."

Lucy felt cold all over for an instant. There were ghosts in the garden with them, unhappy ones. She must pull Elsa back, all the way back into the present, however unsatisfactory it was.

"No more of such talk," she said sternly. "There is no need. What does it matter what Charlotte or anyone else thinks. You are safe now, Elsa. No one is going to harm you or Clara. Do your best job at the church and ignore everything else. Come now. I see Clara on the porch."

Clara waited for them, hovering by the door, her tall, thin frame quivering. With her long dark hair and huge dark eyes set above high cheekbones, Clara should have been beautiful, could have been. She made Lucy think of a horse or a dog whose bloodlines were so pure all the hardiness and resilience had been bred out, and there was nothing left but brittle nerves. Clara sensed something was wrong, but more in the way a child or animal would. She sent Lucy a beseeching look.

"Is she all right?" Clara asked. "Are you all right, Elsa? Elsa, what's wrong?"

"Nothing's wrong," said Lucy firmly. "Coffee would be lovely and perhaps a little music."

Lucy excused herself a little while later, leaving Clara playing a Chopin nocturne, her hair tumbled loose from its old-fashioned bun, while Elsa sat near her on a straight-backed chair, determined to stay awake, to keep watch over her prize.

Lucy took a last sip of wine and said another prayer for Elsa and for Clara and for the soul of Annaliese. Then, as she often did, she recollected the day and prayed for everyone she had met, including dreadful Charlotte Crowley. She prayed for Gerald Bradley and his wife Anne. Such a lovely woman and, Lucy sensed, so unhappy. She prayed for their children, Katherine, the twins and for the boy who had died before they came to the Church of Regeneration. She prayed for poor Mildred, whom she had dodged, and adorable Frankie and his handsome father. She even prayed for Rick Foster, though he hardly seemed to need praying for. She prayed that he would use his talents well and not judge harshly those who'd made a hash of their lives. At last she prayed one of her favorite prayers.

Keep watch, dear Lord, with those who work and watch and weep this night and give thine angels charge over those who sleep. Tend the sick, Lord Christ, give rest to the weary, soothe the suffering, comfort the afflicted, bless the dying, shield the joyous and all for thy love's sake. Amen.

Then she sat quietly, listening to the night, the insect song and the low purr of her cat, a few notes of Chopin's nocturnes lingering in her mind. The dew began to fall, and the earth smelled sweet as it gave up its stored heat to the cooling night air. At the same time a delicious warmth stole over her as if someone who loved her very much had gently wrapped her in a silk shawl, in some tenderness, light as light yet penetrating to her core.

My dearest love, she prayed silently, *you are my joy. Shield me.*

CHAPTER SIX

Katherine did not want to go the Fosters' barbeque, not even if there was a pool. Prescott and Dickie Foster were scary boys. They went to a different school than her, like all the kids at the country club pool who Katherine did not know. That's why she wished her mother would let her bring Frankie swimming, so she would have someone to play with besides Peter and Janie. Peter and Janie had to stay in the baby pool unless her father was there to take them in the big pool. So she usually played by herself. Sometimes the other kids ignored her, and sometimes they made fun of her, because her bathing suit had a skirt. Her mother would not let her wear a tank suit, which was another reason she did not want to go to the Fosters' house and swim in their pool.

Peter and Janie didn't have to go to the party. She'd heard her mother tell her father she didn't think they were old enough to be babysat at a party by some teenager the Fosters hired. She was afraid they'd hit their heads, fall in the pool and drown, so they were being dropped off at Aunt Rosalie's. Aunt Rosalie wasn't their real aunt, but she was her mother's best friend, so they called her that. Aunt Rosalie had two girls. Lisa was Katherine's age and Barbie was the twins' age. They lived in a small house with a big garage in the basement, because the father (who they did not call uncle; he was too mean) fixed people's cars. Aunt Rosalie liked to bake. She was always baking a cake and letting the girls take turns licking the spoon and the bowl.

"I want to go to Aunt Rosalie's," she had begged her mother.

"Well," her mother began to change her mind, "I don't see why you shouldn't. To tell you the truth, I'd rather go to Aunt Rosalie's, too. I'll talk to your father."

Katherine's room was on the other side of the bathroom from her parents' bedroom, the smaller bathroom that only the family used. If Katherine got up to go at night she sometimes fell into the toilet, because her father left the seat up. He also dropped cigars in the toilet. They turned the water brown and the leaves floated on the top.

"I don't care, dear!" He said he didn't care, but his voice was angry. "You know Rick invited the children to the party. He made a point if it. I think at least one of them should go."

If her mother said anything, Katherine could not hear her. When she came back, her mouth was a small straight line, her eyes were down.

"Get your bathing suit, Katherine, and hurry. Your father doesn't want to be late."

It was strange to be with her parents without Janie and Peter. No one knew what to say in the car, so no one said anything. The Fosters had a big driveway that went around in a circle and their house sat at the end of the circle like a big birthday cake with vanilla frosting. Instead of candles it had white pillars in front that made a kind of a porch, but without a screen. The door was a blue that was almost grey, like the window shutters. There was a big knocker with a lion's face on the bottom. Katherine wished she could knock with the knocker. She wished her father would lift her up, so she could get a good grip on it.

"Daddy, can I—" she began, but he was already knocking.

Her mother pressed a doorbell at the side of the door, and she heard chimes that sounded like bells before a grandfather clock rings the hours.

When the door opened, it was not Mrs. Foster, who had hair that was so light, Katherine didn't know if it was white or yellow. It was

Mrs. Green, her friend Aramantha's grandmother. She was wearing a black dress and a white apron.

"Good afternoon, Reverend Bradley!" she said. "Mrs. Bradley. Come in. They all having drinks on the veranda."

Katherine did not know what the word veranda meant, but Mrs. Green let the word roll around on her tongue and float off into the air like it tasted good just to say it.

"Mrs. Green, good to see you," her father said, and he shook her hand like he did everyone's when they walked out of church. "Missed you and your family this morning."

Mrs. Green laughed as if her father had made a good joke. "Fosters hired us to do the barbeque. Been here all day."

"Hot work," said her mother in her friendly voice.

"I see you brought your bathing suit, honey." Mrs. Green bent down as if Katherine couldn't hear her unless she came closer to her ear. "There's a bathroom at the top of the stairs where the girls are changing their clothes. You can go on up, and then come right through here, through them big open doors out to the pool. Grace Jones' daughter Nancy minding the children."

Katherine knew Nancy. She had been babysat by her before. When Nancy came to their house she wore pants called pedal push-ers and socks with little bunny tails on the back. Her shoes had no laces. Instead there was a crack where she kept a shiny penny. She tried to teach Katherine how to blow bubbles with bubble gum, but Katherine ended up getting gum stuck in her hair. What if Nancy told Dickie and Prescott that Katherine could not blow bubbles? She held tighter to her mother's hand.

"Do you want me to come upstairs with you, Katherine?" her mother asked.

Katherine nodded.

"I'm sure she'll be fine," her father said without looking at her. "Let's go say hello to our hosts. Katherine, you can find us if you need anything."

Her mother gave her hand a squeeze, then dropped it as she went with her father towards the doors that looked like windows. They would go to the veranda and become part of a forest of grownups where it was easy to get lost, where she did not want to go in her bathing suit. Mrs. Green had disappeared, too. Katherine looked at the wide curving stairs. You couldn't slide on the banister in her house. It was too close to the wall. But this one, this one was perfect, made of smooth shiny wood. Maybe she could just stay in the hall and go up the stairs and down the banister the whole time.

Katherine turned towards the stairs and stroked the curved end of the banister. Before she could start up the stairs, she heard someone whisper her name.

"Katherine! Pssst! Get over here, right now!"

She turned and saw her friend Aramantha peering at her from around a corner. Katherine was so relieved, she felt like her face broke open and the sun was shining through the cracks.

"I am supposed to put my bathing suit on," she told Aramantha. "Where's your bathing suit? Come on, we can go in the pool together."

Aramantha wrinkled her nose till it almost disappeared in her face. "Nuh-*uh*! I ain't going swimming with Dickie-bird and Scottie-dog. You can see their pee-pees right through them nasty swimming drawers. You go on, if you want to."

Aramantha prepared to flounce away. She knew that flounce. Aramantha would let her skirts swirl, then she snapped them. It was the way she made you do what she wanted you to do, which was mostly what Katherine wanted to do anyway. Aramantha only pretended to be mean. Katherine felt safe with her. She could probably beat up Dickie or Prescott if she had to.

"I'm coming with you!" said Katherine, and she followed her around the corner into a big shiny kitchen where Aramantha's grandmother was putting chocolate icing on vanilla cupcakes.

"Child," Mrs. Green said to Katherine. "What you doing in here? You supposed to be at the party."

"I am at the party," Katherine said, puzzled.

"Don't you want to go in the pool?" Mrs. Green pressed.

"No, she *don't!*" declared Aramantha. "She wants to help me put the sprinkles on the cupcakes. Don't you, Katherine?"

"Don't you be fresh with me, missy!" Aramantha's grandma told her, lifting a wooden spoon as if she was going to smack her with it.

"It's all right, Mrs. Green," Katherine spoke up. "I do want to put sprinkles on the cupcakes. And I also want to slide down the banister."

Mrs. Green sighed like a wind that could stir up a storm.

"Now don't you go and get Aramantha in trouble."

Katherine wasn't sure what she meant. Aramantha was two years older than her. She was the one who decided what they would play. Maybe the Fosters didn't let Dickie and Prescott slide on the banister.

"I won't, Mrs. Green," she said.

"I know you don't mean no harm," Aramantha's grandmother said. "All right. Here's the box of sprinkles. Climb up on the stool. Just a few on each cupcake now, not so many you can't see the icing. Show Katherine, Aramantha. I'm going to take out another tray."

She picked up a tray of cheese cubes stuck to Ritz crackers by little sticks with flags on top and left Aramantha and Katherine alone in the kitchen.

Anne resisted the urge to go check on Katherine. If Gerald saw her go, it would irritate him. He said she was over-protective. Or rather he didn't say it, not anymore. It was one of the many things that could not be said. Since Hal's death, another subject, *the* subject for which there were no spoken words. But he thought it. He thought it before Hal's death and he thought it still. She spoiled the children. She paid them too much attention. And she supposed this much was true. Hal hadn't died of her carelessness. Thank God (if there was one) for that. And he hadn't died because of anything Gerald had done or not done, she reminded herself. It wasn't anyone's fault. How many times had she heard that before everyone stopped talking altogether. It wasn't anyone's fault.

It was her fault. The rainy day, all of them cooped up in that tiny vacation cabin. Katherine, a baby then, still colicky. Hal had wanted to go outside and play in puddles, but she told him it was raining too hard. He'd catch cold. Gerald tried to distract him. Let's build that model airplane, he said. But Hal was only just three. The kit was too advanced for him. He kept making mistakes, getting glue everywhere. Gerald lost his temper and swatted Hal, not hard, but Hal started to cry, and then he flew into a rage. He picked up the model plane and threw it on the floor and stomped on it. And Gerald...Anne wanted to stop here. It happened so fast. She was holding the baby. Gerald dragging Hal into the bathroom. Hal screaming, Gerald screaming. Then it was quiet, too quiet.

Gerald, white-faced, walked out into the rain without a coat. She put the baby in the crib and rushed to find Hal on the floor, swallowing his sobs, purple bruises starting to bloom all over his body. Why hadn't she left Gerald then? Why hadn't she packed their things, put the children in the car and left? If she had, maybe everything would have happened differently. Maybe—

Maybe he wouldn't have died almost three years later of silent pneumonia as a complication of measles? It wasn't anyone's fault that the penicillin that should have saved him sent him into anaphylactic shock. No, she told herself again.

Everything that could have been done was done. It was no one's fault.

He died in her arms.

It was no one's fault.

Anne didn't believe it.

Anne looked at her watch. In another five minutes, she would go check on Katherine. By then Gerald wouldn't notice. He was half way through his first martini, talking to Rick's wife, who looked as though she were preparing to edge away. She felt embarrassed for Gerald and, though he deserved whatever he got for trying to flirt with that fake-blonde-preserved-on-ice debutante, she suddenly felt protective of him. The Fosters were hilltoppers, not Gerald's sort of people at all. It was a painful contradiction in Gerald's character: his preaching of the social Gospel yet still wanting to be accepted by the social set. He had married the wrong woman for that. Oh, she had the social background, but she could not play the game at all. Not at all. Literally, figuratively. She and Gerald played tennis now and then at the club. Only with each other. No round robins, no doubles.

Anne surveyed the gathering crowd. They'd been early, of course. This barbeque was not, as advertised by Rick Foster, "just a few friends." Though perhaps that was what Rick had wanted. But entertaining was the domain of the wife. Sybil had invited the entire membership of the country club, it was clear, as well as people Anne had never met, probably friends of hers from New York. She and Gerald and a few others were clearly Rick's kind afterthoughts.

Nor was Rick standing over a backyard grill, knocking back beer with the men while the wives clustered and ran back and forth from the kitchen with casseroles and jello salads. Florence Green's husband, Jimmy, presided over a huge grill, tending steak, chicken, hamburgers and hotdogs for the children. She couldn't see who was tending bar, there was such a crowd around it. Everyone had a drink with decorative sticks skewering olive or lemon. The men wore sports jackets over polo shirts, and the women affected carefully casual dress, khaki skirts, white shirts, but pearl necklaces, the occasional diamond brooch. She felt both over and under dressed in her sleeveless shirtwaist with a pleated skirt and a little jacket to go over the top. She wished she had worn flats instead of her navy blue heels.

She took her cigarettes out of a small, beaded clutch bag that she carried under her arm.

She supposed she ought to make some small talk with someone before she slipped away. People were standing in little clusters, calling out hearty greetings to newcomers, gradually growing louder and looser. She could position herself anywhere, look polite, interested, laugh now and then, secure in the knowledge that she would never let out a bray like Mrs. Parker, the wife of a gentleman farmer who had her own social aspirations.

Anne lit a cigarette, then picked up the ice water that Gerald had brought her in a martini glass. Taking a step away from the outskirts of the party towards its center, she caught sight of Lucy Way loosely attached to one of the clusters. Lucy wore a dress with a floral print, violets perhaps, which looked light and cool despite its long sleeves. The purple made her hair look especially white, even on the warm, overcast day. Anne found herself thinking of whitecaps on the waves, fair-weather clouds, spring lambs—things that seemed fresh and unstilted. She tried not to make too obvious a beeline for a lifeline.

"Lovely party," Anne murmured to Lucy.

Lucy turned to her.

"Is it?" she murmured back.

And they both put their hands to their mouths to muffle the giggles that suddenly overcame them. Then Lucy linked her arm through Anne's, and they wandered back to the sidelines where they were shortly accosted by Nat Crowley, well in his cups, who seemed to think it incumbent upon him to flirt with them both.

Lucy could not blame Anne for excusing herself. Of course she would want to make sure little Katherine was all right on her own. And Nat, though well-meaning and even charming, had gin breath. Lucy herself was drinking Campari with soda in the absence of wine, which she would have preferred. Cocktails, once the province of speakeasies, were all the rage these days, but Lucy was too old-fashioned and continental to appreciate the trend.

"Fine woman, our Mrs. Gerald," Nat commented, watching Anne's slim figure retreat. "You can tell she's got breeding. Doesn't need to make a point of it, or put herself forward."

He laughed and Lucy just nodded, sensing not much more was required of her.

"She's had the good sense not to go head to head with my Charlotte. Charlotte runs that church or at least the distaff side. I suppose I'm not telling you anything new."

"We all appreciate Charlotte's boundless energy and devotion to Regeneration," Lucy said as kindly as she could, wondering if she would have to include lying in her personal confession to her Lord and Savior; she was not Anglo-Catholic enough to confess to a priest, and besides Gerald Bradley was far too low church.

"Yes, yes, I'm sure you do," Nat chuckled, perhaps not as deceived as she thought. "Whatever anyone says, Charlotte's stood by me through it all, through thick and thin. And there has been a lot of thin on my part, I am sorry to say."

Was he really sorry or did he just want sympathy? How early had he started drinking? Lucy wondered. It was only mid-afternoon, too soon to get choked up about the virtues of your long-suffering, insufferable wife.

"Hello, Mildred!" Lucy welcomed Mildred, who could be said to be lurking at an awkward distance, longing to be included but not daring to intrude. It was Lucy's chance to repent for avoiding Mildred the other day as well as for fending off any impulse of Nat's to be overly confiding.

"Hello, Lucy."

Mildred took a couple of sideways steps forward, in the manner of a crab, Lucy thought, immediately chastising herself. But must Mildred always wear brown, a color that did not become her? Was it Lucy's Christian duty to suggest—what would suit Mildred?—a soft peach, perhaps, or forget-me-not blue?

"Hello, Nat."

"Millie, old thing! How are you keeping?"

He clapped his hand on her back, as if she were a man. Millie blushed as if he had clasped her in a passionate embrace.

"Oh, you know," she said vaguely, waving away the importance she craved. "I never change. My nephew is here today. Well, I call him my nephew. My cousin Rupert's oldest son. You remember Rupert, Nat, from the old days?"

"Oh, yes, of course. Fine fellow. Good polo player. How is old Rupert?"

"Dead," Mildred said simply.

"Oh dear." Nat was clearly flustered. "I'm so sorry. Somehow I missed that. I can't think how Charlotte didn't tell me."

Lucy wondered if she must rescue the conversation or if she might legitimately seek the powder room.

"But my nephew," Mildred forged on, "he's one of the heirs to Rosewood and Father Bradley and Mr. Foster have asked to have a meeting with him. They have an idea, you see—"

"Well, that's wonderful, Millie dear. Just the ticket. If you'll excuse me, I really must—"

Giving each of their arms a friendly squeeze, Nat turned away, greeting people as he wove across the veranda, always listing towards the bar.

Lucy did not see so much as feel Mildred wilting next to her, drooping, her last hopeful petals curling up and falling. No wonder she wore brown.

"Lucy," quavered Mildred, "can I ask you a question? About the Gospel of Matthew?"

"I don't know that I can answer," Lucy hedged. "I am not a scholar or a theologian."

"I know," said Mildred. "But in the Beatitudes where it says, 'Blessed are the pure in heart,' I always think of you."

"Oh, Mildred, my dear, I'm hardly…." Lucy stopped, not knowing what to say.

It was astonishing how little anyone knew about how others saw them. She decided not to embarrass Mildred or herself by protesting what seemed to her an obvious absurdity.

"What a kind thought," Lucy amended. "Now what was it you wanted to ask?"

"Well, it's about Matthew 5:21-22 where Jesus says that if you are angry with someone it is as bad as murder, just as lust in your heart is as bad as adultery. What do you think about that, Lucy?"

Lucy hesitated. Sometimes Mildred's theological maunderings struck her as tedious and well, unattractive, as if she were picking her soul, like a nose, in public. But she sensed real anguish in Mildred's question.

"We are all sinners, Mildred," she said carefully. "To me that is the point of the whole sermon and of so many of Christ's teachings. Don't fancy yourself better than anyone else, because outwardly you have kept the Law. It's what's in your heart that matters. He always forgave sinners. It was the self-righteous he took to task. Why do you ask?"

Then it dawned on her. Nat had snubbed Mildred, cut her off in the middle of an eager, confiding sentence.

"I'm afraid Nat has had rather more to drink than he should," Lucy said gently. "I am sure he did not mean to be rude."

"Oh, Lucy, I'm not angry with *Nat*!" Mildred turned toward Lucy, looking utterly stricken for having given that impression. "I could never be angry with Nat! It's not his fault, you know, not his fault at all that he drinks. I know better than that."

"Who are you angry with then?"

As soon as she asked, Lucy regretted her question. It was idle curiosity. If Mildred answered her, she would surely regret her admission.

"I am sorry, Mildred. It is none of my business."

"Oh, Lucy, I need to tell someone."

"Perhaps you should make an appointment with Mr. Bradley."

Mildred shook her head sadly.

"I don't think Father, I mean Mr. Bradley, understands about sin, personal sin."

It was true. Gerald had given more than one sermon inveighing against preoccupation with individual salvation. He seemed to think obsession with one's own moral condition was self-indulgent, something people did to avoid addressing injustice and poverty. She feared Mildred was just the sort of person he had in mind.

"Mildred dear," Lucy said more briskly, "we all say the General Confession, and whatever Gerald's views of sin, he is a priest with the power to grant absolution through Christ. Surely you are no more sinful than the rest of us."

"Oh but I am, Lucy, I am," Mildred insisted. "No matter how many times I confess, I cannot stop hating her. That's why I want to know: is it as bad as murder? Am I a murderer in my heart?"

Lucy did not ask who Mildred hated. She was afraid she knew.

"Oh, Mildred!" Lucy tried to laugh. "That's why we confess every week! Or surely every one of us would be damned."

"Thank you, Lucy," Mildred said. "I would like to believe you."

And before Lucy could think of a way to excuse herself, Mildred, seeing Nat momentarily unattended, scuttled away.

CHAPTER SEVEN

Katherine was not at the pool, Anne discovered, and Nancy, in charge of some half a dozen wet slippery children, couldn't remember having seen her. Which was not at all reassuring. At least she had not drowned. (Anne had scanned the bottom of the pool thoroughly.) She had probably wandered off by herself in the house or the yard and found a tree to climb or a book to read. After a tour of the grounds and gardens yielded nothing, Anne went inside the house. Katherine had been directed to change in a bathroom at the top of the stairs, so Anne decided to look there first.

Sure enough, there were girls' clothes scattered across the floor with socks flung every which way in no relation to shoes. Clearly no one had supervised them. But she did not see the plaid Bermuda shorts and white sailor shirt she'd chosen for Katherine to wear. Since she was in the bathroom, she'd decided she'd better make use of it. She closed the door and locked it, not with the hook and eye she had at home, but a lock built into the shiny doorknob. Though the house was of some vintage—a colonial that had been extended in several directions—the sink and the bathtub looked new, sleek and modern. There was a huge mirror over the sink that no doubt concealed a medicine cabinet. There were theater lights over the mirror so that guests could fix their makeup. If she hadn't been worried about Katherine's whereabouts, she might have lingered in the bathroom as long as she could to avoid returning to the party.

As it was, she ignored her fading lipstick and the sad effect of humidity on her permanent wave. She stepped out of the bathroom into a wide, carpeted hall with a window seat at one end.

"Katherine?" she called, not too loudly, but loud enough to be heard in an empty house.

No one answered, but she heard a sound coming from one of the rooms down the hall. It felt awkward and intrusive to be in the private part of someone else's house, but if Katherine had gone exploring on her own, she must be stopped before anyone else found her. She made her way as quietly as she could in heels, stepping only on the toe. The carpeting was so thick her movement was almost silent. Why she should take such precautions, she did not know. It made her feel like even more of an intruder and yet it felt necessary.

The first two bedrooms appeared to belong to the boys. It was hard to distinguish one from the other. They were unnaturally neat and looked as though they were ready to be photographed for *House Beautiful* as "the sons' rooms." A shelf of sports trophies, a few blue and red ribbons on a bulletin board. Wall paper depicting hunting scenes in one room, sports in another. Matching bedspread and curtains. She walked on quickly, pausing in the doorway of what must be the master bedroom, a study in beige, white, and off-white with a king-sized bed that managed not to take up the whole room, the space was so large.

At the window seat, the hall turned right. Anne again heard a sound. No doubt there was a playroom for the boys, complete with a ping pong table. Why she did not call out again for Katherine, she did not know. Something about the heaviness of the quiet in the house in contrast to the sound below the windows where ice and glasses met and laughter rose and fell as if it were one synchronized flock of birds. When she arrived at the doorway, she was glad for her stealth.

There was Charlotte Crowley humming to herself happily, opening and closing drawers, sifting through files in a vast, clearly masculine desk. Law tomes lined the bookshelves. Two leather easy chairs kept each other company next to a coffee table neatly stacked with a mix of professional and leisure magazines, *Fly Fishing* and the *Harvard Law Review.*

Rick Foster's private lair.

Anne had caught Charlotte Crowley red-handed.

Red-handed. For a moment, Anne was no longer in the Fosters' house on a Sunday afternoon. It was night. In the rectory living room her guests lingered on and on over coffee that had little chance of sobering up Nat or Gerald or even one or two of the women. She had just rinsed and stacked the dessert plates. Instead of returning to the party, she took the kitchen stairs to the landing and went on up to make sure the children were at least in their beds. The twins, to her relief, were fast asleep. On the way to Katherine's room she saw the light was on in the master bedroom. (Gerald seemed incapable of turning off lights.) She didn't want their room all lit up for everyone to see when the guests finally spilled out into the driveway.

In the doorway to the bedroom, Anne stopped still. She must have made some sound, for Charlotte Crowley turned from Anne's bureau. Utterly without shame, she held up a photograph for Anne to see.

The one Anne kept folded away with antique lace handkerchiefs that she never used. The photograph she shared with no one. Hal at about eighteen months sitting in her lap, his face turned up towards her, she gazing at him. One of his chubby arms reached up, and his hand touched her cheek. There was no Madonna and child in the world by any master that could touch this image: she and her first-born son, serene and self-contained in utter adoration.

"Oh, my dear," Charlotte had said. "Is this the one you lost?"

Anne had not been able to speak. She crossed the room, pried Charlotte's fingers from the photograph and replaced it in the drawer. She did not turn around again until Charlotte was gone.

Now Anne watched Charlotte silently, careful not to give herself away, not even breathing. Charlotte had found another prize, another photograph. She held it up to the light of the window, peering at it closely. For a moment Anne felt dizzy. Her eyes swam. She stuffed her hand in her mouth to keep from crying out.

But of course it was not the same photograph. Of course not.

Slowly, soundlessly, Anne backed away. When she reached the window seat, she pivoted and picked up her pace.

She had caught Charlotte red-handed. She would have her revenge.

"Go on outside now, Katherine," Mrs. Green urged her. "You can't hide out here in the kitchen all afternoon. Hotdogs and hamburgers are all ready. Go on. There's a table set up for the children under the trees in the back yard. Nancy will be there. You be all right. Cupcakes and ice cream for dessert. Watermelon, too."

Katherine did not like watermelon. Too many seeds, and if there were boys around, they would probably spit them at the girls. But she was hungry, and she wanted to be outside.

"Come on, Aramantha," she said. "Let's go."

Aramantha scrambled down off her stool, too, but her grandmother grabbed hold of her arm.

"Aramantha have to stay and help me," she said firmly. "We'll eat later. Now you go on."

Katherine wanted to argue, but she didn't dare. Mrs. Green sounded angry, but she didn't know who she was mad at, her or Aramantha. She hesitated a moment, making circles on the floor with one foot.

"Go on, Katherine!" Aramantha sounded angry, too. "Git!"

So Katherine went, back into the hall and through the doors that looked like windows onto a place made of flat stones, like an outdoor floor. In one direction was the pool. There was no one there now, just a lot of towels left lying around. In the other direction, the grownups talked and laughed and smoked. Some of them held little plates in their hands. All of them had drinks. Katherine wanted to find her mother. Her father had said she could if she needed her, and she did need her. She didn't know where the kids' table was, and she didn't want to go there by herself.

She went into the thicket of grownups, weaving in and out, sometimes squeezing to get by, stopping to look up to see if she knew anyone. Most people paid her no attention at all. Now and then a parishioner spoke kindly to her, but no one knew where her mother was. They all pointed to her father who was talking, talking, talking, his cigarette hand waving and making smoke circles, while his drink hand went steadily up and down. Finding her father would not help.

When she was about to give up, the crowd parted for a moment, and she saw Frankie's father standing behind a counter, pouring drinks. With a rush of happiness, she saw Frankie next to him. He was putting olives on one of those little sticks and piling them up on a plate where his father could reach them. Katherine slipped behind the bar and stood next to Frankie.

"Can I put things on sticks, too?"

She and Frankie never said hello. They just started in doing things.

"You don't know how," said Frankie.

"Show me," insisted Katherine.

"Hey, look who's here!" Frankie's father turned to her, reached past Frankie and pinched her cheek, the way he always did. She didn't know why, but at least his pinches didn't hurt. "Frankie was looking for you. You two run along and play."

"But I'm helping you, Pops!" Frankie scowled.

"I got enough skewered olives for now, son. Go on. Have some fun."

"The hamburgers and hotdogs are ready," Katherine told him. "And there's cupcakes with chocolate icing for dessert. I put the sprinkles on."

She wanted Frankie to know he wasn't the only one who could help.

"Okay," agreed Frankie. "We'll go on a raid."

"A raid?" Katherine repeated, not sure what game they were in.

"We're the Indians," Frankie whispered. "Come on."

Putting his hands to his lips to signal absolute silence, he led her into the shrubbery and they began to sneak around the house to the backyard. There, beyond the grill and the table where food was beginning to be set out for grownups, they spied what Frankie called "the enemy," Dickie and Prescott and half a dozen kids from their school, all still in their bathing suits. Nancy kept getting up to pour more lemonade and wipe up spills while the kids ate hotdogs and hamburgers and potato chips. On another table sat the desserts still under wax paper.

"You get the cupcakes," Frankie whispered. "I'll get the watermelon."

"You mean we're going to *steal*?" Katherine asked nervously.

"I told you," said Frankie. "We're Indians. We are raiding the settlers. They stole our land."

"This is Dickie and Prescott's land," Katherine pointed out.

But Frankie was already crawling, belly to the ground, towards the table. Katherine looked around. So far no one had seen them. She dropped to all fours and followed her friend. Frankie got to the table first and reached up his hands, trying to slide the huge platter of watermelon off while still kneeling on the grass. For a moment, he actually balanced it on his head; then he lost his balance and fell back with it.

"Hey," shouted Dickie. "What happened to the watermelon?"

"Someone's trying to steal it!" shouted Prescott.

Before Frankie could get out from under the watermelon and run, they were both standing over him.

"I know who it is!" said Dickie. "It's that big dumb Wop kid. I've seen him at the church. He's a *criminal*. Just like his father."

"My pops is not a *criminal*!" Frankie came up from under, fists ready.

"Is so!"

"Is not!"

"Why was he in jail then!"

Frankie's answer was a punch in Dickie's nose.

"Hey!" shouted Nancy. "What's going on here!"

"He was stealing the watermelon."

Frankie took another swing, and before Nancy could get in between, both brothers started hitting Frankie, and all the other boys and some of the girls joined in. Katherine started hitting, too, but she couldn't get anywhere near Frankie. Someone shoved her and she spun away. That's when she caught sight of Aramantha peering at the fight from the back door.

"Aramantha!" shouted Katherine. "Help! They're beating up Frankie!"

Aramantha hesitated only a minute, and then she sprinted across the lawn, grabbed Katherine's hand and pulled her back into the fight.

Gerald took another sip of his third? (he wasn't sure) martini. He did not know exactly who he was talking to or what they were talking about. But he loved the guy. He was at that stage of intoxication when everything made sense, even when it didn't. Somewhere during the second martini, he had felt that loosening sigh when everything he'd held tight let go. There was more room inside for air—cool fresh air, never mind it was still hot and humid. His shoulders ached with letting go, but it felt so good to let drop whatever it was he was carrying.

(*My yoke is easy and my burden is light*, Christ had said. But it wasn't, Christ knows it wasn't. Gerald deserved a break now and then.)

The haze of the overcast day was brightening, turning golden. Mrs. Green carried out a big steaming pot of corn on the cob and set it on the buffet table. He loved Mrs. Green, too. Someone should have helped her carry that pot. He could see beads of sweat standing on her brow, making her beautiful brown skin shine. (Brown faces were so much more beautiful than white faces, he had noticed. Why was that?) Maybe he should go offer to help. She was his parishioner, after all, but the man, his new friend whose name he could not remember, was still talking to him.

"You know, Father, I admire what you and Rickie are gonna do for those kids. If someone had done something like that for me when I was a kid, my life might have turned out very different, know what I mean, Father?"

The man had called him "Father." And he had called Rick Foster Rickie. Who was he? His skin was almost as dark as a light-skinned Negro, and his hair was very black. He was wearing a dark suit instead of a sports jacket. He must be a Roman Catholic. That was Rick Foster for you, practiced what he preached. Invited Catholics to his barbeque. Jack Kennedy was a Catholic, of course, but Irish. This man was probably Italian. Italians had replaced the Irish on the list of despised immigrants, but that was changing now. Everything was changing. Had to change. For the better. This man might even be Jewish, though he doubted there were any Jews in White Hart.

"It's been a dream of mine for a long time, even before—" Gerald began.

And a lump rose in his throat. Don't talk about Hal, he told himself. If he did, he would cry. Anne hated it when he cried. Not because she loved him. Did she love him? He knew she thought his tears were cheap. Gin tears, she called them once through her teeth, under her breath. But they weren't. This man would understand a man's tears, he thought. He might put his arm around him and say: I understand, Father.

That made the lump bigger.

It would be better not to cry, even if Anne wasn't around anywhere. Other people would not understand. Sybil Foster would not.

Her hair was so blond, blond as Marilyn Monroe's, and her... Stop, he told himself: your neighbor's wife, your next Congressman's wife. She would expect a man to be in control. Like Rick Foster. They were perfect together, like Jack and Jackie.

"I and my associates consider it an honor to help make your dream come true, Father."

The man put his hand on his back—not a slap on the back, just a kind hand like he understood all Gerald couldn't say, all his troubles.

Gerald wasn't sure what his friend meant about helping. Could he be one of the wealthy backers? A man who had come up through the mean streets and made good and now wanted to help others? Before Gerald could ask, Grace's daughter Nancy came rushing up to him.

"Mr. Bradley, Mr. Bradley! Come quick! The kids are having a huge fight. I can't get them to stop. Mrs. Foster can't either, and I don't know where Mr. Foster is."

She grabbed his martini wrist and dragged him towards the back yard.

It was hard to tell what was going on; there must have been a dozen or so kids going at it full tilt. When Sybil Foster saw him, she rushed over to him (as fast as she could in high heels).

"Do something!" She was furious. "Get that bully off my boys. Get him out of here!"

A surge of adrenalin cleared Gerald's head sufficiently that he put his drink down. He picked up a maple twig that still had leaves on it but would do for a switch and he waded into the knot of arms and legs and started swatting and yelling.

"Cut it out, all of you!"

"Don't you dare hit my boys!" shrieked Sybil. "It's not their fault. They were *attacked*!"

Most of the children had jumped back and run to the shelter of their parents. Out of the corner of his eye, Gerald saw Mrs. Green's granddaughter pulling Katherine away. By now other guests had left the bar to see what was going on.

"Frankie, Frankie, Junior!" Frank Lomangino came running from the bar. "Let goa him!

Frankie was the only combatant left. He had Dickie in a headlock.

"Get your retarded monster off my child!" commanded Sybil.

Gerald stepped aside to let Frank deal with his own son. He felt badly for him.

"They're just kids," Gerald began to say, but no one was listening to him, certainly not Sybil Foster.

Just then Rick Foster came through the back door followed closely by Mrs. Green and, of all people, Anne. Where had she been? She looked unusually flushed. By contrast, Rick Foster looked pale, as though he might be about to be sick. The heat and the gin hit Gerald again in a wave of confusion. For one crazy moment he wondered…Rick and Anne?

Then Rick stepped forward and took charge of his son, just as Frankie let go and turned to his father, who cuffed him and then hugged him.

"He hit me, Daddy! He hit me!" Dickie stated the obvious. "He made my nose bleed. And he shouldn't even be here. He wasn't even invited!"

He ran to his mother and wiped his nose on her beige linen dress.

"For God's sake. You! Get some ice!" Sybil snapped at Mrs. Green.

Mrs. Green, who had collared Aramantha, marched away to the kitchen.

Rick Foster stood calmly in the midst of his party, as if it had not just become a shambles. He went over and placed his hand on his son's head.

"Everyone is a guest here, son. Do you hear me? Everyone."

Gerald looked at Rick Foster. The light made his hair look gold, not blond, leonine. It didn't matter that Sybil was looking daggers at her husband. They just glanced off him. They could not touch his innate greatness.

This man was a leader. He could be president someday. Gerald wouldn't even blame Anne if she fell in love with him.

He vaguely noticed that his daughter had come to stand beside him. He did not know what she wanted.

"Daddy," she said. "Can we go home now? Mommy said it was up to you."

"Sure," he said.

But first he needed another drink.

Part Two:
DEATH

CHAPTER EIGHT

Lucy arrived at the church early, not quite at the crack of dawn, but that was when she had gotten up in order to be here in time to prepare the altar for the eight o'clock service. Ordinarily she would have made preparations on Saturday, but Charlotte, her partner on altar guild this month, had been out of town judging a garden show.

"Nonsense!" Charlotte had pronounced when Lucy had said she could prepare the altar on her own. "I won't hear of your doing all the work. We'll meet early on Sunday and do it together. We are both old hands. It won't take any time at all. The flowers are being given by Rosalie Brown, and you know she always insists on her own arrangements of wildflowers in memory of that baby she lost." Charlotte made it sound as though Rosalie had been merely careless, and her disapproval of wildflowers was obvious. "So there is that much less to do."

If Lucy had not been so keenly aware that she would have vastly preferred working alone, she might have insisted on coming on Saturday. She agreed to Charlotte's plan as a form of penance, though really the endless season of Trinity didn't require such a rigorous approach to examination of conscience. She must not become as morbidly preoccupied with sin as Mildred. And so she allowed herself to feel pleased that she had arrived first and had the church to herself for a few moments.

She walked to the eastern side of the nave past the baptismal font beneath the round rose window, not yet illuminated. Though the day was bright and deliciously cool and fresh, the trees of Rosewood next door to the church meant morning came late. The light in the church was still dusky, the rest of the east windows in the little side chapel, also dark. In one, Abraham Lincoln's purple cape looked black, and the waves Jesus treaded, particularly stormy. Between the side altar and the aumbry the gleam candle burned low. The flame meant that the aumbry held reserve sacrament, leftover consecrated bread that the rector would take on his rounds to the hospital or to shut-ins. The Light of Christ, she sang the words silently, making a mental note to replace the candle, for that Light must never go out when the sacrament was present.

The sacristy was to the right of the side chapel, and Rosalie had left the flowers for the day, asters, daisies, larkspur, and loosestrife, beautifully and simply arranged in several vases. Not being a member of the altar guild, Rosalie had not presumed to place them herself. In fact, she rarely came to church, though she sometimes helped in the Sunday school.

Lucy reached behind the curtain of the small altar for the key to the sacristy, the only door in the church that was ever locked, for it housed all the valuables, the candlesticks and the silver used for Holy Communion, the chalices, the cruets, the ciborium, the paten, the lavabo bowl, the bread bowl. Lucy loved all the names of these objects that were at once holy and homely, like the extraordinary number of hand-embroidered linens, which must be hand-washed and ironed dry—never hung out on a clothesline! The sacristy was nothing more—and nothing less—than a sacred kitchen and linen closet. Lucy thought of the sacristy as the place where Mary and Martha met in peace. What could be more practical and mystical than setting the table for Christ's supper? Never mind it was really breakfast for the hardy souls who attended the eight o'clock, always Communion, unlike the ten thirty which was Morning Prayer three Sundays out of four.

Lucy picked up the vases of flowers and set them on the counter next to the sink, so that she wouldn't trip over them as she went back and forth to the sanctuary following the timeworn steps of what her mother used to call the stately dance. She paused for a moment to acknowledge the church's only image of the Madonna and Child hanging on the wall between the silver cupboard and the sink—a sink that emptied directly onto the ground, for any lingering blood of Christ washed out of the chalice must flow directly to the earth and not become mixed up with modern plumbing.

On impulse, she arranged the four vases of flowers on the counter, as if they were an offering to the Virgin Mary. The Roman Catholic Church had just celebrated Mary's birthday, she remembered. Lucy had always liked this portrait, a Raphael. Mary, so young, dressed in dark red under a cloak that could be green or black. She circled her fat, happy baby with one arm. Both their hands held a book, a prayer book perhaps? In the background dawn was just breaking over an Italian hill town. But what held Lucy's attention was the gaze between mother and child, sidelong but intent, as if nothing, surely not the observer, could come between them.

"*Sainte Marie*," she spoke aloud softly. "*Tu as perdu ton fils, aussi. Tu comprends.*"

Lucy said a silent prayer for Rosalie's baby, Anne's—and yes her own, too, though the child had never come to term, and no one had ever known.

No one but Christ and his mother.

Lucy heard the sound of the side door opening in the church. Charlotte, at last. Just like her to interrupt a particularly intimate moment. Lucy sighed and braced herself to greet Charlotte cheerfully. Hello, Charlotte, she rehearsed. Will you set out the linens or the silver? She would defer of course.

But it wasn't Charlotte, unless she had somehow gotten a key to the organ console. Lucy left the sacristy, went past the pulpit and peered into the sanctuary.

"Who's there?" Elsa whirled around from setting up her music. "Oh, Lucy, it's you. You gave me a fright. I thought no one came here this early."

"Charlotte couldn't come yesterday. We're on altar guild, so we agreed to meet this morning. Only she's late. What are you doing here? Is there going to be music at the eight o'clock now?"

"No, no music for the eight. No money in the budget for two services. I come early to practice before the vultures gather to begin sorting for the great rubbish sale."

Lucy smiled and shook her head at her friend's disdain for a fund-raising extravaganza that no doubt helped pay her salary or at the very least bought new music for the choir.

"I hope it won't disturb you if I set up the altar while you practice," said Lucy.

"*You* won't disturb me," Elsa glowered as she seated herself at the organ. "And neither will anyone else."

And with that, Elsa fell on her instrument and Lucy recognized the prelude of one of her favorite chorales, number 106: *Alle Menschen Mussen Sterben*. All Men Must Die.

Her parents were making those awful noises in their bedroom. One time Katherine had rushed in, terrified that some monster might have come to attack them. Her father had yelled at her and told her never to interrupt again. Her mother had explained later that it was just a game grownups sometimes played. A yucky game, she thought.

She stood up on her bed, so that she could look through the window above it. She could see across the neighbor's lawn, and if she stood up on tiptoe and looked around, she could just glimpse through the tall pines at the lower end of the driveway, not the church part, where everyone turned in from the main street with its maple trees all lined up on each side, but the part that sloped down past the barn where the rummage sale toys were sold. Even though she had never seen Frankie's house, she knew Frankie and his father always walked up this part of the driveway. She hoped Frankie might come with his father this morning. Her father had called Frankie's father last night to see if he could fix something in the parish house kitchen before church.

"Or God help us there will be no coffee hour," her father said, "and the WOR will be in an uproar."

She had never seen the WOR, but her father talked about it a lot. She thought it might live in the furnace room in the parish house. She did not think its uproaring could be any worse than the grunts and snorts her father was making right now. Quickly and quietly she jumped down from the bed and found her old Saturday clothes in the laundry hamper. She hadn't seen Frankie since the fight with Dickie Foster. Her mother hadn't told her that she couldn't play with Frankie, but she had heard her mother talking to her father about him when they were eating grownup dinner. Katherine had been playing by herself on the porch, and they didn't know she was there.

"Why must Frank Lomangino bring his son with him wherever he goes? I suppose he's too much for his mother to handle. But his father doesn't keep a proper eye on him. He shouldn't expect other people to keep track of his child. It's an imposition."

Katherine did not know what an imposition was, but it sounded bad. It might be something to do with imps, who she knew were red and had horns and pitchforks just like the devil. And she didn't know if her father had spoken to Frankie's father, as her mother had told him to. But Frankie hadn't come with his father to work that whole week. Then school had started. Frankie went to a Catholic school. He had to wear plaid pants and a white shirt every day. His teacher was a nun. Frankie and his family went to Catholic Mass on Saturday night instead of Sunday morning, so he could come to work with his father if he was still allowed to.

Katherine put on her sneakers, tying them with the bunny ear loops her mother had taught her that made them stay tied. She tip-toed through the house and out the back door. She would hide just out of sight behind the parish house and watch for Frankie. If she saw him she would pop out at him and scare him.

At least in the morning it was relatively quick. Anne could not suppress a sigh of relief as Gerald rolled off her. Oh, he would have been willing to take time with her if she wanted him to. Gerald wasn't selfish, Anne admonished herself to be fair. Although what could you call it when he'd had too much to drink at night and just went on and on. Even if he had "taken care of her" as they both called it, she would end up feeling like a hole in the wall. Of course, drink dulled him. Sometimes he didn't even finish. More than once he'd fallen asleep on her, in her. (It was good she did not have a knife within reach, she could picture herself stabbing him. She knew she should talk to Dr. Aiken about that, but she hadn't.) She'd just rolled him off her. And, once on his back, he would start to snore. She supposed she could have gone to the guest room, but there was something uncomfortable about sleeping where bishops slept—and where their mothers slept when they visited (all too frequently).

She couldn't help wondering. Would it have been different with Robbie, the one she fell in love with on shipboard when she was sixteen? The one who had told her (oh, the irony) that she should marry a minister? She was a girl of high moral standards, he'd insisted, (really she was just young), not someone he, a southern gentleman, would deflower. He loved her too much to marry her, he said, because he knew he could never be faithful to her. Would sex be different with Dr. Aiken? Not that she would ever know. She was supposed to be able to talk about sex with him. He asked her about her sex life. Was she frigid? Technically, frigid meant not being able to have orgasms. Technically, she could have them. She didn't particularly enjoy them. She'd once had an orgasm, her first one, when she'd worked herself into a tizzy studying for an exam she was sure she would fail. They were a form of palpable shame and anxiety. They were what happened when you felt pressured and trapped.

"Was sex different?" Dr. Aiken asked her once. "Before Hal died?"

He was the only one who would talk to her about Hal's death. (Was that why she thought about having sex with him? No, all patients fell in love with their therapists, Dr. Aiken had explained to her kindly, even encouragingly, though she hadn't confessed her fantasies. It was called transference.) But she didn't know the answer to his question. She couldn't remember. Had she ever been in love with Gerald? All she recalled from their courtship was how relieved everyone was that she had a beau, then a fiancé. Even her mother, especially her mother. Her mother waited till after the wedding to start criticizing Gerald.

"Go back to sleep for a few minutes," she encouraged Gerald, pretending wifely kindness. "I'll wake you in time to get ready for the eight o'clock."

Really, she just wanted the bathroom to herself, the kitchen to herself. Gerald wouldn't eat breakfast till after the eight o'clock Communion service. It was something he didn't talk about much, what Communion meant to him. He so scorned any kind of personal devotion. But if there was a real Gerald, an essential Gerald—one that she might never know and yet found she could believe in—it was the one who showed up week after week for people who didn't need music, didn't want a sermon, just that dry papery wafer, that bare sip of wine, that remembrance of a heartbreaking act that must have seemed so futile at the time. Brought up as a Congregationalist on very occasional grape juice and bread cubes, Anne did not find much meaning in Holy Communion, but she could respect those who did. She hoped Gerald found some comfort in it—comfort she could not give.

Anne checked her watch and turned off the flame under the coffee percolator. She set out cheerios and bowls, milk in a pitcher small enough for Katherine to lift. She liked to do things "all by herself." When the coffee was brewed, she poured herself a cup, lit her first cigarette and went outside to the back steps.

This was the sum of her faith: the tide of smoke in and out of her lungs, the rich, bitter taste of unsweetened coffee, the time before she had to put on a good face. Anne sat down on the steps and stared at nothing in particular, not the backyard with its rusting swing set or the honeysuckle bushes that needed pruning or the parish house beyond. Sometimes, if she was lucky, she could go to a place where she felt nothing, because nothing was real. She took another drag on her cigarette and another sip of coffee, then closed her eyes. She thought she could hear the organ, some Bach prelude. She let it become background with the morning bustle of the birds.

She was almost there to the empty place, when someone opened and closed the parish house door, quietly, almost surreptitiously. But then whoever it was threw caution to the winds and ran so quickly across the driveway that Anne could hear the gravel shift underfoot. She didn't really know or care who it was, but some instinct got her to her feet and she peered through the shrubs in time to see a car backing out too quickly. She had never been any good at recognizing car makes or knowing who drove what, so all she took in was a cream and yellow-colored blur of a car that was not a station wagon (the only other category she had was VW bug) tearing downhill to the driveway's back entrance. Then the brakes screeched. Whoever was driving must have had to stop suddenly to avoid hitting something or someone when he got to the street. Apparently there had been no accident. The engine revved again and the car was gone.

Anne, Gerald thought, waking suddenly and jumping out of bed where he'd been half asleep. Anne leaving him. No, there was her car out front as usual. She wouldn't take his car. She wouldn't leave without the kids. Would she?

How did he know what she would do? He turned from the window, feeling bleak, despite the bright morning light. He didn't know her.

He'd heard her go out the backdoor as he drifted back to sleep. Back door, backing away, turning her back. He was always expecting her to leave. But the truth was, she didn't have to. She was already gone. No matter how often he reached for her, how often she acquiesced, he ended up feeling alone, as if he hadn't touched her in all her most private places, as if she hadn't touched him.

Parts, there were parts that went together, like any machine, like a model airplane. But then they fell apart again. He wondered, if his father were alive, would he have found the nerve to talk to him about marriage? He would certainly never ask his mother, who had canonized his father's memory as if someone had died and made her pope.

"Oh, you're up."

Anne came into the bedroom, as if she hadn't rolled away from him as soon as it was over. She handed him his coffee, black with saccharin. Maybe he had imagined all that. Maybe this was the way marriage was. Maybe they were happy, as happy as any couple.

Loyalty, he could almost hear his father saying. What matters is loyalty. She is loyal to you.

Gerald felt his eyes filling with tears and he fumbled in his bathrobe for his cigarettes. Anne lit one of hers and handed it to him.

"Thank you, dear," he managed to say.

"Someone just tore out of the driveway like a bat out of hell," Anne remarked.

Maybe she did love him, Gerald thought. Maybe their troubles weren't worse than anyone else's.

"Why would anyone be here so early?" Anne wondered.

"Probably dropping off something for the rummage sale that's so hideous they don't want to be identified as the donor," Gerald suggested.

A small smile had its way with Anne's face, and the day looked immediately more promising.

"I'm going to check on the children. You'd better get ready. It's half past."

"Yes, dear."

Gerald took a large swallow of coffee and stubbed out his cigarette in the saucer. Before he headed for the bathroom, he looked out the window again. Lucy Way's car was here. That's right, she'd told him she'd be there early for altar guild, and Elsa was here, too. She often came at odd hours to practice. He looked down the driveway to see if Frank Lomangino had come to fix the kitchen sink in the parish house. No sign of his battered station wagon, but he usually walked, leaving the family's only car for his wife. It was a beautiful morning, really, a hint of fall in the air. Beyond the church, the treetops of

Rosewood caught the early light. He should ask Mildred's nephew for permission to walk there, maybe take the kids. Anne would like that.

CHAPTER NINE

"It *is* the same word. It *is* the same word!"

Frankie was picking up handfuls of gravel and throwing the stones against the metal doors to the parish house cellar. Now and then some pieces hit the kitchen window. Katherine didn't know what he was talking about, she only knew Frankie was mad, maybe because his father had run after him and smacked him hard right after he had run out in the street and almost gotten hit by a car. She would have cried if someone hit her like that, but Frankie just grabbed stones and started throwing. If he broke a window by mistake, he'd really be in trouble. She wanted to tell him to stop, but then he might be mad at her.

"What's the same word?" she asked instead.

"God and dog. Dog and God. I don't care what anyone says. I don't care what *you* say, either, Katherine." It was his first acknowledgement of her. "It's the same word."

Katherine pondered, her mind forming an image of a dog, a Dalmatian, her current favorite. To her, God had always looked like a cloud, a big black cloud. What did God have to do with a dog?

"How?" she asked at last. "How are they the same?"

Frankie picked up another handful of gravel and threw it hard. A fairly large stone bounced off the window and made a tiny nick in it. Frankie was going to break the window if he didn't stop.

"They have the same letters, dummy!"

"Don't call me dummy!" she objected.

"Well, you are a dummy, if you don't know that, and so is Sister Mary Alfatso. She's the biggest dummy of all. And so is dumb old, stupid old Mikey Massarelli. I showed him in the reading book. See?

I said. D-O-G, G-O-D. The same letters, the same word. And then that creep raised his hand and said: Teacher, teacher. Frankie said God's a dog."

"Oh!" said Katherine distracted by revelation, seeing the letters floating in the air. All letters and numbers had colors. D was red and O was black and G blue. You could take them and spell God. "They *are* the same!"

She started dancing a little jig in a circle, the way she did when knowing something made her happy. Frankie let his next handful of gravel fall to the ground, and he started hopping up and down first on one foot, and then the other.

"See? See, Katherine?"

"I see!" she said.

"Stupid old Sister Mary Alfatso is too stupid. She grabbed me by the hair and forced me to kneel down on the floor in front of the statue of the Virgin Mary."

"'You say you're sorry, Frankie Lomangino, Junior. You say you're sorry to the Blessed Mother right now for calling her son, our Lord and Savior, a dog.'"

"'No!'" I said.

"'Well, then the Blessed Virgin Mary is not going to let a wicked boy like you come to her birthday party. You are going to stay right here, kneeling before her statue while all the other children go to the procession and eat cake.'"

All at once Frankie stopped talking, put his fists in his eyes and rubbed them hard. Katherine knew what he was doing. He was making the tears go back inside. She knew because she was almost crying, too. It wasn't fair that Frankie didn't get cake. He never said God was a dog.

"You know what I said to her, Katherine? Know what I said to the stupid old Virgin Mary?"

"What?" Katherine whispered. She knew it was going to be bad.

"I'm gonna get you, I told her, I'm gonna get you and your son, and I'm gonna get all your mean old penguins."

Every time he said "get" he made motions like he was punching or stabbing.

Maybe it was because she'd been holding her breath. All at once Katherine felt dizzy. She remembered a place that she had dreamed or maybe she had really gone there. It was a desert, like in the cartoons, and she was way high up on a cliff looking out from behind a huge boulder. Floating far, far below were God, God and Jesus, God the big black cloud and Jesus in a white robe. She pushed the boulder over the edge.

It fell right on top of God and Jesus.

It killed them.

"Frankie," she whispered. "Can I tell you a secret, a really bad secret?"

Frankie looked at her, really looked at her, a long look.

"Not here." He was whispering, too. "Come on."

Frankie took her hand. They both knew where they were going. They climbed over the wall and into the wood.

Gerald was shaved, dressed and fumbling with his Sunday dog collar when Anne came back into the bedroom in that controlled panicked way that always filled him with alarm. What had he done (or failed to do) now?

"Katherine's not in her room. The twins haven't seen her. I can't find her anywhere in the house. I even went down the driveway to check—"

To make sure she hadn't been run over by that car, he silently finished the sentence.

"She's probably just outside in the yard somewhere. It is a beautiful morning." He made what he guessed would be a futile attempt at reassurance. He felt a sudden sympathy for his daughter. Maybe he understood her better than Anne did. "If Frank Lomangino is here fixing the sink, she might have—"

He saw Anne's face slam shut. She knew. She *knew* Gerald hadn't spoken to Frank about not bringing Frankie, Junior with him.

"Then please hurry and go look for her before the service. I've got my hands full with the twins."

Anne didn't say anything more. She didn't need to. If Katherine was running wild with Frankie Lomangino, it was definitely Gerald's fault.

Katherine almost forgot what she was going to tell Frankie as soon as they stepped into the woods, where the birds sang and fairies flickered at the corners of their eyes, watching them from behind the trees. But Frankie remembered. He stopped her at the top of some stone steps that led down from an old road (all cracks and grass growing through) to a bridge over a stream.

"Secret," he commanded. "Tell."

She told him what she had never told anyone but her older cousin, who had ordered Katherine: "Say the Lord's Prayer. Quick!" Frankie listened, he listened more carefully than he had ever listened to her. When she was done telling him, all he said was.

"Good girl, Katherine, good girl."

After that a silence came over them. They stepped softly, listening to the slightest stirrings in the woods, animals moving through the brush, birds calling, the trickle of the late summer stream. Katherine knew that the trees were watching them. They were dryads, and when they wanted to, they could walk and talk and dance. They were still shy, Katherine thought, but she didn't think they minded her and Frankie being here. It felt like the woods had been waiting for them. When they stepped onto the bridge over the stream with its stone wall on either side, the wind in the high branches picked up and the trees swayed.

"Come further up and further in," Katherine whispered to Frankie.

"That's what the trees are saying." Frankie nodded.

They looked at the path on the other side of the stream, leading uphill into deeper woods. They had to go, even if they got lost and never found their way back home. But just as they crossed the bridge, they heard a sound behind them, someone running, coming around the corner from the direction of the churchyard.

"Quick!" whispered Frankie. "Hide!"

And he pulled her after him under the bridge where they crouched together on mud and pebbles. It seemed too small a bridge for a troll to live under, but it was dark and damp and scary to hear the running footsteps coming closer and closer, so close they could hear the panting breath of whoever was running. And then the footsteps went right over the bridge. Not trip trap, trip trap like the Billy Goats Gruff, but pound, pound, pound like a giant looking for someone who had escaped from his cloud kingdom back down the beanpole. Fee fi fo fum. Katherine hoped he couldn't smell their blood of an Englishmun.

The footsteps slowed a little as the giant ran up the hill into deeper wood. Frankie crept out from their hiding place to look. She did not want Frankie to think she was afraid, so Katherine scrambled after him and looked in time to see a black figure with a hood slip into the tree shadow. She thought for a moment she could see black wings sprouting from its back. Maybe it did have wings and flew away into the trees. She couldn't see it anymore. Her heart was still pounding and her hands felt cold and damp as the rocks under the bridge.

"Did you see its tail?" Frankie asked. "It might have had horns, too. Under the hood."

Maybe it was an imp, Katherine thought, or even an imposition since it was bigger than what Katherine thought an imp would be.

"Do you think it was looking for us?" Katherine still whispered. "Because, because we...trespassed."

She had felt so safe in the woods at first, so safe from God and everyone. She wanted the woods to be only theirs, hers and Frankie's.

"It wasn't looking," answered Frankie after a moment. "It was running, running away from something. It doesn't belong in the woods."

"Are you sure?"

Frankie nodded, making his head bob way up and way down.

"It doesn't belong," he declared. "But it may be back. We are going to need weapons, Katherine. We will find sticks and sharpen them to points. We will make...javelins."

"Javelins," Katherine repeated, deciding not to tell Frankie she did not know what they were. The word made her think of jaguars. Maybe there were jaguars in the woods. She would like there to be lions, too.

"Come on, let's look for sticks."

They crawled all the way out from under the bridge and began to walk next to the stream, sifting through the old leaves with their feet for sticks. First Frankie found one, long and thick with little squiggly lines on it that looked like writing. Katherine wanted one with lines on it, too. So they both looked until they found one. Then they went back up on the bridge and perched on the wall.

"Children!"

They turned to stare at each other. Someone was speaking to them. One of the trees, Katherine thought. They both looked around them, and then at once they saw her: a fairy woman with hair like thistledown and a light green dress that floated on the air. She had appeared out of thin air at the top of the stone steps. She smiled a small, secret smile.

"Come home," she said. "Just for this little while, so that your mothers and fathers don't fret."

She understood. She understood that they did not want to leave the wood. Frankie gazed at the fairy woman, too, but his foot was beginning to dig into the dirt.

"We want to stay here," Frankie told her.

"I know," said the fairy woman. "You will find your way back. You will always find your way back to the wood, if it is your heart's true desire."

She spoke like a fairy, like a fairy in a fairytale.

When she held out her hands to them, Katherine went to her. After a moment Frankie followed. They each took one of her hands, while they held their weapons in their other hands.

"We will play a game," said the fairy woman. "Walk between the shadows."

Stepping carefully on the shifting patches of light, Katherine, Frankie and the fairy woman made their way out of the wood.

Lucy Way reached for the children's hands again after they stepped over the wall. She fully intended to deliver them to their parents with an appeal for clemency. But the children did not take her hands again. Instead they drew closer to each other, as if they could fold their time apart in the wood around them like a cloak.

"Your fathers are looking for you in the parish house," said Lucy. "Let's go find them and tell them you were never lost."

Katherine gave her a solemn look and nodded her head and Frankie, who had been about to start kicking the gravel, stopped foot-poised.

"That's right," Frankie agreed. "We knew where we were all the time."

Lucy wondered if she had just given Frankie a lesson in how to obfuscate, but before she could ponder further, the door to the office flew open and Amos McCready stood on the threshold.

"Lucy Way, thank heavens it's you and not some hysterical female. We need a nurse right away. And send those children up to the rectory."

Lucy started forward, but it was clear Frankie wasn't about to retreat.

"Where's my pops?" he demanded.

"He's helping Mr. Bradley, lad, and he won't want you getting in the way. Off with you now. No more nonsense."

Amos stepped forward, brandishing his cane, and the two children ran for the rectory.

"Quick, Lucy!" Amos urged. "They're all in the basement. They sent me up to call for help. The Fat Fenian, the butcher, and the hearse are all on their way."

Which cryptic list Lucy decoded as Chief O'Brien, Dr. Haydock, an absurd enough name in itself, and an actual hearse, which doubled in this small town for an ambulance.

"Who's in the basement?" asked Lucy running up the office steps. "What's happened?"

"The Crowley woman," Amos answered, holding open the door, then closing it after her and locking it. "I fear she's had a wee accident."

"What about Nat Crowley? Is he coming?"

"The sodden husband? I'll call him right now. The man's got a right to know that his fool wife's had a fall. If he's not dead to the world himself with the after effects of strong drink."

CHAPTER TEN

Lucy hurried to the narrow basement stairs, as much as she could hurry through the obstacle course of unsorted rummage, some stuffed in boxes, some uncontained. The work of organizing traditionally began after coffee hour today. But Charlotte, as head of operations, had been puttering about for weeks. Could she have been lying in the basement helpless while Lucy happily prepared the altar? Lucy took a deep breath and resisted the impulse to rush down the stairs. No use in causing more accidents. There was a sharp curve in the stairs where someone could lose their balance if they weren't paying attention, especially if they were carrying something, which Charlotte might have been.

"She's got no pulse, Rev." Lucy heard Frank Lomangino's voice.

"Maybe she's just fainted." Gerald sounded desperate. "Do you know how to give mouth to mouth resuscitation? I was going to take the training at the fire department this Fall, but—"

"I do!" Lucy called, holding carefully to the railing, so she didn't join Charlotte in a heap. She could just see Charlotte's shoes now, her old brogans that only Charlotte would think of wearing with her Sunday best, so worn out that they had no tread left. She had probably walked from home to the parish house. Lucy could not remember seeing her car. "Hold on!"

Lucy arrived at the bottom of the stairs and saw Charlotte lying full out on her back, staring at the ceiling, her mouth agape. Briefly she wondered how Charlotte had managed to land in that position instead of on her side or hands and knees, but then people flailed when they lost their balance. She could have landed on her side and fallen over. Frank and Gerald also might have moved her, not knowing how dangerous it was to move a victim of a fall.

Gerald stood up and gestured for Lucy to take his place at Charlotte's side. Frank remained kneeling, still holding Charlotte's wrist, as if he could comfort her by keeping contact or somehow reverse what they all feared but did not yet want to name.

Lucy didn't take Charlotte's other wrist, but felt her carotid artery. Nothing. She bent over her chest. It was an eerie sensation, like knocking at a door and knowing in your bones no one is home. Next she looked at the angle of Charlotte's neck and head. Her neck did not appear to be broken. Could she have had a heart attack from the shock of the fall or could she have fallen because of a heart attack? For form's sake, for Frank and Gerald's sake, Lucy put her mouth over Charlotte's and breathed twice into that emptiness. Then she did five chest compressions. And back and forth, her mind empty of anything but action. It had to be. Reaction could wait. So could self-recrimination.

"I think she's dead, Mrs. Way." Frank's voice shook. "Holy Mother of God, I think she's really dead."

"Dead?" Gerald also sounded stunned.

"I am afraid she is," agreed Lucy.

And if she were dead, Lucy noted to herself, as she breathed again into Charlotte's mouth that still gave off the odor of coffee and some sort of sweet pastry, she couldn't have been dead for much more than an hour, two at the outside. She was still warm to the touch; though there were the first hints of livor mortis in the discoloration of Charlotte's usually even complexion.

"Say a prayer, Father," pleaded Frank. "Say a prayer. Quick!"

"Oh, God," began Gerald. "Oh, God, um, accept our prayers on behalf of the soul of this thy servant—" he broke off. "I should wait. She hasn't been pronounced yet."

Lucy was not bound by liturgical or medical protocol. She said a swift silent prayer. Have mercy on Charlotte's soul, dear Lord. Have mercy on us all.

"Who found her?" Lucy asked aloud, as she did another round of chest compressions.

"I did," Frank swallowed a sob. "I came downstairs to look for the kids."

"He came running back up," Gerald continued. "Amos and I came down, too. Then I sent Amos to call for help. Someone should be here any minute. I don't want to do anything until the officials see her."

"And is this how you found her?" Lucy asked. "You were careful not to move her?"

There was no point in sparing anyone's feelings now. Only the truth mattered. Charlotte was dead. Lucy would keep on with the futile resuscitation attempt only until the doctor arrived.

"She was lying just like this," said Frank. "But she had this heavy bag of coats on top of her, covering her face. I moved it. I thought she might be suffocating under it."

He gestured to a pile of coats covered in a plastic drycleaners bag.

"They musta landed on her when she fell. Maybe she was knocked unconscious and couldn't move them. So I moved them, but I think...I think she was already..."

There was a sound of doors opening and banging closed and feet in heavy shoes.

"They're here. O'Brien, Haydock and the hearse," Amos announced from the top of the stairs. "And the eight o'clock flock is gabbling and clucking and moving this way led by the wee schnauzer."

Lucy bent to her task one more time.

"Herd them into the church, Amos, and lead them in Morning Prayer," Gerald shouted up the stairs. "Double the lessons and the psalms, if you have to. Tell Elsa we'll have hymns at the eight o'clock today, any hymns she likes. Just put the fear of God into them and keep them in the church as long as you can."

"Aye, aye, Rev. You can count on Amos McCready for hellfire and brimstone."

A moment later Officer O'Brien and Dr. Haydock, both burly middle-aged men, barreled down the stairs in what Lucy feared was a race for precedence and got wedged together just after the turn, only a slightly more seemly predicament than landing on poor Charlotte's body. It was horrible that Lucy wanted to laugh. But she knew that laughter was a response to horror. Poor Charlotte! Was her death to be reduced to farce? Joe Petrone peered over the shoulders of the two straining men, clearly alarmed to see his brother-in-law Frank kneeling by what could be a corpse. Joe was here in a double capacity as junior officer and medic (he had served in the Korean War), called in by Luke Sullivan, the funeral director, to lend a semblance of medical expertise to the hearse.

"Move aside, O'Brien," growled Haydock. "This is a medical emergency."

"Chrisssake, all right! Excuse me, Reverend."

Just before the banister splintered, O'Brien managed to turn sideways and Haydock, suddenly freed, lurched forward, steadied just in time by Gerald and Frank, who sprang to his feet, leaving Lucy the only one still kneeling.

"Nurse Way, is that you?" said Dr. Haydock. "Thank God you're here."

That was the second time someone had said that this morning. But there would have been more thanks due to God if she had come looking for Charlotte earlier.

"Yes, Dr. Haydock," she said. "But I am afraid we may have arrived too late."

All four children, Peter, Janie, Katherine, and Frankie Lomangino, stood or kneeled on the couch looking out the living room window to the driveway. Anne had given up any hope of keeping their feet off the furniture and resigned herself to standing behind them watching bedlam ensue. First the doctor's car, then the police car, complete with a flashing light and siren, then the hearse. Even though Anne knew it doubled as an ambulance, it was a disconcerting sight.

"That's my Uncle Joey in that car." Frankie had pointed to the driver.

Then without warning he had jumped from the couch and run to the heavy front door, which fortunately he didn't know the trick of opening. Anne locked it before he could figure it out. But Frankie did not give up. He kept tugging at the doorknob, and then he gave way to violent pounding. Great. Now in addition to a police car and a hearse in the driveway, she had Frankie Lomangino throwing a tantrum. She took a step towards Frankie, wondering how to restrain him before he hurt himself or something else. Hal used to have tantrums, but he had been younger and smaller than Frankie. Just then she felt someone tugging at her sleeve. She turned and saw Katherine at her side. The twins hung back in the doorway to the living room, awed and fascinated by Frankie's fury.

"He wants his pops," Katherine told her mother.

And then Katherine walked right up to the flailing boy.

"He's all right, Frankie. Mr. McCready said so. He's helping my father."

To Anne's astonishment, Frankie stopped pounding. He put his knuckles in his eyes and rubbed hard, but not before Anne had glimpsed a tear. She was undone. By Katherine's sureness, by the sight of this big rough boy crying for his father.

"Do you want me to call your mother to come get you?" she asked Frankie as kindly as she could.

Frankie shook his head.

"I want to wait for my pops."

Anne did not know any of the details of Frank's arrest and jail time, but she wondered now if Frankie had seen him being taken away.

"Then stay here with us," said Anne. "I am going to make waffles. Do you like waffles, Frankie?"

He nodded but still did not look at her.

"Come on, Frankie!" shouted Peter. "Come back and look out the window. Mr. McCready's waving his cane around. I think he's going to hit someone."

And Anne's children surrounded Frankie and gathered him in as one of their own.

Gerald was no stranger to the inside of a funeral home. No priest was. In his tenancy at Regeneration he had worked with the funeral director Luke Sullivan many times. He never could help wondering if Luke dipped into the makeup box to heighten his own coloring and smooth his own blemishes. There was something waxen about his appearance or maybe it was just the lighting, all artificial, for even though there were windows at Sullivan's funeral home, the curtains were heavy and the carpeting so thick you could not hear a footfall, so that when Luke or his staff entered a room, they did give the impression of having materialized out of the shadowy air.

Whenever Gerald sat with a parishioner here, he was glad of any distraction, however idle, because it was of the utmost importance that he set aside any memories of that other funeral home in Manhattan where he had gone with Anne, who sat so still and cold and silent she hardly seemed to be breathing. How he would have gotten through the ordeal without his senior rector, Charlie Dean, he didn't know. No, he did know. He wouldn't have gotten through it. He would have broken down sobbing on the floor, or worse, run to the nearest bar and drunk himself into a coma.

Nat Crowley had already been in rough shape when he arrived at the parish house, not drunk but woozy with a hangover, eyes bloodshot. (Sunday morning had an unfortunate way of following Saturday night.)

"Charlotte? Charlotte, old girl!" They heard Nat calling as he banged on the front door that Amos had thought to lock.

Doctor Haydock had just pronounced Charlotte dead and given Lucy the nod to closing her eyes and mouth.

"I'll go break it to him," Gerald had said, moving past Officer O'Brien.

"Accidental death," Officer O'Brien noted out loud as he wrote his preliminary report. "Victim fell down stairs, contusion to head, suffocation under heavy coats in plastic drycleaners bag. In other words, just one of those things, a damn stupid shame. Pardon my French. Petrone, go get the stretcher. Rev., we'll wait to move her till you talk to the husband."

"Is anybody there!" shouted Nat. "Charlotte?"

Gerald had opened the door and steered Nat into his office.

"Where's Charlotte?" he demanded, equal parts bewildered and belligerent. "Why is Sullivan's wagon here? Did she break something?"

Gerald managed to get Nat into a leather easy chair.

"I am afraid it's worse than that, Nat. Charlotte took a bad fall and hit her head. She landed with a bag of heavy coats over her face."

"Silly thing. I've always told her she does too much. Getting up with the birds to fuss with the infernal rummage sale. Why can't someone else take the bit for a bit? It won't do, I told her last night. You'll work yourself to death."

Gerald took a deep breath.

"Nat, Charlotte is dead."

The hardest word you ever had to say to anyone. The irreversible word with its cruel reverberating consonant at both ends, a slammed door, a closed box, a coffin.

Dead, dead, dead.

Now Gerald sat next to Nat in Luke Sullivan's office. Luke had wisely and humanely poured Nat a brandy. Gerald would have welcomed one, too, but he waved it away when Luke offered one. It was Sunday morning. He was a clergyman. He had a parishioner in extremis, a desperately lost sheep, who looked as though he would bleat, if he managed to make a sound at all. Nat belted back his brandy. Luke poured him another, and he drank the second one more slowly as tears began to flow down his cheeks. Like many people, men especially, Nat held his breath to keep from making a sound. Luke opened a drawer and handed him a perfectly clean and pressed linen handkerchief. Classy touch, Gerald thought.

"We reached Nat's son, Jonathan," Gerald told the funeral director. "Woke him up, I'm afraid. He's on the west coast. He'll be taking a flight out today. Maybe it's best to wait till he arrives to make decisions. What do you think, Nat?"

Nat blew his nose loudly.

"Whatever Charlotte thinks is best. She's the one who decides things, you know."

Gerald and Luke exchanged a glance and a slight nod. Gerald figured they both knew Nat was in shock, not delusional. He felt an appreciation for Luke as a fellow professional, a fellow human being.

"Don't know, don't know how I will manage without her. She had a plan, you see. I don't know what it was. She wouldn't tell me. Don't you worry, old thing, she said. (We always called each other that.) Everything will be all right. You'll see. Just leave it to me. Now it won't be all right, I don't suppose. Will it?"

He turned and looked at Gerald, his watery eyes like an old man's eyes (though Nat was only sixty), a baby's eyes. How to answer Nat? He didn't know what Nat was talking about, though he knew the Crowley finances were not what they should be, did not at all match those of their social circle. Last winter Gerald had dipped into the discretionary fund to help with their heating bills. He could deal with practical questions when the son arrived. Right now Nat needed comfort. Another clergyman would have had a ready platitude. The Lord will provide or some such nonsense that Gerald could not stomach or believe. Not since Hal's death. And here was Nat, his wife not cold yet, dead in a freak accident. Where was God in that?

Nailed to a cross, on a cold slab in a tomb.

"Christ knows, Nat," Gerald heard himself saying. "He knows how it is with us here. He knows how hard it is. He'll see you through."

He felt his own voice thicken with tears, and he swallowed quickly. Out of the corner of his eye, he saw Luke nodding his head. The funeral director reached for the brandy again and poured a snifter for them all, himself, too, so Gerald would have been churlish to refuse, thank Christ in his mercy.

One of Luke's silent-footed assistants appeared in the office and bent to speak in low tones to his boss.

"Mrs. Crowley's been freshened up." Luke Sullivan turned to Nat. "Would you like to have a few moments with her?"

Nat looked again at Gerald, beseechingly, as if Gerald were Jesus and might at any moment say, Why do you weep? She is not dead, she's only sleeping.

Gerald helped Nat to his feet and they walked into a dimly-lit parlor. Charlotte's body did indeed appear to be resting on a day-bed, for no coffin had been chosen yet, nor had she been made up or embalmed. She was a handsome woman, Gerald found himself thinking, good bones. Odd, he hadn't noticed her looks much in life. Her personality had been so forceful, he hadn't looked past it.

"Come on now, old thing. This just won't do," Nat said.

They had loved each other, it struck Gerald, the drunk and the kleptomaniac. They saw each other's faults and then turned a blind eye. They covered each other's indiscretions. Gerald felt a pang of misplaced envy, instantly repented as the widower sank to his knees, laid his head on his dead wife's chest and gave way to sobs.

"I'll leave him in your hands, Reverend," Luke spoke in hushed tones. "I'll be in my office if you need anything."

Gerald waited till Nat quieted a little. Then he pulled up a chair and sat next to the kneeling man. He had his pocket-sized *Book of Common Prayer*. It had only been when Hal died that he had noticed that though there were prayers for the dead, and for just about any occasion you could think of, there were no prayers specifically for the bereaved. Gerald had written one. He found it tucked in the back of the prayer book with other supplemental prayers typed on thin onionskin paper. There wasn't enough light to read by, but though he unfolded the paper, Gerald knew the prayer by heart.

"Dear Lord and Savior Jesus Christ, who didst weep outside the tomb of thy friend, comfort those who mourn the death of thy servant Charlotte, especially her husband, Nat. Be with us in this place of dust and grief where the glass is still dark and we cannot see clearly. Thou who didst suffer death on the cross and rose again, make us always mindful that nothing can separate us from the love of God in Christ. Amen."

Nat's eyes were closed, and he was so quiet, Gerald thought he might be asleep. Sleep was the only real comfort, but the wrench of waking ruined it. He doubted Nat had heard any of the words. It didn't matter. The prayer was as stark as grief. He could never bring himself to write about heavenly reunions with lost loved ones. That was sugar-coating to a bitter pill. Resurrection was an article of faith. He would stand by it. But it had not undone anyone's stupid, unbearable death. He would not pretend that it had.

Gerald's own eyes closed. He had not had breakfast or lunch; he'd gotten Ralph Smith, a retired priest who did supply work, to take the ten-thirty, not wanting to subject his larger congregation to Amos's excoriations. Now the brandy had spread out into his limbs. He might have dozed off, too, except for the knocking at the door. A moment later, Luke appeared.

"There is someone in my office asking to see Mr. Crowley. I told her there would be calling hours on Tuesday, but she was insistent. She says she's an old family friend."

Nat stirred and moaned a little as he tried to get up from his knees. Gerald and Luke took an elbow each, and finally Nat stood.

"This is very silly, Charlotte," Nat said. "Get up, old thing. You can't leave me on my own. You know what a nincompoop I am."

"Nat!" someone called from the doorway, and Nat turned, distracted from his pleading.

"Who's there?"

Gerald also strained to see.

A shapeless figure in a brown dress.

"Nat, it's me, Millie."

Mildred Thomson! What the hell was she doing here, barging in at a time like this?

"Millie, what are you doing here?" Nat asked far more mildly. "Were you looking for Charlotte? I'm afraid she's dead, Millie."

"I know, Nat. I'm so sorry." She started towards him across the room. "I've come to take you home. Charlotte wouldn't want you to be alone to look after yourself."

The poor man had little chance of that, Gerald thought. Mildred was the advance guard. Nat would soon be buried under casseroles, jello salads, coffee cakes and pies.

"I suppose that's true," said Nat. "Charlotte always said I was helpless as a baby."

Now it was Charlotte who was helpless. Gerald could not help wishing that Charlotte would rise briskly from the dead and put Mildred Thomson in her place.

"Don't worry, Nat. The Lord will never forsake you, and neither will I."

Far meeker than a lamb to slaughter, Nat Crowley allowed himself to be led away.

CHAPTER ELEVEN

Lucy was too tired that evening to do more than make scrambled eggs and toast for her supper. With her last bit of oomph, she had laid a fire in the fireplace. The evening was chilly and she hadn't turned on the radiators yet, but she knew she'd lit the fire more for comfort than warmth. She sat before it now, eating her supper on a tray, sipping tea laced with brandy, Tabitha curled up beside her. She had lit no other lights, so firelight played freely in the room, reflecting on the walls and ceiling. Its sound was soothing, too, reassuring in a timeless way. Gather round me, human creatures. I will make you a little harbor of light, keep the dark and wild beasts at bay. Of course, she had no fellow humans to huddle with, which made the fire all the more companionable.

Not that she minded being alone this evening. It was a relief. Then she remembered with a pang how she had relished her solitude that morning instead of going to find Charlotte earlier. But why would she have looked for her? Lucy attempted to reason with herself. Even if she had known Charlotte was in the parish house checking on some detail for the rummage sale, she wouldn't have disturbed her when she was perfectly capable of setting up the altar herself. Not even if Charlotte were her best friend instead of someone whose company she preferred to avoid.

It was no good, Lucy realized, and she set her tray on the coffee table, her toast uneaten. It was no good trying to reason or justify her actions. Nor was it any use speculating what might have happened if she had acted sooner. She was going to have to live with the only thing she could know for certain: Charlotte Crowley had fallen to her death while Lucy happily smoothed altar cloths and set out communion silver. Nor could she pretend that she had ever liked Charlotte. She would not speak ill of the dead, and she had tried to be charitable about her when she was alive. But the truth was the truth. God knew it, and so did she.

Lucy picked up her mug of tea and put her feet up on the sofa, temporarily disturbing Tabitha, who soon made the best of it by relocating in Lucy's lap. Lucy half-closed her eyes and let the images from the day rise with the steam, flicker in and out of the corner of her eyes like the flame. The prayer practice of St Ignatius included honest recollection of the day, a seeking for God's presence in all the strange crannies of human thought and deed.

Lucy had done what she could for Charlotte, which wasn't much, closing her eyes and, more challenging, her mouth. She'd also smoothed her skirts. They must have flown up during her fall, and her slip and the garter on her right leg had been exposed. Vanity wasn't one of Charlotte's faults; or maybe it was simply that she took her good looks and social standing so for granted, she didn't have to fuss over her clothes (good quality tweeds or linens but threadbare) or her looks. She'd always had abundant hair, casually swept up and held with antique combs, with an occasional pencil or knitting needle thrown in. She hadn't worn much makeup. She protected her complexion with wide-brimmed garden hats. Still, Charlotte would not have wanted to appear at a disadvantage. She never had done so in life despite reduced circumstances. By the time her husband saw her, laid out on a stretcher, ready to be carried to the hearse, she looked like a handsome woman of a certain age who had decided to have a little lie-down. How strange death was, the spirit flown but traces of it lingering for a time in the body it had helped to shape, especially the face.

Lucy hadn't registered her shock until she was alone in the church again, removing the unused communion vessels from the altar in preparation for ten-thirty morning prayer. As she picked up the chalice, her hands began to shake so much she had to set it down again and hold onto the altar. She lifted her eyes to Christ Triumphant and, as always, he seemed to meet her gaze.

"Charlotte?" She sounded the word silently in her mind, uncertain whether she was praying or asking a question. Maybe there was no difference.

"Don't worry, beloved," she thought she heard him answer. "There is a place for Charlotte at my table. There is room for everyone at my feast."

Lucy nodded, feeling heavy, weak, all the adrenalin draining out of her. If she let go of the altar, surely she would sink into a heap.

"Lucy," a distinctly human voice called to her from the nave.

She turned and saw Elsa slumped in a front pew, holding a paper cup from the dispenser by the sink in the vesting room. Lucy went and sat next to her. She forced herself to cough a dry little cough.

"Please, may I have a sip of your water, Elsa?"

"Oh, Lucy," Elsa sighed, not even attempting evasion.

Lucy took a sip, then drained the cup. She had to admit that the shot of straight vodka was restorative.

"We talked about this, Elsa," said Lucy. "You cannot drink during services, especially not today. Gerald will be counting on you to keep things running smoothly."

"Then he better not have McCready take any more services. *Gott in himmel.* He chose the psalm about smashing the enemies' heads on the rocks. And he preached a sermon on the whore of Babylon drinking her fornications. I couldn't help it, Lucy. I had to have a drink. I need another."

"Where is the bottle, Elsa?"

Elsa seemed to consider for a moment the wisdom of revealing her stash.

"Underneath the organ by the pedals."

Lucy put down the paper cup, went to locate the source. Then she poured Elsa a judicious refill, keeping a firm hold on the bottle.

"I didn't like the woman," Elsa said. "All right, so I said she should be shot. But I didn't wish her ill, Lucy. Do you believe me? I didn't wish her dead."

Lucy felt a shiver run through her. Charlotte's death was an accident, she told herself. Clearly an accident. Everyone present had agreed on that. But could there have been an altercation between Elsa and Charlotte earlier that morning? Did Elsa feel in some way responsible? Had anger made Charlotte hasty or careless?

"You believe me, Lucy, don't you?"

"Of course I believe you, Elsa," she said slowly. "But if you know anything about what happened, how Charlotte came to fall down the stairs—"

"I know nothing." Elsa shook her head vigorously. "Nothing but what that bloodthirsty old Scotchman told us."

Elsa drained her cup and held it out for more.

"Darling, you know I can't," said Lucy.

And before Elsa could protest, Lucy took the bottle into the sacristy and poured it down the sink where it would mix on the earth with all the leftover drops of Christ's blood.

Lucy set down her cup of tea, resisting the urge to pour more brandy. Sleep would come soon enough. She must finish her recollection. There were many in need of prayer tonight. The least she could do was keep awake a little longer.

"Can you not watch with me one hour?" Jesus had implored his disciples.

Her cozy couch before the fire was no garden of Gethsemane, not for her. But Charlotte was dead, and poor Nat must be as bewildered and bereft as any of Jesus's disciples.

The rest of the morning had been a bit of a blur. Lucy rather wished Amos McCready had taken the ten-thirty. Ralph Smith, the supply priest, was an old dear but dull as dishwater. Even when announcing Charlotte's death, he made it sound no more than an unfortunate inconvenience. Lucy had dozed, she hoped discreetly, during the sermon. After a dawn rising, an attempt to resuscitate a dead woman, and a shot of vodka, she could count herself lucky that she didn't keel over in the pew. She wished she could go straight home after the service, but an emergency meeting of the WOR had been called for coffee hour, and it would have been disrespectful to Charlotte's memory to skip it, especially since who should replace Charlotte as head of the Church of Regeneration Rummage Sale was the first and only item on the agenda.

Some fifteen or so women had taken their cups of coffee, their crustless sandwiches and slices of coffee cake (those who could eat) and crowded into Grace Jones' office, one of the few places that was not piled with rummage donations. Though people had been speaking in hushed tones in groups of two or three during coffee hour, no one wanted to be the first to speak at an official meeting of the WOR where Charlotte should have been presiding. Here were women who had known each other for years, some as friends, some just as fellow pillars holding up the church. Such service made a particular kind of bond. Most of these women had also known her mother as she had known some of theirs. And they all knew whose children were whose. Whatever anyone had felt about Charlotte personally, whatever her eccentricities, she was part of both warp and weft. With the thread of Charlotte's life snapped, they were in danger of unraveling.

"Well," Ginger Boomer put down her cup and got to her feet, clutching a well-used handkerchief, "I know that as Charlotte's second-in-command, I should...I mean I ought to...wouldn't want to let her down. Oh, damn it all, Charlotte was my best friend."

At that Ginger began to sob loudly. It was true, poor thing. Charlotte had befriended Ginger, a war widow who fifteen years ago had had bright red hair and curves to rival Marilyn Monroe's. Charlotte was the only wife at the time who did not regard her as a man-eating, husband-stealing barracuda. In the intervening years, Ginger had remarried to a Roman Catholic and had a brood of children who went to church with their father. But she had kept her allegiance to Regeneration and to Charlotte. Her bright hair had faded and her curves merged in general roundness, but there was no denying Charlotte's championship of this one-time social pariah.

Ginger wept without restraint while the other women made murmuring, soothing noises. Mary Louise, a southern lady, handed her a fresh handkerchief, but it was Florence Green who got up and put her arms around Ginger and helped her to sit back down.

"Mrs. Bradley," said Florence resuming her seat. "I wish you would lead us in a moment of prayer."

Lucy stole a glance at Anne, who looked taken aback and thoroughly ill at ease. Florence had been wooed away from the Baptist church by Gerald, and though she had taken confirmation last year, no one had explained to her the Episcopalian skittishness about extemporaneous prayer.

"Perhaps we could take a moment of silence to each pray for Charlotte in our own way." Lucy felt compelled to rescue Anne.

Silence fell in the small room. They could hear children playing outside. Although Charlotte's body had been removed, no one could countenance using the basement for Sunday School that week. In the kitchen next door, someone started the washing up. All of it going on as if someone had not died one story down from where they sat. Lucy imagined Charlotte's soul might be quite bewildered at the sudden change. She prayed for her soul's repose.

"Well now, ladies," began Mary Louise. "As the secretary of the WOR I suppose I am next in the chain of command to Ginger, so if y'all don't mind, I'd like to make a proposal."

Lucy was glad Mary Louise had taken the reins. Everyone respected her. She was married to a count from some obscure European country, and she came from an old aristocratic Virginia family. But she pitched in and did her part as if she was nobody special.

"We all know our departments. Most of us have been working the same table for years. Grace, will you be in charge of menswear again?"

The church secretary was a rarity among the WOR, a divorcée who worked full time. She always volunteered for menswear. The less charitable held that she had not given up hope of finding a new husband. There were some rumors that she carried a secret flame for her boss, but Lucy had never detected any animosity between Anne and Grace.

"If Ginger can help me," said Grace. "I have to be in the office to answer the phone weekdays."

Ginger nodded as she blew her nose.

"And, Marge, will you man womenswear with me?"

"Sure thing," agreed Marge, a strapping blonde who'd grown up on a dairy farm and married her father's hired hand.

"And Mildred? Where's Mildred?" They all looked around, noticing the absence of Mildred's unprepossessing presence. "Well, I imagine she'll be willing to be in charge of notions again. I'll call her later. Florence, would you be willing to take on notions with Mildred? She can be a little distracted sometimes, bless her heart, and she can't make change to save her life."

"Yes, ma'am." Florence tried not to beam. She had always helped out and contributed the lions' share of the baked goods, but no one had ever asked her to preside at a counter before. Good for Mary Louise, thought Lucy, to ask her so simply and matter-of-factly.

Mary Louise continued down the list, with everyone present agreeing to keep their traditional post.

"Well then," concluded Mary Louise, "let's all get to sorting. What better way to honor Charlotte than to carry on with the almighty Church of Regeneration Rummage Sale, the brightest star in the WOR's ever so starry crown."

The women began to stand and fold chairs.

"But we have not decided who is to be in charge," objected Sybil Foster, a relative newcomer to the WOR, who'd been coolly observing and not clamoring to volunteer for anything.

Lucy glanced at Mary Louise, who looked bemused and maybe a little annoyed.

"I believe I just finished saying that we all know what to do, sugar. But I forget you haven't been here for donkey's years like the rest of us. We're proud to have you. What department appeals to you? Everyone can use a little help."

Before Sybil could express a preference for glassware or the white elephant booth, Ginger spoke up again.

"I think Mrs. Foster has a point. We need someone to go between the departments and assign the village people jobs. We need someone to keep track of supplies, like labels, masking tape, hangers, making sure there's enough change. And I just don't think, I'm not sure I—"

"Well," Mary Louise sighed.

"We should make nominations and hold a vote," proposed Sybil.

Mary Louise looked politely pained.

"We are not talking about a Congressional race here, honey. But I suppose we do need someone. Anne, I hate to ask it of you, but it might be simplest if you'd be willing to do the honors."

This was a far worse request than impromptu prayer. Anne looked as though she would like to bolt. Lucy struggled with her impulse to help and her own desire to flee to safety. Perhaps if they worked together—

"I know I am new here," began Mrs. Foster, "but I have run important charity bazaars in the city many times. Compared to that the rummage sale is a trifle, and I have some ideas that would bring new life—"

"Thank you. I can manage, Mrs. Foster."

Anne Bradley stood up and faced Sybil Foster. Sybil was a platinum blonde with perfect clothes, all pearls and pleats. Anne could have been called mousy, brown hair, a navy shirtwaist dress. Her expression was almost completely closed, but something escaped some crack, a crackle of hostility, gone so quickly Lucy was tempted to assume she'd been mistaken.

"It's good of you to offer," Anne added, "but we all know how busy you must be with your husband's campaign. If you'd like to help, you could take my place as Rosalie Brown's assistant in the toy department."

Toys, a department Lucy suspected Anne had chosen because it was down the driveway in the barn—a setting that would not suit Sybil Foster at all. Indeed, the candidate's wife looked positively peeved at the thought, but there was little she could do. The rector's shy, retiring wife had trapped and trumped her.

The women worked for the rest of the afternoon, unpacking boxes and bags, running back and forth, trying to figure out what everything was and where it should go. Ordinarily there was lots of hilarity as people encountered bizarre items (such as a sweater with a long turtle neck but no opening for a head). But today the atmosphere reminded Lucy of a forest where the presence of a predator has quieted the birds and squirrels, and even the wind seems subdued. You couldn't quite have heard a pin or a pine needle drop, but it felt dark and sunless inside the parish house. After an hour or two, voices began to rise again and once or twice someone laughed or exclaimed, but the full chorus never resumed.

Lucy wondered if it would over the next few days. Life had a kind of ruthless grace about it, as she had seen often enough in the war when the living carried on while whole streets turned to rubble in a flash and people's lives with them. In the midst of life, we are in death. In the midst of death we are in life.

Lucy gazed at the fire, burning softly now, slowly turning to jewel-like embers. Not quite voluntarily, her eyes closed and she let the faces of the people she'd met that day parade before her mind's eye. In this half-dreaming state she could see each one in a different light, as if she were looking at them, not with her own eyes but with Christ's. They looked so different then, the most unlovable as loveable as a child.

There was Charlotte now, and Lucy could see that Christ got a kick out of her. She made him laugh. How could Lucy have taken Charlotte's insensitivity so seriously, how could she have overlooked her real, if overbearing, kindness? Poor Charlotte. Wherever she was, she was probably fretting over Nat. Lucy did not know Charlotte's son well, but it must break any mother's heart to leave her child behind.

Rest in peace, Charlotte, Lucy prayed silently, rest in peace.

Lucy felt herself drifting into sleep, and she began to let go. It was so comforting, so comfortable, and she was so weary....

Then she felt someone grasping her shoulder.

"*Lucy, Lucy Way!*"

The voice was so close, right in her ear. Lucy struggled to open her eyes, but she couldn't seem to wake up.

"*Lucy, I want you to know that I did not take your mother's coats. I did not. I know everyone thinks I'm light-fingered, but I did not take your mother's coats down those stairs. Lucy, Lucy Way. Do you hear me?*"

Lucy sat bolt upright. Startled, Tabitha dug in her claws, then leapt from Lucy's lap. The room was dark, the fire nothing but coals. As her eyes adjusted, she was not seeing her airy parlor with its graceful antiques. She was seeing Charlotte, eyes and mouth open, skirts askew, and to one side of her body, where Frank Lomangino had moved them, the pile of heavy coats. Her mother's coats still in their plastic dry cleaning bag, the coats Frank Lomangino had carried upstairs for her and hung on the rack that hot August day.

Tabitha jumped back on the couch, but when Lucy tried to stroke her, she began grooming herself vigorously and reproachfully. Lucy sat still for a moment, her hand suspended over the cat, poised on the brink of her next thought, not certain she wanted to think it, knowing she could not avoid it. Her hovering hand came to her side, where it clutched a bit of her soft flannel dressing gown.

Charlotte had had no reason to take those coats anywhere. Even if she'd wanted them for herself, she could have put them in the storeroom upstairs behind the stage with the costumes, hidden them among the shepherds' and kings' robes used for the Christmas pageant. Clothes were not the sort of item Charlotte stole; she was largely indifferent to fashion. As she had put it in Lucy's dream, she was light-fingered. She did not want to heft or haul heavy coats. She liked things she could pocket, letter openers, paper weights, papers, photographs. That's why (when she was not in charge of the rummage sale) she was traditionally assigned womenswear and not jewelry or notions.

Everyone had been so shocked at the discovery of Charlotte's body, no one had thought to wonder what she had been doing on the basement stairs in the first place. The basement was kept clear for Sunday School classes. Charlotte might conceivably have gone downstairs to see if there were any stray boxes, but she would not have been carrying coats. Lucy's mother's coats had been hanging in their proper department for more than a week. The police and the doctor couldn't have known how odd it was for Charlotte to have been carrying those coats. And since the WOR ran the rummage sale so efficiently, Gerald Bradley might not have thought anything of it, either.

That left only herself, Lucy Way, dutiful member of the WOR, to ask questions.

She closed her eyes again and felt the urgency of that touch on her shoulder, heard Charlotte's insistent voice in her ear. *I did not take your mother's coats!*

Lucy felt her stomach tie itself in a ruthless knot that would not easily come undone.

Christ, have mercy.

Had Charlotte Crowley been murdered?

CHAPTER TWELVE

Anne was annoyed with herself for being annoyed. She could not blame poor Charlotte Crowley for her unfortunate death, yet somehow she did, as she hurried to get dressed for Charlotte's funeral, having dropped off the twins at nursery school less than an hour ago. Rosalie was going to pick them up and give them lunch, so at least Anne would not have to dash away from the reception, although she might have preferred to. Ordinarily the reception would have been held at the parish house, but since the rummage sale setup was in progress, the Federated Church down the street had kindly donated their hall. Gerald had been privy to some awkward discussion about the Crowley's finances. He of course had not disclosed the details to her, but holding the reception at a restaurant or catering it was out of the question, nor could the Crowley's dark, cramped little cottage accommodate the crowds expected to attend. As if the WOR did not have enough on their plate with the rummage sale, they were providing the refreshments for the funeral. Ginger, with the help of Marge, had pulled herself together enough to coordinate their efforts. Anne had picked up an Entenmann's crumb cake on her way back from nursery school and shamelessly transferred it from its box to one of her better china platters.

At least work on the rummage sale had been canceled for the morning, though they'd pay for the lost time later. How Anne regretted not letting snooty Sybil Foster run it as she pleased. It was enough to make Anne believe in demonic possession. How else to explain why her vague resentment of the icy blonde socialite would drive her to take on such an onerous, unwanted task.

Anne sat on the edge of the bed and began gathering a stocking, so that it would not snag on a toe or fingernail, a task that could not be rushed. She had debated leaving on her nylons, but had found a tiny run in one. She never could help thinking of Hal when she put on stockings. As a toddler, he'd loved the feel of stockings and if he got the chance he would run his hands over the legs of unsuspecting guests. Until he was old enough to know better, he'd had to be banished from all coffee hours and other social gatherings.

With her stockings snapped into place, Anne went to her bureau to consult her jewelry box. Her dress, also silk, wasn't solid black but had tiny gold and red *fleur de lis* flecking it. She could wear the small gold earrings that Gerald had given her when Katherine was born, and though she usually avoided the reminder, she decided to wear the short strand of pearls that had been Gerald's gift at Hal's birth. They had their own satin-lined box and she kept them tucked away in the drawer with the linen and lace handkerchiefs.

Where she kept Hal's picture, the one Charlotte had found that evening Anne caught her snooping. Anne touched the frame now without picking it up—there was no time for that—just to reassure herself that it was there. She wished Charlotte had not seen it. She did not intend to forgive Charlotte for her desecration just because she was dead. Anne knew she was not a good Christian; perhaps she was not a Christian at all, but at least she would not be a hypocrite. She would wear the pearls to the funeral. Not to honor Charlotte, but to remind herself that she could not lose what she'd already lost.

The church was crowded when Anne arrived. She did not have any customary seat, because on Sundays she sang in the choir; the choir rarely sang for funerals, due to short notice. Anne managed to avoid the ushers, Mary Louise's husband Count Ludwig and Rick Foster who, Gerald told her, had insisted on taking a day off from campaigning to attend the funeral. Both of them looked so distinguished, Charlotte would have been gratified and might even have voted Democratic if she had lived.

Anne slipped into a pew in the side chapel where she could observe unobserved. Apparently Charlotte had left some funeral instructions, hymns and readings. Grace Jones had found the form on file. It was something Gerald encouraged his parishioners to do. Some people thought planning for death was morbid. Charlotte had probably regarded it merely as another social occasion where she would be the center of attention. Anne doubted Charlotte had picked Bach's organ arrangement of the chorale "In peace and joy I now depart" as the prelude, which Elsa began to play with passion and precision, as she doubtless would have for her worst enemy. Charlotte might not have known what a prelude was; she was musically insensitive at best. Just a bit of filler at the beginning while people arrived and took note of who was and wasn't there and who had a new hat or dress.

Anne could not help being affected by the music, another reason she wanted to sit on the sidelines. This piece had not been played at Hal's funeral, thank heaven if there was one, but she had sung it before as a chorale.

In peace and joy I now depart
At God's disposing;
For full of comfort is my heart;
Soft reposing.
So the Lord hath promised me,
And death for me is but a slumber.

Anne did not remember the rest of the words, but it wasn't the words that moved her, it was the music, its lightness, its serenity, the way it moved like water, so sure of its course. Though it was stately, there was a little lilt to it. She remembered Hal once doing a slow half skip down a hall in her parents' old house where afternoon light spilled in from a high window and made a path. He had been full of joyful concentration as he made his almost formal progress.

Had he departed that way, with a light deliberate step into some beckoning light?

She opened her small beaded bag, just big enough for her cigarettes, lipstick and handkerchief. She had no comforting beliefs. But music sometimes got past her guard. She supposed anyone who saw her would think she was shedding a tear for Charlotte. As she listened to the music, she found herself picturing Charlotte's tumble down the stairs, hardly a peaceful or joyful departure, certainly not a graceful one. To her horror, Anne found herself suppressing a giggle. Not for the first time since Hal's death, Anne wondered if she had become a monster no longer capable of ordinary human feeling— except her own grief.

To distract herself Anne surveyed the congregation, what she could see of it between pillars that separated the side chapel from the nave. People were still arriving and seats being found for those who had not come early enough to claim their habitual places. She caught sight of Lucy Way's white curls, peaking out beneath a black cloche hat with a discreet feather on one side. No longer in style, the cloche would have been all the rage in Lucy's youth. Had she cared about fashion then? Lucy always looked graceful to Anne, but her looks had a timeless quality, neither dated nor up-to-date. She sat where she usually did in the middle of the fourth pew on the right. The light from the window depicting Jesus holding a lamb always seemed to rest on her. Ginger, wearing a wider-brimmed veiled hat decorated with some unfortunate-looking white roses, shared the pew with Lucy and Mildred Thomson, who wore a black straw hat with what looked like a left-over memorial day poppy blaring from the rim. Grace Jones and Mary Louise, both with more discreet millenary, filled out the pew.

The second row of pews seated the family, many of whom had arrived from the city on the morning train. Grace Jones had coordinated rides and in some cases overnight accommodations for an assortment of cousins, their young in various ages and stages, and a few frail aunts and uncles from the preceding generation. Curiously, the third row had been filled with four men in dark, formal suits, their hats respectfully removed, their uniformly black hair well and expensively cut. It was unusual to see men in church without wives. Perhaps they were bankers, or lawyers, though Anne doubted Charlotte's estate amounted to much.

At last, the last notes fell and afterwards that silence when you could hear tiny sounds, a rustle of clothing, the slightest shift of weight in a pew. The heavy doors opened and Nat came in on the arm of his son, Jonathan, an impossibly handsome young man who really was not so young anymore. Anne did not know much about him except that he had gone to Los Angeles to try to make his fortune in film. She had never met him, but he looked familiar, perhaps from a cigarette advertisement. Yes, he did look vaguely like the Marlboro man, except the Marlboro man appeared incapable of any emotion but cool self-satisfaction. Jonathan looked bereft and surprisingly unselfconscious. Anne felt her first pang of grief, not for Charlotte but for the son who had possibly adored her. Another, plainer man, of about Jonathan's age, followed Nat and his son. They waited at the pew for him to seat himself first. Jonathan followed, and Nat sat next to the aisle where he would be nearest to the coffin.

Anne hated that part of the funeral. She hated thinking of the body in the box. Thank God Gerald refused to conduct open coffin funerals. He couldn't control what people did at calling hours in the funeral home, so Anne never attended those, even though as the minister's wife she should. She did not go to gravesides, either. People excused her, she suspected, out of pity. They thought it was because of Hal's death, but it went back further than that, no doubt to the death of her younger sister who had died at the same age as Hal. Why she hadn't lost her mind over Hal's death, she did not know. Maybe she had. Wasn't that why she saw Dr. Aiken? He wanted her to talk about her childhood, but she really couldn't remember much about it. Repression, Dr. Aiken called it. He hadn't made much headway with her.

She looked resolutely ahead, bracing herself for Charlotte's final entrance when she heard someone else come in. Tiptoeing footsteps headed towards the side chapel. She turned and saw Frank Lomangino, dressed in what must be his best suit, looking embarrassed and uncertain. It was unusual for people who weren't members of the church to attend funerals, especially Roman Catholics. They usually paid their respects at the funeral home's calling hours. Frank had been the one to find Charlotte, Anne remembered, so perhaps he felt some sort of obligation to see her through. She was sitting in the last pew, so he had to walk past Anne. He genuflected and made the sign of the cross before sitting down. One of the strangers in the front third row turned around and looked right at Frank, an odd look that lasted longer than the glance people usually gave latecomers.

The door opened again, and Anne kept her eyes on Frank Lomangino's dark hair, the curls that he hadn't succeeded in slicking all the way down.

"*I am the resurrection and the life,*" intoned Gerald, his voice several tones deeper than his conversational tone. It was actually a beautiful voice. It might have comforted someone else. "*He that believeth in me, though he were dead, yet shall he live: and whosoever liveth and believeth in me, shall never die.*"

And those who did not believe? What had Hal believed? What about children who died? What about babies? What about their angry, bitter mothers?

Anne shut out Gerald's voice. It was a distant booming, a foghorn for people who did not know how lost they were, how treacherous the rocks.

"Let us stand and sing hymn 471."

There was no doubt Charlotte had picked this hymn, and there was no way Elsa would have ever played it except at Charlotte's funeral. Now Elsa pulled out all the stops and launched into the opening of "Rock of Ages" as if it were carousel music at the county fair. It wasn't nice to mock the dead or their taste in music, but Elsa was. Anne wondered if anyone else noticed.

"Rock of Ages, cleft for me, let me hide myself in thee." Anne began to sing, and then coughed and covered her mouth to hide her laughter. But she couldn't stop. She laughed silently all the way through the hymn until she cried.

CHAPTER THIRTEEN

"Frankie," said Aramantha in that voice that made her sound like a queen. "You may take three umbrella steps forward."

"Umbrella steps!" protested Frankie. "That's dumb."

But he began to spin, like he did when he pretended to be an enemy warplane about to crash, and whirled forward three steps.

"You forgot to say Mother, May I, Frankie!" Aramantha jumped up and down, unable to hide her glee. "Take five giant steps backwards."

Frankie made machine gun-firing noises as he went, but he did go back, obeying the rules, just barely. He almost never remembered to say Mother, May I. He thought it was stupid. Katherine never forgot the words, which was why Aramantha only allowed her to take baby steps as she got closer and closer to the finish line. Aunt Rosalie's kids, Lisa and Barbie, were playing, too, and so were Peter and Janie and two of Frankie's younger sisters, Maria and Sophie, because Frankie's mother was helping at the rummage sale. The little kids didn't understand the rules, but they had fun doing the steps, the scissor steps, alligator steps, and steps Aramantha made up that no one had ever heard of before. Aramantha's cousins Josette and Bobby were old enough to understand the game—and they knew they had to do what Aramantha said. Even Frankie listened to her. Aramantha had promised Frankie they could play Red Light, Green Light next. Frankie always won at that game.

They were playing on the front lawn by the rectory, because the back lawn near the parish house was taken up by a big tent with rolled up sides crowded with everything from couches to television sets to tractors. When any kids tried to go in there, Mr. McCready would chase them out waving his stick unless they could name all the prophets in The Bible in order. Katherine's grade hadn't learned prophets yet, but Aramantha knew all their names even though she was only in fourth grade. Mr. McCready let her sit in a huge easy chair for a few minutes, while the rest of the kids ran around playing Freeze Tag, till Aramantha got bored sitting in the chair and rounded them up to play Mother, May I.

The toy barn, where they used to be allowed to help last year, wasn't so fun anymore. Dickie and Prescott's mother had taken Katherine's mother's place. Katherine's mother was busy all the time now. It was because of the lady who died. Katherine's mother had to do her work. It scared Katherine a little. What if her mother died, too? Who would take care of them? She hoped not Mrs. Foster. She'd brought Dickie and Prescott along with her to the toy barn. They were supposed to count puzzle pieces to see if they were all there, but instead they just spilled pieces out and left them all over the steps to the attic while they read old *Mad* magazines. When Aramantha and her cousins, then Frankie and his sisters showed up, Mrs. Foster said, "Well, I think that's enough for one day. Can you lock up on your own, Rosalie?"

Everyone was glad when Mrs. Foster and her awful boys left. Katherine's mother came to the barn with a pot of coffee and two cups. She and Aunt Rosalie sat down on old chairs and lit their cigarettes.

"You kids go play," Aunt Rosalie said. "We need a few minutes of peace. Go on, all of you."

Before she'd run after the others, Katherine turned to look at her mother. She looked happy sitting there in the sun with Aunt Rosalie, who must be telling her a funny story. First she smiled and then she laughed out loud. Hearing her mother laugh gave Katherine a strange feeling, like when you have a good dream, but you can't remember it. She wanted her mother to live forever and ever. But if she didn't, Katherine decided, she would run away with Frankie and live in the woods. She did not need anyone else to take care of her.

"Katherine, come *on*!" Frankie had called to her, waiting for her when no one else did. "Hurry up!"

Now in spite of all the baby steps and something Aramantha made up called inch worm steps where you had to get down and wriggle on the ground, Katherine was near enough to tag her. She turned and ran as fast as she could, everyone giggling and shrieking with Aramantha in pursuit, Katherine keeping just ahead of her. When she neared home safe, she saw Frankie waving to her to follow him. She crossed the invisible line, and Frankie grabbed her hand and pulled her to the driveway.

"Where do you two think you're going?" Aramantha called after them.

Katherine tried to turn and shrug.

"Hold your horses!" Frankie called. "We'll be right back."

"You better or we're *not* playing no Red Light, Green Light. All right, Barbie. It's your turn to be it. I'll show you what to do," Katherine heard Aramantha say as she followed Frankie.

"Where are we going, anyway?" Really, Frankie was as bossy as Aramantha.

"I saw that lady," Frankie whispered. "She was coming out of your house. We have to follow her. To see if she goes in the woods. Look, there she is!"

Katherine did not need to ask which lady. She could see for herself. The lady with thistledown hair was standing talking to Mr. McCready outside the big tent. She was wearing a light purple dress and a sweater that looked like the color of clouds at sunset, not quite pink or orange.

"We've got to hide," Frankie whispered, and he pulled her from the driveway to the row of cedar trees outside the choir room door.

"When she goes around the tent to the woods, we'll follow her," instructed Frankie.

The white-haired lady stood very still, her head bent towards Mr. McCready, who for once wasn't shouting and waving his stick. At last she turned away, only she didn't go to the woods but towards the lower driveway.

"We can't be seen by anyone," Frankie told Katherine. "We've got to go around behind the parish house. But first we've got to get past the old crazy man."

Quietly as they could, they ran behind the tent, past the gap in the wall to the wood, around the back of the parish house. Katherine's heart pounded and she was out of breath. She felt excited and scared but she didn't know of what.

"Hey, Frankie, Frankie, Junior," someone called from the upstairs fire escape door. "What are you doing? You're supposed to be watching your sisters."

"That's my moms," hissed Frankie. "Run faster!"

They careened out of his mother's sight around the corner of the parish house. They ran so hard that they couldn't stop when they got back to the driveway and they skidded on the gravel, Katherine falling and scraping her knee.

"I didn't know that anyone but a wind sprite could run so fast."

Katherine looked up, too surprised to cry. There was the lady standing over her. Frankie had stopped like a statue in Freeze Tag a few feet away.

"Come, let me take a look at that knee." The lady helped Katherine to her feet. "I have a first aid kit in my car. Or would you rather I find your mother for you?"

Katherine did want her mother, who was close by, but didn't want to say so, especially with Frankie shaking his head and mouthing something to her.

"My car is just down the hill," said the lady. "Maybe you'd like to help me with the bandage, Frankie."

Frankie followed, dragging one of his feet in the dirt the way he always did when a grownup asked him to do something, even when he wanted to do it. Katherine wondered how the lady knew Frankie's name, but it was something she had noticed about grownups. They all seemed to know your name, even if you didn't know who they were.

"Do you know my name?" she asked the lady in a voice just louder than a whisper, but the lady heard her.

"Let me think," said the lady. "What would a wind sprite be called? Zephyrina? No that's not right, is it? Aeola then?"

"Her name's Katherine!" Frankie interrupted.

He was probably jealous that the lady hadn't called him a wind sprite, even though he could run faster.

"You're not a fairy!" Frankie accused the lady when they reached her car. "You don't live in the woods."

He sounded angry, but Katherine knew he was sad. He wanted the lady to be magic as much as she did. But Katherine still believed she was magic. The lady didn't answer Frankie right away. She opened the front of her car and got out a white box with a red cross on it.

"Where's the engine?" Frankie asked.

Katherine wondered what the lady would say. She knew where the engine was, because her father had the same kind of car. Would the lady tell Frankie or would she play pretend? If she did, then maybe she wasn't really magic at all.

"The engine is in the back," the lady said. "Would you hold this bottle for me, Frankie? That's right. Now tip it just a little onto this cloth. All right, Katherine, I am going to disinfect your cut. It might sting a little."

It did sting, but Katherine did not make a sound. She held her breath, and pretty soon it stopped hurting.

"This scrape needs more than an ordinary Band-Aid," the lady announced. "Frankie, will you hold this bandage in place, while I tape it."

Frankie held it steadily. It almost seemed for a moment like Frankie was another grownup. The lady got out white tape and cut four pieces to fit over the square white bandage.

"Now then," said the lady. "That'll do, but we ought to find your mother, Katherine. She'll need to change the bandage later. Do you know where she is?"

Before Katherine could answer, Frankie stepped out right in front of the lady.

"What is your name?" he demanded. "Where do you really live?"

Katherine knew her mother would have said Frankie was being rude, but the lady didn't seem to mind.

"My name is Lucy."

Lucy like Lucy in the Narnia books!

"Lucy Way. I live in an old house with an old cat named Tabitha. When I go to the woods, I remember my old, old fairy blood. You must have fairy blood, too, or you wouldn't have recognized me."

Frankie stared at her, his eyes dark as water at night.

"Is that why we could see the other thing?" he asked at last. "Because we have fairy blood?"

"What thing was that?" asked Lucy Way.

"The black thing that was running away," said Katherine. "It might have had wings."

"And horns," Frankie added, "but we couldn't see because it was wearing a sweatshirt."

The lady named Lucy Way looked at them for a long time without answering. Her eyes were green, Katherine saw, green as a cat's. Green as the woods. Even though she was looking at them, she also seemed to be seeing something else. She must have fairy blood.

"Children," she said at last. "You must know that in an enchanted wood there is sometimes danger. I know you are very brave, but you must also be very wise. Because of what you saw in the wood, it would be best for you not to go there alone."

"We're not really allowed to go there at all," Katherine admitted, though she knew Frankie might be mad at her for that.

"So!" Frankie began kicking at the gravel. "Who cares? We have fairy blood. Those are our woods."

Lucy Way put a hand on their shoulders.

"Perhaps we will all go there together one day. In the meantime, you must not go there alone."

Katherine waited to see if she would make them promise. Or if Frankie would refuse.

"Frankie, Frankie, Junior!" his mother called to him from the parish house.

"Katherine?" her mother called her from the barn.

"Goodbye, Lucy Way," said Frankie.

"Goodbye, Lucy Way," echoed Katherine.

"Goodbye, children," said Lucy Way.

As Katherine and Frankie went to their mothers, they both turned and saw Lucy Way watching after them.

CHAPTER FOURTEEN

It was only four in the afternoon, but in nautical terms the sun had been over the yardarm since eleven in the morning, Gerald reasoned, the time when sailors (depending on latitude) had their first shot. Being a parish priest had some similarities to being captain of a ship. Both could marry and bury people (he'd done the latter only yesterday) and both had to navigate through treacherous waters, buffeted by storms that could blow your ship way off course. Where he was supposed to navigate the Church of Regeneration should be clear: service, solvency, salvation, not necessarily in that order. But as rector of a small town church, one thing he hadn't reckoned on was a murder.

He opened the lower cupboard of the china cabinet—he didn't have a proper bar—and got out the gin and the vermouth. And then he reached to the highest shelf for the martini shaker. (Anne did not make it easy.) For once, he was careful to wipe the counter after smashing the ice. And he put away the lemon after he cut a peel. He did not want Anne to say anything about his early drink, or rather to *not* say anything, but to clean up the counter so spotlessly she didn't have to. He did not want Anne to wonder why he was sneaking (was he sneaking, in his own house?) an early drink. He did not want Anne to think anything when he'd had no chance to think himself.

At least he was alone in the house, though that could change at any moment. There was no quiet place to be during the weeks before the rummage sale. The parish house was full of women running up and down stairs in their loafers or heels, cackling in the kitchen where someone was always making another pot of coffee or a plate of sandwiches. He had met Lucy Way in his office in the house and listened to her suspicions while the children played outside his window on the front lawn. He'd had to ask Lucy to repeat herself more than once, her low, modulated tones (who had said a low voice was an excellent thing in a woman?) unable to compete with the children's shrieks.

"What was that about the coats?" he'd asked. "Wasn't she carrying them upstairs when she fell?"

"That's just it," Lucy had said, raising her voice slightly as if he were deaf rather than deafened by the noise. "The coats were already upstairs. They were my mother's coats. I'd brought them in at the end of August, straight from the drycleaners. Frank Lomangino carried them upstairs for me and put them on the rack in the clothes department."

"Maybe she had some reason for taking them to the basement." Gerald paused, not wanting to make any accusations the dead woman could not answer.

"If you mean she might have intended to keep them for herself," Lucy answered his unspoken suspicion, "I thought of that, but coats were not the sort of thing Charlotte stole."

Lucy came right out and named Charlotte's besetting sin without mincing words. If anyone but Lucy Way had called Charlotte a thief, he would have suspected malice or envy masquerading as righteousness. But Lucy was so matter-of-fact. He could not detect a hint of judgment. Gerald was not ready to ask his next question. He fumbled for his cigarettes, offered Lucy one, forgetting that she did not smoke.

"Please." She gestured to his cigarettes. "I don't mind at all."

Gerald decided his pipe would be less offensive, more gentlemanly. It also took longer for him to fill and light a pipe.

"My uncle used to smoke that blend," Lucy Way remarked. "Old Cutler, I think?"

Gerald nodded, ridiculously pleased. Even though Anne smoked cigarettes, she deplored his pipes. He left them everywhere. They made a mess, he knew, little spills of tobacco and ash all over the place. Lucy wasn't married. She had no husband to deplore. Yet there was nothing old-maidish about her. Maybe because she had been a nurse in the War. She was used to men, didn't mind their habits.

"My father smoked it, too," Gerald said.

He took another puff and they sat silently for a moment. Lucy did not rush him. Maybe she also dreaded his next question.

"So if she had no reason to carry the coats up or downstairs, how do you think they come to land on her when she fell?"

And Lucy told him. What she thought.

Now he had to think.

Gerald took a sip, more like a gulp, of his drink while he was still standing at the kitchen counter. He wondered where he could go that he would not be interrupted. He could close the door to his study. Anne might think he was sequestered with someone; there were so many people around, a parishioner might knock at the door any minute. But if Anne and the children came home, it would not be quiet inside or outside his head.

Jesus Christ, he swore silently, where could a man go to get a break? Or maybe it was a prayer. In the next moment he pictured the empty church. Of course, that's where he needed to be. No one would think anything of finding a priest praying in his own church, unless he happened to be holding a martini glass in his hand. Well, how about a thermos, then? Gerald began rummaging through cabinets till he found a thermos with the picnic things. He poured his drink into it and then the contents of the large martini shaker. Tucking the thermos under his arm, he went out the front door that directly faced the red doors of the church. There were people still parked by the parish house, but the children had deserted the front yard. It was time for their mothers to go home and start dinner. The coast was clear. Gerald made a dash for it.

As soon as he closed the heavy doors behind him and entered the church, he felt calmer. The afternoon light shone thick as honey through the stained glass windows. There was that smell, the smell of his whole life, faintly musty but fresh at the same time with a lingering trace of beeswax from candles or furniture polish, he wasn't sure.

The women took care of that, the women. The women. Why were there so many women in the church, outnumbering and outliving the men? Well, Charlotte hadn't outlived poor Nat. But the WOR had taken him up, taken him over. Gerald must call on him tomorrow, give him some relief from his nursemaids. For a moment Gerald forgot that this death and bereavement were no longer simple pastoral matters.

Then he remembered. That's why he had a thermos full of gin in the pew next to him. He unscrewed the cup and the stopper and poured himself a full measure. He raised the cup to Christ Triumphant, wishing Jesus could abandon his stiff pose and come down and have a stiff drink with Gerald. He bet Jesus would accept a cigarette, too, but he couldn't risk smoking in the church. It would be too hard to hide if someone walked in. He drained half the cup, and then he closed his eyes and let himself see what might have happened, what Lucy believed had happened. What he didn't know if he could believe, did not want to believe.

Someone pushing Charlotte down the stairs. Maybe someone she had faced and fought. Maybe that's why she had fallen backwards. Or someone might have come up behind Charlotte and struck her a blow on the head first and then dragged her down the stairs. Haydock had said she had hit her head, hard enough to knock her unconscious.

But not enough to kill her.

So someone had gone to get the heavy coats, arranged them over her face, to look as if they had landed on her when she fell. No, not simply arranged them, held them there until Charlotte stopped breathing.

It *could* have happened.

Gerald drained the cup and filled it up again half way. It could have happened that way. It could also have been an accident, no matter what Lucy said about the coats. That's what the doctor had said, and Chief O'Brien had agreed. God knows Charlotte was eccentric and highhanded. Who knows what she was doing with those coats?

Maybe she had decided to move winter clothes downstairs in spite of Sunday School classes. There could be half a dozen explanations. Weren't the simplest, most obvious explanations usually correct? Murder was far-fetched, preposterous. If anyone but Lucy Way had suggested it, he would have told her (it would be a woman, someone like Mildred Thomson) that she was overwrought and needed to go away somewhere and take a long rest. Lucy Way or not, it just didn't make sense. Charlotte had been insensitive and intrusive, and yes, a kleptomaniac. Everyone understood that. That's what a parish church was all about. You forgave people their trespasses or at least you shrugged and went on about your business. That's the closest most people came to loving their neighbor. Even when they couldn't stand him—or her—they wouldn't think of breaking the sixth commandment.

That woman should be executed. She should be taken out, placed in front of a firing squad and shot at dawn.

Elsa's voice sounded in his head. Elsa had said that. But she hadn't meant it. She always exaggerated, dramatized. She had played the organ for Charlotte's funeral, even the hymns she hated. Elsa was hot-blooded, not cold-blooded. She couldn't carry out a murder, conceal it and then go play for eight o'clock communion. Which usually had no music. So why had Elsa been there in the first place so early last Sunday morning?

"God," he said out loud. "No."

He drained the cup and would have refilled it, but the thermos was empty. Just as well. He was feeling woozy. Not drunk, he told himself. He might have a migraine coming on and who could blame him. A sudden death, a funeral and burial, the rummage sale. He would tell Anne he had a migraine. He'd get a cough drop from the choir room before he went home to mask the gin fumes. He could leave the thermos in his car. Anne was sympathetic about his migraines. She would tell the children to be quiet. She would bring him broth and toast. First maybe he should rest for a few minutes.

When he closed his eyes, he saw Anne's face, her cold, furious expression.

Elsa's right about that. Charlotte Crowley should be shot—or at least accidentally pushed down a long flight of stairs.

Gerald definitely had a migraine. He should not have to think anymore. He could not think, he would not think about Anne leaving their bed and going outside that morning. But he couldn't stop. He could hear the backdoor opening and closing. Why would she go outside? Because it had been a beautiful morning, he told himself. She went outside with her coffee and cigarettes. She went outside for a moment's peace. She went outside to get away from him. How long had she been gone? He'd dozed off until he heard the car leaving the driveway and woke thinking it was Anne leaving him. But she hadn't left. She had come back with coffee for him. She had remarked about the car herself. She had been friendly for a moment, and then she'd been angry with him again, because Katherine had run outside to play with Frankie. That's right. Frank Lomangino had been there early, too. So had whoever drove off in that car. Not just Anne. Not just Anne.

Oh Christ, he was going to be sick.

Gerald got up and lurched out of the pew. He didn't think he could make it to the rectory. He didn't want to risk running into anyone in the driveway. If he hadn't been so desperate he wouldn't have considered it, but he was desperate. And so ran down the aisle, turned toward the sacristy and fumbled for the key behind the side chapel curtain.

It was a wide sink, an old-fashioned sink, a merciful sink. It did not judge him. After he threw up, he let the water run for a long time; it washed the sink clean, poured onto the ground below, scattering the remnants of his indiscretion so no one would know. Vomiting was the only sure cure for migraine. He'd caught this one early. But he felt the same exhausted peace as if he'd been up all night. He turned off the faucet. Through the open drain he could hear crows calling in the wood and the last songs of summer insects, life that went on despite human folly or cruelty. For a moment he let himself be comforted. He let himself forget the decision he had to make.

Then he heard someone open the side door to the church. Quickly he left the sacristy, locked the door, and replaced the key. When he turned, he saw Elsa standing beside the altar rail regarding him with a mix of sympathy and severity.

"You look like hell" was her curt greeting. "If Lucy Way hadn't poured out every last drop of my precious vodka I'd offer you a drink."

Lucy Way. He had never thought of her as a busybody. She had always seemed quiet and kind, undemanding. Why must she stir up trouble, although stopping Elsa from drinking on the job hardly qualified as trouble, more like discreet intervention. In fairness, she had been discreet today, coming to him first instead of going to the police.

Elsa spied the thermos cup where it must have fallen and rolled into the aisle. She sniffed.

"You wouldn't be setting a bad example for me, would you, Gerald?"

"Elsa," he said, "I won't lie. It's been one hell of a week."

She nodded, and gestured towards a pew. "Want to talk about it?"

It was tempting, tempting to sit and talk to someone who wouldn't judge him for having a drink in the church, but he couldn't talk to Elsa about Lucy's suspicions. If there were to be an investigation, Elsa might be, Elsa might be...a suspect. His head began to ache again. He'd better get back to the house this time.

"Thanks, Elsa. Another time. What are you doing here, anyway? I thought you avoided the rummage sale like the plague?"

"I do. Like the plague. You don't see me at the perishing house, do you? It's choir practice tonight. I came early to write some arrangements for the anthem. I have to put women on the tenor part. Not enough men. I hope Anne is not too worn out to come tonight. She is my best soprano."

Gerald had forgotten it was Thursday. Was it too late to find a babysitter, he wondered? He didn't think he could cope with the kids. Choir was the one thing Anne would desert them for. She'd even leave dishes in the sink.

"I'm sure she'll be there."

"Take care of yourself, Gerald."

Elsa turned toward the organ, then came back and handed him a cough drop. Horehound.

Gerald unwrapped the cough drop and retrieved the thermos. On his way back to the rectory, he stopped and put it under the seat of his car. He could get it and wash it while Anne was at choir practice. The fresh air was having a good effect on his head. Maybe he didn't need to ask Anne to find a sitter. Maybe he'd just let the kids watch television. He slammed the door closed and found Mildred Thomson standing a few feet away, looking exactly like a hunting dog, quivering with eagerness to retrieve a dead duck. Him.

"Father, I mean Mr. Bradley, I've been looking everywhere for you," she said with mingled relief and reproach. "I...I must speak with you."

Gerald felt dizzy again. What if he threw up in front of Mildred Thomson. What if he threw up on her? From whence cometh his help?

As if in answer, Amos McCready ambled by and paused for a moment.

"Hello, Amos," Gerald called out, but Mildred's grip on his arm tightened.

With one shrewd, bemused glance, Amos sized up the situation, shook his head and shrugged.

"Get some rest, Rev!" he advised.

And Amos walked on, a free man, a man who refused to have any truck with women. He wished he could run after Amos, go home to his bachelor digs in the rooming house where all the old soldiers and sailors lived, drinking and smoking their pipes in the peaceful evening.

"I'm sorry, Mildred. Now is not a good time. Anne has choir practice tonight and—"

"I understand, Mr. Bradley. I am sorry to bother you, but it's, it's a matter of conscience. I've even thought perhaps I should make confession, and you are a priest, my priest—"

He had wanted to be a dentist, Gerald suddenly remembered, like his scoutmaster. How much better it would be to have Mildred's mouth stuffed with cotton balls while he extracted a tooth, anything but a confession. A confession! Good Lord, deliver us. Well, even if she had murdered Charlotte, she was going to have to wait.

"This sounds very serious, Mildred. I suggest you call Grace Jones in the morning for an appointment with me. I am sorry, but I have to go now."

He turned away, and she finally released his arm.

I never had to make appointments with Father Roberts, he could hear her thinking, as she stood there boring holes in his back with her basset hound eyes. Maybe he was not cut out for the parish ministry. No, he definitely was not.

Safely inside the rectory, Gerald stood for a moment in the dim front hall. He could hear Anne in the kitchen getting dinner for the children. He could make out the shapes of the kids sprawled on the floor beyond the dining room table watching cartoons. Any other time, he might have gone to the kitchen, tried to kiss Anne before he got a drink. Depending on her mood, he might have asked how the rummage sale was coming along or complained about Mildred Thomson accosting him. But he could not joke about Mildred's determination to confess...what? He could not tell her that Lucy Way suspected murder had been done. Most of all, he could not tell her the terrible thought that had crossed his mind. The thought that made him hesitate to call the police. If indeed he should call the police. Charlotte's death could have been an accident; more than likely it had been. (Never mind about Mildred. Her conscience was a form of spiritual toothache. She should have it extracted—or maybe exorcised.) And if Gerald mistakenly unleashed a murder investigation, he risked destroying his congregation by arousing everyone's suspicion of everyone else.

Gerald found himself tiptoeing up the stairs and lying down on the bed. He needed to think. He needed to talk to someone with a level head. Someone who knew the parish but who wouldn't get hysterical, that is, someone who was not a woman. Someone he could trust as a friend.

Gerald rolled over and reached for the bedside phone.

Anne glanced at the clock on the kitchen wall. It was nearly five-thirty and Gerald hadn't come in to make a drink. Usually when he was home he was mixing a drink at five on the dot, as if he had been counting the minutes till the hour when alcohol consumption was sanctioned—by what or whom she was not sure. There were rules and a whole list of exceptions to them. One could drink after church and before Sunday dinner, for example, and if Gerald was with his clergy cronies anywhere, anytime, it was always five o'clock. Some wives met their husbands at the door with martinis already mixed (the ones who had been counting the minutes themselves). Other wives, like Rosalie, had to have dinner on the table when the man walked in the door, and a beer open and ready. Anne thought it was enough that she had to cook two separate dinners and in between get the children ready for bed if not tucked in. She drew an unspoken line at being a cocktail waitress. Still, she did wonder where Gerald was. She hoped he had not forgotten that she had choir practice this evening. Thursday was her one night a week away from the kids. Not infrequently she had to hire a sitter, because Gerald had an evening meeting, but it would be awfully short notice for a sitter now.

She put the hamburgers into the frying pan and ran up the back kitchen steps to the landing, then down another short flight into the hall. The door was open to Gerald's study, but he wasn't there. She opened the front door and saw his car parked in its usual spot. Maybe he'd gone to his office in the parish house now that the building was closed and the workers had gone home. It had been a long, tiring day, but she hadn't hated it as much as she'd expected to. She'd made her rounds from room to room, exchanging pleasantries, asking if anyone needed anything, making lists, running errands. No one expected her to sort through boxes, size clothes, or price anything, although she might be called on to arbitrate when the pricing began in earnest. That's where most of the quarrels broke out. What she had, as the rummage sale's head of operations, was license to leave any location or conversation that she found tedious. She could always excuse herself by saying she had something else to do—even if it was to slip into her own house and smoke a cigarette in peace.

Of course it was strange taking Charlotte's place. Anne knew her own presence was more neutral, even negligible. Charlotte had had opinions about everything, and Anne had very few. She sensed that people missed Charlotte, no matter what they had thought of her. She made the rummage sale feel like the event of the season, full of suspense and high drama. Who would get the set of antique lace handkerchiefs or the almost complete collection of German Beer Steins? Could the authentic Swiss cuckoo clock be fixed? All of these things mattered to Charlotte, all the people mattered and their gossip and the pathos of their lives. The village workers loved Charlotte, one of the upper crust who remembered the names of everyone's children and knew whose husbands worked where. In the absence she left, Anne felt she could see Charlotte more distinctly than she had in life when it had been necessary to ward her off. She did not want to canonize Charlotte as people were already beginning to do (being dead did wonders for most reputations) but she acknowledged that it was possible to miss, even mourn, someone you didn't like.

In contrast to Charlotte, Sybil Foster was far too alive to be missed even when she left work at the rummage sale two hours earlier than everyone else. It was just as well that Sybil was not in charge. She would have tried to make her mark on the rummage sale rather than allowing Charlotte's strong impression to fade gradually over time. To Sybil's credit, she had showed up for what she clearly considered a hardship post. Anne had stopped by the toy barn in the morning and found Sybil wearing rubber gloves up to her elbows gingerly opening boxes and exclaiming in horror over some worn stuffed animals.

"They might be infested!" Sybil had objected. "Surely they belong in the incinerator."

Rosalie picked up a lion with a tattered mane and sniffed.

"Just a little musty. Some child will fall in love with it. We'll price 'em at a nickel and come down to a penny if need be."

Anne admired the matter-of-fact way Rosalie overruled Sybil. After Sybil left for the afternoon, she'd brought a pot of coffee out to the barn. Though Rosalie recounted a number of amusing incidents from her day with Sybil, there was no malice in her laughter. She accepted Sybil, and anyone else who came her way, without judgment or illusion. Whenever Anne heard that line of the beatitudes, ye are the salt of the earth, she thought of Rosalie. As for herself, she did not know what sort of condiment she would be—something invisible but corrosive, like white vinegar.

Anne flipped the hamburgers and glanced at the clock again. When she had the children seated for supper, she'd wander down to the parish house. Maybe Mildred Thomson had bearded Gerald in his den. Mildred had been behaving even more strangely than usual, attaching herself to poor Lucy Way like an oversized burr. While the hamburgers were finishing, she'd give Rosalie a ring. By five forty-five supper would be over at Rosalie's house and she'd be in the kitchen, doing the dishes or whipping up another batch of brownies to bring to the rummage sale tomorrow. Anne wanted to do some-thing for Rosalie. Maybe she could offer to take Barbie with her when she went to pick up the twins at nursery school, take all the little ones back to her house for lunch and a nap.

Turning down the flame under the burgers, Anne picked up the wall phone, but there was no dial tone.

"Tell you what," said a voice she could not immediately place, "let's look into it a little further first."

They weren't on a party line. Who was that?

"We both know that they were in financial difficulties," the voice continued. "Let's see what we can find out. Once the police are involved, our hands will be tied. Innocent people might get hurt."

"That's exactly what I'm concerned about."

Gerald. That was Gerald. He was talking on their phone line about something important, more important than getting a drink.

"As soon as the idea entered my mind," Gerald went on, "I began suspecting people. You wouldn't believe who I've been suspecting."

Anne knew she should hang up. She didn't.

"My point exactly. It could demoralize the parish. Not to mention the press would have a field day."

There was silence on the line for a moment. Anne held her breath.

"But if there's any possibility that she's right, the police have to know," Gerald spoke again. "We can't take the law into our own hands. That would be even worse."

To her surprise, Anne found herself silently rooting for Gerald.

"Absolutely," said the other voice, one of his clergy cronies maybe. "But when you go to the police, if you want them to take you seriously, you might need to give them something more to go on than where coats are supposed to be hung at the rummage sale. It's up to you, of course. I'm at your service. I'm afraid our friend may have been in over his head. In fact, she even said some things to me, in strictest confidence. I don't know how much I should say at this point, but I could make some discreet inquiries and let you know what I find out."

"Mom-*mee*!" shouted Peter from the other room. "When is it sup-perrrrr!"

Swiftly and as silently as she could, Anne replaced the receiver. She hoped Gerald hadn't heard the background noise. She didn't want him to know she'd been listening. She wanted him to tell her what was going on. Himself.

CHAPTER FIFTEEN

After breakfast Lucy poured herself another cup of coffee and went out into her garden. There was no reason she had to be at the rummage sale at any particular time. Unlike the young mothers, she had no children to get home for by a certain hour. She could stay later. Nor was she in charge of anything. No one would even miss her if she didn't go. Except Mildred. Lucy could not deny that Mildred was the reason she was procrastinating.

For a moment she put all thoughts of Mildred aside as she made her tour of the gardens. The ghostly autumn crocuses had sprung up, growing straight up out of the ground, no leaves, just their pale bloom, contrasting with a riotous crowd of marigolds, blooming as if there were no tomorrow, no such thing as a frost that could take them down overnight. Michaelmas daisies, asters, chrysanthemum, the champion summer-long black-eyed susans still hanging on, all shouted with color in this season just before the changing leaves lifted every eye to the trees. Her tea roses were in their second bloom, leggy branches that she would have to prune reaching for the sun. In a sheltered corner of her kitchen garden lavender and thyme gave out the scent of her beloved southern France. That is where she came to rest with her coffee, sitting on a wrought iron chair, turning her face to the sun like all the other living things.

Lucy loved every season in turn, the mysterious dreaming winter, the excitement of the first spring stirrings, that great resurgence and the wave on wave of bloom and vegetation, each marking a different moment of summer. But there was something about an autumn garden that was particularly moving, the last flowers among the dried remains of earlier ones, poppies, hosta, lilies, bee balm, the spring flowers already sleeping in their bulbs. Life, death, regeneration, all cheek by jowl in her gardens. When she was in her garden, death did not seem terrible. Death was mostly frightening because it was an unknown. In the garden death seemed familiar, almost reassuring. Things have their season, they die, they return, everything held in that great rhythm, that great round.

Except when it was disrupted, usually by human agency. Gardeners were intimate not only with death, but with killing, if she were to be honest. Weeds got uprooted, slugs drowned in beer, Japanese beetles trapped or crushed. Lettuces were thinned, trees pruned, hedges cut back. There was no malice in it. Lucy actually apologized to the weeds, praised their virtues and explained to them they were welcome in other places. But there was no denying that as a gardener she played God. What made murder different? That you perpetrated it against one of your own kind? That it was motivated by malice or hatred? The worst mass murders were done by people who claimed they were saving the world, or their country, or their people. Did they think of pogroms and holocausts as no different than ripping out masses of bedstraw to keep it from choking the flowers?

Murder was different; how was it different?

Tabitha strolled over, a bit stiff-legged, Lucy noted, and sat down to groom herself in the same patch of sun that warmed Lucy. She couldn't last many more winters. She was nearly twenty years old; how many of her nine lives had she expended? Tabitha finished her bath and lay down on Lucy's feet. Lucy bent to stroke her.

"I wish I could spend the day in the sun with you, Tabitha. I've been avoiding things."

Like her growing suspicion that Mildred might have killed Charlotte? And if she had, must Lucy hear her confession?

"I told Gerald Bradley that Charlotte could have been murdered," she confided to Tabitha. "He will go to the police. It is none of my business now."

And she had told Mildred to take her matters of conscience to Gerald. Lucy was not a priest.

But you are a fellow human being, a fellow Christian, something inside her said. Who are you not to hear her? If she is reaching out to you, who are you not to take her hand?

"I'm going." She got up, reaching down and patting Tabitha's head. "I'm going to the rummage sale, and then we'll see."

Lucy's dread of Mildred's confidences and her mustering of Christian charity and courage proved to be in vain. When she arrived at the parish house, Mildred was on her way down the steps, practically taking them at a bound.

"Oh, Lucy," she said breathlessly. "I'm so glad you're here. Will you take my place at the notions department this morning? Florence won't be coming in till the afternoon. I have…I have an important appointment."

"Certainly," Lucy said to her back as Mildred hurried up the driveway.

Lucy waited, curious to see if Mildred would turn in to the rectory, or perhaps the church. She had asked Lucy yesterday whether she thought Gerald Bradley would administer the sacrament of confession. But instead, Mildred got into her surprisingly elegant cream-colored Citroën and pulled out of the driveway rather recklessly.

Lucy had an uneasy feeling about Mildred. She seemed even more unbalanced than usual, but for now Lucy was off the hook. She spent an uneventful morning arranging odds and ends that kept coming in from other departments, thinking that "What an Odd Notion" might be a better name for this table, though there were some useful items, a small jewel-encrusted doodad that she finally figured out was, or could be used for, a bookmark. A tubular crudely knitted item that might warm an ankle? A coffee cup?

The notions table took up one side of the small front room outside of Grace Jones' office. A large doorway (with sliding doors that could be closed during vestry meetings) gave onto the room where coffee hour was held, so most of the WOR stopped by to say hello and exchange pleasantries. The atmosphere today was more relaxed than it had been, almost a lull as people finished the massive task of sorting and organizing. On Saturday pricing would begin in earnest. Everything had to be ready for the workers' sale the following Thursday evening when the most coveted items would be snatched up. A week from this Sunday the place would look as though a storm had roared through it, leaving only tattered remains.

Two weeks from Charlotte's death under Lucy's mother's coats.

As Lucy stowed another empty box under the table, it occurred to her that in the chaos of the last few days, she hadn't thought to wonder what had become of those coats. Yesterday Lucy had helped Frank Lomangino's charming wife Teresa in the children's clothing department, but she hadn't looked in the coat department. Every time she'd taken a break, Mildred had cornered her. There wasn't much left to do in notions, and she didn't want to start pricing till Florence arrived. People who'd come early had gone home for lunch or congregated in the kitchen for coffee, sandwiches and gossip. She hoped no one would notice, or think anything of it, if she went to the basement as she suddenly felt compelled to do.

Lucy crossed the hall and, not quite tiptoeing, she went down the steep narrow stairs, with their potentially lethal turn. She found herself pausing just where she had paused the day she'd seen Charlotte's body sprawled on the floor. Just as she had then, Lucy held tightly to the banister. It was easy to picture Charlotte's body there; it was as if the memory was still imprinted on her retina. But what she looked at now was the raised knob at the bottom of the freshly repaired banister where the doctor supposed Charlotte might have hit her head and knocked herself unconscious, so that she failed to lift the coats from her face. Everyone had decided so quickly it was an accident. Had anyone troubled themselves to look for traces of hair or blood, or chipped paint? Lucy scrutinized the knob now, and could see no signs that the knob had encountered a skull. Of course she wasn't an expert, but she wished someone who was had examined the scene.

Lucy couldn't shake the feeling that the blow to Charlotte's head might have been administered. By a person.

Slowly Lucy continued down the stairs till she stood at the foot. She peered into all the corners of the unlit basement. She could see no sign of the coats, but perhaps she should turn on some lights and check the classrooms. Then she heard a sound coming from one of the rooms and jumped back, nearly losing her balance. She clutched the banister for support and debated bolting back up the stairs. In another moment, she saw Frank Lomangino coming out of one of the classrooms. When he saw her, he startled.

"Who's there?" he asked

Lucy realized that after coming out of a sunny classroom into the windowless room, it would be hard to see much more than a figure, dark against the light of the stairwell.

"It's Lucy, Mr. Lomangino. Lucy Way."

He ran his hands over his forehead as if wiping away sweat and let out an audible breath.

"I don't mind telling you, Mrs. Way, I was a little spooked for a moment there. I'm no more superstitious than the next guy, and I don't exactly believe in ghosts...."

"I know," said Lucy. "Sudden death can leave a strong impression on a place. I feel it, too."

"You do?" He seemed relieved. "I gotta admit, I find it a little creepy down here now."

What *are* you doing here, she almost asked, but she did not want to sound as though she suspected him of anything.

"I'm glad to find you," she said instead. "I was wondering if you knew what happened to the coats. They were my mother's, you know. Did the police take them perhaps?"

"Nope." Frank shook his head vigorously, to add emphasis and perhaps as commentary on police incompetence. "They just left them here. I came down a couple of days later, and the coats were still just where they were when I...when I moved them off Mrs. Crowley. I took 'em back upstairs where they were before. I didn't think about it. I guess maybe I shoulda asked someone first. Geez, I hope I didn't screw anything up, Mrs. Way."

Only a murder investigation manqué, Lucy did not say.

"It probably doesn't matter," she said doubtfully.

She didn't know if you could dust for fingerprints on plastic bags or wire hangers. Several people had already handled the coats: the drycleaner, herself, Frank. If there was a murderer, he might have had the sense to wear gloves—or she. A woman on her way to church could well have worn gloves as part of her Sunday apparel.

"I'll just go see if they're still in their bag." She turned to go up the stairs.

"Wait, Mrs. Way, do you have a minute?"

Frank's voice was so solemn, she turned back and felt a little discomfited to see that he had closed the distance between them and was now standing right in front of her. He was very handsome, and he was close enough that she could catch a whiff of his scent, reassuringly masculine or disturbingly so. She was an older woman, alone in a basement with a young man she did not really know. She hated thinking that way, so she forced herself to stand still.

"Do you think something mighta happened to her, know what I mean? Do you think she coulda been, that someone mighta...."

"What makes you think so, Mr. Lomangino?"

The question slipped out, but Lucy did not it feel right to confide her speculations to Frank Lomangino. She had done the right thing. She had gone to the rector. She must let it rest there. Still, it was notable that the possibility of murder had crossed Frank's mind, too, even if he could not bring himself to come out and say it.

"It's probably nothing," Frank said. "I found a window left open. That's why I was down here. The furnace was going on more than it should this time of year. The window in that room over there was left open. So I shut it."

If there had been a crime, and therefore should have been a crime scene, Frank Lomangino had muddied it hopelessly. Or was he cleverly trying to throw her—and everyone else—off the scent? Oh, she hated it, hated it that she was thinking like an amateur sleuth in a dime store detective novel. This was a matter for the professionals, not for Miss Marple understudies. But if Gerald had contacted the police, why weren't they here asking questions?

If Gerald had contacted the police...and if he hadn't?

"Mr. Lomangino," she said slowly. "If you have any suspicions, I urge you to go to Mr. Bradley. It would not be a good thing for rumors to spread among the rest of us. We might all end up suspecting each other." Just as I, for a moment, suspected you. She felt herself blushing. "When, really, nothing is more likely than that it was an accident, as the police have decided."

"Yeah, they did, but I'm not sure my brother-in-law Joe buys it."

"Why? Has he said anything?"

Stop it, Lucy admonished herself. You don't want to play detective, so just stop it right now as you told Frank to do.

"Naw, Joe's real careful not to spill any beans, but I could tell it bothered him, how quick it all went. He don't say so, but I know he thinks the chief is a fat, lazy bast— pardon my French, Mrs. Way. I guess you're right. I should talk to Mr. Bradley."

"I think that would be best," said Lucy. "I'd better get back to work now. Give my best to Mrs. Lomangino. I so enjoyed her company yesterday."

And Lucy hurried upstairs, glad that at her age she was wearing a shirtwaist dress with a flared skirt instead of a straight skirt, not that she had any reason to believe that Frank was the sort of man to take advantage of the view. It was just impossible to forget that he *was* a man, even at her age.

Lucy found the upstairs unattended during lunch break. There was no sign of the plastic drycleaners bag. She began to search carefully though the racks of coats to see if someone had unpacked them and hung them up according to size or season—or if perhaps someone (someone?) had removed the bag of coats altogether.

CHAPTER SIXTEEN

Anne made her way up the stairs with a bag of supplies from the five and ten cent store, tags for pricing, labels for sizing, magic markers, pencils, safety pins, paper bags. She had taken Rosalie's daughter with her and stopped at the store on her way to pick up the twins at nursery school. Now the children were playing at the toy barn where Rosalie was working—by herself. (Sybil had to attend some important campaign luncheon with her husband.) Anne would take them all to the rectory for lunch and put the children down for naps when she'd made her rounds in the parish house.

As usual, Anne had no idea where Gerald was or when he'd be back. He had muttered something vague about making calls, which sometimes involved lunch elsewhere. Really, it was easier when he was out and she only had to cope with four-year-olds. And his absence gave her something concrete and mundane with which to justify her resentment. If the truth be told (at least to herself and who else was there besides maybe Rosalie) she was not a very good wife. She was not all that interested in her husband's work. She did not do all she could to help him "get ahead in the Church," an ironic phrase, considering the Church's founder. Really, the Church was as much a corporation as IBM (or I've Been Moved, as its veterans called it). To move up in the Church, you had to be willing to move from parish to more prestigious parish to deaneries at cathedrals and so forth, each move worse than the last as far as Anne was concerned.

So in fairness, Anne could not blame Gerald for not confiding in her about that phone call she had overheard last night. In fairness. But she did blame him. She supposed she could have admitted that she had eavesdropped, but then she would be the one in the wrong, and she much preferred Gerald to be in that position. So she waited and fumed, dispirited and yet oddly stimulated. It was so seldom that anything caught her attention, pulled her out of the flat, grey world she inhabited to keep her grief at a safe distance.

In the big upstairs room, Anne found no one but Lucy Way going through the coats so intently that she did not seem to notice when Anne came in.

"Hello, Lucy," she greeted her. "Are you in the market for a winter coat?"

Lucy startled, and Anne regretted her question. She had not meant to imply that Lucy was one of those people who staked claim to prize items so that they could snatch them up at the workers' sale.

"I'm not," said Lucy. "If I were, I would certainly look here."

To Anne's relief, she did not seem offended at all.

"I actually donated quite a few of my mothers' old coats, all horribly out of date, but in good condition. I had them dry-cleaned, of course. Some people like the old-fashioned styles. I wanted to see where they'd been placed. Sentimental of me, perhaps."

Anne forgot her own awkwardness as she sensed Lucy's. Lucy usually seemed so at ease with herself, so frank without being unkind. Could she still be mourning her mother? Had Anne intruded on a private moment?

"It's hard to say goodbye to the things that belonged to someone, especially clothes," said Anne, and then she almost bit her lip. Now Lucy might think she was talking about Hal. She didn't want Lucy to feel that she was asking for sympathy when she'd only meant to extend it.

"I've got the price stickers and tags," Anne said quickly before Lucy felt obliged to say something. "I hope there's enough for all the clothes departments. I wonder where shall I leave them?"

"I think Mary Louise has set up that card table over there for pricing materials," said Lucy. "She should be back soon. I suppose I ought to get back to notions now that I've reassured myself that mother's coats are well-placed."

Anne stopped mid-step on her way across the room as Gerald's clandestine conversation came back to her. *If she's right, the police have to know,* Gerald had said. And his confidant had answered: *But when you go to the police, if you want them to take you seriously, you might need to give them something more to go on than where coats are supposed to be hung.*

Suddenly Anne just knew: Lucy Way must be the "*she.*" And the misplaced coats must have some connection to Lucy's careful search.

"Lucy," Anne called, just as Lucy was about to disappear down the stairs.

Lucy turned back, looking polite, concerned, and yes a little apprehensive, waiting patiently as Anne pondered just how she might phrase her question:

Lucy, last night I eavesdropped on a confidential call of my husband's and I think he was talking about you?

Lucy, did you go privately to my husband and ask him to go to the police?

Lucy, was it your mother's coats that suffocated Charlotte?

Before Anne could think of a polite way to pry into what no one had seen fit to confide in her, she and Lucy were both distracted by the arrival of Teresa Lomangino with her two of her daughters in tow.

(Was there a third daughter? Anne couldn't keep track of them. For Anne, the sullen pervasive presence of Frankie, Junior blotted out the rest of the Lomangino brood. And with all those sisters, what did Frankie want with Katherine? Anne quickly stopped a train of thought that might lead to Katherine's need for a big brother.)

However many children Teresa already had, the evidence of another on the way was fully visible. Teresa was one of those dark, petite women who looked as though they had merely swallowed something round. No swollen ankles or face, no extra weight. Naturally curly hair that required no nightly ritual of rollers and pins, vivid coloring that needed no make-up, though she wore a touch of rouge. Anne found herself wishing that Teresa wore too much makeup, that she did not look so fresh and pretty in the simple floral-patterned maternity smock she wore over slacks—something most women didn't wear outside the house. Anne was accustomed to feeling inferior to and resentful of women with more polished looks, women with accomplishments, needlepoint, garden club, volunteer work. So far as Anne knew, Teresa's main accomplishment was popping out three—or four?—children and holding her household together with help from her huge family while her husband was in jail. Well, to be honest, that was no small accomplishment. But why didn't she look more worn down? Why did she look so…satisfied?

"Hello, Mrs. Way, hello, Mrs. Bradley," Teresa greeted them, a little breathlessly after her climb up the stairs. "Say hello to the ladies, girls, then take your dollies over there and play till Mommy needs you."

While greetings were being exchanged, Anne wondered for a moment if she ought to invite the little girls to come back to the rectory with her and the other children. But really, Teresa had umpteen relatives she could have left them with. Why were the Lomangino kids always ending up here?

"The girls are going to help me with sizing today," Teresa Lomangino answered Anne's thought and let her off the hook.

"What delightful helpers," Lucy beamed.

Lucy liked children, Anne had noticed. Some childless women did, some didn't. Mildred Thomson, for example. And children liked Lucy. It didn't always work that way.

Then before anyone else noticed his entrance, the little girls cried out, "Pops, Pops!"

Scattering their Barbie dolls on the floor, they ran to Frank, Senior who scooped up one daughter in each arm and then went to give his wife a kiss…which she returned.

Anne turned away, not wanting to see, intending to slip down the stairs before she had to look at any more happiness. No wonder Teresa looked like the cat who swallowed the canary. Imagine having a husband your children adored. Imagine having a husband who would take your son with him everywhere.

"Did you find those coats, Mrs. Way?" Frank asked Lucy.

Anne turned back by the stairs. So those were definitely the missing coats. And Frank Lomangino knew about them. Moreover, Lucy must have confided in Frank or at least asked him about the coats.

"They are all here, thank you, Mr. Lomangino."

"Still in that drycleaner's bag?"

She felt as well as heard Lucy hesitate.

"All properly sorted," Lucy said lightly.

"Excuse me, I've got be going." Anne decided to rescue Lucy. "Teresa, all the supplies for pricing are there on the card table. Let me know if there's anything else you need."

"Sure thing, Mrs. Bradley."

Anne felt it as a gaffe on her part and a reproach on Teresa's that Anne had not called her Mrs. Lomangino.

"Oh, Mrs. Bradley," said Frank, as if he had not noticed her before. "Would you know when Mr. Bradley is getting back?"

That dreaded, ubiquitous question. And the all-purpose answer.

"I can't be sure. He's making calls. Can I give him a message?"

"No, thanks, Mrs. Bradley. I'll wait till I see him."

So Frank had something confidential to say to Gerald, too.

"Anne," Lucy Way called after her, catching up with her on the stairs. "I'm afraid we both got distracted. I believe you were in the middle of saying something before the Lomanginos arrived. Such a lovely family."

Anne turned to Lucy at the bottom of the stairs and looked into her eyes. They really were green, like a wood in sunlight or a pool of water in the middle of that wood. She really meant it about the Lomanginos. What would it be like to live without envy or regret? Anne wondered. What would it be like to be content with what you had and who you were? That's what Anne wanted to know, even more than she wanted to know what Lucy felt compelled to hide about the coats.

"It wasn't important," said Anne. "I've got to go collect the children now. Maybe some morning when all this is over, we could have coffee?"

"I'd love to," said Lucy simply.

And Anne found she believed her. As she left the parish house, Anne realized she was not sure what she meant by *all this*. The rummage sale or the mystery that no one wanted to name out loud? She looked back over her shoulder. The parish house of the Church of Regeneration a crime scene? It seemed incredible. But then she herself had hated Charlotte Crowley, at least in that moment when she'd found her holding Hal's picture. Had someone else hated her enough to kill her? And did Lucy Way suspect who the killer might be?

Anne wished coffee with Lucy did not have to wait.

Gerald had just finished with his hospital calls—one old timer from Regeneration in competition with Methuselah and the sadder case of Janet, not a member of the parish but a close friend of Grace Jones', also a divorcée, in the last stages of breast cancer. Her children, teenagers now, had gone to live three states away with their father. Except for staunch friends like Grace, she was very alone. It didn't matter to Gerald that Janet had no professed faith. There were things no seminary course could teach you, that you learned when you put aside the prayer book and your comforting clichés and just sat with someone dying alone in a hospital room.

Gerald could not have put into words what that knowledge was, and he didn't dwell on it now, as he crossed the parking lot to his car. He heard crows cawing and saw a squirrel running along a tree branch with what might be a black walnut in its mouth. The noon whistle sounded, and Gerald debated going home for lunch. It was a short drive from the hospital, but he might arrive just when Anne was trying to put the twins down for a nap and snatch a little rest for herself. If Gerald were there, she would never leave him to scrounge for himself. No, she would serve him in the kind of silence that made sitting with the dying look like a piece of cake. The timing was too tricky. Better not risk it. Although he did not want to look at it head on, the thought that he had, even for a moment, believed Anne capable of murder hovered at the edges of his awareness, a black ragged-winged presence.

Besides, he ought to look in on Nat Crowley today, and his house was conveniently on the way home from the hospital. It might be good to drop in at lunch time to keep the old boy company. He could help him consume some of the army's worth of food the WOR had dropped on him. Women always thought men were helpless in the kitchen. They forgot that in the war men had cooked whole meals over a sterno in their army helmets. Surely he and Nat could rustle something up. He did not intend to tell Nat anything about Lucy Way's suspicions that Charlotte's death might not be accidental. He wanted to wait to see what Rick Foster turned up. But he would encourage Nat to speak freely. If Nat hadn't started drinking by noon, he certainly would when Gerald showed up.

Of course scotch might not help the already muddled Nat make sense of his finances. (That Nat made a scant living as a trustee of other people's fortunes clearly had to do with family connections, not financial acumen.) If Gerald could get some idea of where things stood, he might be able to help, at least go with him to the bank. In the funeral home, Nat had babbled something about a plan of Charlotte's, presumably to get them out of debt. Gerald had tried to talk to the son, whom he suspected of being as queer as a three dollar bill, but apparently one of Charlotte's missions in life had been to relieve her son of any worry for his parents' sorry financial state, so that he could be free to ride off into a Hollywood sunset. Oddly, the longer she was dead, the more admirable Gerald found Charlotte Crowley. Many women married to ne'er-do-wells turned to their sons and tried to shackle them. Not Charlotte. In her son's eyes, she was as glamorous and carefree as a 1930s movie star. No doubt Charlotte had liked being worshipped and had done whatever she could to encourage it, including hiding any not-so-pretty truths.

Morally reprieved from lunch at home, Gerald enjoyed the drive. The Virginia creeper was already scarlet and the swamp maples had started to blaze. Skeins of geese unfurled in the sky, then descended noisily to search for the last grains of corn in a field of dry stubble. Charlotte's death and Nat's troubles at least took Gerald out of himself. *Make us always mindful of the needs of others*, concluded the Grace he pronounced over every meal. Really, what did it matter whether he was happy or not? Life was not about personal fulfillment.

Gerald turned off the state road onto the shunpike, then down another little road. Past a yew hedge, which someone must have trimmed not long ago, Gerald turned into the driveway of what had once been a laborer's cottage on a big estate. There, sprawling haphazardly, so that you couldn't exactly call it parked, was Mildred Thomson's Citroën.

"Shit!" said Gerald out loud.

And he shifted his car into neutral where his hand and his conscience hovered. He could just put the car into reverse. Most of the windows faced the other direction, and Nat and Mildred probably hadn't seen him. Then, although he wasn't usually given to fancy, he could almost hear Christ say, "*I was being ministered unto by Mildred Thomson, and ye came to my rescue. In as much as ye have done it unto one of these the least of my brethren, ye have done it unto—*"

"Christ!" said Gerald; it did not count as taking his name in vain if you meant it. "All right. I'll go in."

And he parked the car right where it was, shifting it into gear and yanking up the hand brake for good measure.

"Oh, Fath—Mr. Bradley!" Mildred answered the door and led him through a dark coat-lined hall to a small parlor with a table set for two in a windowed alcove. "I was just about to serve luncheon. Please join us."

The moment when he could have lied and said "Anne is expecting me" passed by like an express train, he, alas, being at a local stop. Before he could answer, Nat was on his feet heading for the bar.

"Gerald, glad you're here. Scotch or gin?"

Though he had a well-earned reputation as a martini man, Gerald had been thinking of Scotch. There was an autumnal nip in the air, and its amber color was mellow as autumn oak leaves. Before Gerald could express his preference, Mildred sprang into action and through some practically aerodynamic feat landed herself between Nat and the bar.

"Now, Nat, remember we talked about that." Mildred spoke in a low voice, as if Gerald could not hear, or shouldn't.

"But look here, Millie, I have a guest. Charlotte always said—"

"I am sure Mr. Bradley doesn't drink in the middle of the day."

Gerald felt his mouth opening. He looked for words of protest that would not offend Mildred. Christ our Lord always had a wineskin at hand. There were parables about it.

"Actually, I would love—" Gerald began.

"Now, come, both of you. Sit down at the table." Mildred took Nat's arm and motioned Gerald to follow. "I'll just set another place. Lunch won't be a minute."

As he sat with Nat, Gerald had a sudden, vivid memory of Katherine and Hal sitting at the children's table at one Thanksgiving, both of them wearing bibs, despite Hal's angry, tearful protests. Mildred bustled about setting the extra place, apparently already familiar with the location of the tarnished silver and the yellowed linen place mats—no doubt inherited like everything in the Crowley's overcrowded cottage.

"I'll just serve the soup," she said, and for a blessed moment, the men were alone.

"Millie's been awfully good to me, you see," said Nat miserably.

Awfully good, Gerald agreed silently.

"She's made it all right with the bank."

"She's done what?" asked Gerald.

"We won't lose the house now."

Gerald trusted the "we" still meant Charlotte. Most newly bereaved people took a long time to return to the singular pronoun.

"Charlotte had a plan, you know. But then she, well, she died. Now Millie's come up with a plan."

Apparently in Nat's world, that's what women did.

"Do you mean to say she lent you money to pay off your debts?"

Before Nat could answer, Mildred came in with the soup. It was grey soup, the greyest soup Gerald had ever seen, the sort of thing Oliver Twist might have eaten in the poor house, only he wouldn't have pleaded for more. Gerald wanted to call it gruel. Mildred swiftly returned with a third bowl for herself and a plate of thinly sliced, scantily buttered bread.

"Mr. Bradley," she said, seating herself. "Will you please say Grace?"

Gerald could not help wondering as he blessed the graceless meal if he were breaking bread, so to speak, with a murderess. He dreaded Mildred's confession, but he supposed he ought to hear her. The seal of the confessional was inviolable, but he could encourage Mildred to turn herself in to the police. She could probably get off on a plea of insanity. He would not have to break canonical law to testify to the morbid and obsessive nature of her religious—

"Mr. Bradley? Mr. Bradley." Mildred raised the volume of her voice. "I was just saying what a wonderful job Mrs. Bradley is doing directing the rummage sale. It's not just anyone who could have stepped in to fill dear Charlotte's shoes."

Gerald swallowed a mouthful of tasteless soup. Its texture was like that white paste the children used for art projects. Anne always covered the table with newspaper to avoid any unwanted contact with surfaces.

"I don't think anyone can fill Charlotte's shoes," Gerald said. "Not even Anne." Then he added silently: and certainly, Mildred, not you.

Aloud Nat said, "I'll drink to that!"

And before Mildred could stop him, Nat leapt for the scotch and returned to the table brandishing the bottle in one hand and two shot glasses in the other.

CHAPTER SEVENTEEN

"Nix-*on!*"

"Kenne-*dy!*"

"Nix-*on!*"

"Kenne-*dy!*"

It was Saturday morning. Everybody's mother and some of the fathers were at the parish house or out in the tent on the lawn with the furniture. Lots of kids were here, too, from all the schools—the Catholic, the private, and the regular one Katherine went to. The rummage sale was next weekend.

"Today everyone is showing up to be a worker, just so they can go to the workers' sale," her mother had said to her father at breakfast, while Katherine and the twins were watching cartoons. Katherine could tell her mother was mad, but she didn't know exactly why. "They weren't here all week and they won't show up again till Thursday evening when you can bet the ones who did the least will be first in line at the door."

"The last shall be first and the first shall be last," said her father. "It's like the parable of the laborers all getting paid the same wage, regardless of when they showed up to work."

"Clearly," said her mother, making the cups and saucers clatter as she cleared the table, "clearly Jesus Christ never had to run the Church of Regeneration Rummage Sale."

"But he did suffer death on the cross," added her father, making some kind of grownup joke that Katherine didn't get.

Maybe her mother didn't get it either. She had already disappeared into the kitchen, leaving Katherine's father alone at the table.

"Nix-*on*!" yelled the kids on one side the driveway, the side nearest her house.

It made her feel kind of important having everyone in her yard, but it was also scary.

"Kenne-*dy*!" she shouted with the others on her side, nearest the church.

It made her feel a little safer to stand between Frankie and Aramantha, but it was very confusing to see Dickie and Prescott next to Frankie, though she knew their father was a Democrat. Her father was voting for him, too, to help Kennedy run the country and give everyone equal rights, he had explained to her. Why would anyone not want to be equal, Katherine wondered? But there was Lisa, Aunt Rosalie's daughter and her best friend from school, on the Nixon side, along with a lot of other kids from her school. And Lisa always got the highest mark on every spelling test, even higher than Katherine.

"Nix-*on*!" They tried to scream louder than her side. They looked angry and happy at the same time.

Maybe it was just a game

"Kenne-*dy*!" her team shouted.

It was getting a little boring. Wasn't there anything to do but holler the same names over and over? Just then, Dickie Foster bent down and picked up a handful of gravel. Then he threw it across the driveway as hard as he could.

"Ow!" screamed one of the kids on the other side, holding his eye. "Quit it!"

But the fight was only getting started. Soon gravel was flying back and forth across the driveway. Some kids were crying and running away. Some, like Katherine, were just standing there shielding their faces. It was her driveway. Should she do something to stop it? Before she could think what to do, old Mr. McCready came up the driveway shouting at them and waving his stick. His white hair stuck out like porcupine bristles.

"*Their works are works of iniquity, and deeds of violence are in their hands. Their feet run to evil, and they make haste to shed innocent blood; their thoughts are thoughts of iniquity, desolation and destruction are in their highways. The way of peace they know not, and there is no justice in their paths; they have made their roads crooked, no one who goes in them knows peace. Therefore justice is far from us, and righteousness does not overtake us; we look for light, and behold, darkness, and for brightness, but we walk in gloom.*

"Now you miserable offenders, you wretched miscreants, tell me which one of the prophets spewed forth those inspired words, and I'll not turn you over to your fathers to be thrashed, yea, or unto the constable to be cast into some dank and lightless cell."

All the kids stood frozen, as if they were playing Red Light, Green Light or Freeze Tag.

"You're the minister's kid, Katherine," hissed Prescott. "*You* tell him!"

Before Katherine could say she was only in second grade and hadn't learned the prophets yet, Aramantha shouted out.

"Isaiah!"

"Good lass! Let her be an example to the rest of you heathen hooligans."

Katherine had never seen Mr. McCready smile before. He was missing a tooth and looked like a Halloween pumpkin just before it caves in. But it was too late to save them from their fathers. Her father and Dickie and Prescott's father came up the driveway together. Her father had on his white collar and Mr. Foster wore a suit with a "Get America Moving" button on his jacket.

"What's going on here, Amos?" asked Katherine's father.

"A bit of a scuffle. My advice is to lock the lot in their rooms with bread, water, and The Bible for a month of Sundays. All but this lass here," he pointed to Aramantha, "who knows her scripture."

Katherine wished they could all go away now, back to their mothers, or to play a better game. Maybe Aramantha would start one. She knew all the games and all the rules.

Then Dickie Foster went and ruined everything.

"He started it!" Dickie pointed at Frankie. "He started throwing stones. I think he might have blinded one kid."

"I did not!" Frankie turned to Dickie, and he let fly a handful of stones at Dickie's feet. "You started it! You big fat liar!"

Katherine didn't think Frankie had thrown any stones before then, even though he had picked some up, but now she was afraid he would be in trouble.

"See! See!" Prescott shrieked like a girl. "Dickie's right. Frankie started it. He always starts everything."

"Did not!" Frankie said again. "You're both liars. You lie like rugs. You lie like Pinocchio. Someone should break off your noses and make pencils out of them."

Katherine was scared for Frankie. Didn't he know there were grownups here?

"That's enough now, Frankie," Katherine's father said. "No throwing stones or fighting on church—"

But Mr. Foster stepped in, just like he had the day of the fight.

"Now, son," he said, walking past Mr. McCready toward the Kennedy side of the driveway.

At first Katherine thought he was talking to Dickie, but he came and stood in front of Frankie.

"Calling someone a liar is a serious accusation," said Mr. Foster.

Frankie didn't say anything, just looked down at his feet and kicked at the gravel.

"Son?" said Mr. Foster again, and he put a hand on Frankie's shoulder, but Frankie shook it off, turned away and ran down the driveway.

"See? See, Dad?" said Dickie. "That proves it. He's running away."

Katherine wished her father would do something. She wished he would defend Frankie. He was looking down at his feet, too, as if he were a kid, as if he had done something wrong.

"Daddy?" she said, but he didn't seem to hear her or see her. "Mr. Foster?"

He didn't hear her, either, so she went and tapped his sleeve.

He turned toward her. He looked so kind and friendly. How could he have such horrible boys for his sons?

"Yes? Katherine, isn't it?" He bent down as if she were a little kid, like Janie. "Did you want to say something?"

"Mr. Foster," Katherine knees were shaking and she had to swallow a lump in her throat, but she went on, "Dickie did start it. I saw him pick up the stones first."

"Yeah," said one of the kids from the Nixon side. "I saw him, too."

"Katherine?" said her father, as if he hadn't noticed she was there before.

She was afraid he would be mad at her, but he looked sad instead. She waited for him to say something, but when he didn't, she turned and ran as fast as she could down the driveway.

Katherine found Frankie on the other side of the parish house under the fire escape that led from the second floor. He had his pocket knife out and was whittling the point of a javelin. Katherine had asked her mother if she could have a knife, but her mother said no. Pleading that Frankie had a knife so why couldn't she had been the wrong thing to say. Her mother's face had closed and her mouth had barely moved when she said she did not care what Frankie Lomangino was and was not allowed to have. Katherine was *her* child. Frankie said it was all right, he would make her stick into a javelin, too, when he was done with his. Katherine hadn't told her mother that she had seen a pocket knife in the hardware department in the tent at the rummage sale, and she was going to buy it with her allowance. She had helped Aunt Rosalie in the toy barn after school yesterday, and she was going to help today. So she was a worker, too. She would keep the knife hidden under the mattress of her bed.

Frankie did not say anything when he saw her, just kept whittling, so she didn't say anything either, just sat next to him. She got that dreamy feeling that sometimes came over her when she watched someone doing something, Aunt Rosalie stirring batter, her mother setting her hair. It was like stroking a cat or being a cat someone was stroking. So when Frankie spoke, his voice as much as his words woke her up.

"I am going to kill Dickie Foster. Maybe Scottie Dog, too."

Katherine felt scared. Killing was bad, worse than trespassing. She felt hot and cold all over, remembering that she had been going to kill God and Jesus. But you couldn't kill them, they were already dead. Or at least Jesus had been killed a long time ago by some bad men. Would Frankie really kill Dickie?

"Don't, Frankie!" she pleaded. "You'd have to go to jail."

"So?" said Frankie. "So what? What's wrong with going to jail?"

Katherine remembered that Frankie's pops had been in jail before he had come to work at their church.

"You wouldn't be able to go to the woods," she pointed out. "Not for a long time, anyway."

Frankie stopped whittling for a moment. He looked dreamy now, as if he were seeing things that were not right there.

"After I kill Dickie, I will hide in the woods. Like that man we saw, the one with horns. No one will find me there. Then I won't go to jail."

Katherine felt afraid again. She wanted the woods to belong to her and Frankie. She did not want the scary man to be there, the imposition with black wings. And she did not want Frankie to be like that man at all. Frankie was not an imposition, no matter what her mother said.

"Dickie is bad," she told Frankie. "He threw the stones. Not you. I told on him to his father. You don't have to kill him. His father will punish him."

Frankie looked at her.

"You told on Dickie? To his father?"

Katherine nodded.

"Katherine," Frankie said after a moment, "do you want to be my blood sister? I would have to cut you with my knife. Just a little bit. You would have to cut me, too. That's how Indians do it."

Katherine nodded again. She was scared but it was a good kind of scared.

"Give me your hand."

She held out her hand to Frankie. Holding her right hand with his left, he made a tiny cut on her forefinger. It hardly even hurt. Then he gave her the knife and held out his right hand. It was much harder to cut, than to be cut, but she managed with the tip of the blade to prick him enough to draw a bead of blood from his finger.

"Now we mix our blood," Frankie told her.

And they pressed their bloody fingers together and made little circles with the tips to be sure the blood got all mixed up.

"Katherine, now you are my blood sister, forever and ever."

"Frankie, now you are my blood brother, forever and ever."

Then without saying anything more, they got up and went to the edge of the woods, Frankie with his javelin in the hand with the pricked finger. They stood there gazing at the woods that were turning gold with tips of red, like the blood on their fingers.

Someday, when the imposition was gone, she and Frankie would go to the woods any time they wanted to. Someday they would live in the woods. Forever and ever. Amen.

PART THREE:
MYSTERY

CHAPTER EIGHTEEN

With a soupçon of guilt that made her truancy all the more pleasurable, Lucy Way had decided not to work at the rummage sale this Saturday. It would be crowded with all the husbands and children joining in, too. Besides she and Florence had finished most of the pricing in notions yesterday.

You are not needed, a voice whispered to her, such a subtle yet insistent voice that she stopped in the midst of rolling out piecrust and looked up, almost expecting to see someone there in her big, old-fashioned kitchen. It was a bit dark and barnlike, but she'd had windows put in the upper half of a Dutch door and a kindly southern light spilled through them, all the more bright for passing through the yellow leaves of an old maple tree.

It was true. No one needed her to make this piecrust, which she would fill with apples from her own small orchard and the last raspberries from the canes in her garden. But Elsa and Clara would enjoy the pie when they came to supper this evening. She would serve the pie with a choice of clotted cream or a good, sharp cheddar to cut the sweetness. That would be after the main course of *boeuf bourguignon* (the meat even now simmering in the oven), with onions, potatoes and carrots also from her garden, seasoned with her own thyme. They would begin the meal with endives and a dressing made of sour cream and dill weed that she had grown last spring and dried. Of course she would make biscuits, too. There would be no stinting on butter, and her guests would savor every bite as only those who have known rationing can. She would serve French red wine with dinner, a hearty burgundy. And for an aperitif she would offer dry sherry. Elsa knew better than to expect cocktails from her.

Lucy returned to rolling—though she would be careful not to overwork the dough—thinking of the western light that would fill her parlor, how it would shine through the sherry in her crystal glasses. Perhaps, if it were mild enough, they might sit outside the French doors on the terrace to sip their drinks and enjoy her favorite soft French cheese, *Caprice des Dieux*, on thinly sliced baguette.

When they were ready, that is before Elsa drank too much, when the late light rested in the tops of the trees, they would go in to dinner to a table she'd already set, a centerpiece of dark red and white dahlias on a white tablecloth that she had hand-embroidered at the edges in gold thread in a pattern of cross-stitches, the heavy cloth napkins embroidered in the same pattern. Old-fashioned white china, showing its age with a thousand fine lines—like a face, she always thought—with gilt edges. Real silverware, of course, the handles decorated with cast fruits and flowers. She had plain pewter candlesticks and homemade beeswax candles. Nothing on her table had she bought for herself; everything had a story, had belonged to some other woman, handed down, hand to hand to her own hands that laid everything out just so, not out of fussiness, but for joy.

You are not needed, said the voice again, still softly but with a hint of laughter, as if the voice found her amusing. She gave a little shrug, a French shrug, she thought, a gesture inherited from her French grandmother, the one who had taught her to love cooking. Then she got out a brown crockery pie dish and eased the crust into it, patting, pinching, stretching here and scrunching there till it fit perfectly. She lifted a bowl and poured in the apples and raspberries that had been mixed with brown sugar, spices, a hint of lemon and a splash of brandy. She looked with pleasure at the heaping mound of fruit that stopped just short of overflowing the pie dish, and then she dotted it with sweet butter. Gently, tenderly, as if she were returning a baby bird to its nest, she settled the top crust over the fruit and began to flute the edges.

You are such a funny little thing, her mother's voice this time, but with that same light note of amusement. *So housewifely, it is a shame you never married and had a household of your own.* She had never told her blunt, Pittsburgh-bred mother, who barely knew how to boil an egg, how those words hurt her—at least in the early days. She knew her mother loved her, and her mother had always encouraged Lucy to do whatever she wanted, even when it made no sense to her mother. She had never understood Lucy's determination to become a nurse, something, Florence Nightingale notwithstanding, her mother thought was for those less gently reared than Lucy had been. And perhaps her mother was right, but then Lucy had been reared for a world that no longer existed, even for her mother.

"I suppose it is admirable to have a useful skill," her mother had tried explaining it to herself and Lucy had murmured agreement.

For she could never tell her mother what had happened, how mind-numbing hard work, changing bed sheets and bed pans, alleviating pain as best she could, holding a hand in the night seemed the only thing left after there was nothing left.

You are not needed, the voice was offhand now, maybe a little scornful.

"We must begin as we mean to go on," he had said. "We must not need each other. We must choose each other freely. Need is a bourgeois trap. Even worse, it is medieval. Overlords needing their serfs, serfs needing masters, the king needing his nobles, the nobles needing the king, everyone in a stinking hierarchical dung heap of need with a cruel and demanding God at the top. Need is slavery. Do you see, Lucy?"

Lucy saw that his head with its roil of gold hair was like a lion's and that his eyes were dark and mysterious as her grandfather's painting of the Bois de Boulogne. She felt too timid to tell him that she had always rather liked the Middle Ages, smelly and unhygienic as they must have been. The word medieval called to Lucy's mind illuminated manuscripts, with lovingly detailed birds and beasts entwined with the letters or strayed into the margins. It also evoked madrigals and haunting strains played on the lute. She pictured cathedrals where the common people stood like cattle sheltering in a barn, in awe of the brilliant stained-glass windows, comforted by statues of the Virgin. She thought of people going on pilgrimages and crusades, however misguided, because of a faith he would have excoriated.

Lucy finished fluting the edges of the pie and picked up a knife with a long thin blade and a fine tip. In the center of the crust, she cut five small diamond-shape openings that resembled the star at the core of an apple when you cut it sideways, or the petals of a wildflower.

She might have been very happy in a medieval monastery illuminating manuscripts, but on the rare occasions that she ventured to say such things, he would sigh and shake his head.

"You are a hopeless romantic, Lucy," he would scold. "You don't live in the real world."

And then he would kiss her and tell her how beautiful she was, sometimes almost angrily, as if it was her fault that he loved someone who did not understand Marxist dialectics.

Not that he ever said he loved her, Lucy reminded herself as she set the pie on the counter and got a damp cloth to wipe the table. Very likely he had not. But Lucy had loved him, she saw now, with an idolatrous love. She had made him her very god and surrendered her will to him quite utterly. When he informed her that the only honest thing for them to do was to become lovers, (marriage was somehow dishonest) she did not argue with him. She did not know how to articulate her own inchoate beliefs, which he always dismissed as mere conventionality. Nor did she confess, even to herself, her physical reluctance. She sometimes wished that she had been driven by her own willful desire, instead of by her need, yes need, to please him in all things. She could not help wondering if it would have been different. Instead the sexual act had seemed awkward, like a mathematics problem to be worked out rather than a natural fulfillment of passion, however youthful and mistaken.

Lucy got out her big cast iron skillet and lit the flame under it. When the temperature was just right, she melted butter, added a touch of olive oil and began to braise the onions with thyme, parsley and a bay leaf. She leaned over the pan and happily inhaled the fragrant steam. Surely, she thought as she closed her eyes with pleasure, surely someone who loved scent and taste and color and texture as much as she did, surely she could have learned to enjoy the physical side of love. Or perhaps that did not follow. She had never found out.

"It's no good, dear little Lucy," he had said to her one day as they lay together afterwards in the narrow bed in his bachelor digs.

That was the part of lovemaking Lucy liked best, when all the heaving and panting—that seemed so uncharacteristic of him—were over and she could rest and relish his nearness, the warmth of his skin, his long lashes, thick as a child's, softening the angles of his face.

"You see, Lucy, you are ruled by your heart. I live by my head. We would never get on in the long run. I should feel held back by you; you would feel left behind by me. We must set each other free, Lucy, do you see?"

Lucy did not see, not clearly. She still remembered how the room swam and how the sun caught in one of her tears, making it seem as though everything was drowning in light.

"Lucy, don't cry, you must not cry. This is exactly the sort of thing I mean. We agreed not to need each other this way. We agreed."

She had never felt so naked as when she put her clothes on. Her heart beat so loud, the blood roared in her ears, and his voice receded, as if he stood on the shore shouting while she went farther and farther out to sea.

Lucy scooped up the onions, lightly browned, their flesh translucent, small buttery moons. Then she melted more butter for the mushrooms and ground fresh black pepper into the sauté, feeling suddenly so grateful not to need anyone, to be safe and self-sufficient in her own kitchen. No longer alone in the bare London room she had fled to when she found out she was pregnant. She had never told him; she had never told her great aunt with whom she'd spent the summer in Oxford prepping for an entrance exam to St Hilda's (for which she never sat). Not even her mother knew. Although of course her mother would have known, if the child had lived, for Lucy had meant to keep the baby. She had no idea how. That's what she had gone to London to work out.

"You don't live in the real world, Lucy," he would have said.

Really, she thought, it was he who had no idea of the real world. He had no idea what happened when French letters failed and free love ended. He would never be a girl in a cheap boarding house when the cramping and bleeding started. And when it didn't stop, he would never go alone to hospital where everyone believed you had done it yourself and treated you with pity, disgust or contempt. Except for one nurse, who saw that Lucy was bereft, and held her while she wept. Perhaps that was why she had decided to become a nurse. And of course nurses were needed, needed desperately when the war came.

Lucy set aside the sauté, got the stew out of the oven and put the apple pie in to bake. If war was what people meant by the real world, then she had seen plenty. She had witnessed firsthand how the ideologies of people ruled by their heads could lay waste to human life, to whole countries and peoples. Of course by the time the Second War started, she was no longer a naïve young girl. She was already considered, however inaccurately, an old maid, even by her nearest and dearest. They relied on her, they loved her, but they didn't need her. They faintly pitied her. In a horrible way, she supposed the war saved her from her own bitterness, her disappointment in her own life. It was not that her sorrow went away. It was just that it became woven up, a single thread in a much larger sorrow.

With perhaps absurd satisfaction, Lucy began to put together all the discrete ingredients of the *boeuf bourguignon.* It would simmer gently while the pie baked. She decided that the biscuits would be best if she whipped them up at the last minute. She would just set out the ingredients now. Then Elsa and Clara could follow her companionably into the kitchen and watch while she mixed the batter. How much more homey her little party would be than formal entertaining with matching sets of couples all to be seated just so. Not that Lucy would know, she was never invited to such gatherings, though she was sometimes included in larger affairs when children and old people were present. She was useful then, sitting beside someone's ancient mother-in-law or holding a messy toddler in her lap.

Lucy paused for a moment as she opened the cupboard where she kept baking ingredients and measuring cups. The light streamed in through the windows behind her, touched her lightly, warm as a hand, a small trusting hand.

It was the child she missed; it had always been the child. A son, a boy, not like her lover, but like the Christ child. Surely it was wrong to think that way; she was no spotless virgin. She had been stupid, that was all. No, to be honest, worse than stupid, for she knew what she had done was wrong. Not just because of church teaching or the conventional morality that he despised so, but because it was against her own nature. Yet the thought of the infant Christ and Mary his mother had comforted her then. Comforted her still.

Lucy finished setting out the ingredients for the biscuits. Then, almost inadvertently, she sat down at the table with its cheerful red-checked oilcloth. An odd thought came to her. If he had lived, her son would have been thirty-three. Just like Mary's. Surely it was worse to lose a son you had loved so long, and yet surely it was better to have had a chance to love him. She didn't know, she didn't know. Children weren't supposed to die before their mothers, but they did. And mothers died before their children were ready to let them go, even grown children like Charlotte's son, who seemed a bit of a lost soul for all his handsome looks and the young man she supposed was his companion. Lucy had no living son to mourn her that way. She was free, freer than her lover ever could have imagined or predicted.

"I am not needed," she spoke aloud.

To her surprise the words did not sound self-pitying. They did not hurt.

Beloved, the voice was tender now, golden as the light, familiar as her kitchen, *you are not needed. You are wanted. Wanted.*

"Lucy!" said Elsa, pushing back her chair from the table and stopping just short of leaning back in it. "You have outdone yourself. A superb meal. You are a culinary rival to any of the great chefs of Europe. If I could, I would like to light up a fine cigar as a mark of respect."

Poor Clara, who took everything Elsa said literally, looked alarmed, as though Elsa might in fact produce an enormous and threateningly masculine cigar and confirm the worst suspicions of the absent multitudes. Lucy had once wondered how someone as given to hyperbole as Elsa could live with someone who never ceased to be shocked and worried. But after a time, she realized that was part of Clara's appeal, for Elsa loved to shock.

"Thank you, Elsa. But people generally wait till they have withdrawn to the drawing room for port or brandy to light their post-prandial cigars."

Lucy winked at Clara to reassure her it was a game.

"Brandy," said Elsa, regarding her fingers where she might have brandished a cigar, "would be lovely, even without a cigar."

Elsa had eaten so heartily, with second helpings of the main course and dessert, she could likely absorb a small brandy without further impairment.

"Yes, indeed," said Lucy. "You two, go make yourselves comfortable in the parlor, not quite a drawing room, but it will have to do. I've laid a fire in the fireplace. Just set a match to it and I'll be with you shortly."

"Let me help you clear the table, Lucy."

"Why thank you, Clara," Lucy said, resisting the urge to politely refuse the help of her guest, for she knew it would make Clara happy or if not happy, a condition that seemed alien to Clara's nature, more at ease.

Elsa even carried a plate or two, but after she dropped some silverware, Lucy sent her off to light the fire before she broke something.

"I'm glad to have you alone for a minute, Lucy," Clara confided as she carefully set the dessert plates on the counter next to the sink. "I need to talk to you."

Lucy felt herself bracing inwardly and hoped it did not show on the outside. Clara was one of those people who had little idea of when they were standing too close—or in Clara's case, sometimes too far away, like an injured animal who hasn't decided whether to retreat or attack. She had no social graces, poor thing. She was utterly dependent on Elsa to navigate the world for her—a world with which Elsa had her own quarrels.

"Of course, Clara," Lucy said, moving just a few inches away to begin to rinse the dishes. "What is it?"

"It's about that woman who was killed."

Lucy had been afraid of that. She gave herself a moment as she finished with one dish, then reached for another.

"You mean the woman who died," said Lucy carefully, "if you are talking about Charlotte Crowley. The police found her death to be accidental."

"But you don't believe that, do you? You don't, do you, Lucy Way?"

Clara had come up so close beside Lucy that she could feel the woman's breath on her neck. Against her will, Lucy felt a prickle of fear. Clara had been mad or at least been in a madhouse, an institution, Lucy immediately reproved herself. There was no call for dramatic Dickensian language. She finished rinsing the dish and forced herself to turn and look at Clara. Her eyes were dark and luminous at once. But for a certain look of cunning and desperation, Lucy would have called her beautiful.

"Why do you say so, Clara? What is troubling you?"

Lucy knew she was being evasive, which could upset Clara further, but she wasn't ready yet to discuss her suspicions—much less her visitation from Charlotte's ghost—with anyone further.

"Elsa hated her," Clara stated. "And Elsa was there that morning."

"So was I," Lucy pointed out. "So were a number of people."

"Stop pretending, Lucy Way. You didn't hate that woman. You don't hate anyone. You are a saint. You eat with sinners like Elsa and me, sinners and murderers."

Clara's eyes looked wild, showing too much white like a spooked horse. Lucy had to find a way to calm her.

"Now, Clara—" she began.

"That woman threatened Elsa. Elsa refuses to talk about it. But I know how upset she was that night you came to our house for dinner. Elsa talked to you about it, but she wouldn't tell me. You must tell me, Lucy Way, you must. That woman threatened to have me locked up again, didn't she, didn't she? Unless Elsa paid her money. That's it, isn't it?"

At last Lucy had something to get hold of.

"Clara Barker!" Lucy exclaimed, allowing herself something as close to a snort as she could manage. "That is the most absurd rubbish I've ever heard. Charlotte Crowley blackmailing Elsa? Everyone and his brother knows that you and Elsa are poor as church mice."

"Yes," said Clara with a strange mix of triumph and terror. "That is why Elsa had to kill her."

Before Lucy could summon a response, Elsa called out plaintively, "Lucy! Where the devil is that brandy?"

The very next moment, the phone rang.

"Here, Clara." Lucy quickly put three snifters and a brandy bottle on a tray. "Take this in to Elsa. Pour us all a drink and stop all this nonsensical thinking at once. I'll be with you in a moment."

"Yes, Lucy," said Clara, suddenly as meek and biddable as a child.

Lucy did not stay on the phone long. It would have been rude when she had company. Also, she suspected Gerald Bradley had had a good deal more to drink than he should have and she did not want him to regret confiding inappropriately. She would know everything she was meant to know soon enough, and he had not been coherent enough to answer the few questions she put to him. And so, as soon as she could, she said goodnight and set down the receiver. Then she stood quietly for a moment in her kitchen, waiting for her breathing to slow and her heart to stop pounding, waiting to quiet herself enough to send out a prayer.

O Lord, make haste to help us. And take not thy Holy Spirit from us.

Then she went to join her guests.

"What is it, Lucy?" asked Elsa. "You're white as laundry."

Ordinarily Lucy would have smiled at Elsa's misuse of English idioms, now she just sat still, her back straight in the wooden chair she'd chosen, trying to think what to say.

"Here. Have some of this."

Elsa got up and handed Lucy a snifter of brandy. Lucy downed it in one.

"*Herrgott*, woman!" exclaimed Elsa. "You'd better tell us what it is, don't you think?"

"Is someone else dead, Lucy?" asked Clara, anxiously.

She might as well let them know, Lucy reasoned as the brandy hit her bloodstream. Everyone would know soon enough.

"That was Gerald Bradley," she said. "He called to tell me that Frank Lomangino has been arrested for the murder of Charlotte Crowley."

Lucy saw the color drain from Elsa's face.

"*Gott in himmel!*" murmured Elsa. "That poor boy. That poor boy."

Lucy didn't know if she meant Frank or his son or both. Elsa took out a cigarette, but her hands were shaking so badly, Clara had to light it for her.

"It's all right, darling," Clara murmured. "It wasn't you. At least it wasn't you. Now you won't leave me. Say you won't leave me."

"Of course I won't leave you, *liebling*. What a thing to say!"

They might as well have been alone in the room. They had both forgotten Lucy. But Lucy was there and couldn't help watching. She couldn't help wondering.

CHAPTER NINETEEN

After he hung up the phone with Lucy, Gerald went to the kitchen and poured himself another drink, although he knew he shouldn't, just as he probably shouldn't have called Lucy Way when he was already on his third drink. But he had wanted to talk to someone. Anne was upstairs with the children, interminably bathing them or reading them stories. He was glad now she had pleaded exhaustion from the rummage sale and begged off going to the Van Wagner's for dinner. Frank Lomangino's arrest would be public knowledge soon enough. Gerald wouldn't have wanted to go through a whole evening talking about it or being careful not to talk about it. So why had he called Lucy, he wondered as he poured a double? Because it was all her fault, all her fault that the sleeping dog she could have let lie had to get up to scratch its fleas and land Frank Lomangino in jail.

And, he realized as he almost stumbled on the up and down staircase shortcut to his office, he had expected Lucy Way to say something comforting or at least wise. But she hadn't. He had fallen into the well of her silence at the other end of the receiver, and he didn't know if he could climb back out. Then at last she had asked if he'd called Father Vic O'Shea and if he had seen Frank at the jail.

"Of course I did. I was imprisoned and ye visited me," Gerald had blurted out.

That's why he was drunk. It is a terrible thing to see a grown man bawling like a baby.

"I'm so sorry, Gerald," Lucy had said before he could say anything more, and she'd hung up, not hung up *on* him, exactly, but hung up and left him alone to face the possibility that the ex-con he'd insisted on hiring might have murdered one of the pillars of the church. Knocked her right over, down the stairs, like Samson in the Temple.

No, not like Samson at all. He wasn't thinking clearly. He couldn't think. He made his way around to his desk, sat down and rested his head in his hands. Squinting, he saw the handwritten draft of his sermon for tomorrow. Thank God he had gotten something down on paper that morning before Rick Foster had come to see him to tell him what he'd found out. Jesus God, poor Rick, he must be feeling as bad as Gerald, maybe worse. Rick didn't just have to give a sermon. He had to campaign for Congress, against a Republican incumbent, for Christ's sake. Rick had told Gerald he blamed himself for Charlotte's death. But really it was Gerald's fault. He should call Rick, tell him that. Gerald was the one who brought the wolf among the sheep, the fox into the henhouse, who didn't know wheat from chaff, who to save and who to toss into unquenchable fire, which was easy enough for John the Baptist to say.

But Gerald, Gerald had thought Frank was one of these the least of my brethren, just a poor bastard down on his luck who needed a job, like all those hoboes his father had helped in the Depression.

If only Rick had come to him sooner. Lawyers didn't have the seal of the confessional, even if they had worked in the DA's office, like Rick had before he took a leave of absence to run for Congress. Or maybe they did have some kind of Hippocratic Oath, like doctors. What the hell did Gerald know about anything?

Gerald still wasn't clear what it was Frank was supposed to have done to Charlotte (apart from maybe murdering her). Threatened her in some way, blackmailed her? It all had to do with Nat's gambling debt, illegal gambling. Frank knew about it, and Charlotte had wanted it kept secret. Gerald knew Frank had been in jail before for some kind of low level gambling crime, numbers running or something. But Gerald had been so sure Frank was keeping his nose clean. Goes to show, you never really know anyone. Some of the men his father helped had ended up stealing from him. Hell, even his father had made mistakes and everyone had worshipped him like a god-damn saint. So why should Gerald feel so bad?

Because someone was dead. Because a father of four going on five kids might get life imprisonment or worse. If he had known Frank was up to no good, could he have stopped him before it came to murder?

"I advised Charlotte to go to the police," Rick had said. "I should have insisted on doing it for her. In fact, I had it in my mind to make a few calls, without revealing any names, but I didn't do it soon enough. Charlotte must have let slip to Frank that she intended to turn him in. I blame myself."

Gerald wished he could blame Rick, too, but he couldn't. These were his people and the sheep of his pasture. How was he going to face them tomorrow, all his bleating, bleeding sheep, baa-ing their way through a rummage sale at a murder site? He wished the police had shut the whole operation down, but they hadn't. It was too late for police lines and tape on the floor to mark where the body had fallen. The crime scene had been corrupted—by Frank himself. He cleaned everything up. He'd taken the damn coats upstairs. The dry-cleaners bag was long gone with heaps of other trash. Which made it all look bad, very bad for Frank, the one who found the body, the only one there that morning, because Gerald, *Gerald* had called him to fix a sink.

Gerald drained his drink and laid his forehead down on his sermon. He always tried to tie together the lessons and the Gospel and make them relevant to today's world. He tried to remember the readings for this Sunday. Shunamite, the word came into his head. Oh, yeah, the lesson he could never read out loud. He had to get his lay reader, Amos McCready, to take that passage about the son of the Shunamite woman raised from the dead by the prophet Elisha who hadn't lifted a finger for Hal. Not that Jesus had either. Jesus who raised Jairus's daughter from the dead and the daughter of that gentile woman who kept pestering him. No wonder Anne hated him. Not Jesus, Gerald. But it wasn't his fault Jesus hadn't raised anyone from the dead since his own father let him be murdered. All so he could rise again from the dead on behalf of everybody forever, and that was supposed to be enough? Except for Paul raising that guy who went to sleep during one of his sermons and fell to his death out the window. Nobody raised anybody from the dead these days. Why not? Save a lot of trouble if someone would have just raised Charlotte from the basement floor, dusted her off and let her go on annoying people and running the rummage sale.

What the hell was his sermon about anyway? Gerald wondered, lifting his head for a moment and finding his glass was empty. How Saint Paul was such a son of a bitch, even after being saved, he had to be lowered out a window in a basket in the night or someone would have murdered him. John the Baptist was a son of a bitch, too, crying in the wilderness till he got his head cut off and served on a platter. They were all sons of bitches and what was going to happen to Frank's wife and kids? He better talk to Father Vic again. Offer something from the Church of Regeneration discretionary fund, because it was Gerald's fault for hiring Frank in the first place, putting him in temptation's way, because really who hadn't wanted to kill Charlotte Crowley one time or another. Poor bastard probably couldn't help himself. Maybe he hadn't been threatening her at all? Maybe Charlotte threatened him or he thought she was threatening him, because she couldn't keep her nose out of anyone's private business. Anne hated her, too. Anne, at least it wasn't Anne....

Gerald laid down his head again and the darkness closed over him.

Such mercy in the tomb....

Anne came downstairs to fetch Gerald for bedtime prayers. It wasn't much time out of the day to expect him to be a father, and besides, the ritual had been his idea in the first place. They all sang "Jesus Tender Shepherd" and "Our Father Who Art in Heaven" and said a few God Blesses. It was one of the only times God was explicitly mentioned in front of the children, for which Anne was grudgingly grateful. The children seemed to like the songs and the closeness of a father who would be predictable and available for those few minutes. He would give them loud smacking kisses on the cheek and they would giggle and screech about his sandpaper face, the stubble grown to roughness since his morning shave.

When Anne found him with his head on his desk, audibly snoring, the gin tumbler beside him, full of melting ice, she felt the familiar triumphant dismay that came whenever he let her down, again. Usually he waited until after prayers to sneak an extra drink—or to have a nightcap, as he called it when he did it openly. She knew, of course, that he must be upset about Frank Lomangino's arrest. But for heaven's sake, why couldn't he wait till after the kids were in bed?

Her throat tightened and tears rose suddenly as she thought of Frank Lomangino's kids going to bed without their father at home. Especially Frankie, whom she didn't even like, but damn it if she didn't stop thinking about him, she was going to cry. And what on earth was she going to tell Katherine?

"Gerald!" she said in a loud, angry voice that took her by surprise.

He lifted his head, and she instantly regretted not leaving him there in his own drool while she tucked the children in with comforting lies. *Daddy's busy. He'll give you a kiss when you're asleep.* He was in no shape to climb the stairs much less lead prayers. She did not want her children breathing his gin fumes.

"Anne." He looked at her in such a way that she knew he must be seeing double. "Anne, it wasn't you. I am sho glad it washn't you."

He wasn't making sense. She definitely could not let the children see him this way.

"I don't know what you're talking about, Gerald. I'm going to tuck the children in now."

He half rose.

"No, you stay here," she said sharply.

"It wasn't you," he said again, still half standing, his hands on the desk to support him. "You didn't kill Charlotte Crowley. Sorry, sho sorry about Frank. But I'm glad it washn't you."

Anne felt something like an electric shock go through her before she fully took in his meaning.

"Sit down, Gerald," she managed to say. "After the children are in bed, I am going to make you some coffee."

About midway up the stairs it hit her, and she had to stop and hold onto the banister.

Her husband believed she was capable of murder.

Anne shook Gerald awake and put coffee and a large slice of vanilla cake with chocolate icing on the desk in front of him as well as a glass of water. He was going to need to sober up before bed if he was to avoid a debilitating hangover tomorrow. Sundays always started early and tomorrow, especially, he was going to need his wits about him. She sat quietly in the leather easy chair where he often sat in the evening falling asleep over a book. She had brought her mending with her and was darning one of Gerald's socks so that she didn't have to look at him as he ate his cake and drank his coffee in uncharacteristic silence. Darning was one of the few domestic tasks she actually liked, or at least found soothing. It did not require great skill, just a patient weaving over and under back and forth with her darning needle, making something thin and threadbare thick and sturdy again, serviceable. It was work that would never be seen or admired but had to be done, like so much of what she did. Why darning satisfied her rather than filled her with resentment, she did not know.

Nor did she know why she was not offended that Gerald had suspected her of murder. But she wasn't. She had never thought much about how Gerald saw her. She was used to thinking of herself as negligible. A background sort of person. That Gerald might be afraid of her, or for her, sobered her and in an odd way intrigued her. She paused and looked up from her darning. Gerald was diligently eating his cake, as if he were a child forced to finish vegetables, tears streaming down his face.

Anne looked down at her darning again, but it was too late. She had seen and her heart hurt. Literally. She could feel its presence in her chest and she didn't like it. It was so much easier to resent Gerald, to keep score of wrongs. Had she ever loved him? She didn't know. Must she start now? She didn't want to.

"It's all right, Gerald," she found herself saying, as if he was one of the children. "It's all right."

A sob tore out of him and he put his fork down.

"Why are you being so nice to me?" he asked. "Why are you bringing me cake and coffee? You don't usually when…"

You drink, she finished the sentence silently. No, usually she gave him the cold shoulder. Left him to stew in his own juices, so to speak, went to bed with a book, careful to turn out the light and at least feign sleep before he staggered upstairs.

"You're under a great deal of strain," she said at length. "I'm worried about you."

"Because I thought you murdered Charlotte? I must have been crazy. How could I think that about you? Can you ever forgive me? Please forgive me, Anne, forgive me."

Anne considered her response as she guided her needle over and under from one side of frayed heel to the other. She disliked being begged for forgiveness, especially by Gerald. Well, he was the only one who did it, the only one who had cause. There were things she had no intention of forgiving him, ever. But being regarded as a murderess wasn't one of them.

"I don't blame you, Gerald. I'm just a little," she hesitated, searching for the right word, "curious, I guess. What were you planning to do about your suspicions of me? Were you going to go to the police?"

Part of her wanted him to say, yes. That justice mattered more than loyalty to her. Part of her wanted him to say, I would protect your guilty secret with my life. I could never let you be taken away from the children. And then she thought of Frank's children again. If she really were guilty, it would not be right for them to suffer.

Gerald's only answer was a moan. She wondered if he still harbored doubts about her.

"I didn't kill Charlotte Crowley, Gerald. I give you my solemn word. But I suppose I could have. I did hate her. A lot of people hated her. I had the opportunity."

Anne stopped darning as she recalled that morning. The bright sun, the hint of fall in the air...and the sudden disturbance of a car taking the driveway too fast, brakes screeching.

"Gerald, who drives a yellow and cream-colored car that's not a station wagon or a beetle? Sorry, I can never remember makes."

Gerald, who had stopped crying, thank God, took another bite of cake and seemed to be considering. Then suddenly he put his fork down and stared at Anne.

"Mildred Thomson," he said. "She drives a cream and yellow Citroën. Badly."

CHAPTER TWENTY

"Too bad Frankie won't be coming around here no more," said Aramantha. "Now *I'm* gonna have to be your best friend."

Aramantha sighed as if being Katherine's best friend would be hard work, and then she popped another ginger snap into her mouth instead of putting it on the tray she and Katherine were supposed to be arranging for coffee hour. They had been let out of their Sunday School classes early to help Aramantha's grandmother.

"What do you mean Frankie won't be coming around here?" Katherine wanted to know. "Besides, Frankie's not my best friend, he's my—" She stopped herself; maybe being blood brother and sister was supposed to be a secret. "Anyway, why shouldn't Frankie come here? You know he didn't start that fight with the stones. You were there. Why should Frankie be punished?"

Suddenly Katherine felt worried. What if the grownups hadn't believed her, even her own father? What if her father had ordered Frankie's pops not to bring him to work? She hadn't seen her father after the fight yesterday. He hadn't come home till she and Janie and Peter had gone upstairs to get ready for bed. Her mother said he was too busy to come and say goodnight. This morning she had told them to be very quiet. "Your father has a headache." There had been something wrong with her mother, too. A couple of times before church her mother had come to find her. "Katherine?" she'd said, and then she had shaken her head and said "Never mind."

The second time Katherine had asked her mother, "What did I do wrong?"

"Nothing, sweetie. You did nothing wrong. There's just something I have to talk to you about. But there's not enough time now. It can wait till after church."

Now Katherine knew. It must be about Frankie, Frankie not coming here anymore. Aramantha already knew about it. Who told her?

"Naw, it ain't Frankie who's in trouble," Aramantha said. "But maybe you're too young to know what happened. Maybe I shouldn't be telling you."

Aramantha went back to arranging cookies. Aramantha was almost being mean, like she always was.

"Don't tell me then," shrugged Katherine, who had learned how to be almost mean back. "I don't believe you anyway."

Katherine opened a tin of butterscotch brownies, homemade by Aramantha's grandmother, and began to set them out on a tray.

"You a lie, Katherine Bradley." Aramantha took over and began to line up the brownies in overlapping rows. "And lying is a sin. You ought to know that since your Daddy is the minister."

Katherine didn't know what to say back. Her stomach suddenly didn't feel so good, and she hadn't eaten half as many cookies as Aramantha.

"Come on, girls," Mrs. Green called. "Church is out and people on their way down the driveway. Stop eating those treats and get them to the table."

"I'm gonna tell you anyway," Aramantha announced, leaning in close as she picked up a tray. "Frankie's Daddy gone to jail for murdering that lady Mrs. Crowley in this very basement of this very parish house. Right under where we are standing right now."

Aramantha picked up the tray of ginger snaps and headed out of the kitchen. In the doorway she paused and looked back.

"Come on, Katherine, hurry up. Bring the brownies. And don't worry. I *will* be your best friend. I won't let Dickie and them kill you, even though they want to after you done told on them."

Katherine lifted the tray, but her hands were shaking, so that the brownies came unarranged. Just as she got to the table with them, the rest of the Sunday School kids burst up the stairs from the basement with Dickie and Prescott in the lead.

"No more than two apiece!" shouted Mrs. Green over the thundering of feet, "and then outside with all of you all!"

"It's all right, Katherine," whispered Aramantha, who had retreated with Katherine back to the kitchen doorway. "I got you covered."

Katherine knew Aramantha was a good fighter, but she didn't want to have another fight with Dickie and Scottie. She wanted to find Frankie.

Then she and Frankie would run away together. Forever.

Before Aramantha could stop her, Katherine turned, ran out the back door, past the trash bins to the gap in the wall where she stopped. She had only stepped over the wall that one time with Frankie. When Frankie was with her, she always felt brave, even when she was scared. Her eyes fell on the No Trespassing sign. She and Frankie had trespassed that day, the day Frankie had told her he wanted to kill Jesus's mother, Mary Virgin. And she had told Frankie her secret about wanting to kill God and Jesus.

God must have heard them. God must have seen them. Now God had let Frankie's pops kill Mrs. Crowley and go to jail and she would never see Frankie again. She had never been to his house. She didn't even know where it was. The tears Katherine had swallowed into a lump in her stomach came up into her throat and into her eyes, and she started to cry. She cried so hard, she could not see or hear the person who came up and put their arms around her.

"Come on, Katherine," said her best friend Aramantha. "Dickie and Prescott went home. I saved you a brownie."

CHAPTER TWENTY-ONE

It was early on a rainy Monday morning. Lucy had brought her second cup of coffee into the parlor where she could watch the trees sway in the wind and loose bright leaves while she did her *Lectio Divina*, as she liked to think of it, though she did not engage in the practice as formally or faithfully as a Benedictine would. In fine weather, her meditations often found her in the garden. Surely the second cup of French roast coffee was not part of monastic tradition, but morning coffee always filled her with gratitude for creation, for the creaturely pleasures of incarnation. It was chilly in the parlor this morning, and she might have lit a fire, but she would be spending the day at the rummage sale. The fire would have to wait till this evening. As for Tabitha, a devotee of the hearth, she would doubtless find her way under the coverlet on Lucy's bed and pass the day there instead.

In lieu of a fire, Lucy lit a candle and reached for *The Book of Common Prayer* that always lay at the ready on the table next to her chair. She hoped the daily office would settle her before she braved the decidedly unsettled atmosphere at the rummage sale. She had to admit that Gerald Bradley, apart from looking like death, had done an admirable job of informing the congregation that Frank Lomangino had been arrested as a suspect in the alleged murder of Charlotte Crowley. She often found his sermons too trendy and topical, his efforts to make scripture relevant to today's world a bit self-conscious and forced. Yesterday, in spite or perhaps because of his distress, he seemed to drop down below the flashy surfaces to some more timeless place. His sermon was brief, a reminder that Jesus and Paul and most of the disciples had found themselves in trouble with the law and that God often chose as his servants people others considered vile or unworthy.

"I hope you're not comparing Frank Lomangino to Jesus Christ!" Amos McCready had harrumphed loudly enough that everyone could hear.

An uneasy tittering followed. Gerald Bradley just took a breath, while everyone waited to see what he would do.

"In the name of the Father, the Son, and the Holy Ghost, Amen." Gerald ended the sermon and turned to the altar, leading the congregation in the Nicene Creed.

Lucy settled into her chair and opened the table that gave the readings and psalm for the Monday of the week of the Fourteenth Sunday after Trinity. She looked them up and marked them with a ribbon in preparation for reading the daily office. She had her own way of conducting Morning Prayer, reading the priest's part and the lessons silently, but reading aloud the congregational responses and the canticles. She always spoke the Psalm, different each day, and meant to be chanted or sung, the rhythms intended for the ear and the body. You could not comprehend these ancient songs with your mind only.

"*I said I will take heed to my ways, that I offend not in my tongue.*

"*I will keep my mouth as it were with a bridle, while the ungodly is in my sight.*"

Lucy began reading Psalm 39, not one of the easier psalms that spoke of God's comfort or protection or extolled the beauties of creation. If you read a psalm daily, you took the rocky and bloodthirsty with the beautiful.

"*I held my tongue, and spake nothing: I kept silence, yea, even from good words; but it was pain and grief to me.*

"*My heart was hot within me: and while I was thus musing the fire kindled, and at last I spake with my tongue.*"

Lucy read on as the psalm became a confession of sin, then a meditation on the vanity of man's existence, and finally a passionate plea to God to save the psalmist from enemies that *"speak evil of me."* All leading to the concluding declaration:

"And in my innocency thou upholdest me, and shall set me before thy face forever."

Before turning back to the daily office, Lucy sat for a moment with her prayer book still open to the psalm, letting the echo of that passionate, angry, faithful voice take her out of the comfort of her parlor and the peace she had made with her own life. Gerald was right; the apostles were no strangers to prison cells, stoning, martyrdom, trouble of all kinds. Jesus had been accused of rabble-rousing and blasphemy. Moses led a band of runaway slaves to wander in circles for years in the wilderness where some of them grew cantankerous and discontented. The Bible from Genesis on was full of accounts of trickery, betrayal, wars, murder, lust, vanities of all kinds, a stormy love affair between a people and a God who spoke through all that tumult with a voice so small and still few heard it and fewer still heeded it.

Lucy, as a quiet, older, not-quite-maiden lady, had no enemies that she knew of, but she remembered how menacing the world had appeared to her when she carried her child out-of-wedlock in secret. Charlotte had been notorious for insensitive prying, but who would have known till now that she had made a murderous enemy, if indeed she had been murdered? Lucy almost wished that she had never gone to Gerald with her suspicions. Now the peaceful little church was full of suspicion and strife, full of people speaking out of turn and out of ignorance or else holding their tongues, lest they offend, as she was inclined to do. If she knew the truth, would she have the courage to speak it? She hated to think that Frank Lomangino could have killed Charlotte Crowley. The only thing worse would be if he hadn't killed her, but he took the blame for...someone else.

Lucy felt so agitated, she got to her feet and looked around as if some course of action would declare itself. Then, slowly, deliberately, she sat down again, and opened the prayer book.

Dear Lord, she prayed silently, *if Frank is innocent, uphold him in his innocency, set him before thy face forever. Amen.*

And dear God, she added, *You know I am the one who went to Gerald about those coats not belonging in the basement. If I was wrong in my suspicions, show me how to make amends. If am right that Charlotte was murdered, give me the courage to face the truth, however much I dread to know it. Amen.*

Lucy turned back to the daily office and began to recite the *Te Deum.* She got as far as *Thou Art the King of Glory, O Christ* when the phone rang, unusual at such an early hour. She was tempted to ignore it, but a still small voice, located somewhere in the pit of her stomach, whispered that her prayers, God help her, were being answered. Marking her place, she closed the prayer book and caught the phone on the sixth ring.

"Hello, Lucy?" said a woman's voice at the other end of the line.

"Speaking," she affirmed.

"It's Anne, Anne Bradley. I hope I am not waking you."

"Not at all, Anne. I am always up with the birds."

Though they hadn't sung much this morning in the rain. She supposed they found shelter in the eaves or in the thickets up the hill towards Falling Star Rock. If only humans had as much sense.

"What can I do for you, Anne?" Lucy asked.

"Were you planning on coming to work at the rummage sale this morning?"

"Yes, I'll be there by nine o' clock. Unless you need me earlier?"

"Nine is fine. I was just wondering, well, Frank Lomangino is being arraigned today."

They were silent for a moment, perhaps both wishing to avoid words like murder and suspect and pending trial by jury.

"I'm so sorry about all of this wretched business, Anne," said Lucy at length. "How can I help?"

"Would you mind taking over the children's clothing department? I can't imagine that Frank's wife will want to continue with it."

"I'd be glad to, Anne, though I'm afraid I don't know much about children's clothes."

"Teresa's done all the sizing," said Anne. "She was terribly efficient about it."

Anne's use of the past tense sounded funereal, as if Teresa had died or been locked up in jail herself. Lucy felt a pang remembering Teresa's coming in with her little girls, how the children had run to their father and launched themselves into his arms.

"There's just a little more pricing left and of course taking money at the sale."

"I should be able to manage that much," agreed Lucy. "I haven't been much use so far, just filling in here and there. I'm happy to help. I wish there was something we could do for Mrs. Lomangino. Frank was so proud of her ability to get good bargains at the rummage sale."

There was a small silence at the other end. Lucy let it be as she listened to the wind whoosh, tossing leaves in an upward spiral before letting them fall.

"I really ought to call her," said Anne, sounding reluctant and resolute at once. "I could ask the children's sizes, and if she had any particular items in mind. We could set them aside. I know we're not supposed to...."

"But we will make an exception in this case," Lucy agreed. "Don't worry. '*I will keep my mouth as it were with a bridle.*'"

"Oh Lord, Lucy!" Anne laughed a trifle hysterically, Lucy thought. She must be under a great deal of strain. "You are not going to start spouting scripture, like Amos, or...or Mildred Thomson."

"Oh, no!" Lucy felt a small, genuine horror. "Not like that, I hope. It's just that I was reading Psalm 39 aloud this morning just before you called."

Oh, dear, she might be confirming Anne's worst suspicions of her.

"I'm sorry. I must have interrupted you."

"Not at all," said Lucy quickly. Never mind about not completing the *Te Deum*. It would keep. "I was just finishing up. I'll see you in about an hour then, shall I?"

"Thank you so much. Lucy?"

Lucy caught the pause and the question mark after her name and knew that Anne was not ready to hang up.

"Yes?"

"Could you spare me another moment? There's something I need to talk about. Confidentially. And it occurred to me that we'd have more privacy on the phone than at the parish house. That is, if you don't mind...."

Here it comes, thought Lucy.

"What is it, Anne?"

"Mildred Thomson," she blurted out. "I'm pretty sure she was there that morning, the morning Charlotte was killed. Someone tore out of the driveway in a car that might have been hers. I've told Gerald. He said he would speak to Frank's attorney when he gets one. Gerald is terribly worried about who can be found for him. The family likely can't afford much in legal fees, and the Church of Regeneration can hardly hold a fundraiser. I assume there will be some form of investigation."

Lucy let out a breath that she felt as though she had held since Gerald called with the news of Frank's arrest and Elsa had behaved so strangely. Let it be Mildred, she caught herself in what sounded like a petition. Forgive me, she prayed instantly.

"I am sure proper procedures will be followed," said Lucy. "I know this must be so distressing for you and Gerald."

"Especially for Gerald," Anne agreed. "He was so upset, he thought, he was afraid...never mind," she stopped herself. "He's sick about Frank, of course. Listen, Lucy, Mildred Thomson was following you around that first day of the rummage sale. Before she disappeared to become Nat's minder and left Florence to take over notions herself. Oh, I know you helped Florence, too, Lucy. I didn't mean to overlook all you've done."

Anne's words were coming in gusts and rushes, like the wind. Where would they come to rest?

"But I was wondering, just wondering," Anne circled closer, "if Mildred might have said anything to you."

Now would be the time to say: Mildred wanted to confess something to me in the worst way, and I told her to talk to her priest. But Lucy's tongue still felt the restraint of the bridle, though Anne could not be called ungodly just because she disliked excessive scripture quoting.

"She might have if I'd let her," said Lucy slowly. "But I am afraid I didn't listen. I wouldn't listen."

Anne was silent for so long, Lucy thought she might have hung up.

"Would you listen now?" she asked. "If you had the chance?"

"Yes, Anne," said Lucy slowly. "I would. I will."

CHAPTER TWENTY-TWO

Gerald finished his breakfast of black coffee, scrambled eggs and toast in the company of the newspaper—which was not as comfortable a companion as usual. There was a lurid account of Frank Lomangino's arrest, complete with a photograph of the alleged "crime scene" aka the Church of Regeneration Parish House. The reporter noted that the rector, Reverend Gerald Bradley (typically, they omitted The in front of the title) had been unavailable for comment, which made him sound guilty of something. If he had commented, they would have misquoted him, which was why he had refused. That and not wanting his church to become the center ring of a small town circus. Vain hope, especially with the rummage sale going forward as scheduled. Perhaps that had been a mistake, but he couldn't leave the parish house and yard crammed full of, well, junk, to be blunt. The paper noted that Frank's arraignment was set for today. Gerald wondered whether his presence or his absence would do more harm, or any good, either way. Did he have an obligation to represent the church where the victim had been a parishioner and the suspect an employee?

What would his father have done?

Shit, he thought, damn, damn, damn! His father would go to the arraignment, of course. Just as he told Gerald he must enlist in the army, not that he wouldn't have been drafted anyway, because "you must face the challenges of your generation." If a task was unpleasant, you had to do it.

Gerald folded the paper clumsily (he could never get the folds to line up again) and got to his feet. He would have liked to discuss the matter with Anne at breakfast, but she had excused herself after a bite or two to make a phone call, about the rummage sale, of course, which covered a multitude of sins (murder for example). She had used the kitchen phone and he thought he'd heard her say something about Frank's wife and later he caught the word Mildred. Who was she talking to? Did he need to remind Anne not to gossip? It seemed uncharacteristic of her.

Without picking up any of his breakfast dishes, he went to the kitchen to see if Anne was still on the phone, but the kitchen was quiet. She must have gone upstairs to make the beds. Or perhaps she had taken the twins to nursery school. Before he could decide whether or not to look for her, the phone rang.

"Bradley here," he answered. He never called himself by his title.

"Gerald, thank God. I've been trying to get through to you for ages. Quick. I don't have much time left."

"Nat?" Gerald guessed. "Nat, is that you? What do you mean you don't have much time left?" With a sickening jolt, Gerald wondered if Nat had attempted suicide. Another dead parishioner, he couldn't afford that. "What's happened? Are you all right?"

"Bloody hell, man! Of course I'm not all right. Charlotte murdered by the man who trimmed our yew hedge and that madwoman clearing out my bar, going through all my closets, peering under my bed, without so much as a by-your-leave. Thank God, I thought to hide some gin in the toilet tank."

Here Nat paused for breath and, from the sounds of it, a swig.

"You've got to save me," he almost gasped. "She'll be here any minute to make me porridge—*porridge* as if I were a bear and she's some ghastly antique Goldilocks. The only reason she doesn't stay all night is because we're not married. Yet. That's what she says. Not married, yet. I should never have let her pay off the mortgage. What an infernal idiot I am. Now she thinks she owns the house—and me. I can't get her to leave me alone. You're a priest, Gerald. And I'm a miserable sinner and a drunk, I confess, but have mercy on me. For the love of Christ, *do* something!"

Here was an unpleasant task that trumped the arraignment. Sorry, Pop.

"Sit tight, Nat," said Gerald, realizing as soon as the words were out of his mouth that Nat would follow that instruction literally. "I'll be there as soon as I can."

He and Anne almost collided on the landing by the hall as she came down from upstairs and he came up from the kitchen.

"Oh, it's you," they both said and almost laughed. A light moment that would be as hard to hold as a butterfly and, if you succeeded, might be destroyed.

"I'm off to the parish house," Anne volunteered, continuing into the hall. "I called Lucy Way this morning and she said she'd take over the children's department for Teresa Lomangino."

So that's who she'd been talking to, he thought with relief. No communication with Lucy Way could be classified as gossip. How ironic that Lucy Way, the soul of reticence, should have been the one to launch the murder investigation.

"Are you going to the arraignment?" she asked, turning back at the front door.

"I was going to go." He wanted credit from Anne, from his father's soul. "I will go, if I can get there in time. I've got to pay Nat Crowley an emergency call first."

"Mildred," she guessed, more a statement than a question.

He grimaced by way of protecting the seal of the confessional if Nat's panicked call could be called a confession.

"Anne," he said as she opened the door. "You are desperately short-handed at the rummage sale, aren't you?"

"Not really, I just told you, I called—" She stopped as she got his drift. "Why yes, it is only three days till the workers' sale. I hate to put the whole children's clothing department on Lucy. Yes, Lucy could definitely use some help. You may quote me."

Gerald and Anne exchanged a rare look of complete understanding.

It really was rather absurd to put two childless women in charge of children's clothing, Anne realized. Mildred especially seemed at a loss, wandering in perplexity with almost every garment she touched to ask Lucy, or Anne if she were in the vicinity, what the price should be for this hand-made baby sweater or that worn but serviceable pair of corduroy overalls. Lucy was being most patient and attentive to Mildred's questions, no doubt taking seriously her assignment to win a confession from Mildred when the moment struck, but she seemed to lack her usual confidence when it came to pricing the garments. Was the criteria size, quality or both, Lucy had asked Anne anxiously. Then, on one trip upstairs, Anne overheard Mildred trying to excuse herself from the job.

"I must get back to Nat, Lucy," Mildred said. "He is quite lost without me. I am sure you have matters well in hand. You are always so clever about things, Lucy."

"Oh, Mildred, please don't go. There is such a lot to do, thousands of garments left to price. It makes my head spin. I don't think I can possibly manage without your help. You told me yourself that Mr. Bradley is with Nat. Perhaps Nat needs time alone with his priest. You know, Mildred, when death comes suddenly, sometimes people have unavoidable regrets, things on their conscience.... Oh, just look at this darling little girl's jumper. Perhaps I ought to pair it with a blouse and put it with the dresses. Do help me pick one out, Mildred."

And Anne realized Lucy's strategy. Who would have known Lucy Way could be so devious, even in a good cause? So Anne patiently answered all their questions and tabled what had likely been Teresa's idea to separate things into categories and, for example, mark all boys button-downs one price and all tee-shirts another.

By mid-morning, Anne had made more than one round to all the departments. She decided it was high time she made fresh coffee and took a thermos down to Rosalie. She might stay in the barn to help price toys for a while. As usual, Sybil Foster had more important things to do. You would think she was running for congress herself, she was so busy on the campaign trail. Well, in Sybil's mind

Congressman's Wife and Hostess was doubtless the weightier office. It occurred to Anne, as she went downstairs, that she enjoyed disliking Sybil and felt not the slightest remorse for sinning in thought, which was supposedly as bad as word and deed. If there was a God, Anne thought he ought to be more discriminating. There was a world of difference between thinking and doing. Thoughts could be self-contained whereas doing always made such a mess. And because someone actually pushed Charlotte down the stairs instead of merely thinking about it, here they all were in that mess.

"I just put the last price sticker on, Mrs. Bradley." Florence Green greeted her from the notions table in the front room. She triumphantly held up what appeared to be a gilded egg cup, which probably could have been put with crockery.

"Well, that's just fine, Mrs. Green." Anne felt obliged to stop and admire the crowded tables, attractively arranged, ready to be torn apart by grasping, shoving hands. "You're way ahead of everyone else."

"Got to go home now and start baking for the baked goods table," said Mrs. Green.

"You've taken on a lot of responsibility," Anne observed.

"Oh, some of the other ladies be baking, too," Florence assured her.

And she reeled off the specialties of half a dozen members of the WOR. Anne could not help noticing that she had not been asked to contribute. Whether it was out of deference to her position or because everyone knew she relied on Betty Crocker mixes, Anne could not be sure.

"Like Scripture say, many hands make light work," Florence concluded.

Anne wasn't at all sure that saying was scriptural, but Scripture was the ultimate source of authority for Florence.

"Aramantha will help when she gets home from school," Florence added. "If little Katherine want to, she can come on over."

Anne bent over the table, pretending to examine a display of paperweights to disguise her distaste for this friendship of Katherine's. She did not want to admit, especially to Gerald, that she might have prejudices. Not racial, she insisted to herself. It's just that Aramantha, like Frankie, could be, well, rough. She was pretty sure it was Aramantha who had told Katherine about Frank Lomangino's arrest, though she couldn't be certain. Katherine had been crying too hard to make much sense. And when she had calmed down, she had been very quiet, too quiet. She had stayed in her room all afternoon as if she had been sent there as a punishment. Anne knew it was not fair to blame Aramantha for her own mistake. She should have spoken to Katherine herself first thing yesterday morning.

"That's very kind of you, Mrs. Green." Anne straightened up and tried to smile. "We'll see. I may want to keep Katherine close to home today. But thank you."

"I understand, Mrs. Bradley."

Understood what? That Anne was a snob and a bigot? Anne watched uneasily as Florence pulled on white gloves and shouldered her enormous white leather pocketbook that looked as heavy as if she had taken the sins of the world from Jesus and offered to tote them for a while.

"Aramantha says Katherine crying her eyes out for Mr. Lomangino's boy."

Anne felt unreasonably relieved whereas a moment before she might have resented such a familiar mention of her daughter.

"She is very upset," Anne acknowledged. "We all are, God knows."

"Yes, God *knows*," Florence agreed emphatically. "God knows everything. He sees everything. He mark the fall of the sparrow and he marked Charlotte Crowley's fall down them stairs. Don't you worry, Mrs. Bradley. He's gonna straighten this mess."

With those prophetic words, Florence patted Anne's arm and headed for the door.

In the kitchen where Anne hoped for moment's peace to light up a cigarette, she found Grace Jones ahead of her.

"Hold on a minute, counting," said Grace without turning toward her. "Ten, eleven, twelve." She measured out each scoop neatly, the coffee perfectly level in the measuring cup. "There that ought to hold us all for a little while."

Grace turned towards Anne and leaned back against the counter, while she waited for the coffee to begin to percolate. Both of them reached for cigarettes. Grace was quicker on the draw and offered Anne a light. Anne leaned back against the table, though she could never look as cool and nonchalant as Grace—who dressed as though she were the star of a 1940s movie instead of a modern housewife—which of course she wasn't. The word divorcée suited Grace, Anne thought. She still favored the tailored look, a grey skirt, narrowing from hips to knees. White fitted blouse. Lips emphasized with a bright red shade, smooth folds of hair caught in a net that looked elegant rather than frumpy.

"Where is Gerald today?" Grace asked. "He hasn't even called in for messages."

Anne suspected she should have been jealous of Grace. She knew other women gossiped about her, suspected her of being a home wrecker (even though it was her home that had been wrecked by a philandering husband). They probably thought Grace had designs on Gerald.

"Emergency call," Anne said.

Grace just nodded, knowing Anne well enough to know she wouldn't elaborate.

"How is Gerald?" Grace asked instead. "He looked like hell yesterday, by the way."

Anne wondered why she didn't bridle, didn't resent the implication that she wasn't taking very good care of her husband. Oddly enough, she found herself wishing that Grace really could be her co-wife, which was more or less what a secretary was. The biblical patriarchs had them, and the wives, when they weren't bickering, must have made alliances. What if she said to Grace, no, he's not doing well. You take him for a while. Use your counting skills on martinis.

"He's taken Frank Lomangino's arrest pretty hard," Anne admitted, hoping she did not sound to Grace as though she were confiding. "He might go to the arraignment, if he's free in time."

Grace took a drag on her cigarette and exhaled long and slowly. Stagey, Anne thought.

"Gerald really went out on a limb for that man," said Grace. "Oh, I didn't have anything against Frank personally. Good-looking, good-natured, a bit of a flirt, but he never made a pass at me, the way most men do when they find out I'm divorced."

Anne wasn't sure it was wise to hear any more, but she felt curious and embarrassed at the same time, the way she did when she couldn't help reading tabloid headlines at the supermarket. She wasn't about to ask was Gerald "most men" any more than she would pick up one of those newspapers.

"Guess that cute little wife of his keeps him busy, poor thing with her belly out to here, though that doesn't stop some men," Grace alluded darkly, to her past, no doubt. "I did warn Gerald at the time. Frank looked like a decent guy down on his luck. They all do. But when someone has been in the pen you never know who's got their hooks into him. They don't turn you loose from the mob that easily. But your husband always wants to see the best in everyone, God bless him. He took a chance on me, too. A lot of men in his position wouldn't. I hope you don't pay any attention to the gossip about me, Anne."

Anne couldn't help noticing that Grace was blushing.

"I don't," said Anne, and then added boldly. "Should I?"

"No, you shouldn't," said Grace emphatically. "Your husband is crazy about you. Every wife should be so lucky. I hope you appreciate what you have."

Grace sounded almost angry. Did she guess Anne's lack of appreciation? Did she think she could do a better job of being Gerald's wife? Well, Anne felt strangely sad instead of indignant, she probably could. Maybe Grace would match him drink for drink and keep the kids and their toys out of his way when he'd had a hard day. Maybe Grace wouldn't mind having to lie under him while he went on forever. Maybe she'd even like it.

"The coffee's ready," Grace said before Anne could answer. "Pour you a cup?"

"If there's a thermos around here, I'm going to take some coffee to Rosalie and help her for a while."

"No Sybil again? I didn't think her ladyship and the toy barn would be much of a match. I tell you, people shoo their husbands away from me. She's the one they ought to worry about. If you see Gerald before I do, tell him the sheriff's office called. I gather the local keystone cops have been dismissed from the case. I suppose there'll have to be some sort of investigation, however pro forma. Anyway, the sheriff wants a call back pronto."

Grace filled a cup and bustled out of the kitchen, her high heels clicking efficiently as her typewriter or adding machine.

CHAPTER TWENTY-THREE

By mid-afternoon, Anne was ready to pack it in and decided to make one last round for the day. She and Rosalie had finished pricing the toys by lunchtime, and Rosalie had taken the twins home with her. When she went upstairs, Anne found that by some miracle, Lucy had managed to keep Mildred with her, though the lack of progress the pair had made was staggering. She had hoped to spend some time alone with Katherine this afternoon, but clearly she was going to have to help with the clothes at least for a while. Maybe she could persuade Katherine to join her and then take her out for ice cream on the way to pick up the twins.

"Let's see," Anne began. "What about this pile here?"

It appeared to be a mound of flannel pajamas, in varying degrees of fading or disintegration. She wondered what Teresa had been intending to do with them.

"Oh, don't bother pricing those, Mrs. Bradley."

Anne turned and saw Teresa Lomangino and her little girls walking down the length of room where Marge and Mary Louise in women's wear and Grace and Ginger in men's wear had stopped working to stare. Someone did drop a pin and you could hear it, Teresa's children also being unusually subdued.

"I've brought some pinking shears. I thought I'd cut the pajamas up and sell them at two cents a piece for quilting or patches. Mr. Bradley said the pennies could go in a mite box for UNICEF.

Anne had two simultaneous thoughts: what a clever idea, and: what a lot of work. Then the full impact of Teresa's presence hit her.

"Ter, I mean Mrs. Lomangino, I'm glad to see you. Does this mean—?"

"Held without bail," Teresa answered, her voice both flat and fierce. She looked around the room, insistently meeting every woman's eye. "In case you're wondering, he didn't do it. My husband wouldn't hurt a fly. For real. I'm the one has to swat flies in our house. If anyone has anything to say about it or anything about me being here, say it to my face and say it now."

There was another silence, broken only by one of the little girls asking if they could play dolls on the stage.

"Then I'll get back to work," concluded Teresa.

"Mrs. Lomangino," Lucy Way stepped forward. "I'm glad you're here. Mildred and I are a bit hopeless with the pricing, but we'd be happy to cut squares if we can find an extra pair of scissors."

"Lucy, really I've got to attend to Nat," hissed Mildred.

But before she could protest further, Mary Louise stepped forward and put a pair of scissors in Mildred's hand.

"Get to work, Mildred. Leave poor old Nat alone. We've all got to pull together. I admire you, Mrs. Lomangino. You're doing a brave thing."

Teresa nodded and shrugged and she turned abruptly to the pile of tee-shirts, still unsorted. Mary Louise had spoken, and Anne knew that no matter what anyone else thought, they would follow her lead.

"Seems you have matters well in hand," said Anne to no one in particular, preparing to make her getaway.

"Mrs. Bradley," Teresa turned toward her; one look at her face told Anne the woman was fighting back tears. "Could I speak with you for a moment? Confidentially?" she said in a lower voice. "I'll be right back, girls."

"We can use my husband's office," Anne suggested as they headed out of the room. "Unless he's back...." Anne trailed off. Surely Teresa knew if Gerald had been at the arraignment.

"If he is, I need speak to him, too. I saw him at the court house, but I couldn't say anything to him there. As soon as the arraignment was over the reporters were all over me, and poor Mr. Crowley, too."

"I'm so sorry," Anne murmured, not knowing what else to say, but wishing she could think of something. She knew what it was like to have people awkward and tongue-tied around a tragedy they couldn't or didn't want to imagine. They were afraid of saying the wrong thing, and with reason, for there was no right thing to say. Still Anne had resented people's avoidance of the only topic in the world to her, and now she was doing the same to Teresa, as she walked a little ahead of her, leading the way to Gerald's office.

"It's about my brother Joe," Teresa began when Anne had closed the door behind them.

Anne felt hesitant to sit in Gerald's chair behind his desk, but she gestured to Teresa to sit in the leather easy chair reserved for confiding parishioners while she looked around for something else for herself. But Teresa remained standing.

"He's Constable O'Brien's deputy," she went on. "He was there that day, the day they found Mrs. Crowley. He didn't buy that it was an accident even then, but no one would listen to him. And he's sure Frank didn't do it, not just because he's my brother, though of course no one will believe him, because he is. They've taken O'Brien off the case. Joe had to step down anyway on account of his being family. But if it's all right with you and the Reverend, he'd like to look around, ask some questions, unofficial like."

Anne did not know what to say. First of all, she wasn't at all sure of the legality of Teresa's request. She also felt bemused by Teresa's assumption that Anne had any authority at all in any matter. She was just the wife, though some people thought of her as an extra appendage for her husband. She could and should just pass the buck to Gerald, but Teresa had appealed to her. She didn't want to just brush her off.

"Your brother could get in trouble if he interferes with an official investigation," she felt obliged to say. "So could Ger, Mr. Bradley. I believe the Sheriff's office will be taking over."

Anne stopped herself before she could say more than she ought to.

"The sheriff's office won't do squat," said Teresa bluntly. "Long as somebody goes to jail, they don't care who did it. They sure as hell don't care about Frank Lomangino. To them he's just an ex-con bound to go back to the clink sooner or later. But your husband didn't think that way about Frank, Mrs. Bradley. He wanted to give him a fair chance."

Then why are you talking to me, Anne wanted to say. I'm not the saint in this family. She felt suddenly angry, put upon, cornered by this woman and her desperate problems. How did Gerald stand it?

"Frankie, Frankie, Frankie!"

Anne was distracted by the sound of Katherine shouting. She and Teresa both turned toward the window and saw Katherine running pell mell down the driveway. There was Frankie, Junior standing at the edge of the driveway kicking gravel more savagely than usual. He didn't look up as Katherine neared him.

"I can't do a thing with him," Teresa sighed. "He's barely spoken since they took Frank away. Hardly eats. You know how it is. A boy needs his father."

Anne felt that unwelcome twist of pity for Frankie just under her heart where it stirred up her bitterness. Hal. Had Hal needed his father, the one who beat him for no reason, the one who loved him too late? No, she wanted to say to Teresa. No, I don't know how it is. But Teresa had her own troubles, and Anne preferred to keep hers to herself. She watched as Katherine plummeted into Frankie, she was running so fast. Then suddenly Frankie started swinging his fists, and after a stunned moment, Katherine hit back, just as fast, just as hard.

"What are they doing? Stop!" shouted Anne tapping on the window "Stop it, you two!"

"Hey, you kids!" called Teresa without much heat.

The children went on pounding and swinging.

"They'll stop in a minute," said Teresa. "They don't mean nothing by it."

Anne rounded on Teresa. She was sick of being diplomatic and self-effacing, she was sick of playing the bedraggled dove of peace, her words choked back by the olive branch. Your son is a bully, she wanted to scream, a bully and a hoodlum. He's going to wind up in jail like his father. I will not allow him to take out his home problems on my daughter. You get your son out of here!

"See?" Teresa pointed out the window, unperturbed by Anne's silent fury.

Anne looked and saw that the blows had given away to a bear hug that any minute might lead to wrestling and rolling on the ground. Then the children dropped their arms, joined hands and ran out of sight.

"Well, I better get back to work," said Teresa. "Listen, Mrs. Bradley, I don't mean to cause trouble for you or your husband. That's the last thing Frank would want."

Remorse followed on the heels of Anne's rage. Who was she to judge a woman in Teresa's shoes? And if she was in those shoes (loosely-tied white sneakers, Anne noticed; maybe Teresa was retaining water, after all) would she have advocated for her husband so fiercely?

"If he has concerns, your brother should come and speak to Mr. Bradley in person, Mrs. Lomangino," Anne said. "I'll tell my husband to expect him. I'm afraid that's all I can do."

Even as she spoke the words, Anne wondered if they were true. Hadn't she already hinted at her suspicions about Mildred to Gerald? Who was it that had called Lucy Way and asked her to worm her way into Mildred Thomson's confidence? What was she playing at? It wasn't like her to pry or interfere or even care. Was she possessed by the ghost of Charlotte Crowley? She did not believe in such nonsense. She'd better follow her advice to Teresa and leave the investigation to the proper authorities.

"Thank you, Mrs. Bradley."

Teresa turned and followed her swollen belly out of the room.

"We have to catch the bad man," said Frankie, as they stood at the gap in the wall.

Katherine did not have to ask who Frankie meant. The bad man with horns and wings, the one that flew past them, frightening the fairies and bothering the woods, ruining the quiet of light coming down through the trees. The imposition.

"How?" whispered Katherine.

Frankie didn't say anything for a moment, but his not speaking was so loud it almost hurt her ears.

"We have to make a trap," he said at last.

"A trap," she repeated. "A trap that could catch something big, like a heffalump."

"What are you talking about, Katherine?" said Frankie in that voice that sounded almost mad. "Who ever heard of a heffalump?"

"It's in *Winnie-the-Pooh*," she defended herself.

Frankie made one of the noises that sounded like her father making gas, the kind of sound her mother didn't like her to imitate. Probably Frankie didn't know about *Winnie-the-Pooh*. He told her he hated reading. How could anyone hate reading?

"It does have to be a big trap," he said in his nicer voice. "Bigger than for a helluvalump."

Katherine thought heffalumps were very large, but she wasn't sure, so she didn't argue.

"Where will we build it?" she asked.

"In the woods," he said. "Where else? That's where we saw him."

They both stood gazing over the wall. The rain had stopped, but there was no sunlight to show where the fairies flickered. Even with the red and yellow leaves, it looked dark in there and wet. She thought of the fairies in their homes among the tree roots. She wondered if they drank chamomile tea like Peter Rabbit.

"We're not allowed." Katherine felt she had to say it.

"Who cares?" Frankie said as she knew he would.

Katherine thought for a moment. It wasn't just their mothers. It wasn't even just God. Who cares about God, she thought bravely. But there was someone else.

"The lady," Katherine said. "The lady with white hair. She told us not to go to the woods alone."

There. Frankie could not say who cares to that!

"The lady said we belonged in the woods," Frankie said after a moment. "She said we have fairy blood. I don't care if she told us not to go alone. We wouldn't be alone anyways, if we were together."

That was true. Usually. Usually If Frankie was with her, she felt safe. But she had felt scared that day when they hid under the bridge, even with Frankie there. Then Katherine had an idea.

"Maybe the lady could come with us. Maybe she could help make a trap."

Frankie didn't just blurt out no, like he mostly did when she thought of something. Katherine waited, feeling like she and Frankie were balanced on a teeter-totter.

"She's a grownup." Frankie brought his weight down on one end.

"She has fairy blood," Katherine argued.

"She might not tell on us because she's got fairy blood," Frankie agreed. "But she wouldn't help us. She'd try to stop us."

Katherine knew he was right, and she knew that part of her wanted someone to stop them. But part of her didn't. Part of her wanted to go into the woods alone with Frankie. In stories children fought ogres and witches and dragons and giants by themselves. Without grownups. Frankie didn't even read books, and he knew that.

"We have to do it, Katherine," said Frankie. "We have to catch the bad man. We have to catch him and put him in jail."

Katherine nodded.

"Here's how we'll make the trap." Frankie dropped his voice to a whisper, but before he could explain, Katherine's mother called her.

"Don't answer," said Frankie.

But Katherine knew she had to. Her mother had that sound in her voice, a scared sound that would turn mad in a minute. She turned and saw her mother looking around the yard for her. She didn't have to say anything. Frankie didn't even have to know. She decided inside. She let herself be found.

"Oh, there you are!" Her mother sounded so happy, like she was afraid she had almost lost Katherine for a long, long time. "The twins are with Aunt Rosalie. I thought maybe we could stop for ice cream on the way to pick them up. Just you and me."

Her mother smiled at her, and Katherine felt happy like a child in a story who thinks she doesn't have a mother and then finds out she does and her mother is the queen who has been looking for her lost daughter all the time. Then she looked around for Frankie. He had wandered away from them. He was kicking gravel like he always did, making it spray up into the air, as if the stones were a splash of water.

"Can Frankie come, too?" she asked, though her mother never said yes.

Katherine looked down. She wanted to kick stones, too, and not see that sad, mad look on her mother's face. When her mother sighed, Katherine looked anyway, but her mother had turned her face towards Frankie. She couldn't see her mother's eyes.

"Frankie," her mother said, "I am taking Katherine to get ice cream. Go ask your mother if it's all right for you to come with us. She's upstairs."

Frankie dragged his foot instead of kicking. He made a straight, deep line in the gravel. Then suddenly without saying anything, he ran inside the parish house. Top speed.

CHAPTER TWENTY-FOUR

Lucy found herself wishing that she had something stronger than sherry in the house. Elsa had polished off the brandy the other night. Of course Mildred did not drink alcohol at all. So here they were, having another cup of tea and some cucumber sandwiches. The rain had cleared and the late afternoon light was rich. Being inside felt useless rather than cozy. She would have preferred to be in her garden, pulling weeds that the rain would have loosened instead of sitting with Mildred, doing her Christian duty, if you could call it that, trying to extract a confession like a rotten tooth.

It was something of a miracle that she had managed to get Mildred alone at all. Was it just a coincidence that when they left the parish house after an exhausting but fruitless day, Mildred's car had not one but two flat tires, making it necessary for a tow truck to take it to the garage? Did divine providence really stoop to such means, or was there (disturbing thought) human agency involved? Mildred had been an awkward guest, first sitting dreamily in the parlor while Lucy put together the tea, then leaping up to help and nearly tripping her while she carried the tray. Now after half a cup and half a sandwich, Mildred was on her feet again.

"Do you mind if I use your phone, Lucy? I just want to call the garage. My car ought to be ready. It is so kind of you to fetch and carry me from the village. It is too bad Nat wasn't home. Perhaps I should try him again. He could pick me up here and save you an extra trip into the village."

"I don't mind in the least taking you back." Lucy thought quickly. "I have errands to run." (The liquor store; one should always have brandy in case of emergencies.) "Besides, Nat lives on the other side of the village. Coming here would take him quite out of his way. I wouldn't want to put him to any trouble, and I am sure you wouldn't either," Lucy concluded firmly, though indeed she was sure of no such thing. Trouble for Nat, troubling Nat was clearly what Mildred had in mind. Lucy wondered again about those tires. "I left my number with Mr. Nichols at the garage. He'll call when your car is ready."

Mildred sighed and sat again at the edge of the sofa, if you could call it sitting when her hindquarters seemed to hover, hummingbird-like.

"Mildred," Lucy said, "since you're here, I wonder if I could talk to you, confidentially. You see, there's been something on my conscience."

"Really?" Mildred sounded faintly interested and allowed a few more ounces of flesh to settle into the sofa. "But you are so good, Lucy, so kind. I would have thought your conscience would be unsullied as the driven snow."

Lucy found herself irritated by this assumption. Was she really such a bore?

"You know, Mildred," Lucy continued, "sometimes people hide behind their virtues. For example, I am reticent and don't like to pry into people's private affairs, so I sometimes shrink from people's confidences."

"Oh?" said Mildred vaguely, looking out the window. "Can that be a purple martin?"

"Yes, I believe it is," said Lucy, wondering if Mildred was being evasive or if matters of conscience, unless it were her own conscience, didn't interest her much. "I feel I owe you an apology, Mildred."

"Me?" Mildred looked surprised. Lucy had her attention again.

"Yes, you, Mildred. Right after Charlotte's death there was something you wanted to tell me. I am afraid I brushed you off. I am sorry for that. It was cowardly of me. We all need to help each other in this hard time. I want you to know, I am ready to listen."

Mildred smiled a small, secretive smile that Lucy found disconcerting.

"That is very kind of you, Lucy. But it doesn't matter now. There is nothing to worry about. The Lord has heard my prayers."

"Oh?" Lucy said in turn. This was tricky ground. "I am glad Mr. Bradley was able to help you sort things out."

Mildred looked puzzled.

"Father Bradley? Oh, I decided there was no need to talk to him. I don't like to be a bother."

Lucy had a strong and decidedly uncharitable urge to giggle but managed to swallow it along with a bite of cucumber sandwich. Her subtle methods weren't working very well, and the garage might phone any minute.

"Mildred, forgive me. Sometimes it's best to be direct. You were there at the parish house the morning Charlotte died."

To be truthful, Lucy did not know that for certain, so she let her voice waver subtly between question and statement as a sop to her conscience. Mildred just gazed at Lucy, almost serenely. For the first time Lucy felt afraid. Everyone, including herself, had always vaguely pitied Mildred, so lonely, so drab, so tediously pious. It struck Lucy now that Mildred might be mad. She might have been mad enough to kill Charlotte, and here was Lucy alone with her.

"You mustn't concern yourself about that horrible business any more, Lucy. All things work together for good for those who love the Lord. Now Nat and I can be together as the Lord always intended."

Lucy felt perhaps unreasonably irked at Mildred's appropriation of one of her favorite passages of Saint Paul.

"I do not believe for a moment that the Lord intended for anyone to push Charlotte Crowley down the stairs and smother her under a drycleaners bag," said Lucy sharply.

"Your mother's old coats," observed Mildred. "Poor Lucy. That must be upsetting for you. But Lucy, I did not say that the Lord intended for Charlotte to be murdered, just that the Lord can turn anything that happens to good use. And he has. Don't you see?"

Lucy forced herself to disregard Mildred's theology. It was too distressing to realize that she agreed with Mildred. In theory. But theological fine points were not her purpose here. There were more practical questions to pursue.

"Mildred, how do you know that the coats belonged to my mother?"

Lucy did not think that detail was common knowledge. She had told only Gerald Bradley.

"Why I recognized them, of course. Your mother always looked so distinguished in that royal blue coat with the fur trim. I've never had the courage to wear strong colors. But perhaps now—"

"So you were there that morning," Lucy cut her off. "Mildred, I think you had better tell me everything."

The phone rang and Mildred sprang up. Lucy shocked herself by closing her hand on Mildred's arm. Tight.

"The phone can wait, Mildred. The car can wait. Tell me what happened."

"I told you it wasn't important. Let go, Lucy." Mildred's eyes filled with tears and her lower lip stuck out. She looked for a moment not like a faded, self-effacing, middle-aged woman, but a petulant child. "I've been away all day. I've got to get back to Nat. He needs me. I won't let anyone keep me from him ever again. Not even you, Lucy. Why are you trying to stop me?"

"It is important," Lucy insisted, still holding on to Mildred, as the phone stopped ringing, wondering what she would do if Mildred lunged at her. "It's possible that an innocent man may be charged with Charlotte's murder."

Mildred stopped resisting and stared at Lucy.

"An innocent man? What innocent man?"

"Frank Lomangino, of course," said Lucy.

"Frank Lomangino?" Mildred repeated. "But he can't be innocent. He mustn't be innocent!"

The phone rang again, but this time Mildred did not react. She stared into the middle distance, a look Lucy recognized. She had seen it during the war, a look that meant some dreadful scene was replaying itself.

"I'll be right back, Mildred."

When Lucy had made arrangements with Mr. Nichols to leave Mildred's key under the floor flap and the bill on the car seat, she returned to find Mildred still staring.

"You will tell me now, Mildred," Lucy instructed. "You will tell me everything that happened that morning."

Mildred turned her eyes to Lucy, and Lucy noticed their color for the first time, that sort of undistinguished blue of all newborn babies but vague and watery like a much older woman's. Or perhaps they were welling with tears. Lucy did hope they would not brim over.

"She had no right," Mildred began. "She had no right to give it away to the rummage sale."

Lucy waited. Best to let the story tumble out as it would, not try to make sense of it too soon.

"I gave Nat that music box when we were engaged or we were about to be engaged—everyone knew he was going to propose to me. I brought it back for him from Switzerland. It was a hand-carved wooden music box of a perfect little Swiss house. It even had tiny replicas of the stones the Swiss put on their roofs to hold them in the mountain gales. It played a waltz, the one we danced to at my coming out party. The roof lifted up and you could put little treasures inside a velvet lined chamber. I put some Swiss coins there, a lock of my hair and a pair of cufflinks that he still wears. But that wasn't all. I knew Nat loved to take things apart and see how they worked. Then he'd put them back together again. So inside the music box, carefully folded away where it wouldn't disturb the mechanism, I left a tiny letter, a love letter, if you must know, Lucy."

Yes, Lucy supposed, she must know, even if she didn't want to.

"You are brave to tell me, Mildred. Go on," Lucy encouraged.

"I don't know if he ever found the letter, Lucy. He never said. Of course he couldn't talk about it after he married Charlotte. But I am sure he would never have given that music box to the rummage sale. It had to have been Charlotte. I suppose deep down inside she was always jealous of me. She must have known that I was Nat's first love, and perhaps she guessed that I was still first in his heart. Don't you think so, Lucy? Why else was she constantly taking things that didn't belong to her? She knew she could never really get what she wanted."

Lucy made a sound with a lot of m's in it that she hoped was satisfactory to Mildred but noncommittal.

"I didn't want anyone pawing over that music box, Lucy. It was so delicate, so finely wrought. I didn't want anyone probing it, opening it. What if the letter was still inside? So I went early to the parish house. I didn't have a key, but I thought perhaps I could find a way in."

Lucy tried to picture Mildred (in a brown tweed skirt) scaling the porch wall like Frankie and Katherine and climbing in through the window. She failed.

"I tried the door first just in case, and it was open. I tiptoed inside and shut the door quietly behind me. The building seemed empty. I thought I could hear the Lord speaking to me: *My child, take back the token of your innocent love that the wicked seductress has defiled.*"

Lucy had to resort to taking a large swallow of her now tepid tea.

"The notions table is very crowded, Lucy, as I am sure you know. I didn't think anyone would miss one item. I was about to pick it up when I heard someone in the bathroom running the faucets. I should have trusted in the Lord and stayed where I was, but I am afraid I lost my head, Lucy. I picked up the music box and ran for the front door, just as Elsa Ebersbach was coming out of the bathroom."

"'*Mein Gott*, Mildred,' she said—you know, Lucy, it is still taking the name of the Lord in vain even it is in German—'you nearly knocked me over.'"

"I apologized and explained that I was just checking on something in notions. She gave me the rudest look, Lucy, and then she said, 'It makes no difference to me if you are as light-fingered as Charlotte Crowley. Why should she get all the little treasures?' Then she laughed horribly, and before I could explain, she left, to go up to the church, I suppose. I was mortified, mortified that she would think I was no better than Charlotte...."

For a moment, Lucy lost track of Mildred's protestations as an unwelcome fact registered. Elsa. Elsa had been in the parish house that morning. Of course, it didn't necessarily mean anything. There was no bathroom in the church. Elsa had to use the one in the parish house. That's why she had a key. Oh dear, yes. She had a key.

"I could never steal, Lucy, it would be breaking the eighth commandment!" Mildred was going on. "I hadn't thought of it as stealing until then. But, after all, the music box had belonged to Nat, even if Charlotte was in the wrong to give it to the rummage sale. I decided I would simply buy it back at the workers' sale. I thought it wouldn't do any harm just to put it somewhere out of the way where it wouldn't get damaged. I decided to look for a place in the basement...."

Mildred's voice trailed off. She averted her eyes from Lucy's and gazed down at her hands, which she folded and re-folded. In the silence, Lucy tried to imagine what might have happened. Could Mildred have accidentally knocked Charlotte down the stairs and then seen her opportunity? She had known about the coats, after all.

"Tell me the rest, Mildred," Lucy spoke at length. "No matter how terrible it is."

"Oh, Lucy. It is terrible," whispered Mildred, her hands suddenly still. "There was, well, there was this body lying sprawled at the bottom of the stairs with the bag of coats covering the face. I don't know how, but I knew it was Charlotte—yes, I do know. It was those shoes, those awful brogan shoes she'd had for years that she'd wear with anything."

Yes, she had been wearing them, Lucy remembered, she could picture the worn treads. Charlotte had been one of those effortlessly handsome women who did not have to care about fashion. Her indifference to clothes made other women look contrived or overdressed.

"But of course I couldn't be certain," Mildred went on. "I had to lift the bag off her face. When I saw, when I saw that it really was Charlotte staring at me, like a, like a dead goldfish, I, oh Lucy!"

Mildred's voice was so soft now, Lucy had to lean closer than she liked.

"I was glad. I was *glad!*"

Lucy shuddered as Mildred met her eyes again. Had she looked at that moment the way she did now? Terrified, exultant. Mad.

"Then what did you do?" Lucy prompted as calmly as possible, almost as if she were bored, not hearing the crazed confession of someone who had found a dead body and told no one.

"I put the bag back on her face. Then I hid the music box behind some pipes in the boiler room. But when I had to walk past her again to get to the stairs, I got scared. I was scared she hadn't been dead when I looked at her before. Although I swear she was, Lucy. Those awful eyes! But what if somehow I had killed her all the same, murdered her in my heart? I hated her so much!"

Mildred paused again, and put her hand to her mouth as if to stop the words that had already fled from her. Tears started trickling from the corners of her eyes. Lucy did not take the time to wonder at her own lack of sympathy.

"And so you left," Lucy stated.

Mildred nodded and let out the breath she'd been holding.

"I know it was wrong of me, Lucy. But I had to get away. I had to think. I had to pray! When I got home I knelt down before my *prie-dieu—*" (Of course, Mildred would have one of those!) "and I begged the Lord to tell me what to do. I sobbed and sobbed and even rent my blouse (a few buttons anyway) and beat my breast."

Lucy was beginning to feel queasy, but the dam had burst and she could not hold Mildred back now. She poured the last dregs of the tea, but it looked too strong and bitter to drink.

"Then when my tears were spent and I quieted again, I heard the still small voice of the Holy Spirit. *Lo, the mighty are fallen, and the meek shall be exalted. Behold I shall send you a sign and you shall know that your sin is forgiven. Then your ashes and sackcloth shall be turned to garments of joy."*

Mildred's reddened eyes glistened, a tremulous smile made her face quiver.

"Garments of joy, Lucy! That's when I knew, I knew the Lord meant for me to be Nat's bride at last. I thought I would have to make a formal confession first, so that I could be forgiven for my murderous hatred of Charlotte and be made pure for Nat. Then Frank Lomangino was arrested for her murder. I knew that must be the sign that I was forgiven. My hatred hadn't killed Charlotte, after all. Frank Lomangino killed her. He must have! He must. If he didn't…"

Mildred paused again as her premise trembled on its faulty foundations. It was really quite monstrous, Lucy thought. No one was real to Mildred, except as they furthered or hindered her fixation. But who was Lucy to cast a stone? Perhaps everyone was like that secretly, but most people didn't get exposed even to themselves, especially to themselves.

"Oh, Lucy!" Mildred almost wailed. "Why do you say he is innocent? Why?"

Mildred's face turned a ghastly shade impossible to name. Her skin, which had been illumined briefly with unseemly joy, sagged. It reminded Lucy of overworked dough that has started to dry and crack.

"According to the law, Frank Lomangino is innocent until proven guilty," said Lucy sternly. "No one but the person who murdered Charlotte knows for certain what happened. But we must all help to establish the facts. You were at the parish house that morning. You discovered Charlotte's body. You must go to the police and tell them everything you can remember, just as you have told me, and answer all their questions as honestly and carefully as you can."

Mildred recoiled from Lucy as if she were a poisonous snake.

"Oh, Lucy, surely there's no need for me to go to the police! You must understand I can't do that! What if Nat found out? What if he knew I had found Charlotte, found her and—"

"Run away without calling anyone to help," Lucy finished bluntly.

"But no one knows!" Mildred pleaded. "No one but you, Lucy, and you know very well I spoke to you in confidence. I trusted you. I thought you were my friend. But you only pretended. You pity me. I suppose you've always pitied me like all the rest of them."

She wasn't Mildred's friend, it was perfectly true. And she had invited Mildred to confide. She had been rather insistent on it. And her efforts had not been for Mildred's sake. You might even say Lucy had taken advantage of her. But pity her?

"I don't pity you, Mildred," said Lucy. "I don't pity you in the least. That is why I am urging you to be accountable for what you've done. If you are to have any sort of a life with Nat, and it is much too soon for the poor man to know what he wants, you cannot base it on a lie, even a lie by omission. And it is not true that no one but me knows. Someone saw your car. You were driving too fast out of the driveway. Your brakes screeched."

It suddenly occurred to Lucy to wonder why Mildred had hit the brakes so hard. Had she almost hit something, or someone?

"Mildred, do you remember why you stopped so suddenly?"

Mildred was silent for a moment, frowning. Was she realizing that there might be yet another witness to her ignominious flight?

"A child," she whispered. "I thought I saw a child run out into the street. I hit the brakes as hard as I could."

Good Lord deliver us, thought Lucy. First an abandoned a corpse and then a near hit and run?

"When I looked again, there was no one there. It might have been a shadow of a branch waving in the wind or my mind playing tricks on me. For heaven's sake, Lucy, I was in shock. You're a nurse. Surely you understand what happens to people when they are in shock."

And, Lucy supposed, the child might have run back into the shadows. If there had been a child in her path, it had not been hit or everyone would know of the accident. Praise whatever angels had been in attendance. Perhaps a whole squadron of angels followed Mildred's car to protect the innocents in her way.

"Yes, I understand, Mildred," Lucy said carefully. "People do make rash decisions when they are in shock." In fact, sometimes the most callous people became heroes and the most upright, craven cowards. "But you are not in shock now. You must think, think carefully and clearly."

"All I can think is everything was so wonderful, so wonderful at last and now it's horrible again. Charlotte is still ruining everything. Even when she's dead. She always has, she always will."

Mildred's tears that had begun as a trickle were now full spate. Her nose, which Lucy had never particularly noticed, revealed itself, when red, as bulbous. Well, all right. She did still pity Mildred. It was impossible not to. She went to fetch a handkerchief for Mildred, who after first waving it away, then grabbed it and blew her nose loudly.

"Listen, Mildred," said Lucy gently when Mildred had quieted again. "I don't want to alarm you, but it occurs to me that failure to report the discovery of a dead body may be questionable from a legal standpoint. The police can easily find out for themselves that your car was seen that morning. It would be better for you if you told them just what you told me, that you were in shock. And Mildred, I am afraid that if you don't tell them, I will."

Mildred stared at Lucy, the look in her baby blue eyes changing from disbelief to fear to something Lucy had never seen in Mildred before. Guile?

"If you were to do that, Lucy, you would leave me no choice. I would have to go to the police myself. I would have to tell them about your friend Elsa, how she was at the parish house before I was, washing her hands in the bathroom. Like Pontius Pilate."

Which would, by analogy, make Charlotte Crowley Christ crucified, Lucy forbore to mention.

"Or do you think, Lucy, perhaps we ought to keep this conversation to ourselves?"

Lucy had an overwhelming urge to slap Mildred across the face. If she turned her other cheek, Lucy would gladly slap her again. *Lord Jesus, if I slap Mildred Thomson in my heart is it as bad as if I really did it?*

"Of course you would have to tell them about Elsa being there," said Lucy. "That is the point. To find out the truth."

"Truth," said Mildred, in a strange tone between wistfulness and contempt. Lucy wondered if she were about to quote Pontius Pilate. "Well, of course, our Lord did say: *Then you shall know the truth and the truth shall set you free.* Nat is free now, free of Charlotte. But if Nat is angry with me, too angry to marry me, I will never be free from regret. Never."

Lucy felt a sudden sympathy for Pilate and an overwhelming urge to wash her hands of the whole sorry business. But she couldn't. There was Frank, who might be innocent. There was Elsa, who might not be. There was Mildred, who purported to be innocent of murder but was certainly guilty of fleeing, well, the scene of the crime.

There was only one fact that that was perfectly clear. Lucy had had enough for one day. As Christ had said, *sufficient unto the day is the evil thereof...* Lucy shuddered at the thought of the evil that had been done and left its lingering effects. *Deliver us,* she prayed.

"We all have regrets, Mildred," she said getting to her feet. "The garage called a while ago. Your car is ready. Let's go."

CHAPTER TWENTY-FIVE

"Tell me about the arraignment," said Rick, and he took a desultory drag on the cigarette Gerald had offered him. Rick seldom smoked, Gerald knew, except when he felt relaxed, off-stage, off-duty.

They were sitting on the porch of the Golf and Tennis Club where Rick had invited Gerald for a drink after a campaign rally. Now that the rain had cleared and the sun was out, it felt like summer again. One of the far tennis courts had dried out enough for use. Gerald and Rick sat side by side, feet up on the porch railing, gin and tonics in hand, not watching the play of the two men on the court (wives at this hour had other things to do) but lulled by the sound of the ball, going from racket to clay to racket, now and then falling out of play, so that one or the other had to make a virile serve (serves always seemed virile to Gerald, even when a woman wielded the racket). The players kept score in a good-natured fashion, a friendly game between friendly rivals, the way the world should be. Gerald tried to imagine Eisenhower or Kennedy or, God help us, Nixon shaking Khrushchev's hand over the net, dressed in matching tennis whites. The image did not cohere with the irascible leader of the Communist bloc who had arrived today in New York for talks at the UN.

That afternoon Rick had made a hard line speech about holding the Soviet leader's feet to the fire on Berlin and the absolute necessity for the US to close the missile gap with the USSR. Gerald had attended the rally last minute after a boozy lunch with Nat left him disinclined to return to the office. (Had he called Anne or maybe Grace to let them know he'd be gone for the rest of the day? He realized he wasn't sure.) Rick was much more of a cold warrior than Gerald. He'd been in Kennedy's camp from the beginning of the nomination race, whereas Gerald had supported Adlai Stevenson. Watching Rick in action, so like Kennedy with his youth and vigor, Gerald felt more reconciled to the passing of the elder statesmen, gentlemen of his father's class and generation. Whatever his differences with the cold war Democrats, however appalled he was by Kennedy's earlier collusion with McCarthy, Gerald had to admit that Kennedy, like Rick, had the ability to inspire young people to action. They were shaking the next generation out of complacency into public service.

"It went pretty much as you'd expect," Gerald began. "Frank pleaded not guilty to both charges, extortion and homicide, just as you predicted. Since he's already served prison time for a felony there wasn't a prayer of bail."

"Who's representing him?"

"Poor bastard represented himself," said Gerald. (He could be down to earth with Rick; he'd already taken off his dog collar and stuffed it in his pocket.) "His brother-in-law was there, Joe Petrone, the village deputy, one of the officers on the scene that morning. He wanted to serve as Frank's unofficial counsel, but the judge, Carmichael by the way, ordered him to sit down."

Rick nodded, exhaling slowly, thoughtfully.

"That would be a conflict of interest," Rick said, "though I assume Petrone's been taken off the case as law enforcement. He can't investigate a crime involving his own brother-in-law. I'm sure any investigation is being kicked upstairs to the sheriff, after Chief O'Brien's bungling. Still Frank Lomangino can't possibly represent himself at a criminal trial. I can't imagine a judge who would even allow that. Any idea what the family plans to do about legal counsel?"

Gerald took something more than a sip of his drink. He felt the gin spreading out from his belly. He was at the perfect point, mellow as the September light, but not drunk, not at all, just relieved to be where he was, in the company of friend. Yes, a friend. Rick was not just a parishioner.

"I don't know yet," Gerald said. "I'd like to find a way to help Frank on principle, but from a pastoral point of view, I'm in a hell of a position. Frank was employed by the church more or less at my insistence. Charlotte Crowley was the president of the WOR. To top it off, I have her widower calling me drunk at breakfast asking for protection from a one-woman temperance movement."

He regaled Rick with the story of Nat's surreptitious call. Rick laughed out loud when he told him about the gin hidden in the toilet tank. Clearly Rick needed to unwind, too.

"Then Nat insisted on coming with me to the arraignment," Gerald went on. "So there I am in the courtroom with the deceased's widower breathing gin fumes on everyone and, in the front row across the aisle, there's Frank Lomangino's wife, looking like she swallowed a watermelon, the way women do when they're ready to pop."

Although Anne, taller than Teresa, had never looked quite so huge, and it was hard to imagine the sleek, elegant Sybil Foster ever being so encumbered. Gerald suddenly wondered: would Anne turn up for him in similar circumstances? Would she carry herself with Teresa's potent mix of ferocity and pride? Frank had had his back to the room during most of the proceedings, but Gerald had caught the look that passed between Frank and Teresa as he was led away. Frank had appeared as miserable and bewildered as a man could, but Teresa had lifted her chin and smiled at him, actually smiled, with such heat and force that Frank's face broke open. It wasn't a smile exactly, more like he'd suddenly forgotten he had just been charged with murder and remembered something else. Everything else.

"Brave woman," sighed Rick.

There was something in his tone that prompted Gerald to glance at Rick. His face was so unguarded that Gerald felt he had intruded, breached the rules of manly conversation. He quickly looked away again before he could name the look he'd glimpsed. Had Rick, too, tried to picture his wife in Teresa's place? Gerald thought of Sybil, smooth and impeccable as the pearls she often wore. Anne didn't like her, called her an ice queen, hinted that Gerald was blinded by her blondness. It had not gone over well when he teased Anne for being jealous. Nor when he remarked on how well-suited Rick and Sybil seemed, working in harness on Rick's campaign. You can never tell about a marriage from the outside, Anne had said, her tone cold but laced with meanings he did not want to probe. He doubted anyone else knew how Anne had withdrawn from him, even before Hal's death. And then, on the other hand, couples whose circumstances ought to have made them wretched rubbed along happily enough. He thought of Nat's blind or perhaps not-so-blind devotion to Charlotte, how even in his cups he would gallantly retrieve her from her larcenous wanderings. And Charlotte, too, had apparently taken in stride Nat's peccadilloes.

"Another drink?" asked Rick, draining his glass, so that the ice slid into his mouth.

(So, Gerald was not the only one who sucked his ice. He felt absurdly vindicated before the absent Anne's disapproval.)

"Sure, why not?" Gerald said, instantly wondering if the offer was merely polite and he should have said no, thanks, I've got to be getting home. But Rick had already signaled the bartender.

"I'll get this round," said Gerald, fumbling past his dog collar in search of his wallet.

"Not a chance." Rick waved him away. "I've got a running tab here."

Which Gerald, of course, did not. Anne disliked the country club set and suffered their honorary membership because she could not bear to have the children swim in the town pool, a glorified mud hole. The club had a large swimming pool, sparkling with cleanliness and chlorine, and a wading pool for the twins.

"The least I can do to thank you for coming out to the rally after shepherding Nat Crowley at the arraignment."

Their drinks arrived and they raised their glasses with no need for empty words. Just a look of understanding: the world is a tough place. We do what we can to make it better. Gerald offered Rick another cigarette and was glad when Rick accepted it.

"Say," Rick exhaled his first drag, "I know a couple of lawyers, retired but still sharp, who might be willing to take Frank's case pro bono if it interested them. I'll give them a call, if you think it's a good idea."

"It's a great idea." Gerald felt himself tear up, as he sometimes did in unpredictable moments. He knew it drove Anne crazy. When Gerald choked up over a news story or while saying grace at a family gathering, she gritted her teeth. He took a drink to steady his voice. "And you're going to be a great congressman."

"Really?" Rick sounded faintly amused. "What makes you say so?"

"Because you care about the little people." The least of these my brethren. Oh, God, he was choking up again. "And you see the big picture, too."

"Thanks, Gerald. I hope I get a chance to live up to your expectations of me."

"You bet, Rick. There's a new mood in the country." Gerald let out a breath, a small gust of wind to blow away the maudlin moment. "More than a new mood, a new movement. The struggle for Civil Rights is the vanguard. We need people in Washington who understand that, who are willing to fight on the legislative front for the people who are risking their lives in the streets. Jim Crow isn't going to go quietly."

Their feet came down off the railing and they leaned in a little closer as they went on talking. Another round of drinks appeared and disappeared. They both swallowed their ice, barely aware of the chill in the air as they indulged their passion for politics, engaging in a good-natured debate about the tactics of the newly formed Student Nonviolent Coordinating Committee before they turned to a topic closer to home.

"From my last conversation with them," Rick said, "it sounds as though the heirs are on the verge of donating the Rosewood property to the Camp development fund. They have to determine the merits of a tax write-off to a sale, but they clearly want the white elephant (no pun intended) off their hands. By the way, I had a little help in persuading them from Nat's Carry Nation, aka Aunt Millie. Did you know she is from a branch of that family? Turns out she's rich as Croesus."

"Oh yes," said Gerald. "Mildred never lets me forget. The family donated part of the property for the church back at the turn of the century. I tried to talk her out of using her influence with her nephews. Afraid she'd queer the Rosewood deal with her backing of it. I put it down to your powers of persuasion that they want to go forward. But yes, I do have some idea of the pile Mildred's sitting on. She tithes, you know." The part of Gerald still capable of judgment knew he was being indiscreet, but the rest didn't care. "And she's put a down payment on Nat's soul. More than a down payment. She paid off his mortgage. Don't see how he's going to wriggle free now. Poor son of a bitch. Not very bright. Clearly an easy mark, but such, such a…gentleman."

Gerald wished he could stop himself, but Rick was leaning in to hear him. Rick would understand. He wouldn't judge. He wasn't harsh like Anne. Women were supposed to be so soft-hearted, but really they were hard as nails. It was men, men who bled when those nails were hammered into them.

"Would you believe, after the arraignment Nat walked right up to Teresa Lomangino and patted her shoulder. 'I'm so sorry my dear, so sorry about this awful business. Frank did such a good job on our yew hedge. Can't understand it, can't understand it at all. If I can be of any help to you…'

"I tried to lead him away, but Teresa Lomangino put her hand on his arm. 'I'm sorry for your loss, Mr. Crowley.' And then she turned and walked out of the courtroom, and Nat kept muttering, 'Damn fine woman. Spirited. Reminds me of Charlotte.'"

Without warning, Gerald's tears slipped the gate. It was the third drink hitting him all at once. Then he found his head in his hands. And there was a hand on his shoulder. Rick's.

"Sorry, sorry!" Gerald managed to right himself. "Don't know what's gotten into me."

"No need for apologies, Gerald," said Rick sitting back. "Perfectly understandable."

He picked up Gerald's pack of cigarettes from the table and lit one for each of them. There, that was better. Rick was a true friend, knew what to say and what not to say. They sat and smoked for a moment. Now it was actually dark. He should go home or at least call Anne. But he didn't want to. Rick understood better than Anne what he was going through. But wait. He wasn't being fair. Anne was working hard running the rummage sale, even though she hadn't wanted to. This morning she had volunteered to commandeer Mildred.

Mildred.

"Rick, I just remembered something. Might be important, might not be."

"Let's hear it."

"Anne saw Mildred's car the morning of Charlotte's death. Says she was tearing out of the driveway like a bat out of hell, brakes screeching at the end of the driveway. I've got to report that to someone, find out who, exactly, is in charge of the investigation. Don't you think?"

He appealed to Rick who took a long puff of his cigarette.

"I think you're right, Gerald. It should be reported. I just don't know if you ought to be the one to do it. I mean, Mildred Thomson is your parishioner. Frank Lomangino was a church employee. As you said yourself, you're in a hell of a position pastorally."

"But who else would report it?" He paused a moment as it dawned on him. "Anne. Anne was the one who saw the car."

Rick carefully stubbed out his cigarette.

"I don't want to worry you, Gerald. But if Anne saw the car, where was she?"

Outside. Alone.

"If there's a halfway decent investigation, and there will be, especially if we can get Frank a competent lawyer, everyone will have to be questioned. Everyone will need an alibi. Do you know if anyone else was there that morning? Besides Frank, Mildred, and," he hesitated, "Anne?"

Gerald really hoped he was not going to be sick. Tears were bad enough. It was the drinks, the three drinks.

"I don't know. I was in bed. But I thought I heard the organ crashing—Elsa likes to play loud sometimes; she doesn't care what time it is. And oh, I don't know, Lucy Way must have been there early, too, for altar guild or some blasted thing. Oh, God, Rick, what a mess. How could this happen in a stupid little backwater. I wanted to stay in the city, you know, but Anne, after Hal...."

Get a grip, he ordered himself, grabbing his own wrist. Then again, he felt Rick lightly touch his shoulder.

"A word of advice, Gerald. Wait till the proper authorities contact you. Answer their questions, but don't get drawn into speculating about your parishioners. Amateur detectives are all very well in fiction, but in real life they can get hurt and get other people hurt. Meanwhile, I'll see what I can do about finding a lawyer for Frank Lomangino. I'll make sure he has all the facts. Leave everything to the professionals. You've got enough on the docket."

Gerald suddenly felt light, light-headed and light. His whole center of gravity had shifted as Rick lifted the burden from him. *Come unto me all ye who are heavy laden.* (He couldn't help thinking in Gospel terms, professional hazard.) Bear one another's burdens. Rick was quiet about it, didn't mouth pieties or go in for smarmy public displays of civic religion, but Rick was a damn good Christian.

"Thank you, Rick, I appreciate your help."

"Think nothing of it," said Rick. "Glad to be able to do it."

Rick glanced at his watch and got to his feet. Gerald was relieved to find he could do the same.

"Now, for what can't be helped," Rick grimaced.

It took Gerald only a beat.

"Yeah, I didn't call my wife either."

They grinned at each other and gave each other a mock punch on the shoulder. Neither of them was sorry to be late.

At least not yet.

CHAPTER TWENTY-SIX

She was being driven slowly (no, actually, not slowly at all) out of her mind. And there was nothing Dr. Aiken could do about it. Not that she had even seen him since horrible Charlotte Crowley went and got herself killed and left Anne in charge of the wretchedness that was the Church of Regeneration Rummage Sale. She plunged her hands into scalding dishwater, knowing she should put on gloves (her hands had been photographed for their beautiful shape to grace the opening of her college yearbook) but she found the hot water both soothed and stoked her cold fury. And her beautiful hands were otherwise useless now, same as the mind she was losing.

She pictured herself in Dr. Aiken's office. No couch, which was just as well. His desk, so big it made her think of a steamer ship, the kind her family had sailed on to Europe, and an easy chair for his patients.

"So," she told him in her mind, "Gerald disappeared again, right after breakfast. I haven't seen or heard from him since."

The dishwater blocked the sound of the television in the other room where the children were sitting sprawled on the rug, no doubt spilling ice cream all over. Katherine insisted on making what she called ice cream soup, stirring and stirring until the ice cream melted, then sipping (or rather slurping it with a spoon). She had taught Peter and Janie how to do it with such sisterly kindness and care that Anne had not had the heart to forbid it.

The Dr. Aiken in her mind shook his head as though he knew exactly how she felt, as though his days, too, were spent getting children fed and dressed and off to school then home and fed and put to bed and in the interim doing laundry, paying bills, ironing, cooking cleaning up after the half-blind cleaning woman and, if that weren't numbing enough, doing it all with a parade of parishioners outside her window and children asking where's Daddy and then after a while not asking.

He would look at her kindly through the horn-rimmed glasses that so perfectly framed his brown eyes. He would lean part of his six foot two expanse over the desk and say, "Unconsciously you blame Gerald for Hal's death. Naturally he avoids you—and his own unconscious guilt. We've talked about this before, Anne."

"And I don't want to talk about it again!"

Anne shocked herself by answering Dr. Aiken out loud. (She was glad the children had the television turned up loud.) She never even talked to herself, unlike Gerald who was always mumbling to himself, just like his mother. Now here she was talking back to what she called a fig newton of her imagination. Of course Dr. Aiken was always encouraging her to express herself. Repression was a no-no. It led to all kinds of psychiatric evils—psychosomatic disorders, frigidity, and no doubt eventually ax murder, a mild-mannered housewife gone mad.

The plates washed, Anne reached for the frying pan and began to scrub the greasy imprints of the hamburgers she'd cooked as usual for the children's dinner. She did not know how Rosalie managed to get her girls to eat casseroles with hidden vegetables, one ingredient touching another, things her children would not countenance. (Because she spoiled them, Gerald's mother said. Because she was lazy, she admitted to herself, and hated to cook. Because she secretly resented her femininity, Dr. Aiken added in her mind, unbidden.)

There were days when she regretted flushing the tranquilizers down the toilet, dizziness be damned. Today was one of them. When she had pulled into the driveway with the children, Frankie, Junior still in tow, she almost forgave Gerald his love affair with gin and wished she could join him in a binge. Amos McCready hurtled out of the church oblivious to the path of her car. Ever since Frank Lomangino's arrest he had reinstated himself as sexton, and if he ever went home to change his clothes she wasn't aware of it. His beard, more reminiscent of a Viking berserker than a biblical patriarch, had twisted itself into alarming forks and tufts of unruly hair stuck out on his head like goat horns. Today he was brandishing some sort of ecclesiastical implement and shouting while Elsa, armed with something that looked suspiciously like a vodka bottle (half full?) stumbled after him. Anne swerved just in time and stopped so abruptly that the children shrieked before they tumbled out of the car following Frankie's excited lead.

"They're gonna fight! They're gonna fight!" shouted Frankie.

"Stay back!" Anne ordered the children, as Amos turned to menace Elsa with his weapon, long as a spear with a curved spike on the end. Merciful God (if there was one), that thing could easily take out an eye.

"*Will a lion roar in a forest if he hath no prey, will a young lion cry out of his den if he hath taken nothing!*"

Amos sounded like a lion himself, albeit a mangy, elderly one, but Elsa gave no ground, swinging her bottle over her head as if she held a lariat.

"*Sprich nicht mit mir, du verrückter Mann!*" Elsa bellowed back.

Don't talk to me, you crazy man, Anne took momentary pleasure in remembering enough college German to translate. (Anne realized now how strange it was that she'd majored in German during the war. All she knew then was that she loved Bach and her German professor, not necessarily in that order.)

"How many times I tell you: do not come in the church while I practice, Nincompoop!"

The children were now jumping up and down and clapping as they chanted.

"Nincompoop, Nincompoop! Poop, poop, poop!"

"Stop it!" Anne ordered them. "Go into the house!"

But they were much too excited and distracted to heed her.

"Can a bird fall in a snare upon the earth, where no gin is for him? Shall one take up a snare from the earth, and have taken nothing at all?"

And he took another step towards her, but Elsa didn't back off.

"Ybergeschnappt alter schlingel."

Crazy old man, Anne translated as Elsa lifted her bottle, but she was so short it would only have hit his chin, if he hadn't dodged her neatly, at the same time knocking the bottle out of her hand with his makeshift spear.

"Don't talk that kraut gibberish to me, you wee schnauzer."

Elsa made a convincingly non-human sound as she dived for her bottle, which fortunately (or unfortunately) had not broken.

"Children, inside now!" Anne raised her voice more than she liked to.

Anne grabbed Frankie and Katherine by the collars and spun them around with some force, knowing the twins would follow if those two obeyed. To her relief, Katherine made for the porch, pulling Frankie with her.

"Shall a trumpet be blown in the city, and the people not be afraid? Shall there be evil in a city, and the LORD hath not done it? Surely the Lord GOD will do nothing, but he revealeth his secret unto his servants the prophets."

"Who makes you a prophet!" Elsa, upright again, bottle in hand again, almost spat. "You are a nothing but *schwatzer.*" Windbag. "You have no respect for music. You pig bladder-playing Scotchman, you!"

"The bags of the pipes are made of cowhide, you wee *minger.*" Anne was just as glad she could not translate Scots. "Call yourself a musician, do you?"

They both raised their weapons again. Anne looked around for help. But the few workers milling around down by the parish house seemed oblivious. Where were the busybodies when you needed them? From whence cometh any help at all?

"Stop it right now, both of you, or I'll call the police!"

Elsa registered Anne's presence apparently for the first time. She had the grace to blush, the rest of her face turning as red as her nose.

"Anne, Mrs. Bradley. You will forgive me please. I am afraid I lose my temper when this, this," she stopped herself, "when Mr. McCready will not leave when I ask."

"Aye, Mrs. Bradley. It would be best you call the police when an innocent man just doing his job cleaning the candle sconces" (the implement apparently had another purpose besides maiming) "in the house of the Lord is attacked from behind with a blunt object—"

"I ask you politely several times first," Elsa interrupted.

"And I told you as many times, I have as much right to do my job as ye."

"Both of you, please—"

"So as I was saying, Mrs. Bradley, by all means call the police and let us hope they do a better job than they did the last time an innocent person was attacked from behind."

And he made a slight nod of his unkempt head in Elsa's direction; it was not lost on her.

"If you have something to say, man, say it!"

"It is not for me to say aught. I was na there when it happened."

"So *you* say," snorted Elsa.

Had Amos been there, Anne suddenly wondered? He had been one of the first on the scene. He had no motivation that she knew of to knock Charlotte down the stairs, but perhaps it had served his purposes to have Frank carted off to jail. He had been retired against his will from the position Frank had been hired to fill (and abruptly vacated). And could Elsa have crept up behind Charlotte with a vodka bottle and murderous intent? Much as she admired Elsa's uncompromising passion for music, she had the evidence before her of the organist's explosive temper.

"Mrs. Bradley!"

Salvation or anyway distraction appeared in the form of Teresa Lomangino walking up the driveway, her belly in the lead, her little girls trailing her. (What on earth did Frankie want with Katherine when he had so many sisters?)

"Is Frankie still with you?"

"The children are in the house, Mrs. Lomangino. I'll go call him. You two," she turned to Elsa and Amos who were waving to Teresa and asking after Frank, as if he was not in jail awaiting trial for murder, and as if they had not been assaulting each other and making veiled accusations a moment before. "Go home. Both of you. It's been a long day."

"Yes, of course," said Elsa. "After I close the organ."

"I'll just put this away," Amos indicated his weapon, "and lock the sacristy."

And they went off to the church together as meekly as two errant sheep returned to the fold.

When Anne turned towards the house, she saw the children duck behind the porch railing. They hadn't gone inside at all. What had they made of that display?

"I see you there," she said as severely as she could. "Frankie, your mother is here."

He stood up and came off the porch, dragging his feet through the gravel and scowling as he went. What did Katherine see in him? Both she and the twins stood on the porch looking dejected at his departure.

"Time to go, Frankie. Say thank you to Mrs. Bradley."

"Thank you, Mrs. Bradley," he said without looking up.

"I hope he didn't give you any trouble," Teresa added a little anxiously.

"The children have been no trouble at all," Anne assured her, and before she could think better of it, she grimaced and nodded towards the church.

Teresa actually smiled at her, perhaps for the first time.

"Them two," Teresa nodded, "oil and water. Frank told me all about them. Used to make me laugh with his stories about this place."

There was an awkward silence as the impossibility of small talk on this or any subject made itself evident.

"Come on kids, let's go. Thanks again, Mrs. Bradley. And thanks for, you know."

For not dismissing your impossible request, Anne finished the sentence silently, for agreeing to dump it in my husband's lap.

If she ever saw him again, that is.

Anne drained the dishwater and started to dry the dishes. She hated this moment, the shift from rage to fear. It was still only a little after seven, and it was not unusual for Gerald to be this late or later, but it was unusual for him not to call, for her not to know, however vaguely, that he was making calls, or going to a meeting, or that it was his night with the firemen or with his poker-playing clergy cronies. (Her only night was choir night, just across the driveway, and too often she had to hire a babysitter.) Whether or not he forgot to call her during the day, he usually called Grace for messages. Grace had stayed till five today because she and her girls were helping with the rummage sale, and he hadn't called by then. Of course he might have called when Grace was upstairs or when Anne was out, but he should have tried again. He knew what time she fed the children. Or maybe he didn't. Maybe he didn't bother to think about them at all. She tried to retrieve her anger, but it was useless.

What if he'd had an accident? What if his car was overturned off the road and no one had found him yet? Surely if that had happened someone would have seen the car and gotten him to the hospital. What if he'd had a heart attack, like his father? If he was dead, what would she do? As she put away the dishes, she pictured herself and the children on their own (as they were most of the time, anyway). They would have to move out of the rectory, of course, and get a place of their own. Maybe even an apartment. She would have to get a job. What kind of work could she do that would let her be home for the children in the afternoon? Be a secretary, like Grace? She couldn't type. She was not qualified to teach school. She would hate to be a waitress. Maybe she could work in a bookstore. They would manage somehow. It might not be so bad....

Yes, it would, she stopped herself. It would be terrible for Gerald to be dead and he must be dead or he would have called.

Just then the phone rang, and Anne nearly slipped on the damp patch where she'd mopped up Peter's spilled chocolate milk. She got to the phone by the second ring.

"Rectory," she answered.

"Anne, it's Lucy. Are you all right? You sound out of breath. Have I caught you at a bad time?"

"Oh, Lucy, no, I'm fine. I thought you might be Gerald." Or the police, or the hospital, she managed not to say.

"Oh, if you are expecting him to call I won't keep you," said Lucy.

"No, it's all right," said Anne, not sure that it was but not wanting Lucy to hang up.

"What I have to say is rather serious and, well, confidential," Lucy sounded hesitant. "I think I ought to talk to Gerald about it."

"Of course," said Anne, and then she couldn't help it, though Lucy had delicately implied it was none of her business, she couldn't stand any more suspense. "Is it about Mildred?"

There was a silence as Lucy no doubt consulted her conscience. And Anne's conscience snapped to attention. If Mildred...if Mildred was the murderer and Lucy had found out, she could be in danger, terrible danger, and it would be all Anne's fault.

"Are you all right, Lucy?" Anne asked breathlessly. "Are you safe? I should never have asked you to—"

"I'm quite all right, Anne. And I don't believe Mildred is dangerous, or at least not murderous. I'd better tell you. Mildred was there that morning. She found Charlotte's body. She was almost certainly already dead, but Mildred didn't report the body. She fled the scene."

"Good Heavens! That's a crime, isn't it?" asked Anne.

"I'm not sure," said Lucy. "But it is something the police should know, and I thought Gerald ought to hear about it first."

"Yes, I suppose he should," said Anne, knowing she should simply say, I will have him call you when he gets in, and end the conversation. But she found she desperately wanted another adult to talk to, one she was not married to, not furious with. "Teresa Lomangino wants to ask Gerald if her brother Joe Petrone can investigate, unofficially."

Lucy was silent again and Anne hoped she did not disapprove of her for being indiscreet, which she realized she had been.

"That's a sticky wicket," said Lucy before Anne could apologize. "I'm sure there will be an investigation, and we must all cooperate. You are the one who heard Mildred's car that morning, so you might as well know. Mildred did slam on her brakes at the end of the driveway because she thought she saw a child, but then whatever it was ran back into the shadows. She thinks she might have imagined it because of the shock. Thank God no one else was killed."

Anne was silent for a moment, pondering. A child, a child darting back into the shadows on that Sunday morning, that Sunday morning when Katherine disappeared before breakfast to play with Frankie. She wasn't sure where the Lomanginos lived, but she did know that Frank sometimes walked to work.

"Lucy," said Anne, "I think it was a real child. I think it might have been Frankie, Junior and if it was...."

Just then Anne heard the front door open.

"Lucy, Gerald just came in. Shall I get him?"

"Oh, no. Not if he's just come home. I'm sure he's had a long day. If you wouldn't mind telling him, I'll call in the morning to make an appointment to see him."

And before Anne could ask if it was all right to tell Gerald what she now knew, Lucy said goodnight. A moment later, Gerald came down the back steps to the kitchen, stumbling and stubbing his toe.

"Damn, damn, damn, damn, damn!" he swore furiously.

Anne wondered if somehow Lucy had intuited that Gerald might be in no condition to take her call.

CHAPTER TWENTY-SEVEN

Katherine leaned against the railing and looked out over the stairs. She had to walk out on tiptoes to do it. Behind her was the first part of the stairs going down to the place they turned and below her was the rest of the stairs that led to the landing where you could go one way to the kitchen and the other way to the front hall. If she leaned her head out, she could see the darkness of the front hall. It was like a lake at night. The light slipping out from her father's door was light from the motorboat he took out on the lake where they went in the summer when he went fishing after supper. If he caught a fish, the camp cooks served it to him for breakfast, lying on its side with its eye still open. Everyone in the dining hall clapped, but she did not like to look at the dead fish or see her father lift up its skeleton.

Craning her head out and around, she could also see light from the kitchen tiptoeing upstairs to the landing. She could hear the sink turning on and off and her mother's footsteps going back and forth. In what her mother called her mindseye (the one that could look everywhere) she could see her mother cleaning and cleaning the messes her father made with ice cubes and lemons and cracker crumbs. She wanted to call for her mother, but she was afraid. Her mother might be mad at her. Or mad at her father. She didn't know.

Her father had fallen asleep on her bed when he came in to say goodnight. He had not come up for prayers. Her mother told them he'd had a long day. Maybe he would say goodnight after they were asleep. Katherine had lain in bed awake, watching her open door, bright white with the light from the hall shining on it. Then her father came in swaying from one side to the other like he was pretending to be a bear. He sat down hard on her bed, and it made a creaking noise, and then he leaned over her and made everything dark and too hot.

"Good night, sleep tight, and don't let the bedbugs bite," he said and gave her one of those loud smacking kisses. She could feel the bristles on his cheek that he called sandpaper. Then instead of getting up and going out of her room, he scooped her up like she was Janie or Peter and leaned back against the headboard of her bed, holding her a little too tightly. She held her breath and stayed very still. She was glad she had her Tigger with her. Slowly her father's arms dropped away from her, but he still didn't get up, and she didn't dare move. Then he started to snore like a dragon. She didn't know what to do. At last her mother came into the room.

"Gerald," her mother said in a loud mad whisper. "Gerald. Wake up!"

Her father snorted awake. Katherine rolled away as he got up abruptly and padded out of the room after her mother without looking back.

Katherine had tried to sleep, but she couldn't. Her pillow smelled like her father and her sheets were all out of shape from his lifting her up. She wanted her mother to tuck her in again the right way, to make the sheets smooth and cool the way only her mother knew how. She waited and waited for her mother, but she didn't come. Finally Katherine got up and tiptoed into the hall. She peeked into Janie's room and saw that her bed was empty, so she must be in Peter's room. One or the other of the twins usually snuck out of their room and went to the other one's bed every night. They weren't allowed to, but they never got in trouble.

It wasn't fair.

When she was little, her mother told her, younger than Peter and Janie, before they were even born, she used to climb out of her crib and get into bed with her big brother Hal. She didn't remember him, but sometimes, when she was falling asleep, she remembered feeling warm and snug, surrounded by stuffed animals, safer than she ever felt now.

It wasn't fair that Hal was dead.

Once she asked her mother if she was going to die, too, when she was five. Her mother said of course not. The sickness that happened to Hal did not happen to most people. It would not happen to her. Now she was seven, older than Hal had ever been in his life, which did not make sense to Katherine for an older brother. When she pictured Hal in her mindseye, he was still bigger than she was, at least as big as Frankie. Katherine wished Hal were here with her now, both of them sneaking out of bed, leaning over the railing together. If she did not look to see that Hal wasn't there, she could pretend he was.

Just then Katherine heard her mother's steps on the kitchen stairs coming up to the landing.

"Lean back," she imagined Hal saying. "Don't let her see you."

If her mother came up the stairs, she could run back to her room, but her mother didn't.

"The coast is clear," whispered Hal just the way Frankie would have.

And she leaned out in time to see her mother carrying a coffee cup stepping down into the darkness of the front hall. Then light pushed away the dark as her mother opened the door to her father's office.

"Come on," said Hal. "Let's spy on the grownups."

Spy on the grownups was a game she and Frankie played at the parish house. She had never played it by herself, but she wasn't alone, not really. Hal was with her, even though she couldn't see him because he was dead. She crept down the stairs keeping her feet close to the wall the way Frankie had showed her so the steps wouldn't creak. Maybe if she was quiet enough she could be invisible, too, like Hal.

"Stop here," said Hal when she got to the landing. "If anyone comes out, run!"

Katherine sat crouched at the corner where the landing met the stairs into the hall. Her mother had turned out the lights in the kitchen, so even with the light coming from her father's door it was dark on the landing, dark enough to pretend Hal was hiding there with her. Then the door to the office closed and it got darker. She might have been scared, except for Hal being so near.

"Listen," he told her.

She tried, but she could not hear what they were saying. She could hardly hear her mother's voice at all, but her father's roared and rumbled. He might have turned into a bear, like the pictures he used to draw for Valentine's Day. Her mother had let her see them once. Her father was a big bear and Hal was a bear cub. Her mother was a tall, upright rabbit wearing a dress (unlike the father bear who only had fur) and Katherine was a baby rabbit. Katherine leaned against the wall and let herself see pictures. They all lived in a cozy den, like in a Beatrix Potter book. The mother rabbit sat in a chair, knitting by the fire. The father bear smoked a pipe and read a newspaper. Smoke rings floated around his head. The brother bear and the sister rabbit had a train set with a track, and the train made a sound like a real train. The engine was dark green and shiny, and of course the caboose was red.

She could see it all so clearly, Katherine didn't know it was turning into a dream and she was falling asleep until suddenly she wasn't.

"Damn it, dear! You know I can't trespass on the official investigation!" her father yelled.

Katherine was shaking all over. Can't trespass. Trespass, trespass. Her stomach felt hot and upside down. It was dark, and she didn't remember why she was there by herself in the dark hall. Hal, Hal had been with her, but now he was gone. And her father was shouting about trespassing. Maybe her father knew, knew about her and Frankie. Trespassing. Maybe God had told him.

"You shouldn't have encouraged them."

Her father was still yelling. He did know. He did. Her mother was saying something, begging him not to punish them, but Katherine couldn't hear the words.

"Stop fussing at me!" her father roared. "I told you Rick Foster's going to find Frank a lawyer."

There came the sound of something crashing and breaking. Katherine was afraid, but her mother was in there, alone with her father, her mother rabbit. She had to do something brave, like Hal would have or Frankie. She wished she had her javelin. She stood up and went down the stairs, through the hall and to the closed door to her father's office.

"What? No! I'm sorry, dear, I didn't mean to. No, let me. Of course, I'll call and talk to him. Wait, dear."

Katherine put her hand on the door knob, but she was shaking too hard to turn it. Then all at once the door swung open and knocked her down. She started to cry.

"Katherine," her mother said, not bending down to comfort her. "What are you doing out of bed?"

She found she was crying too hard to make words.

"Did you have a bad dream?" her mother asked in her nicer voice.

Katherine didn't know but she nodded and finally said, "I need you to tuck me in again."

She needed her mother to protect her, from her father, from God.

"Go on upstairs," her mother said. "I'll come up when I've cleaned up this broken cup."

Katherine saw that her mother was holding broken pieces of the cup in her hands, but Katherine didn't want to go upstairs alone.

"No!" She started to sob.

Then her father was there in the doorway, blocking out all the light.

"No, dear, don't you take her!" her father pushed her mother aside. "Katherine, you've got to stop bothering your mother. Can't you see she's had a long day? Can't you see, she needs a rest from you kids!"

Her father grabbed her arm hard so it hurt and began pulling her to the stairs. He was going to punish her, punish her for trespassing.

"Gerald!" her mother said, but she didn't stop him.

On the landing Katherine twisted and tore out of her father's grip. She ran the rest of the way up the stairs and got into her bed and hid under the covers. A moment later she heard her father lumbering up the stairs and down the hall. She could hear her father breathing. In her mindseye she could see him standing against her door, but he didn't look like her father. He looked like a robot she had seen against that door in a nightmare with a square head and a square body. If he came towards her bed, she would hear him clanking. But he didn't. He just breathed for a while longer, horribly, loudly, and then he went away.

Katherine stayed awake for as long as she could, waiting for her mother to come. She needed to tell her mother that she and Frankie hadn't done anything bad. The sign said No Trespassing, but she and Frankie belonged in the wood. The fairy lady with the thistledown hair had said so. But what if her mother didn't believe her? What if only she and Frankie could see the lady? No, she couldn't tell her mother about the lady. Frankie wouldn't want her to. They would just have to run away to the wood, where even God couldn't get them, run away and not come back till they caught the bad man and put him in jail....

CHAPTER TWENTY-EIGHT

Lucy stepped out of Gerald's parish house office aware that her feathers had been ruffled more than she liked or was accustomed to. She paused on the steps, letting the fine morning soothe her, a perfect September morning, warm sun, cool air, Virginia creeper garlanding the edge of the overgrown Rosewood estate. She hoped the weather would hold for the rummage sale, though no doubt people would stand in line in the pouring rain if they had to, especially this year when everyone wanted to see where the murder had happened, though, of course, since Frank's arrest the basement had been locked. (She wondered if she could persuade the proper authorities to search behind the pipes for Mildred's hidden music box.)

After a moment or two, Lucy's feathers began to settle. Poor Gerald looked awful, as though he hadn't been sleeping well. His being under so much strain would also explain why he was more abrupt than usual, not quite rude but definitely dismissive, even (here's where the ruffling came in) condescending. She had always had the impression that Gerald respected her. Why, she didn't know; she would have thought she was too far on the Anglo-Catholic end of the Episcopal spectrum for his taste. Yet he was usually deferential towards her, which made her determined to be tolerant of his insistence on the Gospel's relevance to what he persisted in calling today's society (as if Christians were a gaggle of earnest debutantes). Of course the Gospel was relevant, she had more than once wanted to say to him; eternal verities always are.

Given his passion for the Social Gospel, as he called it, Lucy had thought Gerald would have been more enthusiastic about information that might possibly help clear Frank Lomangino of murder charges, but she supposed his caution was correct.

"Even if Mildred Thomson did slam on the brakes to avoid hitting Frank Lomangino's son," Gerald had reasoned, "we don't know whether the boy's father was with him. Frankie could have been going to the parish house to look for his father. If the kid was out on his own, it's more likely he'd be careless crossing the street."

Lucy had to acknowledge the logic of this scenario.

"But surely the authorities should be told," Lucy said. "Mildred should be questioned. All of us who were there that morning should be questioned."

"I assume that's why Sheriff Harris wants to meet with me," Gerald said with a note of impatience. "By the way, I'm expecting him any minute."

Lucy took the hint and got to her feet.

"Not that I don't appreciate your coming to me. But listen, Lucy. Amateur detectives are all very well in fiction, but in real life they can get hurt and get other people hurt. This is not an Agatha Christie novel."

"And I am not Miss Marple," Lucy said before he could say it and not only dismiss but offend her.

Well, she had been a little offended, she admitted to herself. She did not like to be viewed as a cliché, even a clever literary one, and even if she had already made the comparison herself. Apparently she was not as immune to vanity as she'd liked to believe. Lucy sighed. People were beginning to arrive to work at the rummage sale, and she ought to join them, though what she could (or could not) say to Teresa Lomangino made her heart quail. Would it be permissible to inquire if Frankie, Junior had dashed off that fateful morning unaccompanied? Wasn't that exactly the sort of question she ought to leave to the professionals? After all, she had just protested that she was not Miss Marple. She was Lucy Way, a quiet, older woman who preferred to mind her own business, or beeswax, as people said, which led to nostalgic and irrelevant thoughts of polishing pews in the empty church. Feeling somewhat restored to herself, Lucy started down the steps.

"Deputy Petrone!" she heard someone call in a sharp voice. "May I ask just what you think you are doing on the premises, and don't give me any malarkey about how you're working the large appliances tent."

Lucy knew she should keep going, make her presence known, but instead she stopped. Peering around a shrub, she saw Sheriff Harris squeeze out from behind the steering wheel of his official vehicle, which he had parked haphazardly in front of the main entrance to the parish house. Sheriff Harris (whom she privately called Sheriff Harass) was a bald, egg-shaped man who always made her think of illustrations of Humpty Dumpty in *Through the Looking Glass*. He was not a member of the Church of Regeneration, but Lucy knew him from her days as a rural nurse. She had once testified on behalf of a woman who tried to have her husband arrested for assault and battery. The woman's case was dismissed; unjustly, Lucy thought.

"And good morning to you, Sheriff," Joe answered him. "No, I am not working large appliances, but it so happens my sister is in charge of children's clothes. And she is not going to let her husband being arrested on hearsay stand in the way of her official duties."

Sheriff Harris had a rolling gait as if he walked on ship deck. She supposed he might suffer from arthritis in his hip joints and she ought to feel sympathetic.

"I'm not discussing the case with you, Petrone."

The sheriff walked up so close to him that Joe could have been forgiven for stepping back, but he didn't. If Joe hadn't been so thin and wiry, they would have been belly to belly.

"And you are not discussing it with anyone else, you read me, Petrone, not anyone. You and Chief O'Brien are off the case, and you can thank your lucky stars you're not out of a job after that display of incompetence and possibly worse."

"What's that supposed to mean, Sheriff?" demanded Joe.

Sheriff Harris didn't answer for a moment. Lucy remembered how she had always feared he was about to spit. She winced at the thought of his expectoration hitting the driveway, or worse, Joe Petrone's carefully polished shoes.

"What do you call it when the local authorities at the scene of a possible crime allow a witness, maybe a suspect, Goddamnit, Petrone, the same guy who found the body, to dispose of the evidence? And what if one of the aforementioned authorities is a blood relative?"

Lucy had to restrain herself from popping out from behind the shrub to explain that in-laws were related by marriage not by blood.

"I thought you told me you weren't going to discuss the case with me, Sheriff," said Joe, who still hadn't moved.

"Don't get smart with me, Petrone."

The sheriff grabbed the other man's shirt and tried to pull him nose to nose, a gesture that would have been more effective if Joe hadn't been a head taller than the sheriff. As it was, the sheriff appeared to be addressing Joe's Adam's apple.

"That no-good jailbird brother-in-law of yours is in way over his head. If you care about that pretty little sister of yours, you'll keep your nose out of my investigation. Take that long dago schnoz of yours and go smell the daisies unless you want to end up pushing daisies."

Sheriff Harris loosed Joe's shirt and started rolling towards the steps to the office where he would surely catch Lucy at her eaves-dropping post, unless.... Quickly and quietly, Lucy retraced her steps and then opened and closed the door as if she had only just come out of the office.

"Good morning, Sheriff Harris," she said as he rounded the shrub that had been her cover.

"Oh, Miss Way, it's you," said the sheriff. "Reverend in?"

He kept going up the steps, so that she had to shrink back out of his way. A gentleman would have waited for her to descend the steps.

"Yes," she said. "He's expecting you."

She shouldn't have said that, she realized. The sheriff turned and eyed her with what could only be described as suspicion.

"Terrible business," he said at length.

"Yes, indeed," she answered, and she continued down the steps.

Sheriff Harris would be interrogating her soon enough, she told herself, and she would tell him what she knew. There was nothing else she could do. Just because he was an unpleasant, bullying little man did not mean he would not do his job.

And yet and yet...hadn't he just threatened Joe Petrone? What did he mean when he said Frank Lomangino was in way over his head? Lucy paused again at the bottom of the steps, aware that she was on a slippery slope. She had just lied, not in word, but in deed when she opened and closed the door to make it seem as though she had not overheard the exchange between the two men. She looked down the driveway. Joe Petrone appeared to be heeding the sheriff's warning and leaving the premises, though every few steps he stopped and kicked the gravel just like his nephew Frankie. Should she call out to him, run after him? If she took it upon herself to tell Joe about Mildred's flight and her near collision with Frankie, Junior would she be helping him, endangering him, or simply meddling?

Joe stopped, turned towards the parish house, took a step or two back up the driveway. Before she could consider the right or wrong of it, Lucy found herself waving. Joe waved back tentatively as if uncertain the gesture was meant for him, and then he turned again and trudged away.

"He who hesitates is lost," Lucy said out loud, not sure whether she meant herself or Joe.

Lucy wished she could talk to Anne, who clearly shared her suspicions. But she knew she should not. Anne's husband (and Lucy's rector) obviously disapproved of their speculations. Perhaps he was afraid for his wife's safety, and rightly so. If Frank was innocent, someone else was...guilty.

(Not Elsa, she prayed again, please don't let it be Elsa. Forgive me, Lord, she added at once. For it was an absurd prayer. It either was Elsa or it wasn't. Only God and Elsa knew.)

Lucy found herself turning away from the driveway where she could hear women remarking on the sheriff's car in hushed and excited tones as they maneuvered around it. She needed to calm herself before she went inside the parish house where gossip and speculation must be running rife. She made her way around the furniture and large appliances tent to the gap in the wall that led to Rosewood. After effectively lying to Sheriff Harris, she believed she was more than equal to a spot of trespassing.

Lucy felt better as soon as she stepped into the wood. She could still hear the sounds of cars pulling into the church driveway next door and people calling out greetings, but it felt as though some invisible curtain hung between the two worlds. The wood had its own non-human concerns; spiders waited in webs made luminous by early light. Now and then, even without a breeze, a leaf detached from a branch and made its spiraling journey to ground still damp from yesterday's rain. Moss made its slow, determined progress on the old stone wall beside the carriageway. The estate had been abandoned shortly after the First War, when the staff required to keep up a mansion and extensive gardens became too costly. Lucy had never seen it in its heyday, but she rather liked it in its tangled state that called to her mind the tale of Sleeping Beauty. The wood felt enchanted, in a benign way, as though it protected something worthy or was worthy of protection. She knew that Gerald Bradley and Rick Foster had plans for turning the estate into a children's camp. She hoped not too much asphalt would be involved. Children had enough of that at public schools and certainly in the inner city, as Gerald called it. Lucy thought of Katherine and Frankie in these woods, their sense both of wonder and belonging. Aloud she murmured a few lines of a Yeats poem:

Come away, O human child
To the waters and the wild
With a fairy, hand in hand,
For the world's more full of weeping than
you can understand.

Lucy walked down the old road where grass had already thrust through the pavement here and there, scattering bits of gravel, leaving potholes to turn into puddles, as some of them had in yesterday's rain. She stopped at the stone steps that led to the bridge over the stream where she had found Katherine and Frankie the morning Charlotte was killed, intent on playing, oblivious to the disturbance their disappearance had caused. They hadn't wanted to leave the woods. Who could blame them? She'd had to use her own memory of what it was like to be a child to entice them to come back. How indignant Frankie had been when he met her again in the church driveway as an ordinary grownup. He had accused her of not being a fairy, a charge she had more or less denied, claiming to remember her old fairy blood, assuring them they had fairy blood, too. Was it lying to encourage children in their fantasies?

Lucy sat down on the top step; the sun had found it long enough for it to be dry. A breeze deftly wound its way through the wood as the autumn stream trickled around and over stone. The real world is a hard place, some might argue, not a fairytale. Yet the children who inhabited fairytales were always encountering dangers, cruel or foolish parents, ogres, witches, people who would trick them or hurt them for gain. To survive, they had to rely on wit and bravery and the magical help that came if they were kind to an animal or a beggar. Frankie and Katherine, like herself at an early age, had already suffered loss. If it gave them comfort and courage to believe in their fairy blood, in the magic of the wood, where was the harm? Why shouldn't they?

Because, Lucy answered herself sternly, unlike in a fairytale, no one was in charge of life's plot. The children had already run off once without telling anyone where they were. Old fairy blood or not, Lucy the grownup could not encourage children to defy and frighten their parents or endanger themselves. To make her point without further disillusioning Frankie, she had played on their fantasy of the black winged thing—or was it horned—that they'd seen running away.

Seen running away....

Lucy stood up abruptly, then almost sat again as her knees turned weak. She put out a hand to the wall to steady herself and pictured the children again, combing the stream banks for sticks which they'd clutched in their hands as they walked back with her. The knees and cuffs of their pants had been wet and muddy as if they'd crouched down, crouched down while someone ran past, winged or horned they couldn't be sure, because, Frankie had said, it was wearing a sweatshirt.

Not Elsa, she had prayed. Not poor brave Frankie's father, who had told her he'd found an open window in the basement while mistakenly clearly away all the evidence and making everything worse for himself. And if someone had been hiding in the basement, couldn't he have escaped through the window and run into the woods?

She was so intent on her thoughts, Lucy hardly knew she had walked back up the carriage road until she found herself stepping over the gap in the wall.

"Miss Way?"

Someone called her name. She focused and saw Rick Foster rolling up a flap of the large appliances tent to let in some light and air.

"Are you all right?" he asked solicitously. "You look as though you've just seen a ghost."

"Yes, Mr. Foster," Lucy said. "I do believe I have."

CHAPTER TWENTY-NINE

Anne wanted a divorce, though she knew she would never do anything about it.

She was too busy.

This morning she'd had to get a hungover Gerald out of bed to take Lucy Way's call, make a bromide for him, run to the store (while the children were still in their pajamas with only Gerald to watch them) to get tomato juice which he claimed helped "settle his stomach" code for hangover, especially with a surreptitious splash of gin in it. Then she made his breakfast and hurried him out the door to meet Lucy before the sheriff was due to arrive. Meanwhile Katherine had spilled the milk she got out of the refrigerator by herself (Anne had forgotten to put it in a small pitcher) and she'd cried over it, even though Anne had not scolded her. (Unusual for Katherine to cry, who prided herself on being so much more grownup than the twins; she was worried about Katherine. And was divorce always worse for children than marriage to a man who passed out drunk in his daughter's bed? She made a mental note to ask Dr. Aiken.) The twins had played with their food as usual, building what Peter insisted were igloos out of the sodden marshmallow pieces in their Lucky Charms cereal. When she finally got Katherine off to school, in a tizzy because her favorite jacket had a rip that needed to be mended, and dropped off the twins at nursery school, Anne remembered she had to rush back and straighten up the house, because it was half-blind Bernice's day to pretend to clean.

Now Bernice was wiping the kitchen counters Anne had just wiped, humming and moaning to herself quite happily, Anne suspected. Bernice's marital status was vague or at least no one had ever explained it to Anne. It was possible that her husband had simply disappeared, less messy than divorce, Anne considered, and with a certain appeal. Anne poured herself the last dregs of coffee from the pot and went out the back door to sit on the steps and smoke a cigarette before she took up her duties at the rummage sale. She hoped no one would see her there or if they did would be tactful enough not to approach her. She often wished she could just disappear from her life and turn up somewhere else, some*one* else without having to make any tedious decisions and arrangements. She supposed that was an escape fantasy, though when she had confessed it to Dr. Aiken, he had suggested that she might have a death wish. Not that it mattered one way or another.

Through a gap in the honeysuckle hedge that inadequately shielded a rusty swing set and her clothesline—(which reminded her: could she ask Bernice to hang out the wash? She usually didn't, fearing that Bernice might tumble down the steps, but she really should get to work at the rummage sale)—Anne could see the sheriff's car. She wondered if Gerald would admit to the sheriff that Anne had been outside the morning of the murder and effectively had no alibi. Of course, she had seen Mildred's car and heard the brakes squeal, and now Lucy had Mildred's confession of finding the body, so perhaps the timetable conclusively cleared Anne? But there was only Anne's word for it that she'd been on the back steps and not lurking in the shrubbery (having just killed Charlotte) while Mildred turned tail and ran. It was disconcerting to Anne how unmoved she felt at the prospect of being a suspect. But of course it would be terrible for the children, especially Katherine. The twins had each other. So far they seemed oblivious to the added tension and commotion caused by the mayhem in their midst, but Katherine was older and so sensitive. Anne wished she knew more of what went on inside her daughter's head. (Perhaps she should take her to see Dr. Aiken?)

Last night after clearing up Gerald's mess, Anne had gone to check on Katherine, who was still half awake or half asleep and wholly incoherent, at least to Anne. She kept talking about an imposition (how on earth did she know that word and what did it mean to her?) An imposition with wings that she and Frankie had to catch and put in jail. Katherine also appeared to be terrified that she herself would be sent to jail—or Frankie would. Of course Katherine knew Frankie's father was in jail. It must be terribly upsetting to a child to think that a parent could be taken away like that. She did her best to reassure Katherine that she was safe and Frankie was safe and that Katherine's own father would do everything he could to help Frankie's father. Katherine kept saying "we trespassed." God forgives our trespasses, Anne tried to tell her, but perhaps Katherine could sense Anne's utter lack of faith in any such thing. Finally she offered to tell Katherine a Tigger story. She rubbed Katherine's back till she fell asleep. By then, Gerald had also fallen asleep on top of the bed with his clothes and shoes still on.

The dregs of the coffee were bitter, and it was time to get to work. Anne dumped the coffee off the side of the steps onto the ground and then carefully stubbed out her cigarette. (She would take the butt inside and dispose of it properly as she was always begging Gerald to do.) Just then, a large station wagon with wood trim parked by the gap in Anne's hedge and Sybil Foster got out. Anne had seen Rick Foster pull up by the large appliances and furniture tent earlier, so apparently husband and wife had driven separately, which didn't necessarily imply marital discord. Rick probably had to go off campaigning somewhere later on, generous of him to come and put in an hour or so at the beginning of a busy day. She could understand why Gerald liked him, but she felt embarrassed by what sometimes seemed like fawning on Gerald's part.

Well, she decided, she would make up for it by looking for flaws in the wife, chief of which, to Anne's mind, was her flawless appearance. She always looked lacquered as though she had just come from the beauty parlor. If she had been a brunette, she no doubt would have cut her hair to look like Jackie Kennedy's. As an (un)natural blonde she could have gone for a Marilyn Monroe look, but she wasn't blowsy enough. Today Sybil's hair was piled up in a chignon held with a tortoise shell comb. Instead of a workaday shirtwaist dress, she was wearing khaki pedal pushers (as if she was twenty years younger than she was) and a tailored white blouse and loafers with tassels. The effect was at once sophisticated and youthful, innocent and seductive. As she sauntered down the driveway (no doubt quite aware of her shapely posterior) she waved to someone who was emerging from the large appliances tent.

Not her own husband.

In fact the husband in question belonged to Mary Louise: the tall count from some European country Anne could never remember, except that it was not Transylvania—a favorite quip of the good-natured count. His features were in fact rather homely, but he was very tall, had a head of close-cropped silver curls and of course a charming accent. Clearly Sybil was charmed and so was the count. The pair stood together in the middle of the driveway (so that people had to drive around them) his large head bent slightly towards her as if he could not bear to miss one scintillating remark. She remembered Grace's tart observation that Sybil was the one wives should beware of. Perhaps Gerald (who had a thing for blonds and joked that she had deceived him because he'd met her in the summer when her mousy brown hair could almost pass) would have an affair with Sybil Foster and she could divorce him for adultery. But what if they went on to marry each other? (Would Gerald be defrocked? She wasn't sure of the church rules.) But she did know one thing: she wouldn't let that woman near her children. There would be murder done first—

"Excuse me!" someone called out from the parish house. "If you wouldn't mind, Sybil honey, I'd like to borrow my husband back for a minute. Manly muscle is in short supply around here."

"Oh but you can have *my* husband!" Sybil joked (or was she joking; maybe the Fosters' marriage was on the rocks?)

Anne waited till she saw the count trotting obediently towards his wife, and then she took her cup into the kitchen, dropping her well-extinguished cigarette butt in the waste basket, and tiptoeing through the soapy flood Bernice was unleashing with the mop she never seemed able to wring out. Anne would have to damp mop again later to get the soap streaks out. Surreptitiously, Anne washed her cup herself and headed out the front door.

Elsa had just arrived and was standing by her tan VW (which, when they were both parked, Anne could not tell apart from Gerald's unless she looked inside to see which kind of detritus lined the seats). Elsa now held a stack of worn-looking sheet music and gazed down the driveway at the sheriff's car. Either her hands were shaking or else a breeze that touched nowhere else rifled the paper. She did not seem aware of Anne's presence.

"Good morning, Elsa," Anne called out, not wanting to come up behind her and startle her. "How are you?"

"When will the interrogation begin?" Elsa said without turning around so that Anne wondered if she were talking to herself.

Then abruptly she faced Anne. She looked terrible, Anne thought, as bad as Gerald and no doubt for similar reasons.

"I have no alibi."

"I don't either," Anne said.

Elsa snorted dismissively as if to say: who would ever suspect *you*? My husband did, Anne thought of answering, and she found herself feeling momentarily appreciative of Gerald.

"I believe all of us who were on the premises that morning will be questioned," Anne tried to reassure her, "not as suspects but for information, including Lucy Way."

"Yah," said Elsa, "but Lucy Way was never in the parish house. I was."

"Oh?"

This was the first Anne had heard of it. If Lucy knew that Elsa had been there, she had not mentioned it to Anne. Was Lucy trying to protect Elsa or simply being discreet? Anne wanted to know more, but Gerald had told her, rather rudely, to stay out of it, apparently forgetting he also had been party to Lucy's foray into espionage— which had in fact borne fruit.

"Yes, I was. And if by the grace of God that poor young man is found innocent, they will come after me."

Anne did not know what to say but some response was required surely.

"Why do you think that, Elsa?"

"Because, because that awful woman saw me!" Elsa burst out.

"Charlotte saw you?"

Before or after she was dead? Anne felt momentarily confused. She knew from Gerald that Elsa hated Charlotte as much as she had—and perhaps had more to fear from her. Anne suddenly felt cold all over. What if—

"No, no," said Elsa impatiently. "The other awful woman. She thinks she can sing. I throw her out of the choir; that was before your time, Anne. But even now you can hear her warble from the congregation. Belief me, if I would kill all the people who desecrate music, she would be top of my list."

(Now that Charlotte was gone, Anne couldn't stop herself thinking.)

"Do you mean Mildred Thomson?" Anne said.

Elsa nodded.

If Mildred was telling the truth (and had not actually killed Charlotte herself and made up the story about finding the body) then her account of that morning could put Elsa in a dubious light. Anne wondered again if Lucy knew about the encounter. If Mildred had confessed her flight to Lucy, surely she would also have told her about seeing Elsa in the parish house. Then again, maybe Lucy already knew Elsa had seen Mildred and had used her knowledge to force Mildred's confession.

"She was stealing from the rummage sale," Elsa stated. "Just like the Crowley woman."

Lucy had not told her about that, either. But then they had not spoken for long last night, and Lucy had seemed hesitant to say anything at all, which showed admirable discretion, Anne supposed. Or maybe, maybe Anne and Lucy just weren't friends, not really, not the way she and Rosalie were. Not the way Lucy and Elsa were. Elsa was not Anne's friend either. To Elsa she was the minister's wife, a passable soprano (at least, she hoped, not on Elsa's hit list) someone incapable of malice and murder.

"You must tell the sheriff, Elsa," Anne said. "Tell the sheriff everything you know."

"They will come after me," Elsa said again. "Even with the boy in jail. Belief me, Anne, if I could I would disappear. Take Clara and disappear, but that would make it worse for Clara, if I run and they find me."

Suddenly Elsa clutched Anne's arm. Elsa was terrified, Anne realized. Paranoid, Dr. Aiken might diagnose her. Maybe schizophrenic, too? She and Clara had met at an insane asylum where Clara was an inmate. Was there more to the story?

"Listen, Anne, if anything should happen to me, you and Gerald, you will see that Clara is cared for? She is so delicate, so fragile. Please!"

"I am sure Gerald will know what to do," Anne tried to comfort her without promising anything. "Would you like to speak to him after he's..." done with the sheriff, she finished her sentence silently.

"No, no." Elsa shook her head. "Do not the trouble the man now. He has enough on his platters. I will be in the church when the sheriff calls for me."

And with a toss of her head that was at once sad and defiant, Elsa clutched her music to her chest and headed for the side door of the church.

Anne decided to go look for Lucy. Surely it was not indiscreet or interfering to say: your friend needs you. Maybe Lucy could comfort Elsa, reason with her, or (Anne she wished she could prevent the thought) extract another confession....

As she neared the parish house (where the sheriff's car blocked the front steps, deliberately?) Anne glanced in the large appliances and furniture tent to see if Rick Foster was still working. To her surprise, she saw Lucy Way sitting upright on a hideous leather reclining chair (the kind that you could get stuck in if you were foolish enough to shift the lever and let it dump you backwards.) She was sipping a glass of water and next to her, on a vinyl kitchen chair, sat Rick Foster looking concerned and solicitous. Anne stood uncertainly, wondering if she could approach them or if she would be interrupting a *tête-à-tête*.

Just then Lucy saw Anne and waved. Rick Foster looked around and then stood to greet her.

"Hello, Anne. I'm afraid Miss Way has had a bit of a turn," said Rick.

Had he always talked like a character from a Victorian novel, Anne wondered, or was that Lucy's effect on him?

"I'm quite all right now," said Lucy. "Mr. Foster has been most kind."

Anne did not understand or approve of her sudden impulse to roll her eyes, but at least she managed to hold it in check.

"I guess we're all on pins and needles," Anne said, glancing towards the sheriff's car. "Lucy, if you'd like to come up to the rectory to rest for a while, you're more than welcome."

"Thank you, Anne, but I'm fully recovered." Lucy rose from the recliner with the unnecessary but gentlemanly assistance of Rick's hand under her elbow. "Mildred isn't here yet, and I believe Mrs. Lomangino is on her own with the pricing."

And Teresa was more than equal to the task, Anne was sure. What she didn't know was whether Lucy had taken Anne's offer of respite at face value or whether she was avoiding a possible exchange of confidences. She wished Rick Foster would excuse himself so that she could ask to have a private word with Lucy.

"Ladies," said Rick Foster, reaching for his jacket, as if he had read her mind, a rare trait in a man, "if all is well, I must be on my way—"

Just then the peaceful morning air was rent with screams, worthy of a banshee, coming from somewhere down the driveway.

"Good heavens!" exclaimed Lucy. "Who's being murdered now?"

An image flashed through Anne's mind of some child struck by Mildred Thomson's car, but the children were at still at school.

All three of them ran towards the sound which rose in pitch and desperation.

"It's in my hair! Get it out! Get it out!"

A moment later, they saw Sybil still screaming tearing out of the toy barn like a bat out of hell with Rosalie, holding a child-sized butterfly net, chasing after her.

"Sybil!" shouted Rick. "Good God! What's the matter? You, hey! What are you doing to my wife?"

"Get it out, get it out!" Sybil screamed, her chignon destroyed, her stiff white-blond hair (that had been sprayed into place) now sticking out straight like a cartoon of electrocution. "Rick, don't just stand there. Do something!"

Rosalie, on the plump side, caught up, panting, and Anne could tell from one quick look, trying her best not to laugh.

"It's not in her hair, Mr. Foster," said Rosalie. "I got it. Look, Sybil, it's right here. It's as scared as you are."

"Poor little thing," murmured Lucy.

Rosalie held up a safely captured bat, which had folded itself into the smallest shape possible. Far from being comforted by the sight, Sybil began to shriek again.

"Thank you, Mrs....." Rick hesitated. Rosalie did not exactly move in the Fosters circles.

"Brown," Anne supplied. "My good friend, Rosalie Brown."

"Thank you for rescuing my wife, Mrs. Brown. Perhaps the bat should be—"

"Exterminated!" screamed Sybil. "It's rabid. It attacked me!"

"I'll take care of it," Rosalie assured Rick. To Anne she said in a low voice, "She wasn't bitten. It just grazed her hair. She startled it, trying to hang some overpriced 'authentic' Dutch Girl costume from a rafter. But I suppose I ought to call the pound or something. Can I use your phone, Anne?"

"Sure. You know where it is."

Anne forgot for a moment that Bernice was there, but since she was almost as blind as the bat perhaps she'd take no notice.

"Sybil," Anne tried to be solicitous, "would you like to come to the rectory and refresh yourself—"

"No, I would not!" Sybil turned her full fury on Anne. "I'm going home, and I am not coming back. I quit, do you hear me, I quit! I will not take any further part in this cheap, ridiculous, badly run—"

Rick Foster, looking both grave and pained, began to lead away his wife.

"I am so sorry, Anne," he said.

"Don't you apologize for *me*!" Sybil rounded on him. "It's all your fault we're here. We could have gone to St Luke's in-the-Field where we belong, where *I* belong! But no, you were so impressed with Charlotte Crowley's pedigree and Mildred Thomson's money, fat lot of good that—"

Sybil's tirade passed beyond their hearing as Rick loaded her into the passenger seat of their station wagon.

"Anne," said Rick before getting in, "if Gerald needs me, I'll be at the campaign office this afternoon. Oh, and is it all right to leave my car here for now?"

"Certainly, and if you need a ride—"

"Oh, I can walk back and get it. The exercise will do me good."

At last Lucy and Anne were alone. They turned and looked at each other, both of them biting their lips.

"Some people are terribly afraid of bats, poor things, they can't help themselves." Lucy made an attempt at Christian charity.

Then they both burst out laughing at once. They laughed so hard they had to hold their stomachs and double over to keep from falling down. Before they had recovered themselves, Gerald opened the door to his office.

"Lucy?" he called, a little taken aback by her mirth. "The sheriff would like to speak to you first."

CHAPTER THIRTY

It did not seem fair that it was only ten o'clock in the morning, far too early in the day to have a drink unless you really were an alcoholic, which Gerald was not. (No matter what Anne thought.) There must be something he could or should be doing. Somewhere. The sheriff had commandeered his office in the parish house for interviewing the people who had been on church premises the morning of the murder. He paused in Grace's office on his way out. She was busy working on Sunday's bulletin and doing her best to pretend (at least) that she didn't have an ear cocked for the conversation in the next room. Unless someone had a very loud voice, which Lucy Way did not, or unless you were listening at a keyhole (as poor old Charlotte could no longer) you couldn't pick out words. Good to know, since people were supposed to be able to speak to the rector in confidence.

"I guess I'll go work in my office at the house," he said to Grace. "Or maybe I'll go see if they need help in the tent."

"Rick Foster just left," Grace informed him, rightly guessing that Gerald wanted to chew things over with him. Sometimes he felt that Grace knew him better than Anne did. "He had to take the harpy home. She needs some of her happy pills, maybe washed down with gin."

Gerald paused, his hand on the door, almost tasting the gin, before he registered what Grace had said. Gerald was aware that Grace had no use for Sybil. She and Anne had that much in common, but Anne would never have been so cheerfully catty.

"Is that who was screaming? What was the ruckus about?"

"I don't know. I admit I peeked out the window. Her hair was sticking up on end, which would be enough to put her into a tizzy.

Anne, Lucy and Rosalie were there, so I didn't think I needed to add myself to the mix. Hubby had matters well in hand. I swear that man should be running for sainthood, not just congress."

"I don't know," said Gerald with the little smirk that drove Anne crazy. "I think all you ladies are just jealous of Sybil, because she's a natural blond."

Grace made a most unladylike noise in the back of her throat.

"If you believe that, I've got a bridge I'd like to sell you. Run along, Gerald. Go work on your sermon. Matthew 21:31, one of my personal favorites."

"'Verily I say unto you, That the publicans and the harlots go into the kingdom of God before you?'"

"That's the one," said Grace lightly, keeping her eye on the page she was typing.

Gerald wasn't sure, but he thought she might be blushing. Could Grace have a crush on him? Anne said she did. He wondered if he could have an affair with Grace. Or if he even wanted to. He didn't think he did, which was just as well, he supposed.

"You bet," said Gerald, his hand now on the doorknob. "I could preach on that one in my sleep."

"And you might have to if you don't get some rest before Sunday," said Grace. "Go on now, shoo! I'll get the phone and say you're busy unless it's an emergency call."

Gerald stepped out into a beautiful September morning, wishing he could take the day off, go for a walk in the woods next door, but he felt obliged to be available to the sheriff as long as he was here. The large appliances and furniture tent was empty now, the men of Regeneration being at work at what Gerald sometimes thought of as real jobs. It's not that Gerald didn't work hard. Anne complained that he worked too much, was never home (at least not when she wanted help with the kids) but what was it he did, exactly? Visited the sick and the shut in? Went to meetings, organized charitable work, all things that women did, too. On days like this one, when there were women all over the place, he felt like a barnyard rooster amidst hens who were busy laying and brooding and, truth be told, didn't really require a rooster to get on with the business of, well, life, he supposed, just life. In general, men were more or less in the way.

Gerald paused and looked into the tent, past the furniture to a couple of lawnmowers, an old wood stove, an ancient washing machine that hardly looked mechanized, and a table full of esoteric woodworking tools whose functions Gerald could only guess. He wondered what a man like the sheriff thought of ministers and priests. Probably didn't see much past the collar, gave the office a knee-jerk respect.

Gerald didn't much care for Sheriff Harris, a Republican, like all the other local officials, part of the machine that controlled the county. Rick was the first Democratic candidate for Congress with more than a snowball's chance in hell of winning, and he wouldn't have that much if he had been up against an incumbent. But Woodleigh Stanton, who'd held the seat for decades, had just retired. Rick's opponent, a Tom Smith, with about as much to distinguish him as his name, didn't have much charisma or experience, except at the county level; he'd had a couple of terms as a legislator. Gerald was surprised the Republicans couldn't come up with someone more noteworthy, handpicked by Stanton as his successor. The most interesting thing about Smith was his possible connection with a covert local branch of the KKK, though Rick had never been able to turn up conclusive enough evidence to use it in the campaign. And it might have backfired if he had.

Gerald didn't know where the sheriff stood on civil rights—or rather he was afraid he could guess. His interview with the sheriff had given him cause for concern, which was why he wished he could talk to Rick, find out what progress he'd made on finding a lawyer for Frank. After Gerald had given the sheriff a list of who had been present the morning of the murder, the sheriff had waved away any additional information like Mildred's screaming brakes, the possibility that she might have just missed hitting Frank's son. Most of his questions centered on suspicious behavior on Frank's part that Gerald might have noticed and not just in relation to Charlotte.

"I'll tell you this in confidence, Reverend. Looks like Mrs. Crowley might just have gotten in the way, and Lomangino lost his head. Mr. Crowley may be in danger, too. This could be a lot bigger than Lomangino. Unfortunate, very unfortunate for the Crowleys, this murder may be a case of the tail wagging the dog, if you get my drift."

Gerald guessed the sheriff meant the mob. He'd always suspected the sheriff's office might have its own direct or indirect involvement with organized crime. He supposed tying Frank to the mob as well as to a murder might clean up the sheriff's reputation in an election year. It was all very disturbing. It seemed as though Frank's guilt was a foregone conclusion. And if Frank was guilty then Gerald was guilty too—of being a bleeding heart liberal dupe.

Gerald took one more look around the tent to see if there was something useful he might do. Most of the items had color-coded price tags that Anne would have understood, but Gerald had never been that hands-on with the rummage sale. All the regulars, men and women, had their own turf. On the other side of the tool display, Gerald spied a card table with a radio and a couple of clocks dismantled for repair. That was Marge's husband Hank Van Wagner's bailiwick. (He had a fix-it shop at the back of his dairy barn.) Gerald knew better than to touch a single screw.

He turned away, glad that the driveway was at last deserted, all the busy worker bees inside the hive of the parish house. Worker bees were neutered females, he considered vaguely as he walked slowly up the driveway. Elsa was assaulting the organ, with Bach no doubt. Anne would probably recognize the piece. It sounded ominous and violent and strangely modern, much more modern than someone like Beethoven. He had once asked Anne about the dissonance in Bach, thinking to engage her on a subject she loved. "I don't know, I'm just an amateur," she had answered him impatiently, even dismissively. "You'll have to ask Elsa." But he never had. It wasn't Bach he cared about.

"Rev!" someone hailed him. "A word with ye!"

He turned and saw Amos in the shadow of the church, perched much too precariously on a ladder (which was how he'd come to grief before) cleaning the gutters.

"Amos!" Gerald called out. "What are you doing up there? The leaves haven't even fallen yet."

"Aye, but there's a bird's nest clogging up the works. His eye may be on the sparrow but who is going to clear the shitty old nest out of the drainpipe? Not the Lord God Almighty."

Amos tossed the offending clump of twigs and guano to the ground.

"No," agreed Gerald. "He'd be too busy marking the fall of a stubborn old Jockie. Come on now, Amos. You know you're not supposed to be up on a ladder by yourself. Our insurance has already been raised once because of you."

"Come hold the ladder then, and I'll come down meek as a lamb."

"A lost sheep, you mean," said Gerald, taking a firm hold as Amos began a descent made more precarious by a tricky hip.

"Maybe so, maybe so," said Amos amiably. "I'll not deny it. If you ask me, the whole bleating flock is lost. They need a shepherd with a good strong crook."

Gerald stood back as Amos found the ground with first one tentative foot, then the other.

"Let's just set the ladder on its side around the back," said Gerald, ignoring Amos's extension of the metaphor. "The barn is full of toys, floor to rafters."

And he didn't want to run into Anne who might be there in Sybil's place. His mere existence was enough of an annoyance to her.

"What's on your mind?" Gerald asked, feeling in his coat pocket for his pipe and tobacco pouch, as Amos did the same. "Want to talk in the house? The sheriff is using my office."

Amos shook his head and went to sit on the back steps that led out from the vesting room next to the choir room. Gerald sat down beside him, both of them looking out across the driveway to the rectory backyard where Bernice was hanging out wash in slow motion with very little accuracy. A clothespin missed its mark and a pair of his boxer shorts (a Campbell plaid) fell to the ground. Bernice went right on fastening the pin to the empty line.

"What I have to say can be said in the open air," declared Amos. "And forebye I will say it to the sheriff, too, if I get half a chance."

"He'll be interviewing everyone who was there that morning," Gerald assured him. "You're on the list. In fact, maybe you should save what you have to say for him. I'm in this mess as much as the rest of you—"

"But you're not a sheep," Amos interrupted. "You're the shepherd and it's up to you to spot the wolf in sheep's clothing."

"I may be a pastor, but I am not a detective," Gerald protested. "It's my job to keep the church going in a difficult time, not my job to figure out who committed the crime."

"And if an innocent man is accused?"

Amos allowed Gerald a moment's respite as they both relit their pipes. The scent of tobacco smoke was soothing, the same brand his father had used, his father who had only had to deal with the Great Depression and an endless string of hoboes at the back door, none of whom had murdered anyone, at least not on church property.

"What makes you so sure Frank Lomangino is innocent?" Gerald asked.

"And what makes you so sure he's guilty?" countered Amos.

"I'm not sure. I'm not sure of anything. I'm sick about it, to tell the truth, Amos."

Amos was silent for a moment.

"Ye're carrying a heavy burden, Rev, I know, seeing as the Papish Wop was your pick. Well, let me ease your load, if I can."

"Go on," Gerald sighed resigned.

"This mur-r-rder," Amos gave his r's an even more emphatic roll than usual, "has a woman's hand all over it."

"Why do you say so?" Gerald asked.

"First of all, it's women hated Charlotte Crowley, not men. Sure she was light-fingered and had her long nose in everyone's business, but she made no bones about it. She had a way with men, husband of hers was besotted with her, but she lorded it over the other hens, always at the top of the pecking order. Women are the ones who gossip, and women are the ones with secrets.

"And look at the crime—no weapon, no knife, no gun, no strangling, no body dragged off to the woods. Women aren't strong enough. It was a nasty, sneaking, sniveling crime—a knock on the head, a shove down the stairs. And who but a woman would have thought of smothering her with a bag of dry-cleaning? Who but a woman would have known where to find those coats?"

Frank Lomangino, Gerald did not say. Lucy had told him that Frank had carried the coats upstairs for her. Gerald stopped listening as Amos went on ranting about the perfidy of women. It must be eleven o'clock by now. Maybe he would just see where Anne was, make sure she was not in the house, and then he would have a small before-lunch drink.

That comforting plan was nipped in the bud by Grace Jones running, as best she could in her heels, up the driveway towards the rectory.

"Grace?" He stood up. "Over here!"

"Gerald!" She was out of breath. "Nat Crowe—" She caught sight of Amos and stopped herself. "Phone!"

Even Amos ought to acknowledge that a discreet secretary's price was above rubies.

"I'll pick it up in the house," Gerald told Grace.

Once inside he went to his office and closed the door.

"Nat?"

He listened as the virtuous Grace loudly set down the receiver.

"Gerald! She's kidnapped me. She drugged me and kidnapped me. I should have known to be suspicious when she let me have a drink. She slipped me a mickey."

"Where are you now?" asked Gerald.

"That's just it. I don't know. I woke up in some sort of motel cabin. In the mountains somewhere. She's gone, she's gone to get a justice of the peace. She left me locked in. I climbed out the window of the john and found a phone booth in back of the office. Gerald, listen, I think, I think she killed Charlotte, and if I, if I don't marry her, I think she intends to kill me. Gerald, help me. Oh God, she's back—"

And the line went dead.

"Don't worry, Gerald," said Grace. She must have picked the phone back up again quietly. "I'll see if I can trace the call."

Above rubies. Definitely. Gerald opened a drawer, reached into the back, found a pint of gin with just a swallow left. With a mint lifesaver as a chaser. he set out at a run for the parish house.

CHAPTER THIRTY-ONE

"Dickie and Prescott's mama got bitten by a bat!" Aramantha told the kids gathered around her on the lawn in front of Katherine's house. Even though Katherine lived there, it was always Aramantha who told them what to play. "She's probably gonna get rabies!"

"Like Old Yeller?" Peter asked, his eyes wide and round. He'd had nightmares about that movie.

"Mmm hmm!" Aramantha's head bobbed up and down. "Exactly like Old Yeller. Her mouth gonna foam up and she might even try to bite her own kids. Then they'd have rabies, too!"

Katherine didn't think her mother would want Aramantha scaring Peter, but she didn't know how to stop her.

"They'll have to shoot her!" Frankie sounded happy. "And Dickie and Prescott, too!"

"People don't get shot," said Aunt Rosalie's daughter, Lisa, who always got a hundred on all her tests in school. "They go to the doctor to get shots, so they don't get rabies."

"Then how come, how come Old Yeller didn't get a shot!" Peter shouted, which Katherine knew meant he was about to cry.

"That was the old time days." Aramantha took charge again. "They didn't have shots in the olden days."

"Dickie and Prescott will get shots," Janie piped up. "In their bare bottoms."

And all the little kids, Peter and Janie and Frankie's sisters, Lisa's sister and Aramantha's cousins started to giggle about bottoms.

"No, no, no!" insisted Frankie. "They're gonna get shot. In the head!"

And he made his finger into a gun and made pow, pow, pow noises, and some of the boys started to shoot back and fall down and pretend they were dead.

"Cut it out, y'all!" ordered Aramantha. "Don't be stupit, Frankie! Now let's play a real game!"

"Hide and Seek! Hide and Seek!" shouted Aramantha's younger cousin Bobbie.

Aramantha put her finger to her cheek and took a moment to think about it.

"All right," she said. "Here's the rules. You can only hide outside around the church, around the parish house, around Katherine's house. When you get found, you have to go back to base, and when the one who's it hollers 'olly, olly in free,' everybody got to come back to base. Base is this big old tree."

Aramantha walked up to the maple tree outside Katherine's bedroom window. Its leaves were just starting to turn orange.

"Now we got to figure out who's it," Aramantha announced.

And she had them all shoot different numbers of their fingers into the middle. Katherine never understood how it worked, but finally Aramantha stamped her foot and admitted she was it. "*Again!*" Nobody liked to be "it." Aramantha was fair that way and always took her turn, which was why everybody let her be so bossy.

"I'm gonna close my eyes and count to a hundred," announced Aramantha. "Everybody remember the rules. Get ready, get set, go. One, two, three, four, five, six, seven...."

Aramantha counted loud enough so you could hear her, and she never skipped or speeded up the way some of the boys did. Katherine could still hear her as she ran towards her favorite climbing tree, a big hemlock down the driveway on the lawn nearest the woods. Aramantha hadn't said they couldn't climb. But before she ducked under the low-hanging limbs that Katherine thought of as a door to the tree's living room, Frankie caught up with her, grabbed her wrist and started pulling her around the big tent to the gap in the wall.

"We're supposed to hide in the yard," she protested.

"Who cares?" said Frankie. "I'm not playing stupid old hide and seek. We have to make the trap. Aramantha won't look for us in the woods. No one will look for us there."

On the other side of the wall, Frankie squatted down, carefully moved some leaves and picked up their javelins.

"I finished yours for you, Katherine. See? The point is sharp now."

Katherine forgot all about Hide and Seek as Frankie handed her the javelin. She touched the point. This was not a game. They had gone to another world just like Lucy in Narnia where there was danger, and they had to be brave. They walked on, putting their feet down softly so they didn't make a sound.

"How are we going to make the trap?" Katherine whispered as they reached the steps.

"I found my pops' fishing line in his tackle box."

He reached in his pocket and brought out some tough looking thread wound so that it looked like an eight.

"Are we going to make a big spider's web?" Katherine wondered.

Frankie put his finger to his lips and whispered even more softly.

"We're going to tie the line between two trees. When the bad man comes, he'll trip and fall. Then we will spear him with our javelins."

Katherine's stomach felt hot and jumpy. She didn't know if she could do what Frankie said. Lucy had carried a dagger, but Aslan had told her he didn't want her in the battle. Lucy also had a magic cordial and just a drop would heal any wounds. She wished she had cordial in a crystal vial and not just a javelin.

"I'm going to tie one end to that tree over there." He pointed to a tree on one side of the steps. "And then, let's see, that one. Do you know how to tie knots, Katherine? Real sailors' knots?"

Katherine hesitated. She wanted to say yes, like when she had said yes in kindergarten when the teacher asked who knew how to snap their fingers. She had stood with all the other kids who knew how and had made her fingers move. No one could hear that they made no sound. But if she tried to tie a sailors knot and it came undone then the imposition would get away.

"I can tie my shoes with bunny-knots," she said, which was true. "I don't know if that's the same as a sailors' knot. Can you show me?"

"No, no, no!" Frankie shook his head so hard that his whole body moved from side to side. "We don't have time for that. You can stand lookout. If you see anyone or even hear anyone, come tap me on the shoulder and we'll hide."

Hide for real, Katherine thought, not like a game where the worst that could happen was being found by Aramantha. She stood as still as she could on the steps while Frankie went to tie the fishing line around the tree, looking first one way, then the other way, one way, then the other. Frankie had just finished tying one end of the line when Katherine saw someone at the top of the hill they had never gotten to climb, someone wearing black. She couldn't see the black wings because it was facing towards them, but she thought she caught a flash of horns. Her legs were so wobbly at first she didn't know if she could run, but somehow she did. She tapped Frankie on the shoulder just as he was standing up. Quickly he hid the fishing line under some leaves, and then he picked up his javelin (she was still holding hers) grabbed her free hand, and they scrambled down the bank and under the bridge just as they had before, only now it was wetter. Katherine was wearing her school shoes, leather saddle shoes. She hoped she would not be punished for ruining them.

In a moment she forgot all about the shoes as the footsteps came closer and closer. The man was not running this time. Katherine wished he was; he was taking so long to cross the bridge, not like a billy goat at all but a slow giant sniffing for blood. At last, they heard him climbing the steps, and the footsteps stopped. Frankie started to lean out to look, but Katherine held tight to him. For once she was stronger than Frankie or anyway he stopped straining. They both held their breaths longer than for going past the graveyard at the outside of town.

The colors behind her eyes started going dark and swirly, when she heard the steps again going farther away down the carriage road, and she let out her breath. She wondered if she would have died if she kept holding it and what it would be like to die. It was so good to breathe, she didn't mind crouching and waiting until they couldn't hear anything but the trickle of the stream. Then the birds, who had stopped singing, began to chirp. Slowly she and Frankie crept out from under the bridge into the leaf-yellow light. Frankie went to where he'd left the fishing line. It was still there, and so was the sailors' knot. Katherine took up her lookout again as Frankie unwound the line so that it crossed the path at the top of the steps.

"Come hold the line tight while I tie it," Frankie whispered when he wound the line around the other tree.

Katherine held the line so taut it cut into her finger as Frankie knotted it.

"There!" Frankie said. And they both went to look at the line across the path fine as a spider's web, almost invisible. "When he comes back this way he'll trip and fall down the steps."

An awful thought occurred to Katherine.

"Do we have to stay here till he comes? Even if it's night?"

She did not want Frankie to think she wasn't brave. But her feet were cold, and her mother might worry about her or be mad the way she was when Katherine's father was late. They didn't have any food with them. When Lucy, Edmund, Peter, and Susan had started out together through the wardrobe into Narnia they had taken sandwiches and worn fur coats.

"Olly, olly in free!" Aramantha hollered so loud they could hear her voice all the way in the woods.

"No," said Frankie at last. "We don't know when he's coming back. It might be a long time. When he does come back, he'll trip and fall down and break his leg. Every day we'll come, and when we find him, we'll spear him."

Lucy was not sure Aslan would want them to spear someone who had fallen down and broken his leg. It did not sound like the sort of thing the High King Peter would do. She did not want to believe that Frankie was more like Edmund when he ate the White Witch's Turkish Delight.

"I thought you said you wanted to catch the bad man and put him in jail, so they'll...so they'll let your pops out."

She was worried for a moment that Frankie would get mad at her for talking about his father being in jail or so sad he might have to push his tears back into his eyes.

"Olly, olly in free!" Aramantha sounded good and mad now. "Frankie! Katherine, I know you cheating."

"Okay," said Frankie. "Here's what we'll do. When we find him, we'll tie him up. I'll bring more fishing line. Then I'll stand guard and you can go get my Uncle Joey to come and arrest him."

Katherine felt relieved and decided not to worry about how she would find his Uncle Joey. Some grown up would have to help her. Maybe even her father.

"But if he tries to get away," Frankie added. "I'll have to spear him."

With the plan clear, Frankie and Katherine ran down the carriage road till they turned for the gap in the wall. Before they stepped into the church yard, they hid their javelins under the leaves. Then they leaped over the wall, raced around behind the church, and made it back to base before Aramantha.

CHAPTER THIRTY-TWO

Lucy woke at dawn and for a blissful moment knew nothing but comfort. Tabitha lay curled at her feet. Her light silky quilt was just the right weight and warmth, her bed just the right firmness and softness. Her small room was dim and glowing, just like the sky outside. She would move soon enough, swing her legs out of bed and her bare feet onto the bare wood floor. She would find her slippers and robe, go downstairs to put on the coffee, and the day would begin. Another day that the Lord had made, and she would be glad and rejoice in it.

Then abruptly, prematurely, Lucy remembered and sat up suddenly, disturbing Tabitha who meowed and quit the bed with a most unfeline-like thud.

There had been murder done, and now they were all caught up in it willy-nilly, whether they liked it or not. If they were in a detective novel, this would be the point at which Lucy would want to put the book down, although of course she never did. One had to go on grimly reading to find out who done it. But that was not why she read detective novels. She chose them for their miniature portrait of a world, their cast of eccentric characters, and when all the characters got caught up in solving the mystery (or obscuring it) she could not help feeling that they became diminished, one-dimensional. She sensed it happening to herself, to all of them. Their varied lives, private and intermingled, had been reduced to this single question: who killed Charlotte Crowley? Oh, and perhaps one other: why?

Really, only two people knew the answer to the first question (despite the sheriff's ill-concealed assumption of Frank Lomangino's guilt) and one of them was dead. As to the second question, maybe only one person knew. Charlotte was hardly the soul of sensitivity.

She did not know the effect her intrusive nature had on people like Elsa. (Why was she thinking of Elsa in particular, Lucy fretted?) Oh, bother Charlotte. If she wanted her murder solved, her ghost should be more forthcoming. Apart from that one forceful declaration—"I did not take your mother's coats down those stairs"—Charlotte had been silent as, well, the grave.

Lucy got up, put on her slippers and robe. She pulled back the covers to let the bed air out. She remembered her mother scolding a maid (in the days before the First War when there still were such things) who'd made a bed precipitously. Apparently there was something "not nice" about tucking in the heat and scent of the body (or bodies) that had slept in a bed. Lucy hardly thought her chaste slumbers worthy of such precautions, but she would wait till after breakfast to make her bed, as she always did, with perfect hospital corners. Lucy knew that faithful performance of even small domestic duties could get one through the worst catastrophes. Well, the men who played on the deck of the Titanic had drowned, of course. But they died with unshakable dignity. You couldn't ask for more than that.

Lucy ground coffee beans and relished their rich scent. Her life was awash in small comforts and pleasures. How silly to compare herself with the gallant gentlemen who played music while the ship went down. She was in no danger. She had no heroic part to play in finding Charlotte's murderer. She had done all she could. She had told the sheriff everything Mildred had told her as well as everything she remembered from that morning, concluding with her theory that the murderer might have escaped to the woods. She had even overstepped herself, urging the sheriff to find out from Teresa Lomangino whether father and son had set out together or separately the morning of the murder. If they had both been on their way to the parish house after Mildred discovered Charlotte's body, Frank Lomangino would have an alibi. This line of reasoning had earned her a glower and a snarl.

"I think I know how to do my job, Miss Way."

Whether or not the sheriff had followed her unsolicited advice, Lucy did not know. Shortly after her interview with him, the sheriff had taken off with his lights flashing and his siren blaring. Gerald Bradley had followed close behind him, leaving a dismayed Anne standing in the driveway. (There were times when Lucy positively rejoiced in being a spinster.) To tell the truth, everyone had ended up in the driveway. Lucy had let herself be carried along with all the other alarmed and curious rummage sale workers.

"Now what can be happening?" Charlotte's one true friend Ginger fretted. "I wonder what on earth poor Charlotte would think of all this commotion and disturbance."

She would have loved every minute of it, Lucy did not say out loud. It did seem a shame that Charlotte's death had generated a mystery she was not here to probe.

"Don't ask me," said Anne, for of course everyone was looking in her direction.

And of course everyone now knew that Gerald had not taken the time to let his wife know where he was going.

"Are they going to bring Pops back?" Teresa's youngest daughter wanted to know.

Of course, Lucy realized, the child's father had been taken away in a police car. It made sense that she would look for his return in the same conveyance.

"I don't know, baby girl," said Teresa, picking up the child. "Do any of you know anything about where the sheriff went? If you do, for the love of Jesus, tell me."

She looked around at the women who all shook their heads, except for Grace Jones.

"Sorry, honey," the secretary said. "Nothing to do with your husband, I'm afraid. I have to assume the matter is confidential at this point. In fact, I know it is." Grace looked straight at Anne as if appealing to her. "I was eavesdropping. On the other phone."

All at once Anne, who'd been avoiding everyone's eyes, looked at Grace and actually smiled.

"I declare, Grace Jones, you are incorrigible!" Mary Louise managed to make her scolding sound like a compliment. "Come on everyone, back to work."

Anne Bradley began to turn toward the toy barn, but Grace signaled to her with quick a nod of her head, and Anne followed her into the office instead. It was gracefully done, Lucy thought. How generously Grace had put herself in her place without Anne or anyone else having to do it.

Lucy poured herself a cup of coffee and added a dollop of fresh cream from the top of the milk bottle and poured some into a pretty pale blue saucer for Tabitha, who had got finicky about food in her old age, but could never resist cream. Cradling the warm cup in her hands, she walked through the house to the French doors and stepped out to see what sort of a day it was. The sun had found the top of the oak at the end of her lawn, a red oak, so named for the bark, but this one also had leaves that flamed one branch by one branch amidst the dark green, not turning all orange until late October. Sunrise helped put in some perspective the human messes they all made. No matter who was guilty, and who innocent, today would be another of those autumn days with blue-drenched sky that could lift or break your heart.

Lucy was tired, she admitted to herself, more tired than usual. Even though the morning was chilly, she pulled her robe closer around her and sat down on a garden bench. She still felt ashamed at how overwrought she had gotten with her theory that the murderer had fled through the woods. Well, it had seemed more than a theory when it came to her. It felt almost like a flash of second sight, except that she could not see who it was. The figure was shadowy as if it really was a phantasm with wings and horns. The sheriff had not shown much interest in her introduction of an additional unknown suspect, and she had not thought it prudent, after she'd annoyed him once already, to instruct him to dust for finger prints on basement windows and see if he could see any signs of running footsteps trampling a trail.

But the matter had weighed on her mind as she had continued cutting up the old pajamas into quilting squares while Teresa worked on finishing the pricing. Mildred had never reported for duty (hardly surprising after Lucy had treacherously coaxed her home and cornered her the day before). The afternoon wore on. Children came back from school and rushed in to leave their lunchboxes and books with their mothers, taking the younger children with them when they went outside to play. Their shouts and laughter filled the golden afternoon as if no harm had been done, as if some of those children did not have a father in jail held without bail for murder on these very premises. Against her better judgment, Lucy summoned the nerve to ask Teresa if Frankie usually accompanied his father to the parish house or if he ever walked on his own.

"Of course he goes with his father," Teresa answered almost angrily. "Unless like today, I'm here." She lowered her voice so only Lucy could hear. "Frankie, Junior was with Frank that day. I told Frank: tell the judge. I mean who's gonna bump off an old lady with his kid playing outside? Judge didn't care. They treat him like he's an animal with no human feelings."

Lucy saw a tear escape Teresa's tightly controlled face. She rubbed it away with her knuckles, just like a child.

"Listen, Mrs. Lomangino," said Lucy placing her hand on Teresa's arm. "I don't want to say too much. It might make things worse if I interfere, but make sure the sheriff knows Frankie was with his father that day. And if you can remember the exact time they left the house, it could be important."

Teresa was silent for a time as she fought with more tears.

"Thank you, Mrs. Way." Lucy noted the Mrs. that Frank also used. "I doubt the sheriff will listen to me. He has it in for Frank and for my brother, too, but I'll shout it from the rooftops, if I have to. When Frank gets a lawyer, I'll get him to put me on the stand."

When Lucy finally finished cutting the squares and arranging them in a basket, she asked Teresa where to put them.

"How 'bout over there at the end of that table near the fire escape?" Teresa suggested.

As Lucy set the basket down, she realized that the fire escape would afford an excellent view of the murderer's escape route if he had climbed out of a basement window and run into the woods.

"Excuse me for a moment, Mrs. Lomangino, I think I'll just step out for some air."

"Sure thing, Mrs. Way."

Outside on the fire escape, Lucy looked down and thought she saw some evidence of disturbance in the brush: a broken twig here and there. If the sheriff did not return with a forensics team, she decided she must go over his head somehow and report him for negligence. With her eyes, Lucy traced a possible trail through the woods. Then, through the dense understory, she thought she saw movement. Yes, someone was walking on the carriage road. The murderer, she thought at once, though surely other people walked there, too, as she had herself only that morning. Yet she could not ignore the fluttering in her stomach, the trembling in her hands.

Absurdly, she tiptoed down the fire escape. At the bottom she realized she must not disturb evidence by crashing through the undergrowth, so she headed around the parish house, thinking to approach the woods through the gap in the wall beyond the large appliances tent. But just as she reached the tent, she saw the walker coming toward the gap. She turned back and ducked behind the hedge next to the steps by the office, the same hedge she'd used for concealment earlier. She was mortified when she saw that it was only Rick Foster. Fortunately, he did not see her crouching behind the hedge. He'd simply come to retrieve his car, which he'd left behind earlier when he'd driven his shrieking wife home in her own car.

Lucy waited until he had driven up the church driveway and turned before she crept out from behind the hedge, just as Anne came up the driveway from the barn.

"Lucy?" Anne had been understandably startled. "Were you... hiding behind that hedge?"

"I was," Lucy admitted, hoping to regain her sense of herself as an honest person after obfuscating and sneaking about, activities that were not consistent with what she hoped was her character.

"Oh?" said Anne, clearly too polite or confused to ask why.

"I'm afraid I was acting the fool, Anne," Lucy felt obliged to explain. "You see, I had such an odd, well, premonition isn't exactly the right word, since it's already happened...."

"Lucy, would you like to come to the house to have a cup of coffee with me?"

"Yes, Anne, thank you. I would."

Anne invited Lucy into the living room, but the kitchen seemed the place for confidences, though it had recently been damp-mopped and still smelled of pine soap and ammonia. Lucy waved away Anne's apologies for her cleaning lady (another of Gerald's good works, apparently) and sat down at the kitchen table. Sparing no detail, she told Anne how she had found the children in the woods the morning of the murder. Then she went on to recount her second conversation with them, their account of a man in a black sweatshirt (possibly horned and winged) running away.

"So despite your good husband's admonitions, I took it upon myself to see if I could detect an escape route. Through the woods, I saw someone walking on the carriage road. I am sure Miss Marple would not have leapt immediately to the conclusion that it was the murderer, but I did. I went and crouched behind the hedge. I felt so embarrassed when it was Mr. Foster. I trust he did not see me. I am afraid I may be coming more than a little unhinged."

Anne had looked at her a little strangely, as well she might.

"You saw Rick Foster coming out of the wood?" she said.

"He'd come back to get his car," Lucy added.

"Oh, yes, that's right," remembered Anne. "I offered him a ride, but he said the walk would do him good. I never thought of it, but I suppose the other end of the Rosewood estate opens onto Three Partners Road where the Fosters live."

"Yes, I believe it does," agreed Lucy. "Well, that explains why he was walking through the wood to get his car. Much shorter and pleasanter than by the main road. It's extraordinary what an overexcited imagination can make you think. I must say I am surprised at myself and a little horrified."

And Anne again had been strangely silent. When the phone rang, Anne had jumped up and slipped on a damp patch. She would have fallen if Lucy hadn't caught her arm and steadied her. Grace must have picked up the phone in the office, because the ringing stopped, but Anne lifted the receiver anyway. Lucy rose, thinking to excuse herself silently and tiptoe out. But Anne, horror battling with amusement for control of her face, held up a hand gesturing for Lucy to wait.

"Gerald, I'm here, too, on the house phone," Anne said at length. "No, I understand this could take quite a while. I won't expect you for dinner. I'll just keep something warm. All right. Bye."

"Oh, Lucy!" said Anne when she hung up the phone. "I really don't think I can keep this to myself. I know you won't tell anyone."

"Of course not, but perhaps you shouldn't...I mean, if Gerald...."

"They caught them!" Anne burst out. "Mildred drugged Nat's drink and kidnapped him. They caught them at a motel in the Catskills. She had locked him up and gone to get a justice of the peace to marry them. They're taking her to the police station!"

For the second time that day unseemly mirth overtook them.

"Oh hell's bells," said Anne when she'd recovered herself. "I just remembered I was on my way to the grocery store to pick up a few things for Rosalie and me while she's still here in charge of the children."

Lucy felt a moment's wistfulness at her lifelong exclusion from the cozy, companionable club young mothers seemed to form so effortlessly.

"Her husband expects her to be at home with dinner on the table at five, just the opposite of Gerald. I never know when to expect him. I'll have to hurry. I am sorry to rush you out the door, Lucy."

"That's perfectly all right, Anne," said Lucy, reminded again of the joys of spinsterhood. "By the way, whatever happened to the poor bat?"

"It clearly wasn't rabid. Don't tell Sybil, but Rosalie let it go."

Lucy followed Anne up and down the landing stairs and out the front door.

"It looks like Elsa's gone," Anne observed just before she got in the car. "Lucy, I wonder, I wonder if you should speak to Elsa when you get a chance. She seemed, well, she didn't seem quite herself this morning."

And before Lucy could ask any questions, Anne had gotten into her car and driven off, a careful, competent driver, who would be unlikely to need to slam on her brakes.

She hadn't called Elsa last night, Lucy realized, getting up and going inside the house. She had been so tired when she got home. She'd had a glass of wine with her supper and then gone straight to bed. To be perfectly honest, she had forgotten about Elsa until just now. It was not yet seven o'clock in the morning. Too early to call anyone unless it was an emergency. She would make a point to phone Elsa before she left for the rummage sale, and if Elsa was not at home, she would seek her out at the church even if it meant interrupting her practice.

By the time she had finished her breakfast, baguette with soft cheese and homemade preserves, tidied the kitchen, and made her bed, leaving a small cat-shaped lump under the spread, it was still only seven-thirty. She poured herself a second cup of coffee, as was her not terribly ascetic custom, and sat down in her parlor, with the lovely morning light now streaming in, to read the daily office. She comforted herself by reciting aloud *Benedicte, omnia opera Domini*. She loved the canticle because it invoked the vastness of creation and put the merely human in perspective. In a wavering soprano she suspected Elsa merely tolerated, she decided to sing her favorite verses:

O ye, sun and moon, bless ye the Lord;
  O ye stars of heaven, bless ye the Lord;
O ye showers and dew, bless ye the Lord;
  praise him and magnify him forever.

O ye winds of God, bless ye the Lord;
  O ye fire and heat, bless ye the Lord;
O ye winter and summer, bless ye the Lord;
  praise him and magnify him for—

And then the phone rang, louder, shriller, and more commanding than her voice. She would have liked to keep singing. She wished there was nothing to do but praise God and creation. But there was her neighbor. There was—what a strange thought, how abstract it had always seemed—her enemy or Charlotte's enemy. Someone's. Lucy put down the prayer book and went to pick up the kitchen phone.

"Lucy, Lucy!" said a breathless voice she did not immediately recognize.

"Speaking," she answered.

Then the sobs started, wrenching sobs that made Lucy's own chest ache.

"Who's there?" she finally asked. "How can I help?"

"Lucy, they've...taken...Elsa!"

"Clara? Is that you? What's happened? Take a deep breath. Speak slowly, tell me everything."

"They've taken Elsa to the police station. I don't know anything more."

"Clara," said Lucy, wishing smelling salts worked over the phone. "Sit down. Stay calm. I am coming right over. Don't do anything or go anywhere without me. Wait for me. Do you understand? Wait for me."

"Yes, Lucy," she said, sounding like a lost child.

"I'll be there in ten minutes."

Lucy hung up the phone. Without bothering to get a coat, she picked up her pocketbook and her first aid kit, always waiting on the bench by the door, and left her house.

CHAPTER THIRTY-THREE

Gerald sat alone in the church, in a pew a few rows from the front, where Lucy Way usually sat, he realized. Fitting. She had started the whole fiasco when she came to him with her suspicions. No, that wasn't fair. It wasn't Lucy's fault that Charlotte was dead, Nat widowed, Frank still incarcerated for extortion, Elsa behind bars, Mildred in the mental hospital. Now, to top it all off, he had to contend with Anne's wild suspicions. And tomorrow was the workers' sale followed by a weekend of rummage sale mayhem, crowds lined up the length of the driveway and even down Main Street.

Late afternoon light shone through the stained-glass window of Jesus the Good Shepherd. (Oh, to be a sheep, he thought, a stupid sheep with nothing to do but eat, bleat, be lost and be found.) By rights it was more than time for a martini, but he couldn't drink with Anne there possibly losing her marbles but still able to watch, count, judge, condemn. Even if Anne had been on his side, at his side (had she ever been?) he had too many parishioners in extremis. His whole parish was a shambles. He supposed he ought to call the bishop before the bishop called him. Again. (Grace had taken several messages.) He had no one else to talk to, not even Rick, especially not Rick. How could he tell Rick what Anne had said?

Gerald shielded his eyes from the sun blaring through the white sheep in the window and looked up at the wooden cross where Christ stood, not in naked agony, but triumphant in his bishop's raiment.

Talk to me.

Gerald heard a voice, inside his head, outside. Maybe he was going mad, too.

It's called prayer.

The voice spoke with a hint of irony Gerald found immensely reassuring.

I don't believe in that kind of prayer, Gerald heard himself answer.

I know. It's sentimental, smarmy, and self-serving, the voice laughed at him. *Try it.*

I don't know how.

Yet Gerald found himself slumping to his knees, leaning forward with his head against the pew as he wept.

That's right. You don't need words. Show me.

Without even summoning them, scenes from the last twenty-four hours began to run, as if his memory were a projector and this presence the light that cast them onto a screen he could not escape. So he watched, still helpless, helpless as some poor fool nailed to a cross.

"I did not kill Charlotte, I swear to you!" Mildred screamed, trying to fling herself at Nat in the driveway of the Pine Acres Motel, despite being restrained by the two officers the sheriff had summoned as backup.

The scene was all the more ghastly because Mildred wore what Gerald guessed was her wedding dress, under an ugly brown raincoat. Miss Havisham had at least had a kind of macabre dignity. Poor Mildred had cast hers to the winds that had blown her bedraggled veil askew.

"I swear to you, my dearest love, you must believe me! How could you do this to me? How could you do this to *us*? Don't you love me, Nattie? Don't you want to be with me at long last?"

Words to that effect, over and over, till the police, in their mercy, managed to wrestle her into the squad car, allowing Nat to go with Gerald. Neither Nat nor Gerald had any alcohol with him, which was probably just as well, Gerald reflected, since they both could really use a drink. For a while, Nat sat stunned. Then the silent tears started. Gerald kept his own silence, knowing that Nat would speak if and when he was ready.

"I want to go home," he said at last. "Will you take me home, Gerald?"

"We have to go to the police station first," answered Gerald. "Mildred kidnapped you. You'll have to decide whether or not to press charges against her."

Nat said nothing for so long Gerald wondered if he heard him or understood.

"God," Nat finally spoke. "God. The woman is mad. I never knew. Charlotte must have suspected. Used to tease me about old Millie still carrying a torch for me. I thought it was just a joke. I never thought, how could anyone…it's mad, she's mad. She ought to be locked up before she, before she—Oh God. Charlotte."

Gerald pondered for a moment and decided Lucy's confidence did not carry the seal of the confessional.

"Nat, we can't be sure, but I don't think Mildred killed Charlotte."

And he told Nat about Mildred finding Charlotte's body and fleeing the scene, perhaps almost running over Frank Lomangino's son.

"If that's so, then the boy, that young Italian, didn't kill Charlotte, after all?" Nat managed to make the connection. "I must tell Charlotte. She'll be so pleased. She liked him. Shameless flirt, my Charlotte. I should have been jealous. But I always knew she loved me best…."

He began to weep again and eventually, after blowing his nose loudly on a handkerchief, he dozed off, no doubt worn out from shock and whatever drugs Mildred had slipped in his drink. But the ordeal wasn't over yet.

There followed grueling hours of interrogations and statements and an appearance before the local judge. In the end, all charges against Mildred were dropped, provided she agreed voluntarily to "take a rest" at the Gables, the private and well-regarded mental hospital where more than one overwrought woman of a certain age had made a respectable retreat. Thank God, Mildred's nephew had been able to come and take charge of her along with John Collins, the family lawyer, who had clearly never expected to be called upon to do anything but estate planning. Charges related to fleeing a crime scene had also been dismissed. Mildred's account of the morning of the murder proved coherent enough to corroborate statements by both Teresa Lomangino and Gerald. Frank Lomangino's alibi for Charlotte's murder was now firmly established.

Gerald had finally gotten Nat home, in such a state of exhaustion that the old booze hound didn't even want a drink. Helping him into a dressing gown, Gerald put him to bed where Nat rolled toward the middle, unconsciously reaching for Charlotte.

Gerald sat still, slumped in the pew, aware of the light dimming in the west windows, the lost sheep a little duller, the shepherd, too. Only *one* lost sheep? What were the odds of that?

Keep looking, the voice said.

Gerald sat across the table from Frank Lomangino in the visiting room at the county jail where he'd felt compelled to stop last evening, even though he knew he should go home. Despite Frank's alibi for murder, the poor bastard was still being held on charges of extortion. Because Gerald was a clergyman, he was allowed to see Frank alone. They were permitted to smoke and Gerald had lit up, but Frank was too sunk in misery, his face buried in his hands. For the second time that day, Gerald was witness to a grown man's tears. No one had told him in seminary about this part of the job. New Testament Greek, what good did it do him now?

"Teresa ain't mad at me," Frank said at last. "She ain't mad at me. I'm a fool. I'm such a goddamned idiot. How can a woman like her love a man like me?"

Gerald didn't know the answer to that one—for Frank or for himself.

"I saw Mrs. Thomson's car that morning," Frank went on. "I told the judge I left the house with Frankie, just like Teresa told me to, but I didn't tell nobody that I'd seen that car on accounta Frankie almost got hit, and if he had gotten run over, it woulda been my fault. Teresa makes the kids wait with her when they cross a street, and look both ways, but I let Frankie run ahead. Teresa is always telling me: that boy needs a firm hand and you gotta be the one to give it to him. But behind her back, I let him get away with way too much. I didn't want to be like my pops, always beating up on us whether we did something or not. I'm a softie, a great big softie, that's what Teresa says. You better believe I swatted Frankie good after he ran out in the street and almost got hit. But I was so ashamed, I never told nobody. Now look what I put my family through. I'm a dope, a big, lousy dope."

It was pretty stupid, Gerald considered, without a shred of judgment. Frank could have spun the story to make the near accident all Mildred's fault. Or he could have sworn he told Frankie, Junior to wait at the corner, and he disobeyed, but the poor sod was too honest....

Some thought flickered at the edge Gerald's mind—like heat lightning or fireflies, gone before he could pin it down.

"It's all right now, Frank. However it happened, you've got an alibi now, a good, strong alibi. It's all right now."

Gerald spoke as much to himself as to Frank. He had not strong-armed the vestry into hiring a murderer, after all.

"All right?" Frank, who had been sitting slumped with his forehead in his hands, looked up, straight at Gerald. "Naw, it ain't all right. They can still put me away for a long time on this phony extortion charge. Whose gonna believe me? There's people behind this, and if they want me to go down, I'll go down."

"What do you mean?" asked Gerald, startled. "What people?"

Apparently Frank didn't know that Charlotte had confided in Rick Foster about Nat's gambling debt and the promises and threats Frank had made.

"You know...people." Frank shrugged and looked around uneasily. "People that don't like it when you go straight. People who think you might know too much."

Was he being conned, Gerald wondered? Was all that poor me, I'm such a big dope part of a con?

"But you believe me, don't you, Reverend? You wouldn't of taken a chance on me otherwise. Why would I go and do a terrible thing like that to a lady who was nothing but kind to me, giving me extra work, her husband, too. I didn't need the money. Teresa and me, we may not have much but we were getting by. We were happy."

Frank's head went down again, and Gerald realized his own head was swimming. He was exhausted. He hadn't eaten lunch or dinner.

"Don't worry, Frank," he found himself saying. "The truth will come out."

And who would it set free, he wondered?

"You think so, Father? Say, will you, I mean I know I'm Catholic, but I could use all the prayers I could get. Will you say a prayer for me and Teresa and the kids?"

"You bet, Frank," Gerald said, stubbing out his cigarette and pushing the rest of the pack across the table. "You bet."

Was it prayer to sit here in his empty church, anguished and uncertain of anyone's innocence or guilt, including his own?

You bet, Gerald, you bet, said the voice.

But he knew he wasn't done, praying, that is.

Like Nat, he had been too exhausted to drink when he got home at close to ten o'clock in the evening. He'd sat at the kitchen table eating the meatloaf and mashed potatoes Anne had kept and re-heated for him. He gave Anne a minimal account of the day. She had been attentive and solicitous of his needs, never once reproaching him for being so late, but he could tell she was agitated about something. She was usually catlike, with her tail silently lashing in displeasure, but now she made him think of a bird, darting and flashing in distress at some threat to her nest.

"Is something the matter?" he asked.

He felt her hesitate, teetering on the brink of confiding.

"It can wait," she decided. "You're exhausted. Get some rest."

She spoke with a kind of maternal authority that he found impossible to resist. So he did as she said. It seemed like he had been asleep only a few minutes when Anne shook him awake, but it was full daylight.

"Gerald," said Anne urgently. "I wanted to let you sleep longer, but this is an emergency."

Another one?

"It's Elsa. She's been arrested."

"Was she drunk?" he asked in confusion.

"She's been arrested for Charlotte's murder."

"I didn't do it," said Elsa in a flat voice, hours later, when he sat with her in another small visiting room in the county jail.

I was in prison and ye visited me, sick and ye came onto me. Between hospital calls and visits to the county jail, he had a good portion of Matthew 25 covered. He handed Elsa a cigarette, which she almost couldn't hold, her hands were shaking so badly. He hoped she was not having the DTs on top of everything else. He wondered if he should smuggle in some vodka.

"But I have no way to prove it."

"In this country the burden of proof is on the state."

Elsa snorted, "Believe it!"

Then her tears started, as silent as Nat's.

"Clara!" she finally burst out, letting go all the breath she had been holding. "Clara!"

Gerald waited while she tried to smoke and sob at the same time.

"Clara's all right," Gerald tried to reassure her. "Lucy's taken Clara home with her."

Elsa shook her head, squeezing her eyes shut, damming the tears.

"But if I get life, if I am executed, what then? Even Saint Lucy can't keep Clara forever, and she may...she may go mad again."

"Don't think that far ahead," Gerald pleaded, not just with her but with himself. "There's only Mildred's testimony that she saw you coming out of the bathroom. And Mildred just got carted off to the Gables. "

"I had opportunity and motive," said Elsa bluntly. "Everyone knows I hated Charlotte Crowley. *Mein Gott.* I make a public display of myself right in the church driveway. That old Scotchman heard me and that Fosterling man running for Congress. I am so *blödsinnig*, so stupid. And you, Gerald. You will have to testify against me."

"Elsa," said Gerald, "if I have to testify, I'll testify that when you've been drinking your language gets a little colorful, that I've warned you about it before. If you really had a plan to kill Charlotte, how likely is it that you would be shouting about it in the drive-way? As for motive, why would you kill Charlotte for probing into your private life? Everyone knows about you and Clara, and nobody really cares. And everyone knows you met at the mental institution. It's motivation for gossip not murder."

Elsa sat for a moment, sucking the last bit of smoke out of her cigarette. Then she reached for another and lit it from her first one.

"They will find something else then."

"What do you mean?" asked Gerald. "Who is they?"

"Whoever needs me to take the falling down."

"The fall?"

"Yah, the fall."

"Elsa, you are in America now. You are innocent until proven guilty. You can't afford to be so fatalistic."

She gave him a long look, longer than her first drag on the newly lit cigarette and a seemingly endless exhale. In her eyes, he saw prison camps, refugees, bodies wasted from starvation.

"I am in America, but I am not American. I am stupid, but I am not naïve."

Gerald was getting a crick in his neck and his knees were tired. He sat back in his pew and looked at the cross again. He supposed Jesus could have said the same thing. He'd taken the fall for the Fall, which Gerald had to confess had never made sense to him. How had the world changed since that long-ago execution?

There was no answer from the carved wooden figure or maybe that was the answer. Look at me. In the end I got resurrected. I got cleaned up, got a new suit of clothes and twenty-five bucks to start over.

Gerald, the voice said, *you're not done yet.*

When he had gotten home today, maybe only an hour ago, though time seemed distorted, stretched out, stretched thin, like the silly putty his kids played with, Anne had ushered him into his own office in the house and closed the door.

"How's Elsa?" she asked first.

He told her what he could and assured her that Lucy had taken charge of Clara. Almost before he was done, she interrupted, rare for Anne. She was so agitated that she got up from the wooden Trinity College chair while he remained in his leather easy chair.

"I have to tell you something that I haven't told anyone yet."

He felt himself bracing. It sounded ominous. Why couldn't his home be a haven from the storm?

"Do you remember the barbeque at the Fosters' house?" she began. "I think it was just the weekend before all this started."

All this? Murder. Suspicion, one arrest after another. Work on the rummage sale careening on like a juggernaut the whole time.

"What about it?" he prompted.

Anne was actually pacing, pulling at one hand with the other. He'd never seen her like this before. Depressed and withdrawn was her usual mode.

"I wanted to check on Katherine," she continued. "I couldn't find her anywhere outside. I went in the Fosters' house to look for her.

Last I'd seen her, she'd gone upstairs to change into her bathing suit. She wasn't in the bathroom where all the kids had left their clothes, so I walked down the hall and took a quick look in each room, the boys' bedrooms, the master bedroom...."

Where was she going with this, Gerald wondered? Anne was usually a woman of few words.

"Finally I came to what looked like Rick's study. There were law books on the shelf, leather chairs, a coffee table with magazines, a big desk...."

"That sounds like his study," Gerald agreed. "I've met with him there from time to time. Was Katherine in there getting into mischief?"

What could the child possibly have done that Anne would have concealed it from him all this time?

"Not Katherine. Charlotte. Charlotte Crowley. She was going through Rick's desk. It looked like she was studying an old photograph."

Relief flooded Gerald. This big build up and that was *it*? Charlotte doing what she always did? Everyone knew Charlotte was a snoop.

Had been, that is. Had been.

"Maybe it was silly," Anne went on, "but I didn't want her to know I had seen her. I wanted her to get caught. I wanted her to be punished, for, I guess I never told you about it, for the time she went in my bureau and took out Hal's photograph."

So that was why Anne hated Charlotte so much, so...murderously. Oh, God, oh, God, please God no. Don't let this be a confession.

"So I tiptoed away and went to find Rick. I asked if I could speak with him privately. We went inside the house to the living room. No one else was around. I told him what I'd seen Charlotte doing. I told him she'd found a photograph. I thought he could go upstairs and catch her in the act, but that's when the big loud fight broke out with the children, and he went outside instead."

Anne stopped and waited, waited for him to draw some conclusion.

"Why are you telling me this now?" he asked at length. "Is it, is it because of Elsa?".

Because of Elsa taking the blame for your crime? He couldn't say it.

"Elsa?" Anne seemed momentarily puzzled. "I don't like to think Elsa could have killed Charlotte. But we just don't know, any of us, what we might be capable of."

Gerald felt confused, dizzy, and he hadn't even had a drink. What was she trying to tell him?

"No, it was something Lucy said," Anne continued. "I had forgotten all about that day at the barbeque. Or at least I hadn't made the connection. Then Lucy got this idea that whoever killed Charlotte might have escaped through a basement window and run into the woods. Remember when we couldn't find Katherine that morning? She and Frankie apparently ran off into the woods. They told Lucy they saw someone in a black hooded sweatshirt running through the woods."

"Wait!" Gerald actually held up his hand. "I'm sorry, dear, I'm just not following. What does any of this have to do with Charlotte snooping in Rick's study?"

Anne looked surprised, as if it was all so obvious.

"Lucy saw Rick coming out of the woods," she said slowly, patiently. "He'd had to drive Sybil home because she thought she'd been attacked by a bat. They live on the other side of Rosewood. He walked back through the woods to get his own car."

She was having a breakdown, Gerald thought. She was not making sense, leaping from one thing to another. Then he made the connection. Charlotte snooping in Rick's study. Rick taking a short cut through the woods, the woods that Lucy believed had been the murderer's escape route.

"Are you trying to tell me that Lucy Way suspects Rick Foster of murdering Charlotte Crowley?"

There was a long moment.

"No," said Anne at last. "Lucy doesn't suspect him. I do."

Gerald put his face in his hands again, wishing there was some-one to sit with him and witness his anguish the way he had sat with Nat and Frank and Elsa.

He knew he was supposed to believe Jesus was with him. He was a minister of the Gospel for Christ's sake. No offense to God incar-nate intended, but right now he wanted another person, another flesh and blood person, someone to minister to *him*, and there was no one.

"Tell me what to do," Gerald prayed silently. "Tell me how to talk to Anne."

Because they would have to talk about her, well, her crazy suspi-cions. When some child wasn't caterwauling. That's what had hap-pened this afternoon. Janie started screeching just beyond the front porch. Apparently Peter had been pulling her in a wagon, and she ended up on her hands and knees in the gravel. "It was on accident," Peter insisted over Janie's screams. Gerald had gone outside with Anne to help, but Janie had only wanted Anne. When Gerald tried to talk to Peter, he had started wailing, too, and clung to his mother's skirt. Gerald didn't think any of them had even noticed him walking away, seeking refuge in his own church where not even Elsa would interrupt him now.

Oh, God. Elsa. He wondered if he could find where she'd hidden the vodka. No, he shouldn't even look. He had to keep his wits about him.

Anne, Anne.

He did not seem to be able to do anything but pray her name. Gerald leaned his head against the pew again. He was so tired, so tired.

He must have dozed off. He hadn't heard anyone come into the church, but all at once he was aware of someone sitting next to him.

"It's all right, Gerald, take it easy. You've been having a tough time."

A comforting voice, a hand on his shoulder.

Jesus?

He had asked for someone to sit beside him. Had his prayer been answered? Gerald turned to look.

Jesus! Of all the people to turn up...oh, Jesus!

CHAPTER THIRTY-FOUR

Anne wished she could talk to someone before she talked to Gerald again, or maybe they wouldn't talk. They were so practiced at avoiding anything painful between them and since almost everything was they usually had very little of consequence to say to each other. And, in general, Anne preferred it that way. Her unhappiness was hers, and she was used to guarding it. What else did she have? But now she and Gerald had to talk. They had decisions to make. Granted, her theory might be far-fetched, and Rick was Gerald's friend. But so was Elsa. Why should Rick Foster be exempt from the list of suspects? Why should she? Charlotte Crowley had pried into all their lives. That's what she had to get Gerald to see.

Not long after she had gotten Janie's scraped knees and elbows cleaned and bandaged, someone rang the doorbell. The children had already gone back outside. She had been upstairs putting away bandages and disinfectant, tidying up the bathroom. Let Gerald answer the door. She was in no mood to deal with anyone right now. But the doorbell had rung again. Where was Gerald? She'd assumed he'd retreated to his office at home with a stiff drink.

She had gone to look out the bedroom window, which had an all too ample view of the driveway (only Katherine's little room and the bishop's room afforded any privacy). The doorbell rang a third time. She was just resigning herself to going down to answer the door when she saw Rick Foster step away from the front porch into the driveway. He hesitated, apparently debating whether or not to leave. As if she were in some Alfred Hitchcock film, she ducked away from the window and watched him through the curtain. He glanced towards the parish house, then turned and looked at the house, almost as if he suspected he was being watched. Then, with something just shy of a shrug, he crossed the driveway and went into the church.

If he wanted Gerald, the church was the least likely place to find him, Anne thought. Maybe Rick just wanted to pray.

Somehow she found the thought chilling.

The children were having their supper now. She was letting them eat in the dining room so that they could watch The Mickey Mouse Club and she could have a moment to collect herself. Where was Gerald? She thought she had heard him come in while she was settling the children at the table, but when she returned to the kitchen there was no sign of his having mixed a drink. Now might be her only chance to make a call before she had to sit down and have dinner with him. But who could she talk to? Not Rosalie. Her husband became irate if she talked on the phone for more than a few minutes when he was home. Poor Lucy had her hands full tending to Clara. She needed someone who knew how to listen, someone who knew her, but was not directly involved.

Dr. Aiken. She usually never called him except to make an appointment, but he had said she could if there was ever an emergency....

She opened the wooden cabinet under the phone and found Dr. Aiken's home phone number on the emergency list. She wrote it down, and then she went to use the phone upstairs in case Gerald came into the kitchen to make a martini. Sitting down on the edge of her bed, she lifted the receiver.

"And there's something else...."

Anne heard Gerald's voice. Of course, he'd gotten caught on the phone. That's why he hadn't made his drink. She started to put the receiver down.

"And what is that?" prompted the other voice.

Dr. Aiken? Dr. *Aiken*!

"I think, I think...I think she tried to seduce him."

"Very interesting," he said in that attentive but neutral tone she knew so well. "Why is that?"

"She told me that she had found Charlotte Crowley, that's the woman who was murdered, snooping in his study. Well, it might have happened the other way around."

"In what regard?" asked Dr. Aiken. "I am not sure I am following you."

That made two of them, Anne thought, holding her breath.

"He told me, my parishioner whose house we were visiting that day, that Anne asked to speak with him privately. He took her to his office, she, uh, I gather, she, uh…"

"She proposed to have an affair with him," said Dr. Aiken with his usual sangfroid.

Anne covered the receiver with her hand, so they couldn't hear her breathe, but she kept listening.

"Yes, that's what he said." Gerald's voice was ragged, as if he were about to cry.

In the midst of her shock, Anne felt a stab of pity and rage so sharp she had to bite her tongue to keep from screaming.

"He turned her down, of course," said Gerald.

Of course?

"He's…he's not just a parishioner. He's a good friend."

And what was she? What was *she*?

"He ushered her out and found Charlotte wandering in the hall, claiming to be looking for a bathroom. He suspects Charlotte probably heard the whole exchange."

There was a silence on the line. It seemed endless. She knew Dr. Aiken was waiting for Gerald to spit it out, his worst fears.

That Anne had a motive for murder or for framing Rick for murder—or both?

"Dr. Aiken, I don't know what to think. I don't know what to believe," said Gerald.

Anne could hear Gerald holding his breath and gasping and holding his breath again as he swallowed his sobs. Part of her wanted to go to him as she would to one of her children, and part of her wanted to put down the phone, pack an overnight bag, walk out the door and never look back.

"You mean you don't know whom to believe," Dr. Aiken said coolly.

She could almost picture him, sitting at his desk (though of course he was at home, a place she'd never seen). If he wasn't on the phone, he would be gazing intently over his glasses, his two pointer fingers making a triangle at the base of his clean-shaven chin, with the cleft in it that Anne admired so much, like Gregory Peck's. Gerald didn't have one.

"That's it." Gerald let out his breath. "One of them has to be lying."

"Not necessarily," said Dr. Aiken slowly.

"What do you mean?" said Gerald. "They can't both be telling the truth. They're in direct contradiction with each other. I, I have to choose, but how can I possibly choose...."

That's right, Gerald. You have to choose. Anne felt strangely calm as she sat at the edge of the bed, gazing at the pines in Rosewood that towered over the church, higher even than the steeple. A light wind tossed them. Her fate was in someone else's hands, Gerald's hands.

"Listen, Gerald, may I call you Gerald?"

"Sure, sure."

"I don't know if you fully realize how fragile Anne is. She is held together by scotch tape."

She should put the phone down, Anne told herself. She didn't want to know this. She didn't want to hear this.

"I know she's never gotten over Hal's..."

Death, Anne finished the sentence silently. Gerald couldn't say it, even on the phone with Dr. Aiken. That's why she hated him. That's why she couldn't hate him. He'd never gotten over Hal's death either.

"It is possible that she never will," Dr. Aiken said. "It's more than simple grief. You see, Gerald, unconsciously she blames you for his death. She feels you have failed her as a husband, as a father."

She had been through all this with Dr. Aiken before. She did blame Gerald. It was not unconscious at all, just private. Or it had been till now.

"That gives her a strong unconscious motivation to turn to a substitute," Dr. Aiken continued.

Bizarrely, Anne thought of the substitute teacher, Miss Myers, who Katherine complained was mean and unfair.

"Unconsciously Anne wants to hurt you, and yet, also unconsciously, she wants to be close to you, so she chooses someone you admire and respect. He spurns her. Then her unconscious rage is transferred to a new object. She seeks to destroy this friend of yours through false accusations. She even enlists your aid in destroying him, thereby trying to reconcile with you—"

"Wait, wait." Gerald sounded confused. "Are you saying that in order to reconcile with Anne I have to play along with her suspicions of Rick Foster?"

"No, no, of course not. I am merely trying to explain to you how internal psychological and emotional pressures meeting with traumatic external events, like a murder, might have brought Anne to a crisis point, possibly even a psychotic episode. It is possible, even probable, that she is not lying deliberately, that she has persuaded herself that her version of the event is true."

There was a pause. If she put the phone down now, they would hear the click of the receiver.

"So in layman's terms," Gerald spoke at length, "you're telling me my wife is nuts."

"I'm telling you that she may well be delusional. We can hope that it is a temporary, treatable condition."

"But what do I do now?" Gerald sounded panicked.

Anne felt sick. Why did it not occur to Gerald that she might be telling the truth? A dreadful thought came into her mind. What if she wasn't? Could she have imagined seeing Charlotte in Rick's office? Why would she do that? Then an even more dreadful thought arose. Could she have more than one personality like the woman in that terrifying movie *The Three Faces of Eve?* Could one of her personalities have killed Charlotte Crowley unbeknownst to the others?

Rubbish, a voice spoke distinctly inside her head. (Now she was hearing voices?) It sounded a little like Lucy Way's voice, kind but firm. Sensible. *Keep your wits about you.*

"Just keep her quiet tonight," Dr. Aiken was saying. "Don't say anything to excite her and get her in to see me as soon as possible. I'll tell my secretary to expect a call from you."

Anne barely listened as Gerald and Dr. Aiken said goodbye. She had to think. Gerald had it right the first time. Either she or Rick Foster was lying. And if it was Rick, then he had a reason to lie—and a reason to discredit her in Gerald's eyes.

She heard the click as Gerald hung up, and she put down the receiver carefully as though they could still hear her. She sat very still, hardly breathing. That is what rabbits did when danger was near. They didn't run; they couldn't fight. They froze, hoping not to be seen.

She was in danger.

Gerald didn't believe her. Dr. Aiken didn't believe her. Who would? The sheriff?

Lucy. Lucy Way.

But even Lucy had not believed that Rick Foster could be guilty. She had sat with him in the large appliances tent and confided her theory that the murderer had fled into the wood. But that was before Anne had remembered that Charlotte Crowley had snooped in his office and before Lucy's dear friend Elsa had been arrested for Charlotte's murder.

She must tell Lucy what had happened. Lucy ought to know. But then Lucy would be in danger, too. Anyone who believed Anne would be in danger.

Then Anne thought of someone, someone who would want to know, who might know what to do. She didn't have much time. She opened a drawer in the bedside table and got out the telephone book. Thank God, he was listed.

"Anne?" Gerald called up the stairs anxiously. "Anne?"

"I'll be right there," she answered.

Praying that he would not come up to check on her, she lifted the receiver and dialed.

CHAPTER THIRTY-FIVE

They were running away from the bad man. He had chased them into the church driveway. Frankie had gotten way ahead of her, all the way down to the end. He turned and shouted at her:

"Hurry up, Katherine! Hurry!"

She tried to run but her legs wouldn't move. She tried to scream but no sound would come out. Then a car came and hit Frankie. He went flying up into the air. The lady caught him and they both came flying towards her.

"Fly Katherine, fly," called the lady. "Remember your fairy blood. Fly!"

But it was too late, the bad man grabbed hold of her, he turned her around, and made her look at his face. His mouth was open and he was yelling at her.

"Leave your mother alone. Don't you know she needs a rest from you kids? You're just like your brother Hal."

He was shaking her, his mouth open wider and wider like a monster till the whole world went black.

"Mommy, Mommy."

She could feel the air pushing in her throat, pushing and pushing but still there was no sound.

Then she found herself sitting up in her bed. She could see the hall light shining on her open door.

"Mommy," she called again, her voice only a whisper but she could hear it. She called again louder, "Mom-*my*!"

She listened for the sound of her mother's feet and her door creaking open, but it didn't come. There was only a rumbling sound, rising and falling like the bear going over the mountain.

"Mommy!" she called again as loud as she dared, and then she got up out of bed, walking like an Indian the way Frankie had showed her, so that her feet just breathed over the ground and came down soft like clouds. She could not help the door squeaking as she opened it a crack. But the light from the hall did not fall on her mother's head with its pins and pink curlers.

Her mother wasn't there.

Her father's slow bear snoring turned into a pig snort, and she closed the door quickly so he wouldn't see her.

Where was her mother?

What if she had gone away, gone away because Katherine wouldn't let her rest?

Katherine's knees began to shake and tears came out of her eyes, but she did not call again. She would be very quiet. If she found her mother, she would not ask for anything, not for a drink of water or to be tucked into bed. She just needed to find her. She crept down the dark stairs, holding onto the banister.

On the landing, she stopped. The hall was dark. The kitchen was dark. She did not think she had ever been awake so late, later than Santa Claus on Christmas Eve. The mice must be asleep. She imagined them tucked into their walnut shell beds wearing nightcaps, safe from cats. She wished right now she was a mouse.

Then she heard a sound. Her mother clearing her throat, sighing, her mother awake downstairs in the dark living room.

Katherine tiptoed down the stairs, across the cold floor of the front hall to the living room door where she hesitated. There was a little orange glow near the couch. Her mother's cigarette, held between her fingers resting over the coffee table. Night light from the window found her mother's face and made it look like the lady in the moon. And then Katherine saw the rest of her mother, half-lying on the couch with her knees up making mountains.

Her mother never lay on the couch in the day time. She did not know this mother lying by herself in the dark. This was who her mother turned into in the night, someone not her mother.

The tears came back. Without meaning to, she let out a little whimper.

"Katherine?" her mother said.

It was her mother, her mother's voice. She sat up on the couch and put the cigarette in the ashtray.

"What are you doing up?"

Katherine didn't answer. She didn't want to bother her mother.

"Are you resting?" Katherine finally asked.

She could feel her mother looking at her, even though she couldn't see her eyes now that she'd turned her face from the window.

"Yes, I am resting," her mother said. "I couldn't sleep, so I am resting instead."

Her mother lifted the cigarette to her mouth. The light made her face look like an orange mask. Then her mother put it out, and it was dark again.

"I am resting, too," Katherine said.

"Would you like to rest with me for a little while?"

Katherine didn't speak, just ran across the room to her mother. Her mother put her feet back on the couch and pulled Katherine into her lap, so that Katherine's legs lay on her mother's legs and her head rested under her mother's chin.

This was better, better than being a mouse in a walnut shell bed.

"Did you have a bad dream?" her mother asked after a moment.

Katherine nodded, feeling her head move against the bone of her mother's chest.

"What did you dream?"

Her mother was asking. It wouldn't be bothering to tell her.

"I dreamed about the bad man."

Her mother was so quiet Katherine wondered if she had heard her.

"Who is the bad man, Katherine?"

"The man in the woods," she answered.

"The one you and Frankie saw? The one with horns and wings?"

She nodded again, not sure how her mother knew. She and Frankie had never told anyone but the lady.

"Katherine," her mother spoke, then stopped. Katherine turned in her arms and laid her ear on her mother's chest. Thud-a-thump, her heart was very loud, thud-a-thump, like it was a rabbit hopping away. "Did you and Frankie, did you ever see the bad man's face?"

Katherine's dream came back to her, and she turned her face all the way into her mother's chest.

"Daddy," she said.

"What? I can't hear you, Katherine, what did you say?"

She lifted her head and sat up facing her mother.

"Daddy is the bad man."

"In your dream?"

"I dreamed the bad man was chasing us and then...it was Daddy."

Katherine's mother was quiet for a moment, and then she took Katherine's face in her hands.

"That morning in the woods when you and Frankie saw that man, Daddy was home asleep in bed. He's not the bad man. Dreams get things mixed up sometimes. Daddy's not a bad man, he's just a sad man."

Katherine settled back into her mother's arms trying to understand.

"Why is Daddy sad?" she asked.

"I don't know," her mother said.

And Katherine could hear in her voice, her mother was sad, too. Her mother and father were both sad, though most of the time her father just seemed mad and mean. It was because of Hal, Katherine knew, even though they never said so. She was sad, too.

"Mommy?" she said after a little while. "Who is the bad man?"

"I don't know," her mother said again.

She wished her mother had said the bad man was just her imagination, the way she often did when Katherine was scared. She wished she had said, the bad man is only a bad dream, but she didn't. Her mother's heart was so loud: thud-a-thump, thud-a-thump, and her arms tightened around Katherine.

"You must promise me," she said, "promise me you and Frankie won't go into the woods again."

But Katherine couldn't promise her. She had already promised to help Frankie catch the bad man. They had made a trap. They had javelins. The lady had told them not to go in the woods alone, but she didn't make them promise. She said she would go with them some-day, because they all had fairy blood. The lady knew her mother, so maybe she wouldn't worry if they went with the lady.

"We won't go in the woods again without, without Lucy." Katherine spoke her name as if it were a magic charm.

"Lucy?" her mother said. "Lucy from the Narnia books?"

"Lucy," Katherine said again. "Lucy Way."

CHAPTER THIRTY-SIX

Lucy put down the phone for the second time that morning, praying that it would not ring again until she had had a chance to collect herself. Thank heavens she had thought to put Clara to work polishing the silver. Having something to do with her hands seemed to calm her. Lucy's own hands were shaking. Her heart pounded so frantically, like a trapped bird. She wished she could open her chest and let her heart fly out of her into the soft swirling clouds that she could see outside the window on the landing.

"O had I the wings of a dove for then I would fly away and be at rest."

The line from the psalm sprang to her lips, giving her fleeting comfort, but there was no escape from this strife, and now she was in the midst of it, right in the middle between husband and wife, the last place she wanted to be.

Gerald had called first, speaking in such a hushed voice that at times she'd had trouble understanding him.

"A lot on your plate, I know, but Anne might listen to you...." His voice dropped again. Lucy strained to hear. "Refused to go see her doctor, said she was too busy with the rummage sale."

"I'm sorry, Gerald," Lucy said. "I am afraid I missed some of what you said. Is Anne ill?"

There was a pause.

"Worse than that, Lucy. Her doctor thinks she might be having a nervous breakdown. She might be delusional."

Lucy did not know what to say. It made no sense for Gerald to call her. He must be beside himself to be so lacking in discretion and judgment.

"Gerald, I am sorry to hear that Anne is not doing well. I wish I could help, but," here Lucy dropped her own voice, "I have Clara with me. I promised to take her to see Elsa this morning. But perhaps later, depending on how things go—"

"No, no, Lucy," said Gerald in a more normal tone that also sounded forced. "Forget I asked. You are doing too much as it is. And by the way, thank you for arranging an attorney for Elsa. Rick Foster offered to make inquiries, but...."

His voice dropped again.

"Think nothing of it," said Lucy. "Mr. Barnswell has been my family's solicitor for years. He'll be able to recommend someone if—"

"Excuse me, Lucy," Gerald practically whispered. "I have to go. Will you, will you...pray for Anne?"

He sounded both desperate and embarrassed.

"Of course," she answered, but he had already hung up.

She had hardly had time to reproach herself for not asking more questions or offering to find some way to help when the phone rang again.

"Lucy, it's Anne."

"Hello, Anne," she said, then found herself tongue-tied.

"Lucy, I have remembered something that may be important. Would you be willing to hear what I have to say or would you... would you rather not? I tried to tell Gerald, I did tell Gerald but...."

He didn't believe you, Lucy finished silently. And bless you, you are giving me a choice and I almost wish you'd just blurt it out. Then it wouldn't be my fault for hearing you. Dear God, what do I do?

"Go on," Lucy heard herself saying.

As Anne poured out her story, Lucy sat down on the edge of the worn Victorian chair on the landing. Her back did not touch the straight wooden back, and she did not settle in enough to feel the prickliness of the horsehair cushion. Though she stared out the window, she did not see the leaves from the yellow maple eddying as they fell. She saw Charlotte bent over a desk, pulling open drawers, holding up a photograph, her insatiable curiosity momentarily satisfied or piqued.

"I tiptoed away and went to find Rick," Anne was saying. "I wanted to see Charlotte Crowley have her comeuppance. I never dreamed anything worse than that would happen."

"I see," said Lucy slowly, trying to collect her thoughts. Is this what Gerald meant by delusional, her suspicion that Rick Foster might commit murder over an old photograph? It did seem rather fantastical. "How did Mr. Foster respond?"

"He didn't say much, just thanked me for telling him. I was about to excuse myself when the big fight broke out between the children. He went outside, and so did I."

"And so you never found out what photograph Charlotte unearthed or if she pocketed it?"

"No," said Anne. "I never spoke to Rick Foster about the matter again. I never even thought about it until you mentioned the idea that the murderer could have escaped into the woods. And then we both remembered that Rick lives on the other side of the woods."

We, meaning Anne and herself. The pronoun made Lucy uncomfortable.

"Forgive me, Anne." Lucy decided she'd better be direct. "I don't doubt for a minute that Charlotte Crowley snooped in Mr. Foster's office, but we," she used the pronoun judiciously, "we can't assume that what she found gave him a motive for murder. I don't mean to sound harsh, but if you honestly suspect Mr. Foster, you should go to the police, not to me."

Anne was silent for a moment, just long enough for Lucy to be filled with self-doubt and reproach.

"I have gone to the police," Anne said at length. "Well, sort of. I didn't think the sheriff would believe me."

Lucy could not argue with that.

"Even my own husband doesn't. He doesn't even believe that Charlotte snooped in Rick's office." Anne rushed on before either of them could think better of it. "He thinks, he thinks I tried to seduce Rick Foster and that Charlotte overheard."

"My dear girl!" Lucy was shocked. "Why on earth would he think a thing like that?"

Anne paused for a beat.

"Because Rick Foster told him so."

Lucy wished she were standing, so that she could sit down. Her hand moved to her heart and clutched the soft fabric of her lavender cashmere sweater.

"Lucy?" said Anne after a moment. "Are you still there?"

"I'm here," she managed to say.

"Gerald thinks I'm crazy. He called my psychiatrist last night. I picked up the other phone and eavesdropped. He tried to get me to see Dr. Aiken this morning. I said I couldn't possibly take the time because of the rummage sale."

I know, Lucy did not say out loud. She couldn't tell Anne that Gerald had just called. She couldn't, could she?

"I'm so sorry, Lucy. I know you've got Clara with you and you're worried about Elsa. It's just that, well, I'm frightened. If Gerald forces me to see Dr. Aiken, I could end up at the Gables with Mildred. If everyone believes Rick's story, I could, well, I suppose I could even end up next door to Elsa—or take her place. If that happens, I need someone, someone to know...."

Anne might not be insane, but she was verging on hysteria. Lucy could hear it in her voice. She had to calm her down.

"Now, Anne, it is no good thinking that way," said Lucy firmly. "You must stay calm. If I can think of what to do with Clara, I will be at the rummage sale after I see Elsa. Meanwhile—"

"Oh, Lucy!" It sounded as though Anne had been holding her breath and finally let it out. "If you come, you could bring Clara. She could help Rosalie in the toy barn. No one would bother her there."

That might be a good plan for Clara. It was best to keep her busy instead of brooding, and Rosalie would know how to protect Clara. But even if she believed Anne's admittedly unsubstantiated theory about Rick Foster what would Lucy's presence accomplish, apart from being another pair of hands at the workers' sale?

"I will be there if I can," said Lucy cautiously. "But I can't promise anything. Meanwhile, you must promise me. Don't do anything rash. We don't know yet who killed Charlotte." She used "we" deliberately. "But I agree it is possible that the murderer is still at large. Stay where people can see you. And Anne, when you said you told the police, sort of, what did you mean by that?"

There was another silence.

"I called Joe Petrone."

"But he's been taken off the case!" protested Lucy.

"I know, but I didn't know what else to do."

Except to call Lucy and pull her into the maelstrom.

"I'm sorry, Lucy." Anne seemed to read her thoughts. "I'm afraid...I'm afraid I may be putting you in danger, too."

"Nonsense," said Lucy before she could think. "Anne dear, I must go check on Clara now. I'll see you later this morning if I'm able. Goodbye."

She'd hung up the phone.

Then she must have stood up, for she was still standing by the window, one hand holding onto the other to still the trembling. Silently she began to repeat the ancient prayer: *Lord Jesus Christ, Son of God, have mercy on me, a sinner.* She prayed it over and over until her breathing slowed to match the rhythm of the words. Slowly her breath and heartbeat took over, then they became the prayer, the ground for her thought.

She was not caught between husband and wife. She did not have to believe one over the other. She had to face the truth, about herself first. She had been blind to the possibility that Rick Foster might be the killer, for no other reason than that he was polite, even courtly, and he reminded her of someone she had once adored, and she had not even known it till this moment. She had forced herself to beware of her own biases about Elsa and Mildred, and even Frank Lomangino. She had guessed, even hoped, the killer might have been someone else. It was true, as she told Anne, they still didn't know who the killer was. But dear God, if it was Rick Foster, charming Rick Foster who was running for Congress yet took time to help at the Church of Regeneration rummage sale, well then, she had sat with him, sipped the water he kindly brought her to help her recover from her shock, and confided in him her theory about the murderer's escape route.

And if Anne, if Anne was telling the truth, then Rick Foster was lying. (All right she did have to choose.) And if everyone, starting with Anne's own husband, believed Rick, he could effectively discredit Anne as a witness, which left only....

"Lucy!" Clara called from the bottom of the stairs, plaintive and childlike. "Lucy, I finished the silverware. What should I do now?"

"Let's get ready to go, Clara!" said Lucy turning from the window and coming to the top of the stairs. "We'll visit Elsa and then we'll go on to the rummage sale." Before Clara could protest, she added briskly, "Rosalie Brown needs help in the toy barn."

CHAPTER THIRTY-SEVEN

Gerald was hiding out in his office in the parish house, not that it was a very good hiding place, but he didn't know what else to do. He could and perhaps should be visiting Nat or Elsa or, God help him, Mildred, not to mention making his usual rounds to shut-ins and hospital patients, but he did not want to leave the premises with Anne in such a fragile state. He could have holed up in the office in the house, pleading a sermon to write, but it felt like shirking (something his father would never countenance). Of course he knew he was also avoiding Anne. She was less likely to seek him here than at home. So he sat hunched over his desk, working on a fund-raising letter for the children's camp. Miraculously, Mildred's nephew still seemed willing to sell Rosewood, or perhaps not so miraculously, Gerald considered. Other buyers might be scared off a property next door to a church where murder had been done. Maybe the family wanted to be shed of the costly albatross as well as any proximity to the drama that had driven dear old Aunt Millie round a shockingly sordid bend.

But now that they'd found a suitable property, the mysterious benefactors had mysteriously disappeared. Grace had spent an entire morning looking for a bank statement she was sure she'd filed that reflected a significant donation. She had asked Gerald to call the bank, but the bank had no record that matched the one in Grace's memory. "I must be going nuts, then!" Grace had muttered over and over before she finally gave up. Gerald hadn't wanted to press Rick any further about the men he'd met at his barbecue. Rick had mentioned something about the donors' company suffering losses they had to recoup before making commitments to a charitable organization.

After the election, win or lose, Rick promised to turn his attention to the camp funding campaign. Meanwhile Gerald was crafting a letter to other potential donors as well as looking into state and federal grants.

He had started the same paragraph over and over again: "The Hal Bradley Memorial Camp is dedicated to promoting understanding and friendship between children of all races, creeds, and economic backgrounds. Prejudice is rooted in ignorance of others that can all too easily be twisted into hatred and fear, as history has demonstrated time and again. At Camp Hal...."

He could not concentrate. The outward din of the rummage sale competed with the inward clamor of his anxious thoughts. The project, which had seemed so exciting and visionary, now felt stale even before it got off the ground. Maybe he was just tired. He had woken in the night to find Anne gone from the bed. Certain she'd left him, he tore downstairs, so relieved to find her dozing on the couch with Katherine he'd almost fainted. He'd gone upstairs to get a blanket to cover them. He'd stood watching for a moment, child and mother resting so comfortably together. Why couldn't it be that easy for Anne and him?

It had never been easy, even before the children. He'd thought Anne might change in time; married life was a big adjustment. Then he saw her change overnight when Hal was born. She opened, she melted—but not for Gerald.

To him she remained mysterious, unfathomable. Last evening he had expected her to badger him about Rick or to punish him for not responding as she wished. But she had said nothing; it was as if their earlier conversation had not happened. (Could she be schizophrenic?) She'd cooked and served dinner, put the children to bed, put her hair up in curlers, gone to bed herself with a book, all as usual, except ordinarily he knew she was in some way displeased with him. Last night he could sense nothing. It felt as though she had vanished, leaving behind an Anne automaton to fool him. Today when he suggested she take the morning off and see Dr. Aiken, she had not reacted except to remind him the workers' sale was tonight and she'd be needed here. "I'll make an appointment for Monday," she had assured him, and she picked up the phone and dialed before he could even think about slipping off to call Dr. Aiken again.

Then she had taken the twins to nursery school and gone straight to the parish house when she'd gotten back. He knew, because he had watched out the window. He had trailed after her, but he did not want her to think he was following her, so he'd gone to the office where he'd found Grace already at her desk.

"Could I ask a favor of you, Grace?" he'd said after they sorted through mail and messages.

"Sure, boss," she said.

She called him that sometimes; it was entirely unaffected and affectionate. It filled him with yearning, not for Grace exactly, but for simplicity.

"What can I do you for?" she prompted when he didn't answer right away.

"I'm going to be working on the fundraising letter for the camp this morning. I can answer the phone. I wonder if you would mind helping out with the rummage sale today and...sort of keeping an eye on Anne?"

Grace raised one dark (rather beautifully shaped, he noticed) eyebrow so high it looked as though it might keep going all the way to the ceiling. It was so easy to read Grace.

"Anne's been under a lot of strain," Gerald explained. "I mean the rummage sale is bad enough. But all this other business...." He trailed off.

"Whatever you say, Gerald." Grace got to her feet. "I've been meaning to check out the merchandise before the sale tonight and size up the competition, you know, who I'm gonna have to deck or trample to get the mink stole. I'll try to be subtle or Anne'll get the wind up. She's a smart cookie, Gerald, and tougher than she looks."

She clicked in her high heels out of the office, leaving Gerald reassured and bemused. Held together by scotch tape, tougher than she looks? Which description of Anne was true? Damned if Gerald knew.

Gerald put down his pen and rubbed his eyes, then just rested them against his knuckles, looking at the swirling green and black, red and gold behind his eyelids. He remembered doing that as a kid. When Hal asked him about the colors he saw when he closed his eyes, Gerald knew what Hal meant. One of his better moments as a father, which was sad in itself. No wonder he kept losing steam when he tried to write that letter. Nothing could make up for Hal's loss, and nothing could make up for what he didn't do when he had the chance and, worse, what he did do.

We have done those things we ought not to have done and we have left undone those things we ought to have done, and there is no health in us. The General Confession summed it up. He was a priest, the one who granted absolution in God's name. Why did he never feel forgiven?

Gerald opened his hands and rested his face in them, his elbows on the desk. He was tired, so tired. He let himself doze off, vaguely aware that he'd been doing that a lot lately. When he heard the knock on his door, he came to with such a start he almost gave himself whiplash.

"Come in," he managed to say.

The door opened and there was Rick Foster, dressed in a natty blue suit, his gold hair well-brushed but not slicked; his face looked calm and rested.

Gerald did not feel ready for him; he did not feel equal to him.

"Rick, uh, hello, have a seat."

He gestured toward the easy chair between Gerald's desk and the window.

"I won't keep you long," said Rick, sitting down. "I know it's a busy day here, and I've got a League of Women Voters' lunch in a little while. I just wanted to see how you are...after our talk yesterday."

After you told me my wife is a would-be seductress who missed the mark, Gerald did not say, but he found himself feeling cornered.

"Fine, uh, everything's fine. I spoke with Anne's doctor. He says she may, uh, she may not be remembering everything clearly. She has an appointment for a psychiatric evaluation. She hasn't been the same since our son's death, you know."

Gerald was aware that he was teetering on the brink of lying, and it made him feel sick and sweaty. He hated himself for talking about Anne this way—and he knew Anne would, too. But then she had betrayed him, or tried to, and got humiliated for her efforts. Hell hath no fury like a woman scorned, the famous line sounded in Gerald's mind. How had Anne spent that fury?

"Good, good," said Rick, as if he sensed Gerald's discomfort. "I knew you would know the best way to handle things. You're a good man."

I'm not, Gerald immediately thought. I'm not. I just pictured my wife pushing someone down the stairs and smothering her to death.

"Listen, Gerald, I wanted to ask you something else. How much do you know about Elsa Ebersbach's background?"

"Not much," Gerald said, recalling himself to the present moment with an effort. "German war refugee. Came to the United States by way of Switzerland and England. Some sort of tragic love affair put her on the wrong side of the Third Reich. I don't know the details. She doesn't talk about the past unless she's very drunk and then she's not coherent. Lucy Way might be the only one who knows the whole story. She's probably Elsa's closest friend here."

Rick paused for a moment, as if debating whether or not to say more. Gerald rather wished he wouldn't.

"I'm afraid there may be more to it than that," said Rick.

Gerald began to massage his temples where he could feel a headache beginning.

"What do you mean?"

"You've been following the Eichmann case?" asked Rick.

"Sure," said Gerald.

Who hadn't? His dramatic capture in Argentina last May had brought the atrocities of the Holocaust back into the forefront of everyone's mind. The Accountant of Death had done more than perhaps anyone to engineer and carry out genocide on an unprecedented scale.

"I'm sure you know there are plenty of Nazi war criminals still at large."

"I know Mengele was spotted in Buenos Aires, but he gave the Shin Bet the slip." Gerald's skin crawled at the very thought of The Angel of Death, as Mengele was called. Gerald could not connect him with anything angelic. "What does any of this have to do with Elsa? You can't seriously be suggesting she's a war criminal hiding in plain sight, not even bothering to change her name?"

Rick hesitated again.

"Just because she's using a German name doesn't mean she didn't change it," Rick cautioned. "It wasn't hard to get a new identity after the war. Everyone was buying false papers. There were safe houses all over Europe for escaping Nazis. Even the church was involved, the Catholic Church, that is."

"So I've heard," said Gerald. "The Church has a lot to answer for, and, as Christians, all of us, Protestant or not, have to face that. But Elsa—"

"I'm not saying she was a war criminal, Gerald," Rick interrupted, "but she may be harboring secrets. If someone in her family is on the wanted list and she knows where they are, that's a crime. Even if her family was merely associated with the Third Reich, she may have been so frightened and ashamed that she would attack anyone who pried into her past. By the way, she would have been the right age to join the *Bund Deutscher Mädel*, you know, Hitler Youth for girls. Given the climate of those times, it would have been surprising if she hadn't."

Gerald's head began to throb and he felt the twinge in his gut that confirmed it as a migraine. Maybe a cup of coffee would help.

"Elsa only ever cared about music." Gerald felt as though he were speaking from a long way off, from underwater, over the sound of wind. "She studied in Heidelberg."

Gerald felt rather than saw Rick shake his head.

"I would like to think that love of music makes people more humane, Gerald. Maybe you don't know that half the Vienna Philharmonic orchestra were members of the Nazi party. After Austria was annexed, they expelled their Jewish members."

Gerald hadn't known that. He didn't want to know anything more.

"So are you saying," he spoke slowly, feeling as though the conversation was like a jigsaw puzzle with different colored pieces swirling into bizarre coherence, "are you saying that Charlotte Crowley was a Nazi hunter and that she somehow uncovered something on Elsa? But it's too incredible, it's—"

"Sadly, I am afraid it isn't," sighed Rick. "I remember Charlotte Crowley approaching me after church, not long after Eichmann's capture, asking me if I thought there might be Nazi sympathizers in our midst. I knew what she was implying, and I tried to make light of it. But she might have pursued it. Even if she had no evidence, she could have put Elsa Ebersbach in a panic."

Gerald needed to take some aspirin right away. Excuse me Rick, I am not feeling well, he said the line in his head as if practicing it.

Aloud he said, "Charlotte wanted me to fire Elsa, because she wouldn't play schmaltzy Victorian hymns, but she never complained to me about anything else. And Elsa hated Charlotte because she felt she was a threat to her and Clara."

Rick waited a beat.

"Well, if she was digging around in Elsa's past, she was."

Mercifully, Rick stood up.

"I've got to get going. I just wanted to warn you. This case could get ugly."

With Gerald now the former employer not just of a mob lackey and a murderess but of a Nazi sympathizer? Gerald couldn't speak.

He couldn't say thanks for the warning. He didn't feel up to pointing out that homosexuals and the mentally ill had been on Hitler's hit list. He just, he just needed to stay very still until he could get some aspirin, black coffee and a shot of whiskey, if he had any. Gin didn't go well with coffee.

"Say is that Joe Petrone out there?" Rick asked. "Talking with Lucy Way?"

Gerald pushed himself up from the desk and looked out the window. Maybe it was better for his head to stand up. Maybe he needed to go for a walk.

"Yeah, that's Joe," Gerald confirmed.

"I thought he was taken off the case."

"He was," Gerald confirmed. "And he's been staying out of it. Probably just stopped by to see how his sister is doing. She and Lucy are working children's clothing, I think Anne said."

"Poor woman. Too bad her husband is such a fool," said Rick.

Which woman, which husband? Gerald couldn't help but wonder.

"Good luck with the workers' sale." Rick made for the door. "Wish I could help out tonight, but I've got a Democratic committee meeting. Too bad you can't make it, but I know you'll be tied up here."

"If only I could," sighed Gerald.

"Take it easy, old man." Rick put a hand on his shoulder before he headed out. "You don't look so good."

"Grace?" Gerald called when Rick was gone, and then he remembered she wasn't in her office.

He wished he could go find Anne. She was always nice to him when he had a headache. She would make him coffee and get him a cold cloth. Of course she wouldn't understand about the whiskey. Well, he better dose himself before he got sick at his stomach. Leaving his unfinished letter still rolled in the typewriter, he headed for the office door. He wouldn't risk walking through the rest of the parish house.

Of course he still had to run the gauntlet of the driveway. He paused and looked in every direction. The coast seemed blessedly clear. Rick was gone. So was Joe Petrone. Lucy Way must have gone to her post. Right now, especially now, he didn't want to talk to Lucy. He made a break for it, walking hurriedly with his eyes on the ground, so that even if someone saw him they might leave him alone. He made it all the way up the driveway, his foot on the front porch.

Then, "Rev, say Rev!"

He turned and saw Amos McCready coming out of the church where he'd no doubt been doing something useful and life-threatening on a ladder. Not now, Amos, he wanted to say, but he didn't.

"Are you going to be visiting our lady prisoner today?" Amos asked as he crossed the driveway.

"Maybe later," Gerald managed to say.

"When you go, would you give this to the wee schnauzer?"

He reached into a deep pocket of his workman's overalls and handed Gerald a pint bottle with the label carefully removed.

"I reckon you being a man of the cloth, they won't be searching you for contraband."

"I'm sure she'll appreciate it, Amos." Gerald accepted the bottle and stored it in his own pocket. "Amos, do you think—"

Elsa could be a Nazi sympathizer? He could not bring himself to say it.

"Do I think she's capable of mur-r-der?" Amos gave a generous roll to his r's. "Oh, aye. No doubt we all are. Doesn't matter to me if she's guilty as sin. As one of the least of my brethren, the Kraut witch deserves a drink."

Then he reached into another pocket and took out a hip flask, which he uncapped and handed to Gerald.

Gerald took a large swig. Whiskey, the good stuff, maybe a single malt.

"Sheep Dip?" he asked, handing back the flask, though really he shouldn't. If Amos was swigging this while he worked, no wonder he'd fallen off that ladder.

"Aye," Amos said, but he pushed the flask away. "Give it back to me when it's empty. I think you need it more than I do at the moment. You're looking a little green around the gills."

"Thanks, Amos. You're a true Christian."

Feeling better already, Gerald went inside to make some coffee with an aspirin and Sheep Dip chaser.

CHAPTER THIRTY-EIGHT

If she believed in God, Anne might have been tempted to ponder his mysterious ways. It was indeed a wonder to find herself actually relieved to be working at the rummage sale in the midst of the WOR whom she had spent so much time trying to avoid. For starters, everyone treated her as if she were sane. No one needed anything complicated from her. She went to the kitchen to get a cup of coffee, and there was Florence, cleaning out the refrigerator so that it was fit to store her cakes and pies till the workers' sale.

"I'll be baking more for tomorrow," Florence assured her, "if everything sell tonight. Don't you worry."

If there was anything Anne was not worried about it was the quality and quantity of Florence's baking.

She lingered in the kitchen to drink coffee and admire the astonishing array from Angel food to Devil's food, as Florence pointed out, as well as Lemon chiffon, velvet spice cake, butterscotch brownies, shoofly pie, sweet potato pie, and of course apple, and a dark moist banana bread for which Florence was famous.

"And this one Aramantha make all by herself." Florence pointed out a chocolate cream pie. "Do Katherine like to bake?"

"She loves to lick the batter out of the bowl," said Anne. The batter made with a Betty Crocker mix, she did not add. "Maybe Aramantha could teach her to make a pie someday."

"Anytime, anytime. Aramantha love nothing better than schooling people."

And they both laughed. Anne felt some of her tension ease.

On her way up the stairs to the clothing departments, Anne heard the click of Grace's heels coming up behind her, catching up with her on the stairs.

"Gerald told me to get lost," Grace said cheerfully. "Need any help with anything?"

"Everything's pretty well organized," said Anne. "The pricing is finished. I think people are mostly just scouting for bargains and subtly or not so subtly staking claims."

"I told Gerald that's exactly what I intend do," said Grace as they entered the crowded upstairs room. "Oh, no! That is *not* Ginger Boomer trying on my mink! She must be stopped. You have to be tall to wear that style. Anne, help me to convince Ginger that the stole makes her look like a fat little woodchuck."

Anne laughed again, even harder this time. She felt like doubling over, but she did not want to appear giddy, or worse, hysterical.

"Now Grace," she said with mock severity, "you know the minister's wife must never take sides."

"More's the pity," murmured Grace as she sauntered over to Ginger to make her case.

"Oh, hi, Anne honey!" Mary Louise waved to her from the evening gown rack as she riffled through satins, velvets and chiffons. "I think we're going to need a few more aprons for making change. You know the kind I mean, with the pockets for quarters, nickels, and dimes? They have them at the Five and Dime."

Anne felt a surge of gratitude for Mary Louise. Without ever being bossy and overbearing, she had made sure Anne knew what to do to make the rummage sale run smoothly, and by example she had kept gossiping and speculating about the murder at a minimum.

"Oh, dear, look at this! I just found a stain on this sweet little cocktail dress." Mary Louise held up a strapless bit of black satin. "Such a shame. I wonder if there's time to dry-clean it."

Anne went over to peer at a subtle yet distinct stain that marred the gown just over the left breast where some fashionable woman had no doubt missed the mark with a juicy canapé.

"I could take the dress with me and find out," said Anne. "I'm going to have to go to town. In fact, I better start making a list."

Before she could even look around for pen and paper, Mary Louise handed them to her.

"We're going to need change, too," said Mary Louise. "Plenty of it."

Her errands were beginning to sound legion. She did not want to miss seeing Lucy Way. If Lucy had Clara with her she might not stay very long.

"Anyone else need anything?" Anne addressed everyone.

"A few more hangers," called Teresa Lomangino over her shoulder from the children's department where she was arranging some of the better outfits for display. "And lots of paper shopping bags."

Anne noticed that Teresa's voice sounded flat and tired. Anne watched her put her hands on the small of her back where Anne could so vividly remember feeling the ache of overworked muscles during her own late pregnancies. Teresa must be due any day now. She did not turn around to look at Anne, which probably meant nothing. Anne couldn't help wondering if Teresa knew Anne had called her brother for help. And if she did, was she angry, frightened, wary? Anne wished she could ask, but Teresa seemed so unapproachable.

Anne looked around for Grace. Maybe she could ask Grace to do the errands. There she was at the other end of the coatrack from the mink, helping Ginger try on a snappy hot pink coat with black velvet piping that to Anne's surprise really did look striking on Ginger, bringing out the red in her faded hair and making her look voluptuous rather than merely squat and round.

"That looks sensational on you, Ginger," said Anne, wondering who was this friendly, chirpy woman who suddenly seemed to have jumped into her skin. "Grace, you have missed your calling."

"Do you really think so, Anne?" Ginger, pink with pleasure, almost matched the coat.

"I do," Anne assured her. "Grace, we're going to need lots of change and more aprons, do you think—"

"I'll go grab some petty cash and get the parish checkbook," Grace said before she could finish. "Would you like some company? Errands always go more quickly when there's two people, I find. I'll be back in a jiff."

Without waiting for an answer, Grace clattered down the stairs, leaving Anne nonplused.

"Are you sure you don't mind dropping off the dress?" Mary Louise asked holding it out to her. "I could pick it up tomorrow on my way here. You wouldn't have to think about it again."

"Not at all," said Anne. "I'll let you know when it will be ready."

Anne trailed down the stairs. Through the landing window, she saw Amos McCready walking across to the church from the rectory front porch. She noticed he was weaving a little. At least Grace did not drink on the job, not that she knew.

"Okay, all set." Grace met her at the front door and they stepped outside to the roofed entryway.

"Did Gerald go back to the house? I just saw Amos McCready lurching away from our porch."

"He's not in his office, but he said he would answer the phone, so he must have decided to work at home. So noisy here. My car or yours?"

Anne suddenly felt balky. It was not that she didn't like Grace, but they weren't even friends. Grace was squarely in Gerald's camp. Anne smelled a rat.

"No offense, Grace," said Anne. "It's not that I don't appreciate your company, but—"

"You want to know what the hell is going on, and why I am all of a sudden sticking to you like glue?"

"Well, yes."

"I told Gerald you would be suspicious. Cigarette?"

Grace pulled hers out of her suit pocket as Anne was hampered by holding the dress. Marlboro wasn't her brand, but she accepted. They smoked in silence for a moment, poised before the steps.

"He asked you to keep an eye on me," Anne stated.

Grace nodded and took another drag and exhaled before she spoke.

"Gerald's worried about you," she acknowledged. "He says between the rummage sale and 'all this business,' as he called it, you've been under a lot of strain. But if you ask me, which of course you haven't, of the two of you, I think Gerald's the one more likely to crack."

Then shouldn't you be shadowing him? Anne did not say.

"What makes you say so?" she said instead, trying to keep her tone neutral.

"Buck stops with him, doesn't it?" Grace turned toward Anne and leaned back against the porch banister. Anne did her best to mimic Grace's posture. "He feels responsible for everything and everyone. Two people hired on his watch are in jail. (Thank goodness I wasn't around that morning or it might be three!) He's got the bishop breathing down his neck along with the sheriff's department. On top of all that, there's the big donors pulling out of the camp fund last minute—or beyond the last minute if you ask me. I still don't understand that missing statement, unless I'm missing some marbles."

Grace spoke as if Anne knew what she was talking about. And maybe she should have, but she had kept a distance from the Hal Bradley Memorial Camp. It was Gerald's project from the get-go, his way of grieving—or atoning. She wanted nothing to do with it, but she wasn't about to reveal her animosity for Gerald's pet cause.

"Anyway, he looked just awful this morning," Grace went on, "like something the cat drug in. I tell you, the man needs some serious TLC and a long vacation."

Anne took a drag on her cigarette and looked away from Grace, not wanting to respond to the not-so-veiled implication that TLC was in short supply at the rectory. Grace didn't know the half of it. How about: Gerald believes I tried to seduce his best friend, whom I suspect of murder, which as far as Gerald is concerned means I must be psychotic. Try that on for size. She exhaled slowly.

"I think you're right, Grace," she said quietly.

Then before she could say anything more, Anne saw Lucy Way hurrying towards the parish house from the toy barn, head down and hugging her shoulders as if she walked in a cold wind, though the damp day was really quite warm.

"Excuse me, Grace, I've got to speak to Lucy for a moment. Privately."

She glanced at Grace who raised first one eyebrow and then the other.

"All right," she said. "I'll stop in the ladies'. Listen, Anne, do you want me to go with you or not? My cover's blown, and you seem all right to me. Up to you."

Maybe you should go babysit Gerald, part of her wanted to snap. Mix him a martini and feed it to him in a bottle. But then she thought of driving downtown alone. *Stay where people can see you.* It was unlikely that she would run into Rick Foster while doing her errands, but just the thought of it made her hands shake so much a long ash from her cigarette fell to the ground.

"Come with me, Grace," she said. It didn't matter if Grace were her friend or not. Men liked to say that women were catty and two-faced, but Grace had been refreshingly blunt, unlike her husband, sneaking a call to her psychiatrist behind her back, setting his secretary to spy on her. Right at this moment, Anne felt as though women were all that stood between her and some terrifying brink. "And thank you."

"Here," said Grace. "I'll hold the dress."

Then Anne ran down the steps to meet Lucy.

"Oh, Anne," said Lucy finally looking up. "There you are!"

"You can use my office, you two," called Grace. "Anne, I'll wait for you out front."

Anne sat in Grace's swivel chair and Lucy took one of Gerald's Trinity College chairs. Neither of them spoke for a moment. The din of the rummage sale went on over their heads and in the kitchen that backed on Grace's office.

"How's Elsa?" said Anne at last.

Lucy closed her eyes for a moment and shook her head.

"As you might expect. She rallied for Clara, of course, joked and made light of the situation. She promised me that she won't answer any questions without her lawyer present. I believe there is to be what Elsa calls an interrogation this afternoon. On the bright side, her lawyer, an old friend of mine, has assured me there is no hard evidence against her. Everything rests on Mildred's having seen Elsa at the parish house. Of course Elsa very sensibly did not deny that she was there that morning, so they can't catch her out in a lie. I don't believe Mildred is guilty of anything more than the malicious cowardice she's already admitted, but I must say I don't understand why the sheriff's department doesn't regard Mildred as a suspect. She and Elsa were both at the parish house at the crucial time. Mildred even admits to having been in the basement."

"Mildred has money and family connections, I suppose," Anne sighed. "And she's already been put away."

"Sadly, I am afraid that is true," Lucy agreed. "Elsa is poor as a church mouse and has no family in this country. They'll have to come up with something besides being blackmailed as Elsa's motive."

"When is the arraignment?" asked Anne, almost embarrassed not to know. She and Gerald had so much not to talk about that they hadn't talked at all.

"Tomorrow at eleven," said Lucy. "I am praying they will set bail."

"But who will post it?" wondered Anne. Surely Gerald could not use the church discretionary fund, supposing there was enough in it.

"I will," said Lucy, looking down at her lap, as if ashamed to be caught in a good deed. "Elsa is my friend."

Anne refrained from reminding Lucy that Frank Lomangino was still being held without bail. Perhaps they would treat Elsa differently, though Anne didn't know why they would.

"Oh, Lucy," was all Anne could find to say.

Lucy's face looked as white as her hair, all the sprightliness and youthfulness gone out of it. Anne should not have called her. She should not lean on her. Anne should be the one helping Lucy.

"There's something else I must tell you, Anne." Lucy held onto the arms of the wooden chair as if to force herself to stay seated in the chair or to launch herself out of it. "I spoke with Joe Petrone this morning. He was about to leave just as I was arriving. I sent Clara down to Rosalie in the barn, and we spoke. Briefly."

"I wonder why he didn't come and find me?' said Anne. "I am the one who called him."

"He has to leave."

"Leave?" repeated Anne. "Leave town?"

"Go into hiding," Lucy clarified. "He has been investigating, trying to find out things about Rick Foster. He thinks, he thinks—Oh, it seems so preposterous."

Anne waited, torn between wanting to hurry Lucy and wanting to stop her from saying the rest.

"He believes Rick Foster may have ties to organized crime, that through Mr. Foster the criminals may have been using Gerald's Camp Fund for money laundering."

Jesus. God. Gerald. What had Grace said about a missing statement? Could it be possible? And Gerald didn't have a clue, Anne would lay odds. He didn't have a clue about anything.

"There's more. You know Frank Lomangino was in prison for bookmaking. Joe Petrone says he took—what is the expression—took the fall for his superiors then. It was child's play for them to frame him for Charlotte's murder, especially because of Nat's illegal gambling debt. That's why the extortion charge is likely to stick, despite his alibi for the murder, which Mr. Petrone is strongly inclined to believe Mr. Foster committed."

Anne sat for a moment, trying to take it all in. She had suspected Rick, almost instinctively at first. Then Rick had lied to Gerald to discredit her. But it did seem preposterous. Handsome, successful—hell's bells—blond Rick Foster involved in a money laundering scheme with some professional criminals? It sounded like a bad 1930s gangster movie plot, the kind she could never follow.

"I don't understand. Why would thugs," it felt surreal even to talk about it, "want to help Rick Foster get away with murder? What's in it for them?"

"I don't pretend to understand it all," said Lucy. "I am beginning to realize that despite living through a war, I've led a very sheltered life. According to Mr. Petrone, Frank Lomangino, though a small fish, might be able to sing, as they say, about the bigger fish, who would be happy to 'put him out of commission' as Mr. Petrone expressed it. They don't take it kindly when even small fry decide to go straight. They were especially unhappy when Frank found employment as a janitor at one of their laundromats, so to speak. A janitor with a big ring of keys and access to every room in the parish house. They were probably afraid he might snoop in the office files and figure out what they were up to."

"I see," said Anne slowly. "Grace just told me there had been a mix up about a bank statement for the camp fund." And Gerald had muttered something about needing to work on a new fund-raising campaign, but she hadn't paid any attention. "But I still don't understand what any of this money business has to do with Rick Foster."

"He is running for Congress," Lucy pointed out. "It is always useful for criminals to have friends in high places. I hate to think it, but they may be helping to get him elected in return for favors."

"Yes," said Anne. "I can see what's in it for them, the criminals. But what I still don't understand is what's in it for Rick Foster? He is a successful lawyer. His horrible wife's family is wealthy and well-connected. Sybil brags about raising money for charities through chic bazaars. Even to win an election, albeit against a Republican, why would Rick be involved with organized crime or money laundering schemes?"

Lucy was quiet for a moment.

"If we knew the answer to that question, we might know whether Mr. Foster killed Charlotte Crowley and if he did, why."

"But doesn't Joe Petrone have enough evidence to go to the police? Couldn't they protect him?"

Lucy shook her head. "He told me he would need tangible evidence like bank records—and they may have been removed, destroyed, and replaced—or people who would be willing to risk taking the witness stand. He's still working on it. We agreed that he can call me from a pay phone or send me any documentation he finds, and then I can go to the police, the state police. He thinks the sheriff may be on the criminals' payroll."

"But why you, Lucy? Why not me? I am the one who called him."

"Anne," said Lucy patiently, gently as if she were speaking to a child. "You live at the church where the crime—or crimes—have occurred, if Joe Petrone is correct, and we don't know that yet. Not only that," she hesitated, "you have children. So do Frank and Teresa. He is not just leaving to protect himself."

Anne's hands flew to her heart. Joe must have come to the church to say goodbye to Teresa. That was why she wouldn't turn around to look at Anne. She was too scared or angry or both. What had she done to this man, to his family with her frantic call?

"Lucy, what can we do?" Anne breathed. "There must be something we can do."

"Yes, there must be," said Lucy slowly. "I suppose I can go to the state police myself, with my, well, I'd have to call them suspicions. I couldn't reveal my source. If only we had something tangible...."

They fell silent again. Anne found herself looking into Lucy's eyes. She saw no fear there, only something sad and ancient and yet at the same time full of a light that seemed timeless.

"There is something I would like to try, Anne," said Lucy at length. "I will need your help. With Clara. Will you keep Clara here with Rosalie this afternoon and maybe you could give her supper? No, never mind, you'll be too busy with the workers' sale."

"Don't worry about that. I'll manage," Anne assured her. "But, Lucy, don't put yourself in danger. Remember what you told me: stay where people can see you."

"Yes, and you must, Anne. If Mr. Foster is indeed guilty—and we don't know that yet—then he knows you suspect him. And as far as he is concerned, I don't. Or I never would have confided in him that day I came out of the woods."

"Will you tell me what you are planning to do?" asked Anne. "I should at least know where you will be."

"I won't be in any danger," Lucy insisted. "I am merely going to do my long overdue Christian duty and take a casserole to Nat Crowley. Mildred shooed everyone away while she was there. And I know for a fact she is a dismal cook. I am sure he is in desperate need of a good home-cooked meal."

"Absolutely," agreed Anne, getting to her feet. "Let's check on Clara. Then off you go, Miss Mar—"

"Don't say it," Lucy stopped as she pushed herself out of the chair. "Don't even think it!"

"All right, Lucy Way."

CHAPTER THIRTY-NINE

Just before the workers' sale, Katherine and Frankie sat on the back steps of the rectory trying to get her money out of her piggy bank. Katherine's mother was too busy at the parish house to help her, and Katherine's father was busy having a drink with Miss Barker.

"You want me to babysit Clara?" she had heard her father say to her mother earlier.

"Just till Lucy gets back," her mother said. "Children make Clara nervous, and they'll be swarming the toy barn. Besides Rosalie's had her all day."

It seemed strange that a grown-up would need to be babysat. Nancy Jones was babysitting Peter and Janie during the workers' sale and tomorrow night, too, when everybody in the village would come to the rummage sale. But her mother had said Katherine could go to the workers' sale by herself and buy what she wanted with her own money.

Except she couldn't get her piggybank open.

She had tiptoed into the living room where her father was sitting with Miss Barker.

"Excuse me, Daddy," she had said the way her mother had told her to when her father was with a parishioner. In fact Katherine had said it three times, and he still hadn't answered.

"Can you help me get my piggybank open?"

Miss Barker was sitting on the edge of the couch with a drink and a bowl of peanuts in front of her on the coffee table. Her father was sitting in the yellow easy chair, reading the paper, as if Miss Barker wasn't there, which seemed strange, but maybe that was how you babysat grownups. His drink was on a table next to the chair, and he held a cigarette between two fingers while he held the newspaper with his thumb and another finger.

"Hello," said Miss Barker; she sounded shy. "You are Katherine, aren't you?"

"Yes, Miss Barker."

She didn't seem like one of those grownups who hated children (like the bishop who had a neck like a turtle, even though his head didn't quite pull in all the way). Miss Barker had a face that made Katherine think of a horse and very black hair wound into a bun at the back of her head. Katherine wished she could see how long it was. She bet it would look like a mane.

"I can't get my piggybank open," she confided. Even if she was being babysat, Miss Barker was a grownup and might know what to do.

"Hmm. What?" Her father finally lowered his newspaper.

"Excuse me, Daddy," she said again. "Can you help me open my piggybank?"

Her father lowered the newspaper and took another puff of his cigarette then set it, still burning, in the ashtray while he took another sip of his drink.

"Only one way to open a piggybank," he said. "You have to break it."

Katherine held more tightly to her piggybank. Her piggybank's name was Rosy, and she was pink with darker pink roses around her neck and feet. Katherine did not want to break her.

"No, Daddy," said Katherine. "She has a plug, but I can't get it out."

"A plug! I thought you were talking about a piggybank not a bathtub."

Sometimes her father could be funny and silly. She tried to laugh.

"The only real way to open a piggybank is to smash it," he told her again, stubbing out his cigarette.

"But she says it has a plug," Miss Barker almost whispered.

Miss Barker did sound like a child. She had tears in her eyes. She was not a normal grownup.

"Sometimes you have to break things." Her father shook his head. "You have to be willing to lose something to gain something. That's the way life is."

Her father took another large drink, what her mother would call a gulp, like when she said, don't gulp your juice so fast, you'll get hiccups.

"Gerald," Miss Barker spoke sharply. "She is only a child!"

"Never too soon to learn to face reality." He was smiling what she called his mean smile; it was small and it turned downward but not the same way a frown did. "Katherine, I'll go get my hammer and help you break it."

"No, thank you, Daddy."

And clutching Rosy the piggybank, she ran through the dining room and out the back door. She almost tripped over Frankie sitting at the top of the back steps, waiting for her.

"What took you so long? The sale's about to start."

"Frankie, I can't get my piggybank open, and I, I don't want to smash it."

And she had burst into tears. She thought Frankie would make fun of her and call her a crybaby.

"Give it to me," he said, and immediately he turned Rosy over and found her plug. "We just need a knife. Lucky for you, I have one."

They sat on the back steps, and Katherine watched as Frankie patiently pried the plug loose with the tip of the blade. They took turns shaking out the nickels, dime, pennies, even a few quarters.

"That's a lotta loot!" whistled Frankie.

"Be back in a sec," said Katherine.

Tenderly she replaced Rosy's plug and ran to put her back in her room. Then she opened her top drawer and found a beaded, zippered pouch for the money. When she got back, Frankie had arranged the money in piles.

"You got almost three dollars, Katherine. Come on, let's go buy you the knife. Hurry. We gotta be the first one in the tent or someone else might get it."

Katherine and Frankie ran to join the crowd of rummage sale workers gathered outside waiting for the doors to open. Aramantha was in line next to her cousins. When she saw Katherine, she came bounding over to her. Only Aramantha could run like that in patent leather shoes, like she was flying between steps.

"What you gonna get, Katherine?"

"Don't tell," Frankie hissed at her.

"Shut up, Frankie Lomangino!" Aramantha flounced her skirt at Frankie. "Nodody axed you."

"What are you going to get?" Katherine asked.

"I'm gonna get me a real leather pocketbook with a gold clasp. Grams says I'm old enough now. And some real ballet slippers with long satin ties. I'm not even gonna go down to the toy barn at all. Nothing I need there. You should come with me, Katherine. I'll help you find something nice."

"Now you just hold it right there, little lady,"

Frankie talked like he was a cowboy on television.

"Little, who you calling little, shrimp?"

Aramantha didn't need to stand on her tiptoes to be taller than Frankie, but when she did she looked like a giantess. No, giants in the Narnia books were lumpy and ugly. Aramantha looked more like a dryad, a willow girl. Frankie laughed, not his mean laugh. Just laughed because Aramantha really could be funny.

"Shucks, ma'am," said Frankie still being a cowboy, though he usually wanted to be an Indian. "There is something Katherine has to get right away. But it's a secret."

Aramantha put her hands on her hips.

"Do she have a tongue?" she demanded of Frankie. "Do you have a tongue?" she turned to Katherine.

"There is something I need," said Katherine. "And it's not a toy."

"Hmmph," said Aramantha, pretending to be mad, at least Katherine thought she was pretending.

"But you know you are my best friend, Aramantha," said Katherine solemnly.

"Who he then?" she kicked a little gravel Frankie's way.

Katherine looked at Frankie. He had his hands in his pockets. He was looking at the sky, like he couldn't hear her or didn't care. And suddenly Katherine didn't care whether Frankie liked what she said or not.

"Him?" she shrugged. "He's my brother. I guess."

Before Aramantha could think of a retort, the doors of the parish house opened and Aramantha was off like a shot.

"See you later, alligator!" she called over her shoulder.

"In a while, crocodile," Katherine called back, but Aramantha had already disappeared into the crowd, and Frankie was tugging her arm, pulling her into the furniture tent.

The knife was still there on the small table with other tools where it had been since she'd spotted it. A jackknife, almost exactly like Frankie's. Only instead of a dark handle it had a whitish, yellow one the color of old piano keys. It cost seventy-five cents, almost a dollar.

"You have enough with a lot left over, Katherine," urged Frankie. "Get it."

She picked it up in her hand. It felt heavy and real. Something a grownup might have.

"Uh-oh," said Frankie as they turned to go pay. "It's Crazy McCready."

Mr. McCready stood by a table, where people were going in and out, wearing a change apron. His stick was propped up against the table where he could easily reach it.

"Get out two quarters, two dimes and a nickel," prompted Frankie.

Katherine fumbled with the zipper, trying to hold on the knife at the same time.

"Here, give me the pouch, I'll find the money."

While Frankie searched for the right coins, Katherine walked up to Mr. McCready, who drew his bushy eyebrows together and glared down at her. His hair was white and stood on end and so did his beard. He looked like a wizard, but she didn't know if he was a good one or a bad one. Wizards could be either.

"Katherine Bradley," he said. "Do your parents know you are buying a danger-r-r-ous weapon?" He did what her mother called rolling r's. Because he was from Scotland, her mother said. She and Frankie had tried to learn how to do it. Frankie almost could, but he usually ended up making a raspberry by mistake.

"My mother said I could buy whatever I want," she said, and that was true.

"And your father?" he prodded.

"He's babysitting Miss Barker."

And to her surprise, Mr. McCready laughed. You never knew with grownups what would make them mad and what they thought was funny.

"She has the money," said Frankie in his talking-back voice, which made her nervous. "Here, Katherine." He pressed the coins into her hands. "Give it to him."

Even though she held out the coins, Mr. McCready didn't take them right away.

"And what does a wee lassie like you need with a knife?" he demanded.

What did she need with a knife? You needed a knife to become blood brother and sister and to sharpen javelins and to open piggy-banks. Lots of things.

"Better leave knives to the lads," he added.

"Girls need knives, too!" declared Frankie. "Or else...or else, how can they whittle!"

Crazy McCready regarded Frankie.

"And just what have you whittled, lad?"

Frankie made a noise that could be considered rude.

· "Sticks! Gee whiz, whaddya think?"

The old man laughed again.

"Can I have my knife now, please, Mr. McCready?"

"Tell, you what." Mr. McCready bent over her so that she was afraid his whiskers might touch her. She could smell something sharp and sour on his breath. She tried not to wrinkle her nose. Her mother had told her that was rude. "If you recite me a psalm, the knife is yours."

Katherine felt tears welling up again. She didn't know any psalms. She only knew Our Father Who Art in Heaven. I'm only in second grade, she wanted to tell Mr. McCready. Then she remembered in junior choir Miss Ebersbach had been teaching them an anthem called "The 23rd Psalm." She was in jail now, too, like Frankie's father, so they hadn't practiced this week. But Katherine thought she could remember it.

"I can sing one," she said.

"Oh, aye, go on then."

And she did. When she got to the third verse, she sang the part Miss Ebersbach called the descant. Only the best singers, like Aramantha and Katherine, could sing it. The rest had to stay on the tune.

Yea, though I walk through shadowed veils, yet will I fear no ill, for thou art with me and thy rod and staff me comfort still, thy rod and staff me comfort still.

It was her favorite verse, because of the descant, even though she did not understand how a rod and a staff could be comforting. Mr. McCready must have liked it, too. Maybe because the stick he carried was like a staff.

"Beautiful, lass, beautiful." He wiped away a tear from his eye.

She did not know why the song made Mr. McCready sad. Maybe he missed Miss Ebersbach. Katherine did, too. She reminded Katherine of Mrs. Tiggy-Winkle the hedgehog, small, for a grownup, and prickly but with twinkly eyes. Her mother had told her Miss Ebersbach was best friends with Miss Barker. Miss Barker must be very sad that her friend was in jail. It would be terrible if Frankie went to jail or Aramantha.

"Take the knife, lass, and be very careful with it," said Mr. McCready. "And keep your money. Go buy yourself a wee dolly or something."

"Wait, Katherine," said Frankie. "We need fishing line. I'll buy that."

Crazy McCready seemed to have no objections to selling fishing line to a boy, so Frankie got to pay without reciting anything.

"Come on, Katherine," said Frankie when they were outside again. "We've got to hide the fishing line with our javelins and then we've got to cut branches and make ourselves a hideout in the woods."

The woods.

Promise me you and Frankie won't go in the woods again.

"I can't go in the woods," she said.

Katherine stood very still and looked down at the place where the gravel stopped and the lawn began. In between there was a stone that she had helped paint white last work day.

"What do you mean, you can't!" demanded Frankie. "We have to, we have to catch the bad man or my pops will never get out of jail. Even my Uncle Joey can't catch him."

"Why? Why can't your Uncle Joey catch him? He's a police."

"Because he's gone!" Frankie's voice got louder and softer at the same time. "The bad man is trying to get Uncle Joey. He has to hide."

Katherine felt like a stone in her stomach had dropped right onto her feet. This was bad. When they caught the bad man, Frankie's Uncle Joey was the person she was supposed to find to help them. Who would help them now?

"My mother doesn't want us to go in the woods. I told her I wouldn't unless we went with the lady, Lucy. Lucy Way."

But Lucy Way wasn't here. Her father was babysitting Miss Barker till Lucy Way came back. Then Lucy Way would have to babysit her.

"I thought you were my sister, Katherine," Frankie said.

She looked up and saw him rubbing his eyes with his fists.

"But you're not," he shouted. "You're nothing but a sissy."

Frankie turned and ran into the woods.

"Wait, Frankie, wait!" Katherine ran after him as far as the gap in the wall, and then her feet made her stop.

"Katherine!" she heard Aramantha calling behind her. "Katherine, come on. I want to show you something."

Katherine put her knife and her beaded pouch in her pants pocket and slowly turned around.

"Katherine, what's the matter?" Aramantha demanded. "Why you crying?"

"Frankie's mad at me," she said.

"That Frankie," huffed Aramantha. "He mad all the time. Don't pay him no never mind, Katherine. He's just a dumb boy."

Katherine shook her head.

"He's my brother," she whispered to herself. "My blood brother."

CHAPTER FORTY

Lucy had spent a couple of blissful hours preparing *coq au vin*, almost forgetting everything else in her pleasure at the ingredients (chicken, bacon, mushrooms, onions, garlic, lots of wine and some brandy, too, her stock replenished) all fresh and distinct now married in this elegant but earthy dish. While the coq simmered, she'd made salad with Boston lettuce and chives from her garden and mixed a lemon and thyme dressing. For dessert, she assembled raspberry tarts using graham cracker crumbs and butter instead of a baked crust. She packed a small bottle of cream, which she would whip in situ. When all the food was safely stowed in her wicker picnic hamper, she fetched from her cellar two bottles of her favorite red French table wine. (Some Americans slavishly paired white wine with poultry; that was because they didn't know French peasant cooking.) She put everything in the bonnet of her VW bug, where she could not help remembering she had once transported her mother's fateful dry-cleaned coats, and set out for the Crowleys' house just as the setting sun broke through the clouds that had hovered all day.

Nat was at home alone, as Lucy suspected he might be, with Mildred gone and the rest of the WOR at the workers' sale. Or at least his car was there. She rang the bell twice, then set down her heavy basket and knocked loudly. Still no answer.

Don't be such a goose, Lucy Way, she distinctly heard Charlotte's voice. *Just open the door and go in. It's never locked.*

Which was, of course, what Charlotte herself would have done without hesitation in a similar circumstance.

Picking up her basket, Lucy tiptoed into the little cottage that always seemed dark no matter the weather, surrounded as it was by yew hedges and overgrown with wisteria vines. She went first to the kitchen, relieved to find it tidy, till she realized that Nat very likely hadn't been eating much at all. A look in a refrigerator, empty but for old condiments, stale bread, and some lunch meat she didn't like the look of, confirmed her suspicions. (She suspected Mildred had tossed competing casseroles from other members of the WOR.) Lucy set her basket on the table and went into the parlor, with its dining nook by the one sunny window. She found Nat, still in his bathrobe, dozing on the sofa in front of the hearth. A fire he must have lit hours ago had burnt to embers. Ashes and bits of kindling remained unswept. There was a whiskey bottle on the table, happily still more than half full, and a mug for tea to which whiskey had no doubt been frequently added.

Poor Nat. In the midst of all the chaos and drama surrounding Charlotte's death he had ended up forgotten. She reproached herself swiftly and efficiently, and then set out to make the best amends she could. Placing a very light hand on his shoulder, she softly spoke his name.

"Charlotte?" he stirred. "Give me half a mo,' Old Thing."

She kept her hand on his shoulder.

"It's Lucy, Lucy Way."

Nat opened his eyes to the gloaming. Lucy knew what it was like to wake and have to remember your grief all over again. She waited a moment, then lit a table lamp.

"I've brought you some dinner, Nat," she said. "Would you like to freshen up while I heat things and set the table?"

"Freshen up? Oh my dear, yes. I believe I am in a reprehensible state."

"Not at all," Lucy assured him. "You've just had a little nap. Perfectly sensible."

With her nurse's eye, she watched him get to his feet, ready to steady him if necessary, hoping for the sake of his pride it would not be.

"I do beg your pardon, Lucy. I hope you are planning to stay and dine with me. Let me get you a drink before I go upstairs."

"Thank you, Nat. I've brought a couple of bottles of wine to go with dinner. I'll open one now and let it breathe while I finish cooking."

Nat paused and looked at her with almost pathetic gratitude, and then he shambled, more or less competently, to the stairs.

"Lucy Way," said Nat, pushing his chair back a little from the table. "That was the best meal I have had since Charlotte and I went to Paris for our honeymoon before that awful business with the stock market."

Lucy could not help but feel pleased with the extravagant compliment, almost the first words he had spoken since he began to eat with a single-mindedness that betrayed how hungry he was. Ghastly Mildred must have half-starved him.

"I learned to cook from my Parisian *grand-mere*," said Lucy. "I come by it naturally."

"I'll tell you what's not natural, that you somehow escaped marriage. Look at this magnificent table," he gestured.

While Nat had been in the shower, Lucy had rummaged around finding candles, a tablecloth, and a few purple asters and late black-eyed susans in the garden for a centerpiece.

"The food, the wine," he went on. "Not to mention your gracious and unassuming manner. What a gem you are. I am tempted to propose to you myself."

Lucy was surprised that she was not more offended. She usually was when people expostulated about her single state. She knew Nat could not help but be gallant, even flirtatious. He always had been. She decided to give his knuckles a gentle little rap.

"I hear you have not been short on marriage proposals, *monsieur*."

"Ah, yes," he sighed and reached for the wine, offering to top her glass before filling his. "So you have heard about poor Millie."

"Yes," said Lucy. "I know just about everything, Nat. From Mildred herself."

Even as he sipped his wine, Nat became more sober.

"I went to see her at the Gables, you know, wanted to see how she was getting on. Felt responsible for her somehow."

"That was kind of you, Nat," said Lucy, genuinely impressed.

Ne'er-do-well, perennially tipsy Nat, who couldn't stay away from the racetrack, was nevertheless that rare breed, a gentleman.

" 'fraid it wasn't, Lucy." Nat shook his head. "Her doctor came to have a word with me. Said it was best I didn't see her. Didn't want me to aggravate her psychosis or some such gobbledy-gook. I just hope I didn't lead her on, poor demented thing. If I did…well, hang it all, if Millie did kill Charlotte, I'm to blame. I can't stop thinking about that."

Lucy Way, please tell Nat to stop fretting about that old cow.

"Nat," said Lucy struggling to keep a straight face, "if Charlotte were here now, well, I believe she would tell you to stop fretting about that old cow."

Nat looked at Lucy in wonder, and then laughed, a laugh so rusty it came out as a wheeze.

"Yes, you're right. It wasn't nice, but that is exactly what Charlotte did call poor old Millie. They were second or third cousins, you know. Charlotte never had any use for plain little Millie. Then Charlotte's father lost everything in the crash, and Millie's family somehow held on to their pile. What's more, Millie managed to marry into more money, and Charlotte," he sighed, "married me. Not much of a bargain, and yet Millie seems to feel that Charlotte snatched me away like some prize."

Tell him, Lucy Way, tell him to stop maundering on about Mildred. She's just a red pickle.

"A red pickle?" Charlotte's voice was so distinct, Lucy forgot herself and answered out loud. "Oh, you mean a red herring."

That's what I said. You needn't put on airs and act superior just because I'm dead, Lucy Way.

"What?" said Nat, understandably confused. "What did you say about pickled herring? Don't tell me there's another course to this superb meal."

"Well, I did bring a dessert," said Lucy, rising to clear the table. "But what I meant to say is that Mildred is what is called in detective fiction a red herring." She paused a beat. "So was Frank Lomangino, and so, I believe, is Elsa Ebersbach."

Over Lucy's protests, Nat helped clear and rinse the dishes.

"Charlotte and I never stood on ceremony," he said. "Couldn't afford a cook or a maid. Didn't want her to wait on me. All my fault, the lack of funds."

The kitchen in order, they settled again with dessert, coffee, and some very fine cognac Mildred hadn't managed to seek out and destroy.

"I'm sorry about Elsa Ebersbach," said Nat. "I know she's your friend. Charlotte had her quarrels with Elsa, but I can't believe.... Well, the truth is I don't like to believe anyone did it. I don't like to believe it happened. Sometimes I still don't. Do you know what I mean, Lucy? Sometimes, I can imagine that Charlotte's just in another room or on one of her interminable walks in those awful old shoes.... I'm sorry."

Lucy touched Nat's hand lightly and sat with him in silence while he wept.

Lucy, hissed Charlotte. *Don't get distracted. There's a reason you're here besides seducing my husband with your French cookery. Honestly, Lucy Way. It's only been two weeks!*

Charlotte, Lucy remembered to speak silently, please show a little sensitivity. He's mourning you.

Well, all right, Lucy. But hurry it along.

"Nat," said Lucy after his tears had quieted and he'd blown his nose loudly. "Do you remember how Charlotte used to go wandering, when she, well, when she was a guest in other people's houses?"

To Lucy's relief, Nat chuckled fondly.

"I always had to keep an eye on her, check her pockets. And she had to see to it that I was able to walk. We were a pair, the pair of us."

"Well, Nat, I have a, a sort of an intuition that whoever…"

Don't spare my feelings or his, Lucy. Get to the point.

"Whoever killed Charlotte killed her because she found something that person didn't want found."

"That is," Nat said with effort, "that is possible. And you are not the only one to think it."

"Oh?" said Lucy, hoping he would go on.

"Well, he didn't say so directly, but I think Rick Foster had the same idea. He's been very helpful, really. Offering me financial advice, looking over our bank records. We even spent a quiet hour looking at photograph albums and scrapbooks. I was touched that he would take so much time in the midst of his campaign. Charlotte always admired him, even though he's a Democrat. Used to ask his advice on this and that. He was always generous. Never charged us or made us feel beholden. He'd won her vote, all right. Class traitor, I used to tease her. Ha!"

Lucy's heart sank into her stomach, and all her extremities felt cold.

He didn't find it, Lucy. He did not find what he was looking for.

"Are you sure?" she said aloud.

"Oh, yes," said Nat. "My Charlotte was a fool for a pretty face. Switched parties shamelessly to vote for the most handsome candidate. Ye gods! I suppose she would be voting for Kennedy! She couldn't stand that fellow Nixon's nose or what she called his little piggy eyes. If the ladies rule the day, he doesn't have a prayer."

Hurry! Charlotte buzzed so loud in her ear, it almost hurt.

"Nat," Lucy said; it was now or never, "this may sound like a strange request, but I was wondering if I could have a little wander through the house, the way Charlotte would have in someone else's. Who knows, I just might turn up a clue."

"Why, certainly, my dear. Though, you know, Charlotte never asked permission, she just disappeared."

That's what you should have done, said Charlotte, exasperated. *Have you never heard of excusing yourself to go to the loo? Never mind now. Go!*

In a fevered trance, Lucy went from room to room, pulling open desk drawers, looking under furniture, into the depths of closets, into odd crannies by the staircase with the ghost of Charlotte Crowley spurring her on as if she were a child on an Easter Egg hunt.

Now you're warm, warmer, no cold again, turn around, back to the stairs, yes.

At last in an old dresser in a tiny gabled guestroom, Lucy found herself pawing through antique underwear, bloomers and corsets, of the sort her mother might have worn before the First War. Then her hands felt it, a metal oval, glass front, velvet backing. A photograph. There wasn't enough light from the hall to see what it was. She turned around looking for a lamp or a light switch when she saw the headlights of a car pulling into Nat's driveway.

Take it, ordered Charlotte. *Hide it in your apron pocket. Get out of here as quickly as you can.*

As Lucy descended the stairs, she heard Nat open the front door.

"Rick, old chum, what a nice surprise! Come in, have a drink. You've just missed a meal fit for a king. Maybe there are some leftovers. Doubtful though, not the way I ate. Like a man having his last meal before the firing squad."

Lucy took a deep breath and came down the rest of the stairs and into the hall where she found herself face to face with Rick Foster.

"Hello, Miss Way," said Rick in his usual courteous manner,

His smile was so warm and unstudied, Lucy was thrown into confusion. How could this kind, decent man be a murderer? Maybe Anne had misinterpreted the situation. In her eagerness to prove Elsa's innocence, maybe she had, too.

"So you're the chef Nat's been raving about."

"Guilty," Lucy said before she could think, and she laughed to cover her dismay. "I'm afraid there isn't much left, but I might be able to fix you a small plate before I go."

"Thank you, Miss Way. I've just come from a meeting and my palette has been ruined by doughnuts and bad coffee."

"Then you certainly need a drink," declared Nat, turning toward the living room. "Come along both of you. Lucy's been doing a spot of detecting using Charlotte's favorite methods. Find anything useful, Lucy?"

Lie, Lucy Way! Don't be a goody two shoes. Lie.

"I'm afraid not. Silly notion," said Lucy. "I must say no, thank you, to more cognac, Nat. It's a busy day tomorrow."

"I suppose it is," said Nat, waving Rick through to the parlor, "opening night of the rummage sale." There was a world of sadness in the pause that followed. "I hope everyone will forgive me if I give it a miss this year."

While Nat poured drinks for himself and Rick, Lucy slipped into the kitchen. When she put away the leftovers, she hid the photograph inside the large earthenware crock that had held the *coq au vin* and secured both in her basket.

"Good night, Mr. Foster. Goodnight, Nat," she called through the kitchen door. "No, please don't get up. I'll let myself out."

CHAPTER FORTY-ONE

"The cup of salivation."

Gerald slid a used paper coffee cup filled with vodka across the table to Elsa. Luckily his clergy privileges gave him access to the meeting room, a private windowless box (with stale air that stank of sweat and unvented cigarette smoke) where inmates met with their lawyers or he would not have been able to offer Amos's sacrament, so to speak.

"You are bad, Gerald," Elsa sighed. "A very bad priest. Bless you. And thank the old Scotch terrier. Tell him, I will smuggle in single malt if he is ever, what is your expression, in the chink. "

"Clink," corrected Gerald. "Name of some old English prison."

"And the sound of the cell door swinging shut," Elsa added. "*Zum Wohl!*"

She raised her cup, then drained it, and handed it back to Gerald for a surreptitious refill.

"Take some yourself," Elsa urged. "You look as though you could use it."

Gerald could not argue with that, even though he was not the one who had just been denied bail on a murder charge. Or the one languishing while awaiting trial on charges of extortion.

Before attending Elsa's arraignment, Gerald had visited Frank Lomangino, who'd sat with his head in his hands, too depressed to look up.

"The attorney came to see me this morning," Frank said.

"Mr. Applegate?" Gerald asked, the attorney Rick Foster had found, who'd agreed to represent Frank pro bono.

"Yeah," said Frank. "He wants me to plead guilty to extortion. He says if I do that and give some names of people I used to work for, he can make a case for a short bid."

Gerald waited for a moment, not sure what to say, not feeling capable of giving advice.

"I told him I didn't do it. I never did nothing like that to a lady who was never anything but kind to me. I knew that her old man was in trouble for gambling debts. Couldn't stay away from the track, and people like, well, like what I used to be, they take advantage of people like that. That's how I used to make a living. Mrs. Crowley, she told me about his troubles, asked if there was anyone I knew, any way I could help her, put in a good word for her. I shoulda told her I don't know nothing or no one. Not anymore. But I wanted to do her a good turn, so I said. Sure, I know some people. I tried to find out who was his juice man—"

"Juice man?" repeated Gerald.

"Sorry, Rev. The juice man, that's the guy who collects the debt, by any means necessary if you get my drift. Oh, the Crowleys were in trouble for sure. I felt bad for them. But my nosing around didn't do them or me no good. The higher ups just started watching me again."

Frank's story did not square with what Gerald had heard from Rick. In fact, Frank had never before mentioned Charlotte's confiding in him. He couldn't help wondering if Frank was spinning a story, working on his sympathies. In other words, conning him.

"Mr. Applegate is a good man," Frank went on, "representing me even though I can't pay him. I can't complain. But he don't seem to understand. To the people I worked for, inside and outside don't make no difference. If I name names, I'm a dead man. Who cares maybe, much use I been to anyone, but my family, they might... Teresa, Teresa—"

Frank couldn't breathe through the sob caught in his throat. Gerald was afraid he'd turn blue.

"Take it easy, Frank, take it easy." Gerald wanted to pound him on the back, but the old scratched metal table was between them.

"So I told him, Mr. Applegate, I'm gonna take my chances with the jury, cuz I am innocent of the charges. If I go down, at least no one else will go down with me. So Mr. Applegate says, it's your funeral, Frank. Because Mrs. Crowley can't come back and testify, and it's my word against the word of the state's witness."

"The state's witness?" repeated Gerald.

"Yeah, the prosecution got a witness says Mrs. Crowley came to him and told him I was threatening to rat Mr. Crowley out for illegal gambling unless they paid me. What kind of sense does that make? Trying to get money from someone who's already in debt up to his ears? Maybe I'll get lucky and pull a judge who can figure that one out. But what are the odds?"

Gerald felt as though he'd been hit over the head and little birds were flying out and twittering around him the way they did on the cartoons his kids watched. Frank was right. The charge did not make sense on its face. Extorting money from the Crowleys? Blood out of a stone? Why hadn't he seen that before?

"Gerald!" Elsa said loudly. "Gerald, if you please, the cup of salivation needs a refill."

"Oh, sorry, Elsa." Gerald poured again, then put the bottle out of sight under his jacket. "I have a lot on my mind."

"Yah," sighed Elsa, "yah. I'm sorry, Gerald. I am one more burden on your back."

"My yoke is easy and my burden is light," Gerald quoted, more out of habit than conviction.

"It's no joke, Gerald, no joke."

Gerald decided not to correct her English. For sure, if there was one, the joke was not easy. He didn't get it.

"Gerald," she said after upending the cup. "I need to talk about Clara. There are some things you don't know that I have never told you. Take another drink."

Gerald did as he was told, then waited.

"I believe you know that Clara was patient at the insane asylum, yes, I know you Americans prefer to call it a mental hospital. I taught music there, and she was gifted, is gifted, so gifted, almost as gifted as...well never mind. Until that Rottweiler Charlotte Crowley sniffs us out, only you and Lucy knew I fell in love with Clara there. I always told you Clara was released into my care. Actually, with my help, she persuaded some young doctor to let her sign herself out. (He got in big trouble later, I can tell you.) The truth is, Clara ran off with me. I swear to you, I did not know until later, there was a trust settled on her on the condition that she stay in the nuthouse. When she left, she was disinherited, penniless. That didn't worry me, but we were both terrified that her family, a rich old New York family, might try to track her down. Her parents were dead, but there was an awful old grandfather who did unspeakable things to Clara when she was a child; no wonder she went crazy. It suited the old troll to have her locked up; he didn't want anyone to know the truth. But years went by, and nobody tried to find her. We lulled ourselves into thinking we were safe, that we might have a little happiness."

Elsa held out her cup. They both had another small drink. Gerald wished Amos had given them a larger bottle, but then, as he no doubt realized, it would have been harder to smuggle in.

"Well, that is the secret awful Charlotte Crowley digs up, like a dog after a stinking, rotten bone. They all know each other, these old families. She had heard many times for many years about the disgraceful old Sapphist who seduced the poor insane young heiress. As you can imagine, Charlotte Crowley had things to say about what I ought to do if I had any morals or scruples. She threatened to tell Clara's family where Clara was. Maybe the old bloodhound thought they would reward her in some way, pay her imbecile husband's debts. Ah, Gerald, don't tell me, we have killed that bottle!"

Gerald poured out the last few drops, not Christ's blood. Maybe his sweat, his despair.

"Forgive me, Gerald. I should have told you before. After all, you took such a risk to hire me. But I didn't think it mattered. It didn't matter as long as I could take care of Clara myself. But now, look at me, held without bail, charged with murder, a trial that will be a circus. Lucy cannot take care of Clara forever. I can't ask it of her. And of course I can't ask you and Anne. But I must ask you and Lucy to help Clara somehow. Persuade her to go to her family and renounce me, denounce me for all I care. The horror of a grandfather is dead. The new trustees, surely they can be made to see reason. Defame me all you want, but help Clara, please, please."

Gerald's head was reeling and not just from the vodka.

"Elsa, you know I will do what I can, but you talk as if you know you'll be convicted. If you're innocent...are you innocent, Elsa? No, sorry, I shouldn't have asked you that."

"No, Gerald, you can ask. You of all people have the right to ask. I believe you will believe me when I tell you, no, I am not the one who killed Charlotte Crowley, though I wanted to when she threatened Clara and me. You saw me that day. If I could have killed her right then and there in the driveway, maybe I would have. But since I can't, in a few days, I calm down, little by little. After all, what can Clara's family do to us, disinherit her again? They can't lock her up again. She is a grown woman who signed herself out legally. So I decide I will simply torture Charlotte with dissonant anthems, and she will never again get to cat wail (so off-key) her horrible favorite hymns."

Gerald wished he could laugh, but he felt too heavy, too weary for levity.

"So, you are innocent," he said, sounding more tentative than he could have wished.

"Yah, I am innocent. But will that save me? How strange to escape the Nazis and die in an American gas chamber."

Gerald did not suppose it would be comforting to Elsa to know that she would more likely be electrocuted or sentenced to life imprisonment.

"You know what is even stranger, Gerald, when I am interrogated yesterday, no one is asking about Clara and me. No, they want to know am I or was I ever a member of the Nazi party? They want to know about my family, did any of them hold high level posts in the Nazi party? And where are they now? Over and over they ask me.

And I want to shout, damn you, you stupid people: how can I be a Nazi when I am disinherited because I fall in love and run off with a woman, a Jew, a *Jew*! But I can't, I can't bring myself to speak of her. Or what my family, someone in my family, must have done to her... my fault, all my fault."

Finally the vodka got to her, and Elsa buried her face in her hands and wept. Gerald sat and felt his own tears threatening to overflow their bounds.

"Where does this come from, Gerald? Just because I am a German, they make up this crazy Nazi war criminal story, as if I could hand over Mengele himself. I don't understand."

But Gerald was beginning to be afraid he did.

"Elsa," Gerald hesitated, then blurted it out, "has Rick Foster ever visited you?"

"No, why should he?" Elsa looked surprised and rankled by what must have struck her as an abrupt change of subject in the midst of her anguish. "He is a busy man. Besides, we are not friends. I have never cared for him, and I believe, from things you have said, the feeling is mutual."

It was true, Rick, as a member of the vestry, had understandably expressed concern about Elsa drinking on the job.

"Why don't you like him?" Gerald pressed. "Everyone else does."

"I don't know why. Really, Gerald does it matter? He reminds me of someone. Who is it? I never gave it much thought."

"Think now," he said.

Elsa closed her eyes. Gerald was afraid she had passed out when suddenly she jerked upright, her eyes open.

"Herr Fuchs!" she said. "Mr. Fuchs, I should say. He was an American. Not the face. The voice. I am a musician, so I hear tone and pitch. That is really how I remember people more than the face."

Gerald had never particularly noticed Rick's voice, mid-range in pitch, he thought, but not remarkable. When he gave speeches, he never sounded hoarse or strained. Yet he knew how to build excitement, to inspire.

"Who is Mr. Fuchs?" he asked.

"He was—" She stopped, as if jolted by some connection. "Well, I didn't think about it then. It was before the war, sometime in the early '30s. But he was, he must have been an American Nazi sympathizer. He stayed with my family when he visited Germany, and he and my father seemed to have some serious business together. They went to meetings, to rallies. This was not unusual in those times. There was a son, a few years younger than me, with an awful case of spots on his face. I think his father beat him; the boy used to cringe like a dog when his father came near him. My parents expected me to entertain this boy, but I have no patience. I am afraid I take him to the cinema once with my friends, and we sneak out to go to a party and left him to find his own way back. It was not kind."

For a moment they were both silent. They could hear the clock on the wall and the sound of the guard pacing in the hall.

"Gerald," she looked at him, "these questions, these interrogations. You don't think, you do think, they are coming from him, from Rick Foster?"

"I don't know what to think," said Gerald, but he knew it was a lie.

The truth was, he hadn't thought, hadn't wanted to think. He better think now and fast.

"Anne," he said out loud. "Oh my God! Anne!"

"Gerald what is it?" Elsa was alarmed "Are you all right?"

"No, I'm not all right," he said, getting to his feet. "I'm all wrong. Elsa, I'm sorry. I've got to go."

He had to find Anne. No, he had to go to the sheriff. Help, he prayed over and over in his mind, help!

"Go, Gerald," he heard Elsa say as he banged on the door for the guard to let him out. "*Geh mit Gott.*"

CHAPTER FORTY-TWO

Anne stood looking out the window of the notions department. Behind her, in the room where coffee hour was served, Florence and Bernice (who'd come to fill in for Mildred) bustled and bumbled setting up the baked goods table. How Bernice was going to see well enough to make change, Anne did not know. Maybe she knew a quarter from a nickel by touch. But a one dollar bill from a five or a ten? At this point Anne didn't much care if someone took advantage of half-blind Bernice to rob the notions table blind. She just wanted the whole wretched business of the rummage sale to be over. It was still an hour till the doors opened, and people were already lining up, pressing against the locked doors, crowding the roofed entryway, spilling into the driveway where there was already no parking left. The line (or, more accurately, mob) kept growing as people arrived on foot from both ends of the driveway.

Truth be told, Anne was terrified.

Who were these people? She did not recognize them. Most of the village people of her acquaintance were inside the parish house. Where did these others come from? She felt the same way each year when she took the children to the county fair—hordes and hordes of people with faces that looked somehow both doughy and pinched and inexplicably horrifying like figures in a Bosch painting. When she had tried to explain how she felt about such crowds, Gerald had accused her of class prejudice and gone on about the evils of the class system in America, all the more pernicious, because people pretended it didn't exist.

And where on earth (or in heaven or hell) was Gerald? He had left at ten-thirty this morning for Elsa's arraignment and he hadn't been back since. Nor, as far as Grace knew, had he telephoned. Of course no one was answering now. Grace had closed the office to take charge of menswear with Ginger. Grace's daughter Nancy, babysitting at the rectory, might pick up the phone and take a message. But Nancy wouldn't and shouldn't leave her charges, who included Clara Barker, to push through the rummage sale crowd unless the call was an emergency.

How could Gerald do this to her? True, she had been avoiding Gerald since she overheard his conversation with Dr. Aiken. She didn't dare say anything to him about Joe Petrone's suspicions for fear he would run to Rick Foster or conspire with her shrink to have her locked up. But right now she didn't need to talk to Gerald. She just needed him to be the one to open the doors and to use his authority to stem the tide so that no one would be trampled to death.

She peered out the window at the furniture and appliance tent, hoping to catch a glimpse of Mary Louise's husband Ludwig, but she only saw Amos McCready, standing and fiercely guarding his turf, his stick at the ready. His idea of crowd control would be to roar scripture and bash skulls. At least Rick Foster was nowhere in sight, she noted with a slight loosening of her tensed muscles. To think that once he would have been her first choice to pinch hit for Gerald. And what on earth were she and Lucy going to do about Rick? After dropping off Clara with Rosalie (dear Rosalie) who had kept Clara busy in the toy barn till Nancy Jones arrived, Lucy had vanished for the afternoon. Anne hadn't even seen her, so she didn't know if Lucy's last-ditch attempt at sleuthing had shed any light on anything at all.

Really, there was nothing to be done about Rick Foster now, except stay out of his way. Far from being alone, as Lucy had cautioned against, Anne would be surrounded by crowds all evening. She quailed at the thought of braving the ballooning crowd to look for Ludwig. Maybe Mary Louise would know where to find her own husband. She started up the stairs and nearly collided with Mary Louise who was clattering down them at breakneck speed.

"Oh, Anne, thank heavens you're here," said Mary Louise. "Teresa Lomangino's water just broke, and the pains are coming awful fast. It's her fifth child for heaven's sake. If we don't hurry she'll have it right on the stage!"

"Hell's bells!" said Anne. "Who can we spare to take her to the hospital?"

"No one," answered Mary Louise. "We're short-handed as it is. Lucy's not even here yet. I'll go call Sullivan's. Isn't Teresa's brother one of the medics? Let's pray he's on call; that might be a comfort to her, poor thing. If she has the baby on the way there, at least someone will know what to do."

"Good idea," agreed Anne. No point in telling Mary Louise that Teresa's brother had skipped town.

"And while I'm at it, I'm going to call Chief O'Brien to help with this crowd. He might as well do something to earn his keep on the taxpayer's dime."

Relieved that Mary Louise was taking charge, Anne rushed upstairs to find Teresa Lomangino surrounded by women. Some were mopping up the puddle of amniotic fluid, others wringing out her wet stretch pants, while Ginger and Grace raided women's wear to dress her in a bright orange polka-dotted muumuu that made her look like a gigantic poisonous fruit.

"Mary Louise is calling Sullivan's right now," Anne told Teresa. "It shouldn't take long for the hearse to get here."

"Wouldn't that be a kick? Have the baby in a hearse." Teresa tried to laugh but groaned instead.

"Say, Anne?" Teresa called her by her first name for the first time. "Have you seen Frankie, Junior? The girls are at home with my mother, but Frankie, he's here somewhere."

Anne felt a surge of annoyance, which she quelled as best she could.

"He's probably with Katherine," she answered. "She's at the house with a babysitter."

"I gotta see him," puffed Teresa. "Gotta tell him to be real careful walking home."

"He can stay with us," Anne heard herself saying before she could think better of it. "I'll phone your mother."

"I gotta see him," Teresa said again. "I'm all he's got right now."

And she started walking towards the stairs.

"I can send someone to look for him." Anne ran after her.

But Teresa kept walking, allowing Anne to put an arm around her, pausing now and then for a contraction, but dogged in her determination to find her son. Anne managed to steer her to the office door away from the press of people at the main entrance. Walking behind the appliances tent, they made their slow progress to the rectory.

Inside they found Nancy Jones sitting on the couch with Janie on her lap. (Anne wished Nancy would not chew bubble gum; last time a bubble burst in Janie's hair and Anne had had to cut it out.) Clara also sat on the couch, while Peter and Katherine knelt in front the coffee table. A cutthroat game of Parcheesi was in progress, with Peter earnestly explaining to Clara that she must land next to Janie's player and send it back to the beginning, even if Janie cried, because "it's the rules."

"Where's Frankie?" Teresa's question came out a wail, and everyone looked up startled and a little frightened.

"Katherine," Anne said, "Mrs. Lomangino is going to the hospital to have the baby. Frankie can stay with us overnight. Do you know where he is?"

Katherine turned around and stared up at her mother with those solemn grey eyes that always seemed to be seeing something Anne couldn't.

"Do you know where he is?" Anne repeated.

First Katherine shook her head, and then she paused and nodded.

"I think he's hiding," she said.

"Can you find him?"

She nodded again.

"Then go find him as quickly as you can."

Katherine got to her feet but still seemed to hesitate.

"Hey, the hearse is here," announced Nancy Jones, who had stood up with Janie on her hip.

"The hearse is here! The hearse is here!" echoed Peter bouncing up and down on the couch.

Dislodged by the commotion, Clara rose from the couch and approached Teresa slowly and steadily as she might a wounded animal.

"Katherine, go find Frankie," urged Anne.

Katherine stood, poised to run, and whispered something softly.

"Tell Frankie, I'm gonna have the baby, honey." Teresa tried to lean over to speak to Katherine, but a contraction seized her and she grabbed her back instead. "I'll try to make it a brother this time."

"I will, Mrs. Lomangino," said Katherine just loud enough for them to hear.

Anne did not see Katherine slip away. The medic was knocking on the front door. And Clara, having reached Teresa's side, clamped a long-fingered hand on her shoulder.

"Would you like me to go with you?" Clara asked. "I delivered kittens once."

Teresa looked bewildered, and Anne moved forward intending tactfully to pry Clara loose.

"My Miss Ebersbach is in jail with your Mr. Lomangino," explained Clara.

To Anne's astonishment, Teresa sobbed and threw herself into Clara's awkward arms. The unlikely pair made their way out the door to the hearse.

Katherine ran out the back door and down the back steps of the rectory, stopping when she got to the driveway. It had turned into a noisy river, but instead of water it was people, only they weren't moving the way water moves. They were all clogged up in front of the parish house. She did not know how all those people would fit inside. She was glad she had gone to the workers' sale yesterday. She had her knife in the bottom of her blue jeans pocket. The green hat with the ostrich feather that Aramantha had talked her into buying and the green velvet cape that went with it were in her room. She had gotten them in the ladies department, but really they were for playing dress-up. The knife was real. Katherine reached into her pocket and touched the knife. She might need to use it, and that made her feel brave and scared at the same time.

Her mother had told her to find Frankie. If her mother knew where Frankie was hiding, she might not have let her go. She had whispered to her mother: *Frankie is in the woods*. She didn't know if that counted as telling. Anyway, it was too late now. She had to go. She had to tell Frankie his mother was having the baby. If she didn't, when Frankie got tired of hiding he would look for his mother and not know where she was.

That would be terrible.

Taking a deep breath as if she were going to swim underwater, Katherine plunged into the crowd just as the hearse, the horn honking the whole time, turned around and went out the front end of the driveway onto Main Street. Katherine pretended she was a minnow darting in and out among sharks and whales, and she made it across the driveway without even bumping into anyone. She ran around the big tent, not even slowing down when she heard Crazy McCready call out.

"Just where do you think you're going in such a big hurry, wee lassie!"

Then she stepped through the gap in the wall and into the Wood. All by herself.

She felt scared, but it was a good kind of scared, the way she might be afraid if she met Aslan. *He's not a tame lion*, Mr. Beaver had told the children, *but he's good*. The Wood was the same way, not tame but good. The light had climbed high into the trees. Katherine walked as quietly as she could through the shadowy world below, the coolness rising up from the ground, touching her hands and face.

Bright flashes of new fallen leaves, red and yellow, glowed on the ground, lighting the way for fairies. For her. Because she had fairy blood. Lucy Way had said so. As Katherine came closer to the stone steps, she tiptoed. She wanted to surprise Frankie, maybe even scare him. But when she stopped at the top of the stairs, she could not see him anywhere.

"Frankie!" she whispered as loud as she dared.

At first she heard nothing at all, and then down near the stream bed came a rustling, and a leafy shape rose up, a water or wood sprite, she was not sure which.

"Katherine!" a voice whispered back. "Over here. Watch out for the trap."

In the dim light, Katherine could hardly see the fishing line, but she knew where it was. Stepping over it carefully, she walked down some steps, then scrambled down the steep bank where she found Frankie hidden again behind some branches he had woven together.

"Look!" said Frankie when Katherine crouched beside him. "Look at what I made! You didn't even see me from the steps, did you?"

Frankie seemed to have forgotten to be mad at her.

"It's neat, Frankie!" Katherine said. "It's like a kind of house!"

"It's camel flags," explained Frankie. "Soldiers use it so the enemy can't see where they are."

She did not know what Frankie's woven branches had to do with camels or flags, but she was glad to be hidden from the enemy.

"I knew you'd come, Katherine. I brought your javelin," said Frankie, gesturing to the ground behind him, "and I've got the fishing tackle, too. Now we just have to wait for the bad man."

Then Katherine remembered the message and her mother telling her to find Frankie and bring him back.

"Frankie, your mother is having the baby. My mother says you can stay with us! Your mother says she's going to try to have a brother this time. She's going to the hospital in the hearse."

"In the hearse! My moms is a lucky duck. I got to ride in the hearse with my Uncle Joey one time. I got to lie down where the dead people lie. It was cool. "

Katherine did not think she would like to lie where a dead person had been. She wondered if Frankie's mother minded. Especially if Frankie's uncle wasn't there.

"Frankie," Katherine said, "if your Uncle Joey is gone, who will I go get to arrest the bad man?"

Frankie didn't answer right away. In the quiet, Katherine could hear the birds twittering, louder, then soft again. A squirrel carrying a nut leaped from one tree to another rustling the branches overhead.

"I don't know," Frankie finally said. "But we have to catch the bad man, Katherine, we have to or I might never see my Uncle Joey again and my pops might have to stay in jail forever."

"And Miss Ebersbach," said Katherine.

She did not understand how the bad man had made all the bad things happen. But she knew the badness was real. There was badness in Narnia, too, and children had to fight it. Katherine moved closer to Frankie, and she sat down on the ground cross-legged like an Indian brave to wait. The stream sang a song that repeated the same notes over and over. She gave the notes words from the psalm, thy rod and staff, they comfort me, thy rod and staff, thy javelin, me comfort still...

"Katherine," Frankie's whisper came into her song, "do you have your knife?"

"Yes."

"Good girl, Katherine, good girl," he said, the same way he had when she told him she wanted to kill God.

That was the funny thing with Frankie. He made bad things good.

CHAPTER FORTY-THREE

Lucy hurried towards the lower end of the church driveway. She'd had to park on a side street since both sides of Main Street had cars parked bumper to bumper. She should have arrived an hour ago. She hoped Anne wasn't worrying about where she was. Maybe she ought to have told about Anne that she was going to visit Mildred at the Gables, but she couldn't shake the feeling that the less Anne knew about Lucy's discoveries—or wild goose chases—the safer she would be.

Mildred had graduated to the nonviolent ward and was dressed in her own clothes again. Or maybe they weren't hers. She had on a rose-colored cardigan, a color Lucy had never seen her wear before. It quite became her, and Lucy said so, receiving a rush of gratitude that was touching, if also sad. Mildred had sobbed with relief when Lucy assured her that Nat harbored no ill feelings. In fact Mildred had appeared to be saner—and a great deal more humble and contrite—than she had in a while. Lucy didn't know if it was drugs or being sequestered from the drama of her ill-fated attempts on Nat's affections, or, perhaps (why perhaps?), some form of divine grace and mercy. In any event, she was willing to help identify the woman in the photograph that Lucy had taken from Charlotte's house.

"I'm pretty sure that's Charlotte's cousin Jane, on her father's side. Charlotte and I were second cousins on her mother's side, same maternal great-grandmother or something like that. Jane may have been a more distant cousin and probably once removed. She was at least ten years older than we were, Charlotte and me, our set," Mildred explained. "We all thought Jane was very beautiful—and tragic. Her parents died young, in some sort of accident, I believe. There was some mystery or scandal about her parents, something we young girls were not supposed to know. Anyway, her parents were dead and had left her quite penniless. I know now she is what you would call a poor relation. Her best hope was to marry well, and so Charlotte's family hosted her Season, with the idea, I suppose, of making her look like a catch. I believe she did marry, but that's where I lose track of her. There was no big wedding. No one willing to foot the bill, I imagine. Charlotte never heard from Jane again that I can recall. I see from the photograph that she must have had a child."

The woman held a baby in her arms, a year old, perhaps. Mother and child gazed at each other, rapt as any Madonna and infant Christ.

"Where did you say you found it?" Mildred asked.

Lucy hadn't said, and she didn't intend to say. Unlike her late second cousin Charlotte, Mildred was not a bloodhound. She was easily sidetracked into a theological discussion of sin and atonement.

"I know now I shouldn't have tried to force Nat to marry me, Lucy. My doctor has explained to me that I was suffering from a long-term fixation, which became a mania after the trauma of Charlotte's murder. But what I want to know, Lucy, is if I couldn't help what I did (though when I did it, I know I intended to) because of temporary insanity, is it still a sin? And is insanity the same thing as demonic possession? Was Our Lord healing people like me when he cast out unclean spirits? And if it is the same, who is curing me, the doctor or Our Lord?"

"I don't see why it would have to be one or the other, Mildred. Don't you suppose God is present in the people who help us as much as in those who need our help?"

Mildred's face, which had been gathered into deepening wrinkles, relaxed for a moment.

"Lucy, you are so clever!" she said. "No, more than clever. I do believe you should have been a priest. It is a pity you can't be. Lucy, since you're here, and Father Bradley isn't, there's something else that's troubling me. How do I atone? Especially when...oh, Lucy, I still love Nat, and I still wish he loved me. I am afraid I am still fixated or in a state of sin or both."

Lucy reached out and patted Mildred's hand.

"It's never wrong to love someone," Lucy said carefully. "It's what you do with the love that matters."

Mildred was silent for a moment.

"What shall I do with it, Lucy Way?"

Lucy hesitated, not feeling qualified to play the role of spiritual advisor. But as she had just said to Mildred, God could be present in Mildred's doctor, so why not in Lucy?

"Well, Mildred, one way to atone for what you did and to love Nat might be to pray for him—not pray for him to love you back, just pray for his peace. You could also show your love for Nat by praying for the repose of Charlotte's soul, praying that whoever murdered her will be brought to justice."

Mildred looked thoughtful. "I don't know that Charlotte would want me to pray for her, Lucy. She never liked me, you know. She always looked down on me."

Lucy smiled, thinking of her own recent encounters with Charlotte's spirit.

"That will make your prayers all the more potent, I should think. As Our Lord taught us, pray for those who despitefully use you."

"Oh, Lucy!" Mildred said with a fresh spate of anguish. "I am afraid I was rather spiteful to you about your friend Elsa. Will you forgive me? I did see her at the parish house that awful morning, it's true. But I, I can't believe she did it."

"Of course I forgive you, Mildred," said Lucy. "And I would be very grateful if you would pray for Elsa, and, and...for me."

"You, Lucy?" Mildred seemed surprised by the request. "I will, Lucy, oh, I will! And I will pray for Elsa, too, and for Nat, and, well, all right, for the repose of Charlotte's soul...."

Lucy left Mildred busy with her list, feeling oddly comforted and touched. God knew Lucy needed all the help she could get. She felt no closer to solving the mystery of why Rick Foster would murder

Charlotte than she had. But somehow the photograph must hold the key. She felt the weight of it in her pocketbook as she hurried up the driveway, now joined by a stream of others heading to swell the crowd already waiting to storm the main doors of the parish house. It was a daunting sight. She would never be able to push her way through that crowd to the front door, which would be locked in any event. Surely the office door was locked, too. Grace Jones would be upstairs in menswear by now.

As she got closer to the parish house, Lucy saw a police car parked just beyond the toy barn. That was very wise of Gerald, she thought. This year's mob no doubt included morbid curiosity seekers who wanted to see the site of the murder. She was glad there would be an official presence. She supposed if she could find an officer on duty, she could appeal to him to escort her inside, but that seemed a dubious proposition. Then she thought of an easier solution. She would just go round the back of the parish house and climb the fire escape. It would be locked from the outside, but the children's clothing department was right next to the fire escape door. If she knocked loudly enough, surely she could catch Teresa's attention or someone's and they would let her in—with a good twenty minutes to spare till the doors opened.

Pleased with her plan, Lucy parted from the crowd and slipped round the back. As soon as she was out of sight of the crowd, she sensed someone behind her. Bother. She would have to explain that only workers were allowed inside before the doors opened. Or maybe it was simply another latecomer like herself who'd had the same idea. Just before she reached the fire escape, she turned to look.

There, standing in front of her with the late afternoon sun behind him, lending him its glow, was Rick Foster. He was wearing the black sweatshirt that concealed his wings, though the hood was down, revealing his burnished hair. No visible horns.

Steady, Lucy, whispered Charlotte's spirit.

"Oh, Mr. Foster, it's you," said Lucy.

"Miss Way," he greeted her. "What a lucky coincidence to find you here."

"Oh? Did you need to get into the building, too?" asked Lucy, though she knew he was working in the furniture and appliances tent. "I'm late for my post in children's clothing. I was just going in by the fire escape. I'm sure someone will be glad to let us both in."

She wanted to get to the fire escape as quickly as possible, but that would mean turning her back on him, which would be rude, dangerous or both.

Quick, Lucy.

As she made to turn, Rick Foster closed the distance between them in two easy strides, and also closed his hand on her elbow in a manner that was at once courtly and menacing.

"Actually, Miss Way, I was hoping you could demonstrate your theory for me. Show me the escape route you believe the murderer followed. I might be able to use my influence to get the sheriff's department to investigate further."

Don't, Lucy!

"Thank you, Mr. Foster. I am afraid the sheriff found my suggestions silly. But now is hardly the time to investigate. The doors to the rummage sale are about to open—"

"Not quite yet," said Mr. Foster calmly and reasonably. "We have time for a little stroll. And it's a lovely sunset. Don't you agree?"

"No!" said Lucy. "I mean yes, it's a lovely sunset, but if you could just speak to the sheriff, I am sure that would be best. We must not risk trampling any evidence."

"The rain, the rabbits, and the deer have already seen to that," Rick pointed out. "Forensics doesn't matter in this case as much as it should. It is all motive and opportunity, motive and opportunity."

To Lucy's dismay, he had already propelled her several feet.

Scream, Lucy!

She wanted to. She really did. She could feel the scream starting silently, pounding at her throat to be let out. Or was that her heart? But if she screamed, the jig would be up. He would know she suspected him. Perhaps he was only testing her now to see what she knew, to find out if she was a threat to him. And even if she did scream, who would hear her over the din of the crowd, the excited bustle of preparation?

That is a point. Honestly, Lucy, you're not making it easy for me to help. If you can't scream, keep talking. Blither if you must.

"Well now, Mr. Foster," said Lucy, stalling him before he plunged her into the wood. "Let us give our minds to the conundrum, try to think as the murderer might have thought. If he, or she, did escape through a basement window," Lucy could feel his impatience as he gripped her arm just a little too tight, "he would have crashed through the undergrowth—it's fairly thick here—or do you think he would have walked around the parish house and gone through the gap in the wall where there's already a path?"

She hoped she sounded sincere and persuasive. And if indeed Rick Foster had gone that way and agreed to do so again, they would pass close to the tent where she'd have a better chance of being heard or making a dash for it.

"Miss Way, you have such a flair for deduction. It is too bad more women are not detectives."

Priest, detective. In one day, two missed callings.

"But I must point out to you one thing you may have forgotten," he continued, propelling her forward again. "The furniture and appliances tent had not been set up yet on the morning of the murder. So the murderer would not have had cover if he, or she, fled that way."

"Was it not, Mr. Foster?" Lucy asked while he solicitously moved branches out of her way as he guided her firmly further into the underbrush. "Then where were the furniture and appliances stored?"

"Oh, Miss Way, I am surprised that someone with a mind as sharp as yours and a memory as keen would have forgotten," he chided her in a playful and, to her horror, flirtatious manner. "Furniture and appliances were stored in the barn until the sorting started. The men put up the tent the same afternoon the women went through the boxes."

"Of course, Mr. Foster, you're quite right. It must have slipped my mind," she said, as she slipped on some leaves, and Rick Foster caught and righted her. Thank God she was wearing loafers and not heels, but the loafers had no tread at all. "Still, it must have been quite a bother for the murderer. All these briars."

And, Lucy added silently, you are wrong about the forensics. We are leaving evidence with every step should anyone care to investigate my—

Don't even think it, Lucy. My case hasn't been solved yet. You are not to upstage me.

"Let's stop for a moment to rest and think," said Rick.

Lucy noticed he did not let go of her arm.

"You're right about the briars," he conceded. "It's slow going through the brush. At some point, our murderer would have wanted to get up to the carriage road."

Our murderer. The bizarre assumption of an intimacy between them made Lucy feel queasy. Yet was there not a horrifying intimacy between murderer and victim?

Don't be disgusting, Lucy Way. I'm surprised at you!

"I'm sure you're right," she said. "Once he was out of the sight of the church yard, he would have climbed to the road. Up there around that bend." She pointed.

And maybe, if they got up to the carriage road, she could make a run for it.

"Yes," agreed her captor, so amiably it was hard even now to believe they were not simply an amateur investigative team. "It's not so steep here as it is further on. Shall we?"

As if she had a choice with his grip on her arm still a tad too tight for comfort. They clambered up the slope to the carriage road wall.

"Ladies first," he said.

At last he'd let go of her arm and then, to her dismay, he gave her a boost over the wall, his hands most indelicately positioned.

This is your chance, Lucy. While he's hoisting himself over the wall, run!

CHAPTER FORTY-FOUR

Gerald ran up the sidewalk on Main Street as fast as he could, pushing past people on their way to the rummage sale. Anne, Anne. Her name sounded with every pounding step, with every ragged breath. Anne, Anne. He would never forgive himself if something had happened to her while he'd gone on his fool's errand at the sheriff's office. He had thought vodka didn't linger on your breath like gin, but the sheriff had leaned across his desk and taken an ostentatious sniff.

Well, he had sounded like a drunk or madman, his words tumbling over one another. "...accused my wife of trying to seduce him...accused Frank Lomangino of extorting money from paupers... accused a lesbian who'd run away with a Jew of harboring Nazis..." Gerald was gasping for breath by the time he got his story out.

"Take it easy, Reverend. We'll look into it. Go home now and get some rest."

The sheriff hadn't taken a statement from him. He hadn't even taken notes, and Gerald had wasted all that time.

Gerald turned into the driveway and ran, now blind with sweat, not knowing where to look for her first. Then he saw Anne hurrying from the front porch. He did not know how he could run any faster, but he did, both of them nearly falling over as he careened into her.

"Anne, Anne! Thank God I found you," he gasped, holding on to her as if he would fall or drown if he didn't. "Oh, Anne, I was wrong, I'm sorry, so sorry. Rick, he was lying and I believed him."

"Gerald! Shut up!" Anne screamed as she shook herself free of him, and for a moment he thought she might slap him, which he deserved. "I can't find Katherine. I can't find Katherine!"

In one searing instant he saw it: she had lost one child. The fear of losing another never left her.

"We'll find her, Anne. I promise you. We'll find her."

Lucy ran. Just as she rounded the curve in the carriage road, her loafers betrayed her and she slid, landing her on her knees. In no time, his hands were on her again, not just one but two as he pulled her to her feet, then twisted her arms behind her back.

"Why such a hurry, Miss Way?"

She could feel his breath on the back of her neck.

"Mr. Foster, if you are a gentleman," she summoned her indignation, "you will stop playing this silly game of detective and let go of me at once. I told you before, I am very late. There is a huge crowd about to swarm the parish house. Every hand is needed to help. You ought to be at the tent with Mr. McCready. He'll be wondering where you are."

"You are wrong there, Miss Way," he said. "Count Ludwig is helping in the tent, because I am at a high-powered fundraising dinner, or I will be very shortly as everyone will attest. If you are a lady, you will not want me to be late."

Under the circumstances, she rather thought she would like to ruin his alibi.

"But I will be missed," she pointed out. "The WOR are expecting me. I am not known to shirk my duty."

"I don't doubt your untarnished reputation for a moment, Miss Way, and I'm sure your fellow pillars of the church will wonder where you are. But as you point out, they will be much too busy to go looking for you for several hours. I'm more attentive. I've been following you all day."

Lucy thought of twisting suddenly to break his hold on her and wielding her pocket book as a weapon. Then, to her horror, she felt metal closing on one wrist and, before she could move, the other. She spun around to aim a kick at his groin, but he caught her leg with one hand and held onto her arm with the other or she might have gone over backwards, which would have saved him some trouble if he intended to knock her unconscious.

You'll have to use your wits, Lucy Way. Unsettle him, keep him talking. Don't show any fear.

"So, Mr. Foster," said Lucy, now facing him, "I am going to take your assault on me as evidence that you murdered Charlotte Crowley. I hereby place you under citizen's arrest."

Rick Foster looked at her in amazement, then his face broke open into a laugh, such a pleasant laugh, she almost wished she could join him.

"Miss Way, I find you so delightful. I do. I am genuinely sorry I have to kill you."

"Indeed, you will be sorry," Lucy told him. "You are making the classic amateur murderer's mistake, committing a second murder to cover the first. Don't you know that is how murderers always get caught?"

At least in detective novels, she did not add.

"Ah, but you see. This is not my second murder. It's my third, Miss Way. Three times is the charm."

"What about three strikes and you're out?" Lucy countered. She had not been brought up on baseball. But Rick was American; surely he had.

"Ah, but Miss Way, not if you're the pitcher!" He laughed softly as if at a private joke. "If you're the pitcher, then you've just helped your team win. You're a hero."

Lucy decided to give up on baseball as an extended metaphor.

"Who was your first victim?" Lucy asked almost politely, as if asking a poet the title of his first collection of verse, "assuming Charlotte was your second."

Second? Charlotte sounded a little miffed. She always did want to come first in everything.

"No questions from you, Miss Way, until you answer two for me," Rick said. "First, what were you and Joe Petrone discussing yesterday?"

So he had seen her. She must be careful. She might be about to die, but Joe must escape, Joe and the evidence he was gathering that would free Frank and Elsa and put Rick Foster away for good. For good.

"His sister's baby, of course. Not that it's any of your business. Naturally he's worried about her. All those children and a new baby, a husband in jail, and no one to pay the bills. The burden is bound to fall on her family."

"Why would he talk to you about it?" Rick sounded skeptical.

"I'm a nurse, Mr. Foster, in case you didn't know. As a visiting rural nurse, I've ridden the hearse with Joe Petrone on a number of occasions. He's a trained medic. Korean War. I was a nurse in the Second War. We have a lot in common. He asked if I would help Teresa at home when the baby comes. I was very touched that he would think of me. Really, Mr. Foster. I thought you were in a hurry to get to your dinner."

Well done, Lucy, well done.

All at once, to her vast relief, Lucy realized Rick Foster had no power over her whatsoever. He'd made it plain he was going to kill her. No hope of escape, so why bother to tell him anything? Stupid of him, but then perhaps most murderers were stupid or at least too clever by half. She had that odd sensation of lightness and exhilaration that she remembered from the Blitz. She was walking through the valley of the shadow of death. For the moment, at least, she feared no evil. In fact, Rick looked more frightened and disconcerted than she did.

"By the way," she said, feeling almost cheeky, "don't you think you should have asked questions first. You might have discovered that I know nothing worth killing me over. You could have saved yourself the trouble. Now you've shown your hand."

"You showed yours first, Miss Way," he pointed out, "when you turned to run."

"Touché," she acknowledged.

"Miss Way," he said, a hint of sternness in his voice, as if he were a headmaster reprimanding a wayward school girl, "this is not a game. There are no points to be won. Not for you. Now for my second question. What did you find at the Crowley's house last night?"

Lucy debated. She could say she found nothing. She could hope that he wouldn't look through her pocketbook and that someone else would find the photograph and figure out that it was a clue. But she herself did not even know what it meant. Only Rick Foster could tell her.

"Open my pocketbook," she said. "You will find the photograph."

Keeping her firmly in his sights, one hand on her arm, even though she was handcuffed, he fumbled with the clasp, reached into her pocketbook and withdrew the photograph.

It's your last chance, Lucy. Kick him.

But Lucy found herself riveted on Rick Foster's face as it collapsed into grief, and she realized she had never before seen him without his perfect mask. And all at once she knew what she needed to ask him.

"Rick?" said Lucy softly calling him by his first name. "Rick, who killed your mother?"

He looked up at her, the grief transfigured into a rage just as naked.

"They did!" he said. "*They* did."

And Lucy put at least a couple of pieces together, the poor relation served up for a season, married off and forgotten. He did not need to tell her who *they* were. She knew.

"She used to tell me about New York," he went on without any prompting from her. "We lived in a little suburb outside Chicago, near the meat-packing district. She used to go on and on about it afterwards, whenever he beat her—or me."

Lucy noticed he did not use the words *my father*—or *my mother*. *He, she*.

"When he was out of the house, I'd come lie in bed next to her. She made it sound like the Emerald City of Oz. She kept saying we would go there, next summer, next year. She wrote to them. I saw her, letter after letter. But she never got any letters back."

"How old were you when she died?" Lucy asked.

She kept watching his face, all her senses heightened, especially the sixth.

"Seven," Rick said. "He'd sent me away to school, a military academy for the children of American Nazis. I didn't know till later that's what it was. He told me she died of pneumonia."

"But you don't think so."

"No." He paused for a moment that seemed longer than it was. "No, I don't. For a long time I didn't believe she was dead. I didn't go to her funeral. I don't even know if she had one."

It was strange, so strange to be alone in the wood with the man who was about to murder her and to feel her heart break for him. *Dear God,* she found herself praying, *defend O Lord this thy child from all the perils of this night.*

"And *they* didn't care. That family, her family, for Christ's sake, never cared what happened to her," he said. "But it's their fault. They trussed her up and tricked her out and married her to that man, Hitler's doppelganger." He paused again. "And do you know the oddest thing of all, Miss Way?"

Rick hadn't forgotten she was there. She almost thought he might and she would be able to slip from his grasp, tiptoe away, leaving him alone with his ghosts.

"I never knew who Charlotte Crowley was, never knew she was my mother's cousin," at last he said the word, mother, "never knew she was part of the family that betrayed my mother and abandoned her until Charlotte stole that photograph and tried to blackmail me."

Lucy studied his face. His eyes were unfocused. It was all happening again. Lucy needed to see it, too. Whether she survived or not, she needed to know what happened that morning, how it had led her and her murderer here to this wood.

"Why did she ask you to meet her at the parish house?" Lucy asked. "Why not call you or come to your office?"

"Oh, Miss Way!" Rick looked distressed. "Under the circumstances I can't hope to keep your good opinion of me, but please understand, I did not go to the parish house to meet Charlotte Crowley, much less to murder her! It was not premeditated, if that makes you feel any better."

Oddly enough it did, a little. But not much, considering her own imminent murder definitely appeared to be planned.

"But why were you there at the parish house in the first place?" Lucy prompted. "Charlotte was getting ready for the rummage sale and altar guild, but—"

"That was just her excuse." Rick cut Lucy off. "I caught her, in the parish house office, going through files, sensitive files that I had come to...retrieve."

Lucy breathed a silent prayer of thanks that she had deflected his attention from Joe Petrone.

"And so Charlotte threatened to reveal the nature of the files unless you paid her off?"

Rick shook his head impatiently.

"No, no, Miss Way. I thought you had a better grasp of human nature. If it was only the files, we might have come to an understanding. I already knew she needed money desperately. That wouldn't have been an insurmountable problem. It was her other threat. That's where she made her mistake, her stupid, cruel mistake."

That's hardly fair, huffed Charlotte, *I was only making polite conversation.*

" 'Oh, Rick, by the way,'" He gave a fair imitation of Charlotte. "'I believe we are related....' And she went on gushing about poor dear cousin Jane, as if any of them gave a damn about her. Then Charlotte said, 'But surely your name can't be Foster. I suppose Fuchs is too German these days, especially for a congressional candidate. It wouldn't do to be the son of an infamous Nazi sympathizer.' She dared to say that after what they did to her, knowing, *knowing* who he was, knowing what he was—"

He stopped abruptly, rage constricting his throat, the same rage he had turned on Charlotte.

"When did you kill him, Rick?" Lucy asked. "When did you kill your father?"

"Just after the war," he said, letting out his breath as if it was a relief to say it. "When Pearl Harbor was bombed and we were finally in the war, I wanted to enlist. I wanted to fight the dirty sadistic German bastards my father worshipped. I had my bags packed. I was on my way out in the middle of the night. My father caught me, pushed me down the stairs and beat me senseless with the butt end of a gun. Then he kidnapped me."

Now that he started talking, he hardly paused for breath. Quite possibly, almost certainly, he had never told anyone what he was telling her now.

"For years I didn't even know where I was," he went on, "except it had to be somewhere in South America. I was his prisoner, literally. A prisoner of war. But when he had a stroke, the tables turned. He became dependent on me for everything. He turned over all his assets to me, all his criminal connections. He'd had everything planned for any eventuality, a whole raft of new identities. I could take my pick. When the time came, it was the easiest thing in the world."

He paused for breath, and Lucy heard the chime of the bell that announced the opening of the rummage sale. She could almost feel the ground shake as hundreds of feet surged forward. When would someone come to look for her, how would they know where to look?

"I pushed him down a flight of stairs," he concluded.

"Just as you did Charlotte," said Lucy mildly as if it were a mere point of information, a loose end she wanted to tie up.

"Yes," he said. "But I knocked her on the head with a paperweight first. And she wasn't quite dead at the bottom. By the way, I am sorry about using your mother's coats."

Lucy found herself at a loss for words.

"Come, Miss Way."

Almost as if he were taking her in to dinner, he linked his arm through hers and began to drag her (drag her, for she willed her feet to take root) towards the steep flight of stone steps. And she suddenly got his private joke. He was the pitcher, and he was going to pitch her down the steps as he had his pitched his father and Charlotte before her.

"I'm sorry," he said. "Very sorry. Would it make you feel any better to know your death will not be in vain? You see, I am poised to do so much good for the world, so much good. I am going to help make sure there will never be another Hitler, and men like my father will be found out and stopped. No one will suffer like you suffered. Your death won't have been for nothing. You will be so proud of me, so proud."

Lucy knew he was not speaking to her any more. She understood that he was not just murderous but completely mad.

I'm so sorry, Lucy, whispered Charlotte, *and he got it all wrong, you know, I wasn't—*

Hush now, Charlotte. Leave me to my prayers.

Lord Jesus Christ, son of God, have mercy on me, a sinner. Lord Jesus Christ, son of God, have mercy on him, a sinner, Lucy prayed and balked as best she could. And she breathed, savoring each sweet numbered breath of her life.

Now they were at the top of the stone steps, and Rick turned to her.

"I'm sorry," he said again, "I'll try to make it as quick and painless as possible."

Keeping hold of her with one hand, he reached into the pocket of his sweatshirt where he had apparently secreted a rock. Less obvious than a paperweight, Lucy supposed, easier to chuck.

Then out of the corner of her eye, Lucy saw something strange.

"*Macbeth shall never vanquished be, until Great Birnam wood to high Dunsinane hill Shall come against him,*" she found herself quoting, an old habit and old habits die hard.

"What's that, Miss Way?"

Before she could answer him, Birnam Wood began to bellow.

"Ch e-e-e-ya-a-arge!"

Startled Rick dropped the rock, let go of Lucy and spun around. A second later, he tripped and pitched headlong down the steps. She could hear the thwack of his head as it struck stone.

"I've got him, Katherine, I've got him. Run!"

In the gloaming, Lucy saw Frankie Lomangino astride Rick Foster, a spear in his hand, pointed right at Rick Foster's carotid artery.

"Lucy Way, don't move!" shouted Katherine running towards her up the steps. "There's a trap!"

Hardly able to comprehend what was happening, Lucy watched as Katherine crouched down at the top of the steps, pulled a jack knife out of her pocket and sensibly cut a near invisible piece of fishing line before it could trip someone else.

"I'll be right back!" the child promised.

Lucy's nurse's training took over, and though she was handcuffed and could not be of much use, she began to walk down the steps to where Frankie still straddled an inert Rick Foster, unconscious or dead, Lucy did not know. Before she could reach them, she heard Katherine shouting.

"Mommy! Daddy! Come quick! We caught the bad man! We caught the bad man!"

Lucy turned to look back, and in another moment, Anne, Gerald, and thanks be to God, Joe Petrone, rounded the bend, with Amos McCready, staff at the ready, and in full Celtic battle cry, bringing up the rear.

Part Four:
REGENERATION

CHAPTER FORTY-FIVE

Gerald sat at the top of the wooden steps sipping coffee and looking out at the half mile stretch of low tide. When the tide was high the water came right up the steps, still warm to the touch in October, though the chilly air discouraged swimming. Anne was out there somewhere walking in her rubber boots. Every morning she'd gotten up while he was still asleep, and every morning he'd woken alone, sure she'd left him. And in a way she had, but she'd made coffee first, and the car was still there beside the off-season cottage they'd rented for the week.

He had not wanted to take a vacation. There was so much to clean up, in every sense, back at the church. But Grace and Anne had made an unholy alliance. Wives and secretaries were supposed to be adversaries. It was much safer for men that way. The two of them had gone behind his back to the bishop, who had ordered him to take a vacation or else be suspended from his duties. Ralph Smith was taking the services. Grace and her daughters were keeping the frankly delighted twins. Lucy Way, who ought to take a vacation herself, had invited Katherine to stay with her.

Everyone was happy (perhaps even Anne, though it was hard to tell) including the state Democratic committee. They had drafted a legendary folksinger to run in Rick's place. Bob Wright (you can't go wrong with Wright) was, ironically, about as far left as you could get without being a communist. In fact, he had been blacklisted during the McCarthy era. Rick had run as a cold warrior and Bob was an outspoken advocate for nuclear disarmament. Ordinarily the party would never have considered such a radical. Gerald guessed it came down to name recognition. Wright wouldn't have had a snowball's chance in hell of winning under ordinary circumstances, but Rick Foster's indictment for murder—and for money laundering—was national news, and so this last minute candidacy was high profile. Everyone was happy, maybe even punch drunk, except of course for Rick Foster. And maybe Rick's wife and sons, though it was hard to say. They had decamped immediately back to Park Avenue where they belonged. Sybil had lost no time filing for divorce.

And Gerald. Though he had not lost a beloved wife like Nat and had been nothing worse than an innocent dupe in the camp fund debacle, he was deeply unhappy. More than that, deeply ashamed. He was a bad shepherd. He'd welcomed a wolf into the fold. Worse than that, he'd come pretty close to hero worship of that wolf. And worst of all—he could still hardly bear to think of it—he'd let that man assassinate his wife's character. He'd put up no resistance, and because of his credulousness, he'd almost lost another sheep.

I am a worm and no man, he silently quoted Psalm 22.

What would his father have done in his place? There was hardly any use in wondering. His father never would have gotten into such a mess, would no doubt have seen through Rick, and he would never have doubted his wife's respectability. But then Gerald's mother was so much simpler than Anne, outgoing, direct. *No excuses, son,* he could almost hear his father saying. The one thing Gerald had done that might have made his father proud was to visit Rick Foster the week he was in the hospital under heavy guard and heavily sedated for pain. Rick had broken an arm and a leg and suffered a concussion. They had to keep him under medical surveillance for several days to insure there would be no swelling of the brain. He'd been moved to a jail cell just before Gerald went on vacation. He would visit Rick there when he got back.

I was sick and ye visited me, in prison, and ye came unto me.

It was not easy practicing what he preached. When Gerald had visited, Rick was moving in and out of waking and dozing. But at one point, Rick had opened his eyes and said very distinctly, "Lucy Way."

"Lucy's fine," Gerald assured him.

"Lucy Way," Rick kept saying, agitated until he finally finished the sentence. "Lucy Way was here."

Apparently Lucy had come to see Rick Foster, too. The effect of her visit must have been profound. Last Gerald had heard, Rick intended to plead guilty to charges of aiding and abetting in a money laundering scheme in exchange for protection of his false identity. There would be no need for Joe Petrone to testify or to involve himself in any capacity at all. He also admitted to falsely accusing Frank Lomangino of extortion. Overriding the advice of his attorney, he had confessed to the murder of Charlotte Crowley and to attempted murder of Lucy Way. Frank Lomangino and Elsa Ebersbach had been cleared of all charges and released from jail.

Gerald took another sip of his coffee, cold now on this chilly morning with its rosy clouds, and satisfyingly bitter. He stood up for a moment and looked down the beach. He thought he saw Anne a long way off, poised just where sand turned to water. A long way off, distant. Just where she should be in relation to him. Though she would come back, most likely, at least for today. She had every other day this week. She would make breakfast for him or maybe today he would take her to the diner in town. Then they might take a walk together on the Atlantic side, the surf too loud for much conversation. They would spend the afternoon resting and reading, historical novels, both of them, hers about obscure royals, his about naval wars. When it was five o'clock, he would have a martini. Anne had made a huge concession to him and their vacation and would sip half a glass of sherry. She was being kind to him.

He could hardly bear it.

He had broken down yesterday evening, halfway through his second martini. He had accused himself of everything he could think of, especially of believing Rick, about anything, about everything, about Anne. How could Gerald believe in anything now? How could he ever trust himself again? Look where Gerald's ideals had led him. And dear God, look where Rick's had led him!

"Ideals are not wrong, Gerald," Anne had said when his rant was exhausted. "They're just not enough, not without the little things, the daily things."

Though she did not say so, Gerald sensed Anne was thinking of Lucy.

"You lost your friend, Gerald," she'd said at length. "I'm sorry."

"Don't!" he'd said before he could think.

"Don't what?" she'd asked.

"Don't...don't forgive me!" he'd surprised himself by saying. "Not yet."

"All right," she agreed. "I won't. I don't know much about forgiveness, anyway. Gerald, I don't really think I'm a Christian. Does that bother you?"

Gerald looked up, startled, fascinated. It was the most personal thing she had said to him in a long time. Maybe ever.

"No," he said, "no, it doesn't. And it probably doesn't bother Jesus either."

He had hoped she might say more, but she hadn't. Maybe someday she would. Maybe someday he would have the courage to touch her again. But not yet, not till he could forgive himself, and he was not sure he ever could.

It was almost time to go back, but Anne was waiting, waiting for the exact moment the tide turned, except that it was hardly even a moment, it was a lull, the most exquisite lull, before a breath out became a breath in, like the moment when a sleepy baby stirred at your breast and his eyes opened, then closed, and you saw the tiny veins in his eyelids. Anne stood and closed her eyes now, breathing the scent of low tide, sweet and salt and bitter all at once. Seagulls cried overhead while cormorants stood silently beside her, waiting for the same signals. If Anne had a soul it lived here, between the tides, between earth and water, water and sky. Her soul was made of this.

She wanted never to go back.

There it was: the shift, the breath of the sea itself, and the little wavelets lapping in, thirsty for land. The sea would have its way again, taking and tossing trash and treasures, always the same, never the same. That was the great mercy of the tides, the only mercy Anne knew. She waited till a wave washed over the toe of her boots, and then she opened her eyes, sight flying out beyond the earth's curve before she turned and began to walk back toward the steps, where Gerald would be waiting for her and pretending not to be.

Their marriage was having a lull, she considered as she walked a zigzag, following the wave patterns. The tide had gone out as far as it could go, everything lay rank and exposed (so much prettier on a beach than in a life). She did not know what the next tide would bring, if they would ride it out together or not. Right now she did not want to know, and she was grateful to Gerald for not forcing it—and for not forcing sex. Not that he had ever forced himself on her. He hadn't had to; she forced herself. This week he'd kept his distance or respected hers. She wasn't sure which, but it made it easier to be gentle. She supposed they ought to have marriage counseling at some point. Or maybe not. Certainly not with Dr. Aiken.

Anne had fired Dr. Aiken. She had not gone to see him; she had simply left a message with his receptionist. For the first time, he had called her.

"You see, Anne, unconsciously you blame me, so that you don't have to face the fact that your husband betrayed you."

She had hung up on him. It had given her great pleasure. Of course Dr. Aiken, the despicable worm, could be right. She could be blaming him in order to think more kindly of Gerald. And if she was, why was that a bad thing?

Yesterday when he'd got enough gin in him, Gerald had excoriated himself. There wasn't much more to say about all he'd done wrong. Of course that could be self-protective, reproaching himself before she could. She couldn't help feeling sorry for him, but she hadn't said much. Then he had taken her by surprise. Instead of begging her to forgive him, he begged her not to. As the steps came into view and she could make out Gerald sitting on the top step carefully not looking in her direction, it struck her that she hadn't given the matter of forgiving him much thought. At least not for suspecting her of murder and adultery. His lack of faith in her character weighed on him so heavily, but she was largely indifferent.

How could she tell him, could she ever tell him? She had already never forgiven him. For years. And years.

Since he beat her son. Her son. Did he ever think about that, awake in the middle of the night? That he had beaten his son. Just as (oh this was a hard one) just as Rick Foster's father had beaten him.

Anne stopped in her tracks and turned to look out to sea again. And she knew; she had that much rage in her, oceans of it, typhoons. She could smash Gerald to bits.

Maybe she already had. Anyway, he was broken. That much she knew. Broken.

Suddenly Anne took in a breath, sharp, deep, more air than she had ever had in her lungs, and then she let it out. She turned and walked on. She could see Gerald's face now. He still wasn't looking at her. When she started up the steps, he took his cigarettes out of his pocket, lit one for her and handed it to her when she got to the top.

"Thanks," she said sitting down on the step below him.

"Want to have breakfast at the diner today?" he asked.

"Sure," she said. "That would be a nice change."

Today was the day Katherine and Frankie were going to have a picnic in the woods with Lucy Way. Katherine had gotten to stay with Lucy Way all week. She had her own room with a bed called a sleigh bed, with a satin quilt for a cover that looked grey in some lights and rosy in others. One side of the room had a sloping ceiling and little windows under the eaves low to the floor where Katherine could sit and look out at a spruce tree. The bigger window next to her bed had a view of Lucy's garden where orange and gold flowers bloomed. The last flowers before frost, Lucy said.

Every morning, Lucy made porridge with maple syrup to sweeten it. Instead of raisins, Lucy had blueberries and cranberries that she had dried to keep for the winter. She let Katherine stand on a footstool and stir in the fruit when it was time. Today they had packed a picnic basket with what Lucy called French bread, the kind you broke pieces from instead of slicing. They had cheeses and peanut butter and homemade raspberry jam to spread in case she and Frankie didn't like the cheese, and apples they had picked from a tree in Lucy's garden. For dessert, she and Lucy had made butterscotch cookies with chocolate chips. To drink, they had ginger beer, not ginger ale, beer!

They met Frankie at the parish house. His pops was back at work, and he and Mr. McCready were going to clean the gutters with Mr. McCready holding the ladder for Frankie's father. Frankie's mother had sent homemade salami to go with the picnic. After the picnic they were all going to go to Frankie's house to see his new baby brother Joey. It was funny to be outside her own house with nobody home. It made her feel almost like a grownup, like a parishioner or a worker.

Frankie's father took the picnic basket from Lucy Way and showed Katherine and Frankie how they could carry it between them, each taking one handle. It was warm and sunny in the middle of the day with just a nibble of cold at their cheeks. The three of them set out for the woods with Frankie and Katherine and the picnic basket leading the way. None of them spoke as they walked down the carriage road. The air was so still you could hear the trees let go of a leaf, the swish of the leaf in the air, and the whisper when it brushed the ground. Though no wind moved them, Katherine could see the trees nodding to them. *There they go,* she imagined the trees saying. *They all have fairy blood, you know.*

They got to the top of the steps where the bad man, who turned out to be Dickie and Prescott's father, tried to throw Lucy Way down the steps. To kill her the way he had killed Mrs. Crowley. It still scared her to think about it, and she had had nightmares until she went to Lucy Way's house.

"Put the basket down for a moment," said Lucy Way.

When they set it down on the top of the steps, Lucy opened the basket and took out a soft, silk handkerchief, which she unfolded carefully. Inside was a tiny crystal bottle that Katherine had not seen Lucy put in the basket. Maybe it had been invisible till now. It looked like the bottle that held the other Lucy's magic cordial. Or maybe it *was* that bottle! Maybe Lucy Way had somehow brought it back from Narnia.

"Now children," Lucy unstopped the bottle, "I am going to put a little of this water in your hands, and then I want you to sprinkle it all over these steps, from the top all the way down to where Mr. Foster landed."

"Why?" Frankie wanted to know. "What's it for?"

"When your mother cleans the floor, what does she use?" Lucy asked.

"Water," said Frankie. "And soap, I guess. That water doesn't look soapy."

"It has something more powerful than soap," said Lucy. "Can you guess what it is?"

"It has magic," whispered Katherine.

"Yes," said Lucy. "That is one word for it. This water comes from holy wells all over the world. Just a few drops will clean away the sadness and the fear."

"And the badness," said Frankie. "Dickie and Prescott's father is very bad."

"He did very bad things," Lucy Way agreed. "And bad things were done to him, and no one helped him."

"Will this water help him?" Katherine asked.

Lucy stood still for a very long time, holding the bottle, and Katherine began to wonder if Lucy had heard her.

"Sometimes," she finally spoke, "when people are very sad or angry or bad, they leave parts of themselves behind in a place. The part that is angry or sad gets stuck. That's all any ghost is, you know, something or someone stuck. If anything is stuck here this water will help it go on its way. Then the kindly spirits of the wood, who may have been frightened, will come back again. Will you help?"

They both nodded and held out their hands. Lucy Way dropped a few drops of water into their hands; it caught the sunlight and the gold of the trees. Slowly Katherine and Frankie walked down the steps, shaking the drops from their hands onto the ground while Lucy Way watched from the top step.

When she and Frankie got all the way to where Mr. Foster had fallen, they turned and looked back at Lucy Way standing on the top step, as still as the trees, as golden as the light, her face serious and glad at the same time.

"Well done," said Lucy Way.

And they walked back up the stairs to fetch the picnic basket. On the bridge where the bad man had run while she and Frankie hid underneath, the three of them paused and looked up the hill where Frankie and Katherine had longed to explore.

"Further up and further in!" said Katherine.

"Further up and further in!" repeated Lucy.

Then even Frankie said it. In fact, he shouted it, "Further up and further in!

And with the picnic basket bouncing between them, Frankie and Katherine ran up the hill.

Lucy Way paused in the doorway of what she already thought of as Katherine's room to look back at the sleeping child. It had been a long day with lots of time outdoors. Anne had told Lucy about Katherine's nightmares, and so she had thought of a simple rite to perform at the steps to banish the fear and grief, her own, the children's—and Rick Foster's. She had felt lighter afterwards and the children seemed positively exuberant.

They had spread out their picnic beside the pond where bright leaves floated and fish darted, visible below the surface. There was even a snapping turtle sunning on a log that was fortunately just out of Frankie's reach. After they'd feasted, Lucy rested on the picnic blanket, while Katherine and Frankie had explored the overgrown orchards, the icehouse, the walkway over the dam, the tiny hidden cove on the other side of some stepping stones. She had kept a watchful eye on them, but she need not have worried. With every discovery, they came racing back to tell her what they'd found.

In the late afternoon, they'd walked back to the church, the picnic basket much lighter. Storing the basket in the bonnet (where Frankie still felt the engine should have been) they drove in her car to Frankie's house, a white house with green trim and a green door, which Katherine particularly noticed, close enough indeed to the church that they could have walked.

Frankie ran ahead and opened the door to a house that smelled of baking and beeswax and clean laundry.

"Surprise!" called several voices before Lucy's eyes had adjusted to the light.

"Come in, come in!" Teresa Lomangino came forward and took both her hands.

And then Lucy saw Frank beside Teresa, holding the baby. Just behind them stood Elsa and Clara, both beaming, as well as Joe Petrone, Amos McCready, looking wild as ever, and Nat Crowley, with his customary courtly bearing.

"It's a party! It's a party!" shouted Frankie's little sisters, unable to contain themselves any longer.

"A party for you three," said Frank. "Our heroes. Hey, Frankie, come 'ere."

Frank, Senior held out his arms to Frankie, who, characteristically, looked down and scowled. Then all at once he took a flying leap and hurled himself at his father. Frank, Senior put his arm around his son and reached out to pinch Katherine gently on the cheek. Then he approached Lucy and gravely took her hand.

"How can I thank you?"

"Really, truly, you must not," said Lucy in distress. "It's the children who are the heroes. It was not my idea at all to go into the woods, and if it hadn't been for the children, I might not have come back. And it was Anne Bradley and Joe who solved the mystery."

And here was Nat who was still bereft and Rick Foster's sons with a father who might face a life sentence or worse. How could they celebrate and yet…she saw, they also needed to. They must.

"Don't be so modest, Lucy Way," said Elsa severely. "You ruin my appetite, and I know there is some delicious food in the other room."

"Come on, let's eat!" said Teresa. "We can talk more when our mouths are full."

After they feasted on homemade chocolate cake, ignoring the antipasti that Teresa had also set out, all the children ran upstairs to play some rambunctious game that must have involved jumping on and off as well as up and down on beds. The grownups pulled up chairs around the generous kitchen table, laughing and talking, drinking drinks as sensible as tea, as strong as whiskey and as ill-advised, perhaps, as vodka. Lucy happily accepted a glass of Chianti. Baby Joey made the rounds from one pair of arms to another, except for Elsa and Amos. They found common ground at last, agreeing that babies were not their forte. Clara took more turns with Joey than anyone else, holding the baby awkwardly and speaking to it gravely. The baby, though getting to his fussy time of day, gazed at Clara and treated her with great forbearance.

At last Lucy's turn came, and she held the surprisingly solid little bundle and lost herself in wonder at his face, now at two weeks old beginning to smooth and open like a flower. Life, death, mystery, regeneration. Over and over, on and on. As the child opened and closed its eyes between sleeping and waking, Lucy couldn't help remembering Rick Foster in the hospital. Because they knew she was a nurse, the staff had escorted her past the guard and allowed her to sit with him. When he'd opened his eyes, he had looked at her with the impenetrable wonder of a newborn. They did not speak, and soon he'd drifted back to sleep.

"May I hold him again?" asked Clara softly.

"You know," said Lucy, relinquishing the baby to Clara, "I never did hear how it happened that you showed up at just the right moment, Joe. I thought you had gone away into hiding."

"I was hiding," laughed Joe. "You tell the story, Teresa."

"You see, Mrs. Way, my brother was hiding all the time in the basement at Sullivan's with all the stiffs, a place nobody would think to look."

"Well, not exactly *with* them. But Luke said he could pop me into a coffin anytime should the need arise."

"Smart, huh? Hope his nephew gets his brains, no offense to his father or nothing." Teresa gave Frank a dazzling smile. "So when Mr. Sullivan got the call to take me to the hospital, Joe sneaked out and hunkered down in the hearse. All the way there, I kept having this feeling about Frankie. That he was in some kind of danger. Couldn't shake it, so when we get to the hospital I told him, Joe, you gotta go back and look for Frankie. It's a madhouse there with the rummage sale. Nobody will even notice you. And so there he was, at the right time and the right place. A miracle," she concluded, smiling at Clara.

"A miracle," agreed Clara, looking up with a face so beatified she could have been a Madonna.

"And a much happier use for a hearse!" declared Nat Crowley. "Charlotte would be so pleased."

Everyone was quiet for a moment. A good quiet, Lucy thought, a needed one. Then Frank Lomangino got to his feet.

"To Mrs. Crowley. May she rest in peace!"

And everyone drank to Charlotte's memory.

Now Lucy lingered in the doorway, watching the peaceful rise and fall of Katherine's chest as she slept. They'd come home to Falling Star Farm and had a late supper together in front of the fire, scrambled eggs and cinnamon toast, warm milk with honey. After Katherine had taken a bath and gotten ready for bed, Lucy had read to her till she fell asleep. They were nearly at the end of *The Dawn Treader*, one of Lucy's favorite parts where Reepicheep, the gallant mouse, paddles on alone in his little coracle to the utter East where the salt waves grow sweet.

Katherine had closed her eyes, and Lucy closed the book and tiptoed to the door where she turned back before she left the room.

Defend, O Lord, this thy child from all the perils of this night.

There had already been perils, there would be perils. Who knew what joy and trouble lay ahead for this sweet, solemn child who had saved her life? Lucy prayed she would be there to defend her.

An Excerpt from

ALL THE PERILS OF THIS NIGHT

sequel to *Murder at the Rummage Sale*

Katherine woke up, shaking.

Where was she?

Streetlight came in through a barred window. Outside someone kicked a garbage can and cursed. There was a bed and sheets that didn't feel clean. She didn't feel clean. She had to go to the bathroom, badly. When she got out of bed, she felt stiff, everything hurt. Her head hurt; she might have to throw up. She moved slowly across the room, feeling for a door. Why was she naked? She couldn't go out of the room without anything on. She went back and wrapped herself in the sheet. She just had to get to the bathroom; then she'd figure out where she was.

In a bar of light, a doorknob. She turned but nothing happened. She turned it the other way. It was broken. She shook it and turned it some more.

It was locked.

She began pounding on the door, and finally she cried out, "Help! The door's locked, help!"

And she kept pounding and shouting.

Lucy sat bolt upright in bed. For a moment she hardly knew where she was, it was that dark. But someone had been screaming for help. Someone.

"Katherine?" she called out loud.

And then she swung her legs out of bed, orienting herself by the crack of light under her bedroom door. Of course, she was at home, of course. At home alone. But she couldn't help herself. She went down the hall to the room she now called Katherine's room and opened the door, hall light spilling onto the empty sleigh bed, neatly made, the satin quilts Katherine loved folded at the foot.

"Shirrup with that filthy racket!" someone shouted back, a woman's voice.

"The door's locked!" Katherine called. "Help me, please! I have to go to the bathroom."

"Wot! What's she on about, a bath in the middle of the bloody night."

The woman was English. That's right she was in England. They said "loo."

"I have to go to the loo!" She was almost sobbing now.

"You got a pot under yer bed, ain't you? Now shut yer gob and let decent folk get some sleep."

"Where am I?" she said, this time in a whisper.

She limped back to the bed. She had a limp? Tears streamed down her face, stinging what felt like cuts. She knelt down and felt under the bed and finally found an enamel pot, with a chipped handle, and a mostly gone roll of toilet paper. She pulled it out from under the bed. She was shaking so badly it was hard to squat, but she managed. For a moment there was only release. Then she stood up again, so dizzy she knew she was going to be sick. Her eyes now accustomed to the striped light, she saw a small sink in one corner of the room. She almost knocked the chamber pot over in her hurry to get to it. She grabbed the sides of the sink and heaved. When she was done, she didn't know what else to do but go back to the bed. She curled into as small a shape as she could make and wrapped the sheet around her tight.

And they wrapped him in swaddling clothes and laid him in a manger.

In French class, she had learned that *manger* meant to eat. He slept in the place where animals ate, on their hay. And the cows brooded over him, maybe nosed him a little but they did no harm to him, just as the black angus had never harmed her. Bear, her white dog, herded them and kept her safe.

Where was she?

"Katherine," Lucy spoke her name again, though of course the child wasn't there.

Lucy left the door to the room open as if to hear her if she cried out again and went back to her own room. Pulling a thin cushion from under her bed, her only concession to her years, Lucy knelt by the side of her bed.

"Defend, O Lord, this thy child from all the perils of this night."

No other words came to her, so she prayed them over and over, aloud, then silently. Till she laid her head down on the bed and without meaning to fell into a troubled sleep.

Forthcoming from Imagination Fury Arts

FROM ELIZABETH CUNNINGHAM

The Book of Madge, the secret graphic novel
behind The Maeve Chronicles, limited edition

The 25th anniversary reissues of:

The Return of the Goddess

The Wild Mother

FROM OTHER AUTHORS

Princess Olga by Douglas Smyth

Son of Byford by Juba Kalamka

CPSIA information can be obtained
at www.ICGtesting.com
Printed in the USA
LVOW04*1538150816

500453LV00016B/141/P

9 781944 190002